I0599863

A Story in Stone

A Story in Stone

Kristen Cornwall

Paintwater Press

Copyright © 2025 Kristen Cornwall

All rights reserved

The characters and events portrayed in this book are fictitious. Any similarity to real persons, living or dead, is coincidental and not intended by the author.

No part of this book may be reproduced, or stored in a retrieval system, or transmitted in any form or by any means, electronic, mechanical, photocopying, recording, or otherwise, without express written permission of the publisher.

ISBN-13: 9798992818505

Cover design by: Kristen Cornwall
Library of Congress Control Number: 2025904881
Printed in the United States of America

For the ocean. You're a delight.

1.

She found calm in the long pause between breaths, a sense of replenishing stillness.

Yes, her body moved, but only with gentle undulation, faint echoes of the ocean dancing with air above her, rhythmic and soothing. Here, with limbs outstretched and dark hair like espresso tentacles seeping out into the unseen, somewhere between whale song and the shore, Lil floated. Having long since given herself permission to exist as she was without question, Lil savored the serenity of the ocean, of a cup of tea, of easy moments, but here, cradled by depth, she indulged.

A sudden ripple of water traveled along her back and through her mind. A feeling like fingers combing through her hair induced a sense of hypnotic somnolence, followed by a flash of darkness, and that smell... How it was possible while submerged, she didn't know, but she was quickly overcome by the deep forest scent, spiced, smoldering. Shadows played beneath her, taking form.

Wings, teeth, length beyond measure, and a sense of overwhelming nostalgia. Of waiting. Of absolute certainty, fleeting.

Then it was gone, leaving her awake and alert under a layer of ocean, and the cool light of dawn.

Another dream, she told herself as she broke the surface, opening her eyes to clouds resting on water. Only subtle changes in the grey and white hinted they might be two separate things, instead of one.

Lil emerged onto the rocks of Vancouver Island's western shore, utility belt hanging from her hips, and a small stone cylinder hanging from her neck. The secluded house before her stood half encased in fir trees, sliding doors and a wall of windows facing the ocean. When she reached the back deck, Lil peeled off her swimsuit, slipped into a jersey dress, and made her way inside with a couple jars of sea water.

A deep stone fireplace sank into the wall across from where she entered. A well-warn couch stood against the far-left wall facing two wingback chairs, a coffee table between them. To her right, a utility sink in the corner, shelves housing jars, paint, brushes, supplies, rocks, shells, books, bones, and other treasured bits. In the center of the room, an expansive wooden table supported a seven by three foot blank, stretched canvas. Beside it, a much smaller table laden with jars, bowls, brushes, and paint waited.

The living room wrapped around and opened up into a kitchen with an island, and an open door to the pantry and sunroom, the front door, hallway leading to all the rest. Beside the pantry door hung a framed botanical illustration of an apple blossom in white and muted pinks, with fresh green leaves and emerging buds yet to burst. A housewarming gift from Magnus, and the only piece on her walls she hadn't painted.

A Story in Stone

Lil eyed the canvas as she approached, poured a jar of seawater into a large clay bowl. She opened the second bottle and slowly emptied about half onto the stretched surface, spreading it around with a large brush. When the material saturated, she put her tools down, leaned in close, and inhaled the ocean's scent mixing with the fabric, tasting salt, remembering.

Standing up slowly, she set to work introducing paint, watching as water wicked up the blue she applied in long strokes, she and the ocean working together. Lil danced this way for hours, her body still feeling the water move over her as she worked, the depth that had held her from beneath, the calm between breaths.

As her trance receded, she made her way to the kitchen and put the kettle on. She chose a rounded cup, light grey on the outside, white glaze on the inside. She'd etched a little mark when she'd made it, about two centimeters from the bottom of the handle. It was the outline of a circle with a line going across the top, a touch of the white glaze on it like a thumb print.

Hot water flowed over crushed mint leaves from the garden, and steam carried their vapor up toward Lil, a prelude as she scrolled through the contacts on her phone. There were few names, so it took mere moments to select Magnus. It rang once.

"Lily, what a welcome surprise."

She pictured him in a suit with his silver hair perfectly combed and parted to the side, blue eyes that had seen three times her years. Maybe he was in a helicopter or in a private meeting, though it sounded quiet on his end so not likely the helicopter...

"I hope I wasn't interrupting…"

"Nonsense, I'm sitting with a book," he said, his words warm as always.

"I created your painting this morning. It should be dry by tonight but, I'd like to keep it here until tomorrow to make sure it's, well, how it should be."

"I have absolute faith in you, Lily, dear. As soon as you feel your work is ready to be released, I'll have it shipped to the new Iceland property. I have people on site preparing for my arrival prior to the conference, but it won't be suitable for my stay, of course, until *both* your works are in place: one in house I'll use for entertaining, the other in my private residence. I can't be carting the one I have back and forth between the two houses. That would be absurd."

A smile touched her face, hands wrapping around the steaming mug.

"Do you need any tea for your trip?" She asked. "Nan could put together a package to send along with the painting. I'm headed over this afternoon."

"Yes, but I can pick it up myself. I'm seeing Nan this evening for a stroll in the orchard, then we'll roll up our sleeves in the kitchen. There is something so satisfying about baking with that woman. We made bread last week. It was… good."

Lil heard Magnus pause his speech, but not breath. She may have detected a sigh.

"The painting," he said. "You worked on it this morning?"

"…Yes"

"And how was your swim?"

Lil imagined the look on his face, mischievous and nonchalant. She wanted to tell him about the dream, but not while he was fishing for details…

Those she kept around her knew what she was capable of, the length of time she could hold her breath, for one thing, a knack for horticulture, unintentional atmospheric and occasionally seismic alteration, paintings that carried with them a sense of what she'd felt and where she'd been. She'd been painting for Magnus since she was a child to help with his insomnia. Her work hung in Nan's shop as well, but neither were not driven to test, name, or exploit Lil for what made her whatever she was. Their love was greater than the need to sate that curiosity, so they coexisted as a family.

"You'll have to find out in your dreams, Magnus, in Iceland. Unless you want to take a nap here in the morning," she goaded.

"I'm certainly not coming over to *nap*," he scoffed. Then, obviously pouting, he added, "I'm flying out in two weeks. I'll have to wait until then."

He was disappointed, poor old guy.

"I was thinking of hunting blacktail up at your place," she said. "Will that be ok with you out of the country?"

"Of course, Lily, and I should think it goes without saying. Send word when you head up if it makes you feel more comfortable, and I'll tell my people to look out for you, or rather, to stay out of your way. Gunnar will be there, of course. The forest will be yours."

"Thanks," she smiled. "What time will I see you in the morning? I'll be up by dawn, so, if there's a time that works best for you..."

"Seven o'clock."

"I could make muffins?"

"Will there be butter?"

"Magnus... their milk is for their babies."

"Please..." She could almost hear his eyes roll through the phone. "There are cultures that survive on dairy. I don't know *what* my life would be like without cheese. You won't milk a deer, but you would hunt and kill it."

"The hunt is fair."

He harrumphed.

"Magnus..."

"I'll bring my own butter. Make the muffins."

"Sounds good," she chuckled. "And Magnus, the swim was very relaxing. There were whales."

He released a long sigh. "Their song, it goes right into me; lulls the soul. Thank you, Lily."

"You are sincerely welcome, Magnus. I'll see you in the morning."

2.

The wheels of Lil's truck hit the crunch of Nan's gravel of driveway, the familiar sound of coming home. Nan's consisted of three main buildings with gardens between and, beyond that, a lavender field, apple orchard, and forest. Nan's shop, where they served tea, craft beer, and pastries, was a rustic one level building with a porch out front. Some distance behind the shop stood the old house where Nan lived, where Lil had grown up. To the right, next to the shop but set back almost as far as the old house, stood a barn, a beautiful open space Nan used for workshops, functions, and storage.

Lil opened the weathered wooden door of the shop and walked in to the familiar smell of herbs, ale, and baked goods. To her left, the shop opened up into a modest seating area where three tables were occupied with patrons. Paintings of the ocean hung on the walls, infusing a calm mood into the space.

Lil stood in the doorway, watching Nan on the other side of the front counter. She had her back turned, phone to her ear and cord trailing to the wall. She'd had that phone as long as Lil could remember, same went for the botanical illustration beside it, the page of numbers and weathered chai recipe suspended from a blue thumbtack.

Salt and pepper grey, heavy on the salt, came down to Nan's jawline in curls and waves. A loose, white cotton racerback top, displayed well-toned arms, and grey, wide leg linen pants flowed to the floor. Hanging up the phone, Nan twisted around and smiled, eyes peering over her red reading glasses. She'd surpassed seventy-five years, but her body was fit and her mind sharp.

"Magnus needs a large batch of tea for his trip to Iceland," Lil started. I offered to have you put something together, but he said he'd come pick it up himself…"

Nan took off her glasses. "Did he happen to say what time?"

Lil smirked. "No, but he *did* mention something about the orchard and getting his hands dirty…"

To her credit, Nan kept a straight face. After taking a deep breath, followed but a controlled exhale, she said, "He's coming over to make apple pie. I'm doing a double crust; he'll do one of those crisps."

"With the brown sugar on top?"

Lil watched Nan's thoughts drift for a moment.

"It's just pie," said, a little too uninterested.

"Mmmhmm."

"Use the chamomile and lavender in the barn," Nan said, conveniently changing the subject. "Take your time. Claire will still be here when you get back."

"I want to see the painting before you ship it out!" Claire shouted from the kitchen, popping in an instant later, wearing a green linen apron, blonde ponytail carrying the subtle scent of rosemary and grapefruit conditioner.

She jumped up to meet Lil with a tight hug, one of a handful of people who'd put their arms around her.

Claire was a few years older than Lil, petite, athletic, and had an undeniable thread of sunshine woven into her.

Lil had been adopted by Nan as a young girl, and Claire, being Nan's biological granddaughter, quickly became Lil's closest, perhaps only, friend. And while Claire's childhood home had been in the city, she came to stay with Nan many weekends throughout the year, weeks at a time on school breaks. After college, Claire got her own place in town, somehow managing part-time employment at Nan's. This was impressive, since the rest of her waking hours were spent working for Magnus at The Orn, one of his research facilities. It was a wonder she found time to sleep.

"I painted it this morning," Lil said, "but it's not staying with me long. It'll ship as soon as Magnus gives his approval."

"Which you will get."

"Right, and he's coming by in the morning."

Claire let out a sigh and turned to Nan, pleading. "I need to go to Lil's... just for a couple hours..."

"Fine, but keep it brief. I need at least one of you helping out here when things pick up later. Todd is off doing some surf thing and won't be around until after dinnertime."

"That'll be Lil," Claire winced. "I'm headed to the lab for lunch."

"Nan might need both of us here," Lil said. "She's going to have her hands full in the Kitchen. Will you be baking here, or at the house...?" She added air quotes over the word *baking*.

Nan couldn't suppress a laugh as she grabbed a towel and snapped it at Lil, then Claire for good measure.

"Get going with that tea and be on your way. The sooner you go, the sooner you'll be back to entertain me with your foolishness."

On her way to the barn, Lil passed the garden benches she'd grown up sitting on, the solitary apple tree she'd planted as a child. They had an orchard, of course, but she had wanted to try growing a tree herself. It was one of the last things she'd made before deciding to keep things simple...

The barn, a vast space filled with natural light, was one of her favorite places to be, not for the main room but for the space above. On the ground floor there were tables and workbenches, a bathroom down back, and a separate room for storage. Above, on the second floor, was a modest, unoccupied bedroom, and one of the lesser mysteries of Lil's childhood.

Ascending the stairs, she paused as her feet passed the top step. With wide plank floors and high ceiling, the room was spacious but uncomplicated in appearance. The wall at the far end was a triangle of windows surrounding a door to the balcony facing the shop. It looked like another exit, but there was nowhere to go but down, she supposed.

A familiar bed stood off to the right with a nightstand and chair beside it, abutting a small desk where Lil had left a rolled-out leather mat. Laid atop it were several knives and a hatchet she'd been meaning to work on, a wooden box with a sharpening stone, waiting. More blades rested in the desk drawer, stones of different grits on the shelf. Most of the tools had once belonged to Grampa Pat, a man she'd never met, and came into Lil's possession as a gift from Nan.

There was something meditative about the act of sharpening a knife on stone, blade sliding over the wet surface, the pause before passing over again. Stone and steel. The sound was rhythmic, pulling her into a calm much like the ocean. Lil first heard the sound in Nan's garden on a crisp November morning when the insects had finally ceased their song for the season. The sky had been plentiful with clouds, broken by cracks of sunshine sending spotlights beyond the trees. Lil had been eight or so, poking about in the damp grey and brown of the garden while Gunnar sat on a bench. She and several crows had been observing each other, then there it was, the slow, wet scrape joining what sound a slight wind had evoked from the trees. She'd paused, her eyes closing as he continued.

Lil surveyed the rest of the room: a book shelf, a chest of drawers, an old leather chair. She'd had a room of her own reading material in the house, of course, with plenty of books and places to consume them, but the barn slowly became her own library of sorts over time, evolving into something respectfully off limits to others.

The first time she ventured up the back steps, she'd been nearly six years old. It was mostly storage downstairs then, and she'd been helping Nan unpack boxes. Feeling done before the task was finished, she sought entertainment elsewhere.

Nan was vague in explaining why she maintained the barn room, stating it was for the rare occasion when more company stayed over than she could keep at the house, which had never happened in Lil's experience.

Lil had been so drawn by the scent of the bed, that she'd asked if the mattress was stuffed with moss and resin. Nan removed the sheets to reveal that it was not some custom, hand-fashioned bed but a store-bought standard: double size with springs, foam, and dust mites. Her attempt to demystify the room with mention of pests did nothing to thwart Lil's curiosity, though, so she enlisted Claire's help when Nan spoke of the room no further.

Lil laughed to herself as she remembered, she and her cousin had been about six and nine years old, leaning over the bed, sniffing. *It has a distinct smell,* Claire had said. *Almost like you, but woodsier, and smokier. Nan probably adds stuff to the laundry soap.*

Lil hadn't been surprised to learn that she had a smell, everything else did.

Lil advanced to the bed and sprawled across it, turning her face to breathe in the smell of the mattress through the sheets. It was like the deep woods after rain; earthy and potent, tangled with something warm and spicy, like myrrh and

11

cardamom. Lil felt an undeniable intimacy about taking in the scent; knowing molecules which originated as a part of someone or something else were inside her, that the origins were still unknown niggled at her, but she'd become tolerant of the remaining mystery. The daydreams she'd started having, though, they seemed to tear open the seams that held her curiosity.

Later, as she and Claire approached her front door, Lil asked, "Did anyone ever live above the barn?"

Claire took slow steps beside her, paused, and said, "Do you remember that story I told you about the time ladybugs flew all around me? Memories from being that young are so weird, like fragmented snapshots. I remember being in the garden, I might have been three years old, and there was a man there who worked for Nan. I don't remember his face, but he had dark hair, and he was huge, but I'm sure any adult would have seemed big to me at that age. I guess I was just wandering around doing who knows what, and I saw a ladybug on his finger. He let it crawl onto mine, and talked, then he sang a little song. I don't remember what he said, the song though… I'll never forget that: *Ladybird, ladybird, protect these leaves, eat all the aphids then dance in the breeze*, and then *I swear* the ladybugs, there had to have been fifty of them, they rose from the plants and swarmed around me. It was magical. I'm not sure," Claire continued, "but I feel like he may have lived there. Nan still hasn't said?"

"She brushed me off when we were kids, but I haven't brought it up since."

"Have you had another dream?" Claire smirked.

Lil smiled and rolled her eyes as she put the key in the door. "I'll tell you inside."

She'd told Claire about the episodes, the daydreams she'd had, slipping into moments that seemed somewhere in between, somewhere familiar. In more than one, there'd been a man she couldn't see, and she swore he'd smelled like the room above the barn.

"You know," Claire said, "I'm surprised Magnus never installed a keypad or a print scanner… or cameras at your house."

"He's offered, and I've thought about it, but I'm sticking with one lock, one key. Keep it simple."

Claire's eyes went right for Lil's new painting on the wall.

"*Nice*," she breathed, standing still a moment before making her way over and collapsing on the couch beneath the piece. "This is the *perfect* nap spot," she continued. "But I'm not napping. I don't have time to nap. Way too much going on."

"Relax a minute while I make some tea. I had another one of those dreams and I want to tell you about it."

"Did it have that barn smell again?"

"Yes, oddly enough. I was swimming, and thoroughly submerged when it happened."

"*Shit*. Have you told Nan?"

"No… Just you, Magnus, and Gunnar."

"She hates being last to know, but I get it. Love and worry. We definitely need to discuss your water dream," Claire sighed, burrowing deeper into the cushions. "And I'm expanding my social life a bit. Remember how I went and visited my parents?" she asked, her voice becoming breathy, lengthening. "Hey, what tea are you making? We might need chai."

Lil halted production, understanding Claire must have something significant to discuss. "Chai it is then."

Nan had taught them the recipe as children, kept handwritten copies by the phone in the old house and the shop. She even had a little rhyme that went with it to make it easier to remember. On an unexpected stormy day when they needed something cozy: chai. Whenever they had a conflict, or exciting news to share: chai.

13

Lil set about gathering ingredients, tying her apron strings on her way to the pantry. The apron had once belonged to Nan, but the old woman had embroidered and apple blossom at the top corner and gifted it to Lil when she'd moved out on her own. The addition was subtle and meaningful, adding memories to the light grey linen already altered by a few streaks of pink and indigo at the hem... The blueberry incident had occurred in Nan's kitchen many years prior, Nan's Pinafore having taken the brunt of the assault while Lil's only had a small bit of stain seep in. The results had been rather nice, in her opinion, and Nan's too, it was the only apron Lil had seen her wearing since.

"Claire?" she said, setting down the last of the spices on the counter.

Silence.

Lil smiled, observing the gentle rise and fall of Claire's chest, closed eyes fluttering lightly, wet spot forming on the couch under her slightly opened mouth. *Sleep is such a precious state,* she thought, believing there's something sacred about where we choose to leave our bodies when we journey away to our dreams, about those to whom we entrust ourselves.

As the couch groaned, Lil untied the strings of her apron.

"Oh Lil, it was so relaxing," Claire started, stretching out from toes to fingers. "I was floating in the water, and... It smells so good in here. Were you baking?" She bolted upright, eyes darting around. "How long have I been asleep?"

"I baked two batches of muffins. We need to go. Like, *now.*"

Claire's eyes widened as she got to her feet.

"I put your tea in a travel mug and packed you two muffins for the road," Lil said, ticking her head toward the bag on the counter." Let's scoot, or Nan will be giving me the stink eye all night."

"She hasn't called, has she?" Claire asked, sipping her tea and clutching the bag of muffins.

Lil shook her head, hand on Claire's lower back, gently guiding her toward the door.

"No, she's saving it for when we arrive. Now, what's the story with your social expansion? I made muffins and tea waiting for you to wake up and tell me what you're planning. Conferences?"

"Nope," she said, clearing her throat, then pausing her steps to cough. "I almost aspirated on my muffin," she laughed. "Water dream first, then my thing if we have time."

3.

Waves massaged the shore, in and out, their song soothing and slow, though not as slow as Lil's breathing.

Another rhythm eased in, much closer than the water, a sound like stone grinding on stone, with a smell like spices, and fire.

Lil remembered getting comfortable in a lounge chair on the back deck, but it wasn't the recliner cradling her body, it was sand. Her eyes remained heavy and, as she strained to open them ever so slightly, she saw a man sitting beside her. She couldn't see his face, she never could, but his arms flexed before her, his hands working.

A dream with the familiarity of a memory.

"Why do you do it like that?" A man's voice asked. He sounded young, further away. "You could hollow it easily with your mind, could you not?"

"Vibrations from the stones go through my body. I like it."

And his voice moved through her. She *knew* that voice, and the smell...

"This vessel will hold water. When she drinks from it, she will taste through the liquid to the stone, to the memory of these hands. It will help her wake."

A tapping sound interrupted his words.

A Story in Stone

Lil closed her eyes, feeling herself being pulled upward into the air, upward, and back into herself.

*

His platinum watch caught the light of the morning sun as he reached the front door. Aged by salt and water, the door had felt right for her house by the ocean, weathered, perhaps reclaimed from some sunken ship with big sails and precious cargo... The old metal knocker with its greenish-blue patina had been fashioned from an antique with a simple design: a horizontal rod and hanging ring. He'd picked it up some thirty years prior from an artifact dealer in Scotland of all places. The piece had spent time in one of his private collections, until her home was built.

His fingers grazed over the rod, grasped firmly onto the ring, and knocked.

Lil opened her eyes to a *tap, tap, tap*.

Barefoot, she padded from the deck through the house, where she found her friend waiting with silver hair well-groomed and parted on the side, beard just long enough for every strand to be brushed perfectly into place. He wore a warm smile, fine grey suit over a crisp white shirt, no tie. His smile, though... he held weight behind it.

"Good morning, Magnus," she said, putting both arms around him, inhaling the familiar scent of bergamot and juniper. He reciprocated, but with only one arm. Curious, Lil looked down, spying a small bit of folded brown baking parchment tied with string.

"The butter," he said dryly.

She smiled and shook her head. "I hope you brought enough; I made oat muffins with cardamom, and another batch of rye."

Once in the kitchen, Lil observed contentedly as Magnus caught sight of the large wooden bowl resting on the island. Though the muffins were baked yesterday, their smell still traveled through the tea towel they hid under. Eager,

A Story in Stone

Magus couldn't resist lifting a corner of the linen before giving his attention to the living room, where the painting above the couch caught him by the eyes and chest, pulling him forward.

He walked as if her work had been leading him, and perhaps it was.

"Beautiful. Sublime. I can feel it by just putting my hands out."

He glanced down at the couch, and then to her face as she stood beside him.

"The nap is tempting," he chuckled lightly, bracing himself on one of the tufted seats before sinking down.

Lil relaxed into the couch across from him, carefully considering the lines of his face, the way his eyes drifted. She wasn't one to interrupt silence, but something about him invited concern.

"What are you thinking, Magnus? You've carried some weight here with you, and now you're going somewhere, perhaps to another time."

He smiled softly, the gesture weakening as he glanced down to his hands.

"When Mira passed on, I was lost. I couldn't save her, not with all my resources. We'd had nearly forty years together, she and I. That's longer than you've been alive… Longer than anything constant in your life. Can you imagine?" He looked off through the doors, to the ocean. "Forty years," he whispered, pausing to exhale before he continued. "Nan helped with her tea and her friendship, but then one day I met a young girl sitting in the garden. Precocious, but humble. What an interesting little thing you were. Still are. I felt you studying me then as I walked toward you, and do you remember what you said as I approached?"

Lil heard cicadas in her mind, the words she'd said weaving through the insects.

Bushing, just a little, she rolled her eyes. "You won't let me forget."

When there is disturbance inside me, she'd started, *it affects the things around me, like a rumble deep in the mountain shaking leaves on every tree. I have tools, though, to help me find my calm, like poetry and the rhythm of my breath. The orchard is peaceful, and the ocean helps me a lot but I can't always be there, so I paint it. I use my tools until I need the storm, though I don't know when that'll be. It seems like you could use help finding what your tools are. What helps you?*

Magnus shook his head and smiled, his cheeks pushing up at the wrinkles under his eyes. "You couldn't have been more than five years old, and by lunchtime I was walking out to my car with a bag of Nan's tea, one of your little ocean paintings, and five handwritten poems."

"Well, you wouldn't take my book so I had to jot them down for you."

"Believe me, dear, they were much appreciated, as you well know. I fell asleep that night with your painting on my bedside table, and for the first time in over a year, I dreamed of something other than my wife's limp hands and lifeless eyes. I have slept beside you're work, in one form or another, every night since… had this house built knowing someday it would be yours."

"It was too generous, Magnus," she whispered.

"You could have refused."

"I tried."

"Yes, you did indeed…" He trailed off, his expression once again occupied, troubled even.

"Magnus?"

"There's a developing situation" he started. "Some folks up north discovered an animal carcass, mammoth, partially thawed. Three flew over from the Cambridge Bay research facility last week, took samples, evaluated the site, and returned to the station. Forty-eight hours later, two of the three were dead. By the time they were found deceased, twelve others had already become ill. At that point, the dead remained closed in their rooms while the twelve infected isolated in the dorms, and the asymptomatic kept to the main building, though they've all since perished. Save for one. The survivor, Tom, was the third member of the site visit team."

Lil's eyes widened.

"We believe it to be contained…"

"Magnus," she whispered.

"Though none of those who first discovered the carcass are ill, we still believe the animal is the most likely source. Locals have been advised to stay away from the area. There's a small group standing watch at the site to prevent further exposure until the remains can be safely managed."

"None of the locals ill, though," she pondered. "Perhaps some change occurred within the samples when they were brought back to the facility, a reaction to a chemical stabilizer, a stain. It could simply be that those on the ground never made contact. We'd need to know more about how the pathogen works."

"Precisely. Of the three researchers who originally went to scout the site, only two contracted the illness. The unaffected scientist is indigenous to the area; his family who discovered the animal. I'm hopeful there is some genetic or dietary factor that could be used to combat the pathogen, but we need to know more."

It was contained, he'd said, but that was temporary.

"Lily, dear, I have a very big favor to ask of you."

A favor. Her heart picked up pace, but she kept her breath slow.

"The dead remain where they fell, though most are confined to the dorms. The incident was kept quiet, but not so quiet that the government isn't abreast. A crew will be sent, but I've been asked privately to do what I can before things get on the books, so to speak."

"The favor…"

"I'd like you to go to the facility and retrieve what samples you can before we neutralize the remaining biological threat from the air. Whatever we're dealing with appears to be extremely virulent, and I won't take any chances. If errors are made, the consequences could be devastating, globally."

Though she could make a mistake like anyone else, Lil was uniquely equipped to not bring the ramifications home with her... *The dead remain where they fell,* he'd said, and the bodies would still contain whatever had relieved them of their lives.

"Tom, the one who didn't get sick, could he..."

"Tom's in quarantine, dear."

"Yes, of course."

The investigation into Lil's biological resilience began at The Orn when she was about nine years old. Magnus had encouraged her curiosity as a child, given her free reign to roam his research facility, provided she had an escort. He entrusted his niece's son, Gunnar, with her care, teasing that he'd given her a guard. He'd been nineteen then, with a solid build, short, dark hair, his eyes darker still, so dark, the border of each pupil seemed to blend into his iris. Magnus assured her that he was family, trustworthy, and while gifted in skill, he had a stillness of temperament that she'd be comfortable with. She had been a child, and Magnus had wanted her to have someone with her. He teased that he was giving her a guard, and he had.

She'd been visiting with Nadia one afternoon, a researcher working with varicella at the time. It came up that Lil had never contracted the illness, though when Claire had come down with chickenpox at Nan's Lil had been in close contact. Nadia proposed that Lil had either been vaccinated or had the illness when she was younger, developed immunity either way, and just didn't recall.

I've never been to the doctor, that I can remember, Lil had said. Nadia had understandably looked surprised, and Gunnar appeared a little uneasy with the information being shared.

I don't remember anything from before I was adopted, though, so it's possible.

21

Nadia offered to check her for immunity to the usual childhood inoculations and Lil had no objection. Gunnar, though, was on the phone with Magnus before Nadia had a chance to send her assistant for supplies. Magnus stipulated that he would need to speak with Nan and draw up a nondisclosure agreement and terms of use before a blood draw was initiated.

It looks like you've had all the usual vaccines. I ran the gamut, and there's no way you'd have had all these illnesses without remembering; certainly not polio, Nadia laughed. *I did find it peculiar that you'd been given some of the adolescent vaccines, like HPV and the meningococcal conjugate. Magnus also asked me to…*

Nadia looked puzzled, and then raised a brow as she looked up to Magnus, who'd made his appearance for the results a priority.

Can you roll up your sleeves, so I can see your shoulders? Nadia asked.

Lil obliged, noting Nadia's continued state of confusion as she examined her arms.

Do you have any scarring… a circular scar?

I have no scars, anywhere. Why, should I have one?

She's looking for your smallpox vaccine site, Magnus said with a delighted smile. *But you   don't have one do you.*

It was the four of them; Gunnar, Lil, Magnus and Nadia. Magnus had insisted that Nadia's assistants be dismissed for the project.

Lily dear, would it be alright with you if I ran a few more tests to check for immunity to some less-common pathogens?

Lil consented.

Run her blood with Marburg, CCHF, anything you have lying around, oh, and run it with that thing Matt and Rika are working on. Nadia…

Nadia looked up from her momentary stupor and nodded.

Do remember the nondisclosure agreement and conditions for use of Lily's biological material. Everything you've processed so far will be incinerated before you move forward, yes?

She agreed, of course.

Lil's blood had displayed remarkable resistance to anything they matched it with, prompting Nadia to request further investigation. Whether it was the mention of DNA analysis or the hungry look in her eyes, Lil couldn't be sure, but Magnus shut down the project entirely.

He thirsted for secrets, savoring the veil that mystery provided as much as having the privilege of walking behind it, but he had limits. Others, though, were not able to balance their curiosity with compassion, and would always want more.

It was this insatiable human quality, she supposed, that most influenced her decision not to return to The Orn, of course that didn't happen for some time after Nadia. The other part of the story, why she lived by the ocean and kept her breath easy, had clouds threatening to ripen beyond her window

"Details, Magnus."

"Five-hour flight with a stop to refuel. Gunnar will take you in the small cargo plane, and he *will not* be exiting the craft on site under any circumstances. I mean it. Your work at the facility should take an hour at most, then, just a hop, skip, and a jump to a small private station to drop off what you've recovered, and a five-hour flight home, give or take. You'll need to refuel once on the way and on return. Back by bedtime, breakfast tomorrow at the latest."

"I... Magnus, I'm not sure how comfortable I am with... Well, I know there won't be anyone present to see, but, I'm not sure how comfortable I am with doing things, or what I'd even be *able* to do. It's always been accidental, and I don't... I never practiced. I don't know how I'll be able-"

"No, no..." he soothed. "No, you won't need to do anything, Lily dear, just be your remarkable self and don't get infected with anything while you're there," he smiled. "Walk in, walk out. That's all."

"What of the animal?" She asked. "Will that be left?"

Magnus let out a breathy, "No."

"Why not just get samples there?

"You'll be able to adequately decontaminate at the facility, so that's where you'll be going. I won't ask anything more; even this seems a bit of an overreach, but I felt I must."

Quick. Quiet. It had become apparent during her childhood that becoming *involved* was less than ideal to the point of dangerous, but Magnus knew the risks. He also knew how to be discrete, and he loved her.

"I'm supposed to work at the shop lunch to dinner," she sighed. "Meet Claire after, then go surfing with Todd…"

"Yes, well, that does take priority…"

Lil rolled her eyes.

"I spoke with Nan. The boy will come in with one of his friends; it's all taken care of. I just… I need to hear you say yes."

She sighed. "Gunnar will be there?"

"Just the two of you."

"I'll do it," she said, heart steady, ocean waves outside, slow and steady as her breath. "Yes."

With a great sigh, Magnus seemed to release more air than she thought his lungs capable of holding. "Thank you."

"Is Gunnar already at the plane?"

"No, no, he's on his way here to collect you."

Lil sighed. Of course he was.

"I'll notify the two of you when the plane is nearly ready, and Lily, do please consider getting a little sleep before you leave."

"I'm not going to sleep on the plane, Magnus."

"Very well," he smirked, standing, stretching. "Now that we have that settled, an old man was promised a muffin, but has yet to set eyes on any baked goods. Am I to eat the butter by itself?"

"I saw you lift the tea towel earlier, Magnus," she said, popping up and giving him a nudge with her shoulder. "Let's get you fed. Cider?"

"Perfect."

Lil let the cider simmer with cloves and cinnamon until a sweet, spicy fragrance filled the air around them.

Hands stretching up to an open shelf above the counter by the sink, she paused, fingertips brushing against an unfamiliar surface.

Lil kept eight mugs on that shelf, and knew each one well. She'd made all them. But this… Heart quickening, she pulled the oddity down for examination. Simple, beautiful. The vessel lacked a handle, and appeared to have been carved entirely of river stone. No, she'd not put that there, but she couldn't say definitively that she hadn't seen it before. In fact, she had the undeniable suspicion she'd dreamed of it…

Her fingers slid across the surface, finding damp mud along the bottom, and a deep, fresh scent, but there was something beyond the fertile soil she breathed in; something warm, familiar. Hearing the sound of liquid inside, she paused, slipping two fingers into the cool darkness, then brought one to her lips. Salt water.

"Magnus," she started, turning back toward him. "Did you happen to leave this little treat here for me to find?" It would be like him to have done so, he did love a good mystery, and delighted in sharing puzzles with those he thought worthy of them. But she knew, in her heart she knew it wasn't him.

"No…" he whispered, receiving the vessel with gentle hands, and plucking a pair of reading glasses from his breast pocket.

25

She poured them each a mug of cider while he examined the piece, her heart steady, but quite a bit faster than usual. Could she have manifested the thing somehow?

"You've no memory of it, how it got here?"

She sighed.

"I've stirred something," he observed, watching her.

"I had a dream about it before you arrived; nodded off out on the deck. I saw someone making it."

"A dream. Did it feel like the others?"

She nodded.

"That makes four this month."

"Five," she corrected. "In the water yesterday morning, I saw a massive sea serpent or something."

Magnus raised his brows.

"It's not in the painting," she smiled.

"Might make for an interesting night," he said, eyes returning to the cup before handing it back to her. "What do you make of its physical origins?"

"You don't think I could have…?"

"I think there's a great deal we don't know in regards to what you're capable of, dear. Have you been," he paused, choosing his words. "Practicing?"

"No," she replied, understanding him clearly. "Nothing more than painting, but that's intuitive. This cup was definitely in the dream though, I'm sure of it. Someone was making the cup so that I would drink from it, and wake up."

"Hmmm. Well, as far as I know, dreams are a way for us to communicate with ourselves. Perhaps there is something you're aware of, but need help *waking up* to, so to speak. You and I both know there are parts of yourself left unexplored, intentionally. Perhaps this is your mind's way of whispering, *I'm ready.*"

"Manifesting a physical object from a dream is hardly a whisper."

He dipped his chin and raised his brows with words unsaid.

"I recall the maple, Magnus."

The tree Lil spoke of had once stood in front of Nan's house, until she'd taken a nap after an unsettling experience at The Orn. Magnus had accompanied Gunnar in exporting her home, had stayed on account of Nan, and had witnessed lightning strike the old maple twice, then a third time as the tree burned.

While the unknowing creation of an object existed in a new, impressive skillset, the presentation had been somewhat tame, comparatively, as far as volume was concerned.

"I know I need not remind you that you're welcome in the lab for any purpose, any time. There's no place more secure, except perhaps one of my other facilities, if you want to tinker on something. Explore a little. You've grown beyond needing a chaperone, but if it made you more comfortable, Gunnar is available," He offered. "I'd love to see what you are capable of, not just out of selfish curiosity, of course, but-"

"Flattery, Magnus."

"You know me too well," he said as she poured cider into two mugs, passing one over to him. "Tell me, how are things with the business at Nan's? I understand there's some kind of yoga club now. She extended an open invitation, but I prefer something more private in my exercise."

As if he didn't know exactly what Nan did with her mornings.

"Honestly Magnus, a club? Do you imagine we have a president and a treasurer? Airing of grievances? Do we scrapbook after?"

"I'd love to understand more of what you do at these yoga and scrapbooking functions," he said playfully, taking a healthy bite of muffin after testing his drink.

"I don't do clubs…"

With that impish smile of his, it was hard for Lil to keep a straight face as she went on to explain what Magnus knew already.

"Yoga in the lavender field most days at sunrise. Usually it's Nan or Claire leading, but I go sometimes. There are workshops a few times a month: canning, making balms and herbal remedies, foraging. People can pay a flat monthly fee and come to any and all of the events, or pay as they go. It's a lot easier for Nan now that Claire has taken on more of the business."

Magnus washed down the last of his muffin with a sip of cider.

"Yes, that is understandable. I'd wondered why Claire chose to relinquish what I believe to be her passion for, well, something less demanding of higher education. But then I find myself in the garden, in the orchard, blissfully baking with Nan, and I understand… I feel the pull to slow down… But I'm challenged by the potential for so much to be discovered, at a time when the need is great. And the wheels are ever turning, Lily. We are constantly on the cusp of something groundbreaking, and it's hard for me not to be on the forefront. It's who I am, I suppose, and I do well enough that I can still relax as I need to. I'm sleeping splendidly, of course, wherever I go. Speaking of going… I'm leaving Saturday. First to Boston for a couple days to check in with the bio-med folks, and visit with Mira's younger brother, Martin. Then on to Iceland for two weeks. I'm officially going for business, but if it was only business I wouldn't have moved forward with the house. Boston is a bit busy, but Iceland… Lily, it's beautiful. The offer still stands, I'd love for you to join me. You're always welcome wherever I go, but the Iceland house is something special. The landscape resonates with a feeling I would only insult by attempting to describe."

Magnus globetrotted frequently, with ownership of a private jet and lodging arrangements what seemed like everywhere. Lil had traveled with him before; always with Gunnar tagging along, which she didn't mind. His temperament was much like Magnus's in that he didn't need to make noise to feel comfortable.

Iceland did sound beautiful, and she'd wanted to visit. With a twinge of guilt, Lil thought she could, *maybe*… but she had commitments at the shop. Nan would tell her to go, of course, but Lil knew she should stay.

"I don't think the timing is right with work… but it sounds wonderful, Magnus."

"Oh, you can steal away for a couple weeks. She has the boy there."

Lil chuckled to herself. *The boy.*

"The children's tea party is coming up, Claire and I do a whole thing, dress up…"

"Very well then," he pouted. "The house will still be there, and the mountains, the ocean, and your paintings."

"When can I expect your people to come for it?" She asked, nodding toward her work on the wall.

"Is tomorrow too soon? And same as before, I'll have my people come and retrieve it, but no one you are unfamiliar with. You'll only need to interact with Gunnar. The shipping company will prepare the work up at my home and take it from there."

"Sounds good," Lil said over an empty plate and mug.

"If you're trying to kick me out, it won't work. I've only had one muffin, half a cup of cider, and we haven't been outside yet. Come." Magnus stood, mug in one hand, oat muffin in the other, and started for the back door. "There's still time before Gunnar gets here."

"What, you don't need butter on that one?"

"I used it all on the rye. I'll bring more next time. Take a muffin for yourself and let the food quiet your mouth. You're chatty today, and I want to listen to the waves."

Lil smiled, grabbed a muffin, and followed him out to the deck.

4.

Lil's eyes drifted closed, Gunnar's calm presence steady beside her as the thrum of the plane's engine faded out through some trick of the mind.

A child sitting on the ground at the edge of a mint patch, Lil held her sketch pad while Magnus first made the introduction. Both she and Gunnar remained silent, cautiously assessing one another. Then, Magnus made his way into the shop, and Lil's new guard stayed behind, with her.

She kept to her work initially, capturing the likeness of the pollinators, but she couldn't keep her curious eyes from drifting over to her human visitor. Large as he was, Gunnar's movements flowed with undeniable grace. He relaxed himself on the ground nearby, but not too close, prompting Lil to gather her supplies and settle down beside him. Flat on the ground, she followed his gaze to an unremarkably beautiful flower, and to the crab spider waiting like a deadly jewel amongst the petals.

They remained for some time, she and Gunnar, sharing stillness with the spider, until the honeybee arrived. Four outstretched legs clamped down on the insect's shuddering body. The dance was brief, the embrace was strong, and the remains of the insect were later discarded to the garden floor, food for the earth.

"Tea?" She'd asked, turning toward him.

Nodding, he rolled onto his side, and crouched beside her.

Tilting her head, she stared, unsure what he was doing.

His eyes flicked behind him, then to Lil again, his brows arched in question… Offering her a ride on his back.

Lil couldn't control the smile bursting out, pushing back her cheeks.

She climbed up behind him, arms around his neck as he stood, and she found herself higher than she'd ever remembered being on two legs. He carried her like that through the garden and into Nan's shop.

He visited several more times over the five days following their introduction and, after the first week passed, Gunnar began escorting her to The Orn.

She'd inquired once about the manner of his education, given his age and position.

We were taught martial arts and had weapons training, he'd said. *Magnus went there too, long before my time.*

Magnus went to a military school? She'd asked.

Gunnar had smiled ever so slightly, shaking his head with equal subtlety.

A small private school. We grew our own food, cooked our own meals. Anything we consumed that could be grown, we grew, either outside or in the greenhouse.

Lil liked the idea of children growing things, *really* growing things.

Did you live there, she'd asked.

I started living there around age ten. My nuclear family was able to relocate closer to the school by then, so I still had a home life.

Did anyone else in your family go to school there?

He'd given his head a shake, a little smile working its way to his lips.

Not everyone. My parents didn't go but Magnus did, and his grandfather. It is a legacy school, but not every member of a family is recruited. Generations are often skipped over. Magnus, as the only living relative who'd attended, came to speak with my parents, explaining what he could about the school and the significance of attending. It was a great honor for my family.

A Story in Stone

Do you feel that way still?

He nodded. *We are taught that, while we will go on to do great things, it is our sacred duty to serve the balance of life in whatever it is we do. And now here I am, here with you.*

Lil hadn't realized Gunnar's potential to assist her, physically, until sometime later. She was given full access at The Orn, per Magnus, to observe anything she wanted unless there a justifiable safety concern could be made. Most were curious and excited about her presence, but when workers needed solitude with their projects, she understood, and moved on.

Gunnar could be quiet, big and quiet, like a mountain, and it was just what she needed: something solid there with her. As solid as he was, he could also be fluid, and he had moved so quickly that day.

They'd been moving through a first-floor hallway, one wall made entirely of windows. Ken, a researcher she'd bumped into an improbably number of times, walked a few yards behind them, but Lil suspected he'd been following her.

As she turned into a room after Gunnar, fingers tapped playfully on her shoulder, as if piano keys rested there under her shirt, their music unsettling.

What is it that you do in there? Ken had asked as she swiveled toward him. *You always observe us,* he said in a way that made her skin crawl. *Wouldn't it be fair if I had turn observing you.*

There was a heat in his eyes that shouldn't have been there, though she wasn't quite sure what it was at the time.

He'd stroked his hand down her arm, moving his body in closer. *Why don't you give your friend a break so he can grab a coffee? You and I could talk more about how you got the algae in my lab to respond to your voice.*

Something hadn't felt right. As a warning tingled within her, the blue world outside the glass hallway transitioned rapidly to one of grey and darkness, clouds moving fast and strong as her heart.

33

A blur of movement manifested into Gunnar, suddenly dragging Ken back into the room with him. Lil followed around the corner, watching as Gunnar zip-tied Ken's hands, sat him facing the wall, and instructed him not to speak. Things slowed down again when Gunnar opened his jacket, exposing his shoulder holster as he retrieved a small waxed-paper bag. He held it out to her, an offering.

Lil had dipped her fingers in silently, without question, barely rustling the paper as she retrieved a caramel. It was soft, and had a hint of lavender. *Nan inspired me to try something new in the kitchen,* he'd said.

Gunnar rolled up the bag, returned it to his jacket, then took out a cellphone and made a quick call. Within minutes, another man came in to retrieve Ken. She never saw him again.

"Eyes open, kid."

The engine purred loud beneath is voice. No *way* had she fallen asleep...

Lil opened her eyes to the soft blue sky concealing stars. She may have nodded off a bit, but the atmosphere remained unchanged. good.

Gunnar, to her left in the pilot seat, glanced down at his travel mug, removed the lid, inspected what remained, replaced the lid, and settled back into silence, the only additional commentary being the arching brows over his dark eyes.

What? She asked silently, a little squint in one eye as she regarded him.

"I was hoping you'd dreamed of coffee," he shrugged.

Lil rolled her eyes and smiled, "It doesn't work like that."

He turned toward her, raised his brows, then faced forward.

"Yeah, okay. I don't know how it works," she conceded, catching the tiniest hint at a smirk on his face. They could both smile about it now, but the whole cup incident had been, and remained a little unsettling when she lingered on it. She'd discussed it with Claire when she'd called to break their plans, then with Gunnar when they embarked.

"I could stay," he said, as if sensing her thoughts.

"It was just the once," she said. "But the dreams, the *daydreams*... No, let's just... Let's give it some time, whatever it is."

Colorful houses dotting a patch of snow below, then the larger structures of the research station off to the right as they approached. No official runway existed, but plenty of open ground, level enough for landing, and the Cessna Grand Caravan was rugged enough to handle it.

They pulled in beside two-stories of copper and glass, a maintenance building positioned to the right of it, living quarters for scientists to the left.

Lil and Gunnar observed their surroundings through the glass as the engine went quiet. The land, barren and crisp, lacked trees in all directions, only snow, ice, rock, and liquid water where it still moved enough to resist turning solid.

Lil let out a breath that she supposed could have been a sigh, then felt something press into her palm. She looked down at her hand to find Gunnar's, then glanced up to catch those dark eyes as his fingers slid away from hers, from what he left there. The wax wrapping crinkled as she uncovered the small, amorphic cylinder of pliable amber. She put it in her mouth, placed the folded wrapper in her pocket, and savored the sweet heat of the ginger beneath the caramel. Gunnar had physical strength, and stealth. His temperament eased her, but he also had a way with confections that bordered on divine.

"Something to keep me warm out there?" She asked, then squeezed his bicep before heading into the back. Magnus and Gunnar would have a visual of her journey courtesy of surveillance footage and a body camera, but she'd be going in alone.

Beyond the zippered passage in a heavy fabric partition, Lil surveyed their cargo and found the bag of protective clothing she needed to change into. The nature of transmission was still unknown, and she needed to take as much precaution as possible not to accidentally bring anything back on board.

"All set," she called out once she'd changed.

Lil wore a chest harness with body camera over what looked like adult footed pajamas garnished with duct tape, face peeking out from a tightly cinched hood.

To hold any retrievable specimens, she strapped a satchel across her body, careful not to obstruct the camera. The backpack she pulled on next, large enough for a weekend trip to the moon, held everything she would need for a shower. And the box...

"The cooler inside the box is open," Gunnar said, patting a cube at her feet as he came through the partition. "Before you shower, open the box and place the specimens in the cooler. After you shower, close the cooler and remove it from the box. When you return to the plane, you'll load it into this," he said, referencing another container.

"Specimens in cooler, cooler in box," she repeated.

"Like a turducken," Gunnar said as a means of reinforcement, but with a face so stern she wondered how he'd managed it after referencing a chicken roasted inside a duck inside a turkey.

"I was thinking nesting dolls…" She said, prompting the smile she'd sought. If anyone had the strength to hold out, it was Gunnar, but why should he? "Is the camera up and running?"

He nodded. "I have the feed up in the cockpit. Magnus is watching from his location."

"So, he heard you say turducken."

Gunnar's nostrils flared.

"And," she added, "There's a recording of it."

His eyebrows went up as he pointed to his right ear, "I've got you in this one," then he pulled an earpiece out of his left. "And I've got him laughing himself into a fit in the other."

A chuckle passed between them; a moment of much needed release that faded to quiet smiles as cold air swept in through the open door. The chill seemed more refreshing than biting, something familiar in its touch that called her to wake up, but from what, *to* what, she wasn't sure. Perhaps the wind knew what was waiting for her, and sought to sooth before the task of processing death began.

Gunnar pressed his hand to her chest above the camera. The stone cylinder necklace she refused to take off, resting beneath her disposable clothing, cradled in the V between his thumb and forefinger.

"It's different from a deer," he began. "Shouldn't be, life is life, but it's different when they're human. It's different, knowing they had no one with them, no one easing them into whatever comes after."

"I'm with you," He said, pulsing his hand against her chest. "Remember to breathe, keep your head clear, in and out. My body will be in this plane, but I'll be here," another pulse of his hand on her chest, "and here." He separated his palm from her body, and brought his fingers to the hood over her earpiece and mic.

Lil put her hand on top of his, the absurdity of the glove between them drawing out another smile. Gunnar didn't ask if she was ready, he just held her eyes with his until she removed her hand, and walked off the plane.

After a jaunt through the frigid air, Lil entered the maintenance building by way of the staging and marshalling area. The large room had a couple large stainless-steel sinks, but more useful were the washing stations, each the size of a freight elevator. She put the box down, approached, and turned on the water. A cold stream splashed onto the concrete floor.

"I can shower in here if I need to."

"Good."

She'd need to dispose of her clothing and possibly scrub down after she was through with her work; she was hoping only the former.

The room's primary function was for readying equipment prior to departure, and for cleaning and breaking down equipment after returning from the field. The scientists who'd brought back the pathogen had only been making an initial visit, so there shouldn't have been equipment enough to warrant use of the room. This worked in Lil's favor, as she found the space barren and presumably clean.

Lil arranged her shower supplies, did a walk-through of the building finding no signs of life, and left.

She entered the main building through two sets of doors, pausing before a small circular room partially enclosed in painted glass. Black brushstrokes told a story on the clear surface: a figure with an owl, other birds. It was beautiful.

"Around to the right and straight back."

Following Gunnar's instructions, passing artwork on the walls and on pedestals along the way. She'd done the math; with two and twelve in the dorms, there'd be four dead in the main building where she walked. Bodies waiting to be found.

The unnatural fabric of her clothing rustled too much, too loud, her footsteps echoing from the thoughtfully painted floor and off the walls. She passed an empty kitchen, lecture hall, labs, and seating areas.

"You'll want to find the cold room."

Lil peered into a space with doors that spanned two stories from floor to ceiling, an overhead crane just beyond, and a narwhal on a large stainless-steel table. A portion of the animal's abdomen appeared to have been gnawed on, in contrast to the man-made incisions elsewhere. Its large, spiraled horn, a tooth she had once been surprised to learn, proudly extended from the corpse; a steeple.

"Necroscopy lab," she breathed.

"Head through to the cold rooms," he said, then paused a beat before adding, "Don't linger. The animal has long since passed."

She nodded. "I can feel its emptiness."

Lil found what she was looking for in a small room kept at a controlled temperature for the preservation of specimens: two small screw top containers, crudely labeled.

"Does Magnus know if they made slides or started any work with the material? Should I check the labs?"

Without answer, she headed for the nearest stairs to do a sweep of the second floor. Echoes vibrated out from her, over the walls and back. Lil felt like she was in a mountain cavern, a great stone room lit by the warm glow of dancing flames. She heard another set of footsteps in her mind, anticipated, something had spilled, released onto the floor, echoing until she stopped moving and just breathed, warring within herself with what to grasp for: reality, or the memory flickering just out of reach, like a forgotten word resting on the tip of her tongue.

"Just the cold room," Gunnar said. Apparently, the site crew came home, had dinner, told stories, and went back to the dorms. The sick began to feel ill overnight and didn't leave confinement the following day."

Another pause, an opportunity for her response.

"You still with me?"

She nodded, mute.

"Where'd you go, kid?" He asked, his deep voice whisper, grounding.

"I don't know. Something about the echo as I walked... Brought be to another place for a moment, a familiar place I've never been. The walls were stone lit by fire... I wasn't alone."

"Put your hand on your chest."

She did.

"I'm with you. Do you need to get outside?"

Lil shook her head, replaying what Gunnar had said about the crews activity, what she knew about the illness, all while her hand rested over chest, over the stone resting under her clothes.

"There were three," she breathed, continuing down the second-floor hall, glass-walled rooms on one side of her, a balcony on the other. "Magnus said there were three who went on site, and only two became infected."

Lil paused, looking down to the first floor. Long, curved benches undulated down the corridor like the back of a red dragon moving through sunlit water.

"The third began working excavation logistics in the morning," Gunnar said, pulling her back from another impending drift. "By midday others began to show signs of illness, so any work on the specimens would have been derailed."

Lil had been at the Orn after hours more than a few times. The work day didn't end at dinnertime for many; it certainly didn't for her cousin. Claire had slept in her office plenty of times, and Lil suspected the arctic scientists, who lived on site, might have a similar sense of flexibility about work hours.

"Magnus is trying to get ahold of Tom, the survivor," Gunnar added.

Lil entered a laboratory where equipment appeared to have been in use, a sweater on the back of a chair, notebooks open, personal items at various desks, as if someone had just left to take in some fresh air, to get some lunch. She scanned the workstations and checked the incubator where, after pulling open the heavy stainless-steel door, she was engulfed in the warm scent of soup. Among the stacks of petri dishes, she found a specimen labeled around the top edge with initials, date, time, and the word *mammoth*. In the fridge, Lil found two jars like what she'd gathered from the cold room downstairs. One clearly contained hair; the other had a chunk of tissue, both crudely labeled, though *mammoth* was legible enough.

She put them all in her satchel.

"Magnus has Tom on his end; says you'd better head to the genomics lab and check the incubator. Apparently samples need to cook for a time in the tray wells with buffer. It'll still be in there unless someone tampered with it."

Opening the door to the genomics lab brought a rush of air that smelled not of soup, but of putrefaction.

The male on the floor might have had skin like hers once, minimally melanated and warm beneath the cheeks, but there was no warmth from him. His waxy skin had become purple around his open mouth, blood crusted at the sides and down his neck, staining his clothes. His cheeks were the color of plums and eggplant, the same blotchy violet patches decorating his arms, and what the V-neck of his shirt collar reveled. His eyes remained open under drooping lids, giving a true sense that there was nothing inside.

Lil had witnessed death's stages, though not in a human, and she'd not seen it so... *unnatural*. Unnatural, not in how the subject perished, but in the cold reception surrounding his remains. It was this that horrified her.

The forest and the ocean didn't leave much behind. The dead become food for animals, fungus, and microscopic life. Once broken down, the leftovers become part of the soil, for plants to absorb through their roots. Teeth, antlers and bones, like pebbles and stones, become part of the forest floor, for moss to grab hold of, to erode into soil and sand. The wind would have its way here, too, she supposed, over time.

"I'm right here, kid. You still with me?"

Lil felt a phantom hand on her chest, nodded, and began to search the room.

She found what she was looking for in the incubator: one tray with the writing she'd seen before. It went into her crowded satchel.

"I need you to put on a large pair of gloves over the ones you're wearing. There are spares in your bag if the ones in the room are the wrong size."

She ignored the impulse to take a deep breath.

When the gloves were on, he said, "Take the pink plastic box out of the bag, place it on the workbench and open it."

The box contained a large syringe with a thick needle attached, several smaller packaged needles, scissors, a scalpel, small bolt cutters, glass vacutainers of different sizes with different colored tops, biohazard labeled baggies, and a small plastic screw top container.

Gunnar talked her through drawing what blood she could from the cadaver, harvesting tissue, and removing three fingers. When finished, Lil discarded the soiled layer of gloves, closed the pink box, loaded it into her satchel, then crouched back down.

Sitting on her heels, she rested her hand on the mottled chest of the man beside her. She closed her eyes, lamenting the body's inability to provide as it was meant to, with nothing but tile and steel surrounding it instead of earth and water. What a waste.

Each of us is a potential garden, she thought, interrupted by breath in her ear. It wasn't until the following silence that Lil realized she'd been humming.

"Pull your hand back," Gunnar whispered.

Lil's eyes flicked open as her arm retracted from the green depression at the dead man's sternum.

Tiny mushrooms the color of cream and butterscotch clustered around where her palm had been, speckled throughout the low blanket of moss that spread outward from the indentation. Little white flowers like stars, seven petals each… chickweed.

Lil sucked in a breath. "I didn't mean…"

"It's alright, kid. Go ahead and stand up. Good. Let's get you back to maintenance, okay?"

She nodded, backing away from what remained of the body, now thriving with growth.

"In and out," Gunnar said, guiding her breath with his own. Lil stayed focused on the sound like rolling waves in her ear. Steady and powerful, she synced her respirations with his, timing her steps: in, four paces, out, four paces… until she pushed the front door open and crisp air rushed in to surround her, refreshing and playful.

She leaned into the wind, uplifted by its strength as she drew closer to the maintenance building, Gunnar tracking her with his eyes from the plane.

In the staging room, she stored the materials she'd collected, as instructed, and stood by the shower, her thoughts drifting to what she'd left behind in the genomics lab.

"If all your seams are in-tact and you remove your clothes properly, just wash your face and get back to the plane."

She nodded, slipped the straps off her holster, and looked into the camera.

"I'll see you in a few minutes."

Lil followed procedure, carefully taking off her dirty clothes, cleansing, and wrapping herself in the soft white robe Magnus had provided. She wore clean slip-on shoes to the door, then kicked them off and ran barefoot to the plane, wind pushing her along, Gunnar's eyes pulling her forward.

Stopping beneath him, she placed the cooler inside the box he held. After tucking the cargo away, he set out a large jug of water with a spigot at the edge of the doorway.

Lil began washing her hands vigorously in the stream of water, her steady breath giving in to occasional gasps.

"Almost done," he breathed, then hauled her effortlessly into the plane, his arms grounding, solid.

"I'm okay, it just… It snuck up on me in the hall with the echoes, and then in the lab."

Lil felt his chin rubbing against her hair as he nodded.

"You've adapted with grace to your brilliance," he said, the scent of ginger and caramel on his breath.

He tapped an orange box with his boot. "Toss the robe there, get dressed, and come on up front." He offered a soft smile, then slid through the partition. "And don't worry, there are more caramels."

Lil dressed, and discovered her slippers from home waiting beside her boots. Gunnar. He must have grabbed them from the house.

She found him relaxed in the cockpit, waxed paper bag outstretched toward her as she sat down. They'd made good time, she realized. She could still meet with Claire.

"Only Magnus and I have witnessed the footage from the bodycam and security. No one else will see," he said.

"I hadn't even thought of that," she sighed around the candy between her teeth. "Will they send a team through to clean up?"

He shook his head. "I wasn't sure before you went in, but now… They'll demo the site from the air once Magnus has what you've acquired. Safety measures are already in place to keep the townspeople away from the facility, possible relocation."

Lil's eyes flicked to the research station, the houses in the distance. She felt slightly drained, and more than slightly hungry, clutching an apple muffin she'd eat as soon as the caramel in her mouth dissolved.

Gunnar got the plane moving, bringing them up slowly to an open patch where they could gain speed.

"Over twenty million dollars went into that facility," he said, "but not nearly as expensive as leaving it standing.

*

Roughly an hour later they descended upon a small red rectangle nestled against the white snow, two even smaller buildings beside it. A private research station. Magnus's.

Lil followed Gunnar through the partition to the back, trading her slippers for boots, eating a pear while he opened the back door.

Lil watched from the shadows, just beyond what light leaked in through the archway as Gunnar hopped out. Two parka-clad researchers greeted him, receiving Pandora's Box.

Lil had no interest in conversing with Saul and Martine, though she had heard wonderful things about the couple, and they had Magnus's complete trust to have been gifted what she and Gunnar passed on to them.

The pair looked past him into the plane, perhaps suspecting someone stood in the shadows. They were curious, she knew, of course they were, but Gunnar revealed nothing, not a glance over the shoulder. It wasn't until the door closed behind the two parkas that Lil jumped down from the plane to stretch her legs.

The wind seemed to have been waiting for her, flowing over any surface it could, and through her unbound hair.

Observing the surrounding expanse, Lil observed beauty in the shapes around her. The story of the landscape was told on a different scale, giving an unrelenting sense of time and distance that felt almost as overwhelming as it was familiar.

Though absent of color, the potential for life persisted. Did rock and snow want for such a thing? Lil pictured the dead man in the lab, the life she brought forth from him. It hadn't been intentional, had it? No, not consciously, but she'd asked for something. She'd asked, and answered.

45

Magnus had encouraged her to practice, her own body seemed to be urging her toward something. She had her reasons for not exploring what she was capable of, but perhaps…

Like a mountain settling beside her, Lil felt Gunnar's presence.

"How far out is the mammoth site," she asked, meeting his waiting eyes.

"You'll miss the meeting with your cousin."

She held his stare.

He nodded. "I'll get the coordinates."

Minutes later, she sat in the cockpit with Magnus on the sat-phone against her ear.

"There'll be no hookup for a portable shower, no decontamination equipment. Tom's colleagues described progressive, descending muscle weakness and paralysis like one would find with botulism, but accompanied by high fever, chills, gastrointestinal pain. Muscle paralysis of the diaphragm does not lead to a favorable outcome without a ventilator. You witnessed the appearance of the skin… disseminated intravascular coagulation like what you'd see from septicemic plague, Lily. You cannot get close. I'm apprehensive about you even touching the soil…" He sighed.

She'd had gloves on in the lab with what she'd done. She wouldn't need contact from her skin…

"I'll wear the zip up suit, boots, gloves, and bag everything for incineration before I get on the plane. I'll stay at a distance from the animal. With fresh air and the wind, any remaining exposed skin should be fine."

"I should be able to notify those standing watch before your arrival, so there won't be any surprises."

Lil hadn't anticipated having to speak with anyone… that she might be *seen*.

"You're nervous," he said softly; not an accusation.

"I feel like I need to be there, Magnus. I feel drawn to it, but," she sighed, "I'm apprehensive. I can't have people watching me do what I did inside…" Memories from the Orn flooded back, of being coveted.

"There will be five or fewer," Magnus started, "and they're not the sort who will be holding their recording devices, live streaming miracles. If ever a person walked this earth who should listen to their gut, Lily dear, it's you. Follow the feeling. Gunnar will be there."

Lil looked to her left, meeting dark eyes.

"Okay." She whispered. "Tell them we're coming."

*

White expanse gave way to brown and deep darkness surrounding an undefined protrusion of the ground below. Two small structures stood at a distance in the snow; wooden poles gathered into a conical shape covered with animal skin. Another tent, large and octagonal, surrounded a thin pipe delivering steam into the air. A pickup truck had been parked close by, old but rugged, an ATV sat alongside it. Two individuals stood outside, then a third exited one of the smaller structures as the plane approached.

"I don't have a solid plan. In the lab, I felt a need and followed it. I think I might be able to prompt a useful transformation here, but I don't know what it is yet. I don't even know if I'll be able to. It could be like watching for water to boil."

"Water boils faster with you watching it."

She rolled her eyes. "I meant other people."

"When the tide is quiet, you make the waves roar."

"That's just having fun," she sighed, almost brushing him off before she heard what he meant, that she was adept, effortlessly so when focused and relaxed. It's what she'd been working on her whole life; the breathing, the ocean, finding the mountain within herself, the stillness.

Ginger caramel had already started to soften against Lil's tongue as she looked at him, still facing forward in the pilot's seat, still clutching the empty waxed paper bag in his hands, concern on his face.

It pained him to stay behind.

"I'll come out if I feel I need to," he whispered with strength, but not volume. He turned and looked into her eyes, calm and serious as ever. "The moment the sky darkens, I'm pulling you out. With my hands if I need to."

Lil leaned over, placing her right palm against him, just below his shoulder, one of his hands settling atop hers He grounded her like a megalith, solid and timeless, but the effect was not one sided.

She took his hand with hers against her own chest, pressing into the soft sweater where the stone necklace rested. "Here," she said. Then, with the other hand she tapped her earpiece. "And here."

He lifted an uneasy, but increasingly confident smile. He would keep her steady, root her to a solid foundation, keep her from freefalling, and she would trust him. It's what they did. What they'd always done.

Three individuals waited in boots, gloves, and parkas by the tents as Lil approached in a new onesie with boots, gloves, and hood pulled tight around her face. The central figure, an older woman, stepped forward.

"Hello, I'm Amka. You must be Lil?" She smiled.

Lil nodded, sensing wisdom, caution, and curiosity beneath the hostess veneer. "I'm glad you knew I was coming," she said, feeling the woman's brightness, returning her smile. "A friend of mine said he would try to get word to you, but it was very last minute, and the site is so remote..."

Amka nodded, "Yes, we heard you would come."

"You know what happened to the people who visited before?"

48

"Mmm," Amka confirmed, nodding. "I know what happened to the two of them that Tom came in with. I don't know if the same happened to the other man, though."

"Which one?" She was told there'd been three, including Tom.

"The first one. I was with my grandsons. We came upon the thawing creature, and he was there: tall, broad, long light hair, eyes like honey. He was barely dressed for the weather, but didn't seem cold. He was like you," she said, eyeing Lil thoughtfully. "Not from here."

"And, he was *alone?*"

"He was. The boys were excited, so we left to spread word, and he was not here when we returned. Tom came by plane later with his friends from work. So much joy at the time. Fortunate that Tom was spared what happened to the other boys; men I suppose," she smiled, and then sighed, getting a distant look about her as she went on. "The ground has thawed strange. The weather cycles, have been changing, but this… it's as though the animal was at the center of it, like the earth wanted this. The one I spoke to said you might be able to help, but didn't say how."

Lil wasn't sure either.

They stood together where stones pebbled through snow still stuck to the ground, not too far from where the thaw took over.

"I need to get a little closer, but not too close," Lil began. "I'd like to walk out alone and meditate a bit. The pilot," she added, gesturing to the plane, "he knows me well, and he'll intervene if I sit for too long. I walk out alone," she reiterated, "and I come back alone. Only him, okay?" Lil felt she might have been a little too firm with that last part, but it was important for Amka and her companions to stay back if things got *interesting.*

Amka nodded, making no effort to disguise her puzzled expression.

"We'll be here. You take your time."

The woman may have been confounded, but it was with a sharp mind and eyes like a hawk that she watched Lil walk away.

White, brown, and grey met sky in a solid line, the only interruption being the lump of thawing carcass, a time capsule of hair and flesh, about eight meters out from where she stopped.

Lil knelt, knees sinking into the moist ground, frigid soil sliding around her hands as she pressed them down. Having managed to grow a little garden in the lab earlier with thoughts of life, she supposed she could do it again, but was she safe out in the open as Amka watched from a distance? Would the pathogen survive in the soil and new growth? There would still be risk, even if she grew a redwood from the creature's remains. If another exposure occurred, the impact to human life would be devastating.

The ground trembled beneath her, the earth's voice a low rumble that seemed everywhere, all at once.

Breathe, she thought; *breathe.*

She needed to still herself and just feel.

Breathe, she repeated. *Breathe until everything else fades away, be the mountain that remains.*

Gunnar drew breath like a metronome in her ear, an ocean reaching for land. Closing her eyes, Lil allowed herself to relax into the sound until his breath was hers, and the ocean moved before her. White waves turned orange, flames reaching for her, not to burn her down, but with longing. Fire rolled like the tide coming in, until there was no water left, only inferno. When red and gold licked at her knees, she pulled it closer still, the heat engulfing her with such intensity it almost broke her heart. Lil took it all in, then pushed the fire forward until it surrounded and converged upon the remains of the mammoth. Ice turned to steam, flames relentless against wet flesh until the carcass combusted.

The ocean of fire simmered from a roar to a rumble, then a murmur, until it was only breath in her ear again. The wind had calmed around her, reduced to gentle fingers brushing aside the tendril of hair that had escaped her hood. The light current of air passed like soft lips over her eyelids, coaxing them open.

Lil obliged, first seeing the steam rising from her body, then, what she'd done.

Ash and char remained in the massive bowl of black glass where the beast had been. No smoke, no coals, no embers endured as there was nothing left to burn. Only a rising ring of steam, and the blush of twilight on the horizon.

"Can you stand?" asked the deep voice in her ear.

Pushing up, she tested her balance and found herself able enough.

"Yeah."

Lil stood tall, and turned.

The three onlookers didn't need to speak, the awe on their faces said enough. Amka, though, seemed to sense Lil's vulnerability. The aged woman made to move toward her, but halted, perhaps remembering the instructions she'd been given.

Lil raised a reassuring hand, and made the short walk on her own, playful wind a rustling her suit. The fabric felt too tight against her face, her wrists, covering her in plastic.

She needed to come out of it, to come out of something.

"Please, rest and have some tea, come," Amka soothed.

Lil allowed the woman to guide her back, where she took a seat by the tents. She made to reach up and grab the zipper at her chin, but her gloves were muddy.

"Could you," Lil started with a deep breath and a weak smile, holding up her hands as she exhaled. "Could you help me with the zipper? And maybe the hood?"

Amka removed a mitten, and pulled the zipper down.

Lil wriggled, rolling her shoulders as her hood pushed back, skin still humming. She pulled her arms, drawing the sleeves with gloves attached inside-out and tied them around her waist, letting the upper half of the suit flop down. Lil shook her long hair loose, stretching as she closed her eyes and inhaled deep, filling with crisp air. She felt more than her lungs swell, felt her whole self expanding.

Thankfully, Amka went about procuring a cup of tea instead of staring. The woman unscrewed the top of a large silver thermos, poured hot liquid into one cup, then another; the ritual itself soothing in its familiarity.

"Lichen, berries, and a few other things," Amka said, explaining the contents as she handed a cup to Lil. "We all drink it,"

Lil almost never consumed things from people she didn't know. Her lifestyle supported the preference, so she rarely encountered the need to turn down an offer, but sitting in the privacy of their open expanse, Lil held what Amka offered, somehow absent that undercurrent of instinct to decline.

A sigh slid into the steam as Lil brought the cup closer to her mouth. Subtle floral notes blossomed over her tongue as she took her first sip, followed by undeniable earthiness. The flavor seemed familiar, yet unlike anything she knew. She found it quite pleasant.

"I'll send home with you," Amka smiled. "It's what I do for Tom."

The woman ducked into the tent, later emerging with a tin in her hand.

"I use about two spoons for every cup of water. You can do less, but no more than four spoons."

Lil nodded, expressed thanks, imagined sharing the new find with Nan and Magnus. She'd need the ingredients to make more herself. Magnus. Once she was back on the plane, she'd have him reach out. But that had her thinking...

"The other man," she started, "the one you first saw, how did he arrive at the site?"

"I cannot say, but I saw no vehicle. We didn't speak of it at the time, and then he was gone."

Lil didn't need to take another look at her surroundings to know how odd it was for someone to be alone and on foot in that terrain.

"More will come," The old woman continued. "But what they find will not be the same." A statement, but asking.

Lil sipped what was left of the tea, and returned her empty cup.

"Tell them…" She trailed off, looking out to the dark crater.

"I'll tell them we burned it down," Amka said. "The animal made people sick, and we did what we could to protect ourselves. We sang a song to the ancestors, of course, so the fire would burn strong," she added with a playful wink, then her sincere eyes turned serious. "You have our thanks."

"And your tea," Lil smiled, tapping the tin. She really needed to get the recipe written down.

*

Lil stepped into the open crate Gunnar had set outside the plane, dropped her suit and stepped back out, covering the box and handing it over. He tossed it carefully aside, then reached down, hauled her up, and held on.

"I didn't know what I was doing," she whispered, emotions still sparking. "Your breath was in my ear, then I saw waves turn to fire."

In the safety of his hold, Lil opened her thoughts, but they were moving too fast, unravelling. Gunnar's hand lingered firm on her back, moving up and down until she began to settle again.

"I left nothing but melted rock, Gunnar."

"Then nothing harmful remains."

By the time they lifted off, Lil had moved on to fruit after consumed what was left of the baked goods they'd brought. Lil was as hungry as she was tired. What she'd done in the lab, and with the fire… things like that required energy, she supposed.

"There was another exposure," she said, gravity of the potential outbreak sinking in as she ate the last apple, mentally replaying her conversation with Amka. "He wasn't local. the woman I spoke with said he was first on the scene and hasn't seen him since. Described him as blonde with *honey* eyes, tall, and alone with no vehicle. He was there when she first arrived, and gone when she returned."

Gunnar didn't nod, but he'd heard her. "We'll tell him when we refuel."

Him. Magnus.

In the air, blue sky fading to black, and her head leaning back against the seat, Lil closed her eyes. What was it Nan said she ran on? Salt water and what? Lil smiled, thinking of the ocean rolling over her body, of floating just below the surface.

"Eyes open, kid."

She sighed and did as he asked, tilting her head to the left.

"Green bag behind my seat," he said.

"Snacks?" Drowsy, but already in motion, she reached, driven by a spark of hope after thinking they'd eaten everything… Glancing up, she saw the corner of his mouth lift.

"Sorry, kid. You ate everything, but there's MadLibs and crosswords. Should be pencils in there too."

5.

"There's someone I want you to meet," Claire beamed.

Lil's cousin wore a soft, white, button up shirt with and a sage green cardigan, hair high in a ponytail exposing the tiny malachite stud earrings she always wore. The stones matched the single, spherical bead she wore on a thin, silver bracelet. Very subtle, very green, very Claire.

After returning late from her field trip for Magnus, Gunnar spent the night in Lil's guest room to be sure she was alright, and she'd spent a significant amount of time on the phone with Magnus, acquiescing to his persistent urging that she prioritize practicing, and do so in a safe, controlled environment.

Lil had been vague with Claire regarding the particulars of her need to cancel their prior plans, only stating Magnus had needed a time-sensitive favor. Neither she nor Claire required further explanation.

And now she wanted Lil to meet someone...

Lil tilted her head, issuing a flat stare from across one of the old, wooden tables in Nan's shop. Widening her grey eyes, she silently said, *I thought we were past this.*

"No, no, it's not like that," Claire shot back. "He's-"

"I don't *meet people,* Claire. If this is a set-up, I swear…" Lil turned to the counter, shouting, "Nan… Chamomile and lavender." She took a deep breath and scanned the room. "He's not here, is he?"

"Oh my goodness, Lil," Claire huffed. "Calm down, seriously. He's not here now, but he's coming. And before you say anything, it's *not* like that. I know you're particular about, *doing things,* but I thought you could help him with his research. I was going to bring this all up the other day," she sighed. "But I fell asleep on your couch, then we were rushing back to Nan's, and your dreams, which we're *not* done discussing. Then you couldn't meet last night…"

"What could he possibly be researching that I can assist with? Painting? Ceramics? Oh, bless you Nan, you're an angel," she said as the woman placed an ash grey mug with a poorly defined dragonfly imprint in front of her. During her undergrad, Claire took an entomology class that became an inspiration while she was tinkering at Lil's pottery wheel. Lil made almost all the stoneware at Nan's, except the bug mugs. Those were Claire's, and the dragonfly cup Lil drank from was her favorite.

Inhale and sigh. Lil looked up at her cousin through the steam.

"Okay, so, what does he need help with? And who is he?"

Claire perked right up. "He's pretty great, actually. His name is Brian. Dr. Sullivan, but his first name is Brian, and his research is with whales, and I thought..." She waited for Lil to respond, to finish her sentence, move, do *something*.

Claire sighed, "I thought since you go swimming how you do, and you swim with them sometimes... It just seemed like there was a connection there, and that you could help somehow. Maybe you could get close to the whales and observe something he or his team wouldn't be able to? You really need to talk with him."

"So, is this a first date for you guys?"

Shock spread like cold water over Claire's face. "What?"

"I'm thankful that you respect me enough not to attempt forcing me into a setup, but really Claire, you could have run it by me on the phone. Now I'm moments away from meeting this person. It's like a set-up of a different kind, and I don't like this feeling, like a little of my consent has been taken away." She paused, taking a sip. "What did you tell him about me?"

Claire sat up straighter, refreshed with a new serge of enthusiasm, "Oh, I didn't tell him anything. I invited him to come hang out, and thought you could just *be* here, and we could casually bring up his research, totally natural."

Totally natural. With an understanding smile on her face, Lil looked across to her cousin. Claire, though she had fumbled this a bit, was far from simple. She took kickboxing, taught yoga, and had begun shouldering more of the business responsibilities at Nan's, much to Magnus's disappointment. She worked part time as a research botanist or microbiologist depending on what hat she wore in the lab at Magnus's research facility, The Orn Institute.

"So, he thinks he's meeting just you, and you're going to have a surprise cousin with you, who is a woman, single, and happens to have a connection to something he researches... Claire..." Lil rubbed her face... "Claire, he's going to think you're setting us up."

Claire smiled and shook her head. "No, I don't think so…"

"Oh. My. Goodness... How long have you been seeing him?"

Claire widened her smile. "Ok, so it's only been a couple months but it could be getting kind of serious. Well, I don't know if it's *serious*, but it feels comfortable."

A couple of months was at least *encroaching* on seriousness for Claire. Lil knew her cousin liked to hang with colleagues after work, meet people, and go on dates when she could squeeze it in. She had a shining personality and persistent innocence about her… but she was also very passionate about fitness and her research. Claire made friends easily, a bright light at the office, but, historically, the effort it took to maintain a partner couldn't compete with what she did at the Orn. Maybe now that she was pulling back at the lab and spending more time at Nan's she'd be able to sustain things with this whale guy. Two months though, and Lil hadn't known?

"How can it be serious if this is the first I'm hearing of him? And when do you even have time to *see* each other? You are always working."

"I know it's been too long without an introduction; that's part of why I'm bringing him here. He's never been to Nan's, and this... this place is a really big part of my life. We mostly see each other after work, or before…" she said, rolling her eyes. "We do a lot of reading and paperwork together after hours at my place or his. It's nice to have someone who digs into his work as deep as I do."

At least he understood her, or had the same work rhythm. Lil would have to see them interacting to make any real judgment, judgement she'd keep to herself...

"Has he met Jane and Brad?" Claire hadn't introduced anyone to her parents since that one guy in college, and that had been incidental while they were visiting.

"No, he almost did though. Remember a couple weekends ago I drove down to see them? Brian had a thing at the university so we went together, but it just didn't work out as far as a rendezvous." She shrugged. "His schedule was too hectic."

"I still can't believe I haven't met him yet. That it's been months and I didn't know."

"Well, I may have been a little nervous, too. You're pretty spectacular, and, that can be intimidating."

Lil rolled her eyes. "Claire, you are smart, talented, you can talk research with him, which blows his skirt up, apparently, and these bug mugs are the cutest. I could never upstage you, but if I did, then he's not the guy for you. Look, if it will help take the edge off, I'll harness my tresses," she said, twisting her long hair into a bun. "And I could pick my nose when he walks in, so it looks like he's caught me doing it?"

Claire burst with a spurt of laughter. If she'd been drinking something, Lil would have wound up wearing it.

Smiling, Lil tipped her mug back, finishing her tea. "Nan, I'm going to need another one of these immediately," She called out. "And Claire is going to need some...?"

"Kale Stout!" Claire shouted.

"Well, if you're having the kale stout, you should probably have an apple tart..." Lil shrugged, then both grinned and laughed, shouting, "Two apple tarts!"

It was two tarts later and into her second stout that Claire inhaled suddenly.

Brian had walked in.

Lil guessed he measured up at a few inches under six feet tall, thin, but fit. He wore khakis, hiking boots with red laces, and a moss-colored sweater with a thick weave to it. His hair was dusty brown and thinning, short, but long enough to have some shag around the ears.

Claire stood and waved. When he caught sight of her, he smiled and joined them, hugging Claire briefly before they both sat down.

"Brian, this is my cousin Lil that I've told you about."

Lil cringed inside. She didn't care much for that introduction, as it usually preceded disaster. Inhaling the vapors from her third cup of tea, she readied herself for Claire's embellishments...

"She works here at Nan's sometimes," Claire continued. "She's also an artist. She did that big painting over on the back wall, and all the other ones... She makes most of the mugs and plates here too."

Brian looked around as Claire, doing her best not to feel outshined, referenced Lil's visible accomplishments. Lil felt Claire wilting ever so slightly during the presentation, it weighed on her heart. It was so unlike her cousin to feel dulled by anything, and to witness it was unsettling.

'Lil, this is Brian. We met at the Orn a few months ago."

"Nice to meet you, Brian. Do you work there as well?"

"No, the day I met Claire I was in with a mutual acquaintance. He had a couple short meetings, and the cafeteria at the Orn is *amazing*. Of course, I was only in the public part of the building. Security is *tight* there. I thought I was going to be strip searched before we were done. It was intimidating, and a little exciting," he laughed.

"Oh, you don't know the half of it," Claire started. "You were electronically fingerprinted but at minimum you also had your irises and face scanned... and a reading of your chemical signature taken for our database. Ugh, I probably shouldn't have said that."

"Have you met JD?" Brian asked, turning towards Lil.

"The mutual acquaintance," Claire clarified. "JD works for some corporate international this or that. His company collaborates with Magnus's sometimes, so he's always flying in. I don't know him *well*, but we just kept running into each other over the past year. At some point we started sharing schedules so we could coordinate lunches. He kept pushing to meet up *outside* the Orn, but that was before I cut back at work. I was just juggling too much." She said, then paused enough for Lil to see the gears turning. "You could meet him. We're going to see Brian's friends play at a bar Friday and He's meeting us there. You should join."

Lil rolled her eyes. "Claire..."

"I know, I know. Just think about it. It would be fun to have you come out."

Lil put up a hand, ending the conversation as she turned to Brian. "Can I get you a drink? Claire and I have had a bit of a head start; treats as well."

He looked up at the counter, browsing the chalk board menu. "A Blonde Ale, and..."

"The oatmeal cookies don't have raisins today," Lil offered.

"An oatmeal cookie sounds nice," he smiled. "But I can get it myself, really,"

"No, let me," Lil insisted as she stood and stretched. "I wanted to chat with Nan anyway."

Nan kept a casual appearance as Lil approached, though barely able to contain herself.

"Is that him?" she asked as Lil rounded the counter

"You knew there was a *him*?"

"Claire's been buzzing about the same guy for a month or so. You, who can sense a beetle landing on a leaf a mile down the road, I don't know how you missed it." They both turned, obviously, evaluating the couple. "I'm surprised it's taken this long for her to have him over. Did you come up here just to gossip?"

"Blonde Ale and an oatmeal cookie for the gentleman, and Claire wants me to help him with his *whale* research."

Nan paused reaching for the fridge. "Did she tell him anything about you?"

"No."

"Well, I'm steering clear of *that*, but be cautious. He seems benign from a distance, but you never know for sure at first glance, even at the second. Now, before I forget,"

Lil raised her eyebrows. "As if that would happen."

"Magnus said he invited you to Iceland. You didn't mention it."

"The troublemaker…" Lil started. "It's too short of notice now. Todd can't pick up *all* the slack, and Claire can't be here every day. And the party…"

"We did just fine yesterday while you were off helping Magnus with his urgent whatever-it-was. Todd can get one or two of his friends to help out again. Some days it feels like they've nothing better to do than hang around here waiting for him to get off work. They might as well put their hands to good use."

Lil regarded her with a wordless stare, more than done speaking about it.

With a sigh, Nan gathered up the beer and cookie, and rounded the counter.

"I'm coming over to meet him."

Lil sat back in her seat, wondering if Brian could feel the danger looming beneath Nan's smile, the blueberry-stained apron, the disarming scent of baked goods.

"Brian," Claire beamed, "this is Nan. She's my Nana, but her name is Annabel, so Nan either way. Nan, this is Brian. We met at work."

"It's nice to meet you, Brian. Are you from around here?"

"I just moved to the area last spring," he said with cheerful formality. "I used to work at the university. I maintain affiliation, but currently

I'm conducting research with one of the local whale-watching outfits. I'd never heard of your place before meeting Claire. There's a real special feel here."

"We're a well-kept secret, and we like it that way. I need the business to make a living, but if this were to get too busy, it would lose the essence of what it is." She put her hand on his shoulder. "Enjoy the cookie, Brian."

Nan flashed Claire a quick raise of her eyebrows, turned and walked back to the counter.

Brian put his hand over Claire's.

"It was so nice to meet you," Lil said, standing from her seat. "Claire, I'm going to head out."

Her cousin looked horrified, color draining somewhere behind the alcohol-induced pink of her cheeks. "No, you can't go! Why are you leaving?"

"I feel like a swim, so I'm just going to go home, call it an early night."

"A little brisk out there for a swim," Brian said, tipping his beer back, then he tilted his head with a thought. "Unless you have a heated pool. I say we meet at Lil's next time if there's a heated pool option."

"Ocean. I have a house on the shore."

Brian's brows pinched together, head cocking to one side. "But it's dark out, and it's *cold*. You don't go out alone, do you?"

"Lil," Claire started, "why don't you stay and we'll talk more." Then, turning to Brian, she said, "Sometimes she sees whales out there while she's swimming, right Lil?"

Lil eyed her cousin, not at all appreciative of the contrived segue. "Yes," she sighed, "I swim both alone and with whales, on occasion." It wasn't something she advertised, but he seemed harmless, and it meant a lot to Claire, so she sat back down.

"You swim with whales? What kind? Are you affiliated with any research groups? How often are you on the water?"

"Ok, slow down Brian," Claire laughed.

"Claire," he huffed, delightfully exasperated, "I *research* whales. This is kind of a big deal."

"In," Lil corrected. "*In* the water, not on. I swim alone, and it's not *about* anything. It's relaxing, and sometimes the whales are there too."

Claire gave Lil an encouraging *go on* look. Lil was hesitant, knowing what their conversation would lead to, but she'd just incinerated a mammoth in the arctic. And while Brian had already started to feel like a tag rubbing at the back of her neck, the idea of helping him, whatever that meant, barely registered compared to what she'd been through up north, and it would mean a great deal to Claire.

"If there's anything in particular that you're interested in," Lil sighed, "and if there's a way I could be useful, I'd probably help... depending on what it is you need..."

She could hardly believe her own words, that they existed outside of her body.

Brian gathered himself, packaging his excitement into something intense and serious. "I'm very interested in southern resident orca population stability. We have concerns they're not breeding enough, that their diet might not be diverse enough..."

"Well, at least one is pregnant, so there's that. And some of the non-resident orcas that have been hanging around, teaching locals to hunt for seals."

"No," he shook his head. "That doesn't make any sense. We would have seen something indicating that level of interaction between the resident and transient orcas."

"I don't have an agenda, Brian. These are just my observations," Lil said, closing her eyes a moment, taking a deep breath. Why was she doing this? Claire.

"We'd need an ultrasound or a blood sample to confirm the pregnancy," Brian said, taking a long drink from his bottle of blonde ale. "No, I don't see either of those things happening, but I *could* give you some audio equipment to take recordings."

"If she consents, I can get a sample," Lil offered, figuring it was no different an act than a specialist might perform. It's not like she'd be growing plants from her hands or starting fires… and no one would be watching.

Brian stared, glancing to Claire, and back. "Consent? Would you have her sign forms? And have you even taken a blood samples from an animal before, human or otherwise?"

Lil looked into her empty mug, then to the nearest painting on the wall, reaching for the feeling she'd embedded in the paint.

"Nan?" Claire called out. "Nan, could you bring Lil another tea? I think I'll have one too, and three tarts. They're so good!"

Claire lowered her voice to a stern whisper, attention on Brian. "Lil is *capable*. She could, like, perform her own appendectomy after watching a video tutorial. Honestly, I can get her some stuff from the lab. She'll be fine."

Brian shook his head. "I can't believe I'm entertaining the idea that this is plausible."

"Listen," Lil started, her voice slow and steady, tolerance limited. "Why don't we just forget about it and relax. I'm going to head out to the orchard for a walk before I get behind the wheel. You guys should play cribbage or chess, we've got games over on the bookshelf," she said, nodding over to the corner, looking for a polite way out, but Nan was already standing beside her with a steaming mug for Claire, a teapot refilling Lil's cup.

"Todd will be over with the tarts in a minute," she started. "I'm turning in; my old bones are *tired*. Was nice meeting you, Brian."

"Likewise, Nan," he smiled. Then, as the old woman left, he asked, "Who's Todd?"

"A kid who helps Nan out around the shop," Claire said, pausing to blow on her drink. "She likes to have it just family here, but he's practically family. His grandmother is good friends with Nan; she and his mom come to a lot of our workshops. He was getting in trouble when he was in either elementary or middle school, so his mom asked Nan if he could work here. That was about seven or eight years ago. He works here at the shop and over at the surf school. Nan *really* relies on him, especially with me at the lab so much."

"Nan straightened me right out," Todd said as he rounded the table. "And I'm not a kid, I'm almost twenty."

Todd, tall with an athletic build, wore brown corduroys and a grey t-shirt that said *Stoked* in faded white letters. He had short, shaggy red hair, generalized freckles, and small plug earrings.

He put down the women's tarts but held on to Brian's, eyeing him skeptically.

"Brian, is it? I heard about you."

The table became still.

"I think it's great, you being with Claire, but you need to know up front that just because she doesn't have brothers, that doesn't mean she doesn't have brothers, know what I mean?"

Lil smiled up at Todd, delighted. He was his undiluted self, and Lil loved every gram of him.

Claire looked absolutely mortified.

Brian, caught off guard, attempted to maintain composure. "I think I understand, but clarification would be helpful."

"To *clarify*, I mean she's got people looking out for her. She's like a sister to me, and Lil is a force to be reckoned with, so keep it honest and treat her right, is what I'm saying. Don't get me wrong, Claire could lay you out no problem," He said, shooting her a sideways glance before refocusing on Brian. "Those kickboxing classes are no joke. That being said, these tarts are unreal." Todd placed the last of the desserts down in front of Brian, patting him on the back, and said, "Dig in, bro."

Lil watched Brian's eyes follow Todd as he left to clear some glasses from another table.

"Well, that was… unexpected," Brian began. "Troubled youth, you say?"

Claire raised her head from where she'd rested it in her hands. "I am so sorry, Brian. I did *not* expect him to get weird."

"No, it's ok, really. You have a big heart, and it's good to see your family cares so much about you."

Claire smiled, something silent and sentimental passing between them before Lil lowered the pitch of her voice, said, "Dig in, bro," and they all laughed.

"I want to circle back to the whales," Brian announced. "What's the plan? Should we meet at Lil's? Your place is on the shore, right?"

"Yes, but I don't *entertain company*, Brian. Once you guys get me the necessary equipment, I'll take a swim, then meet you guys here to hand everything over. How soon can you get me what I'll need?"

"The audio recording gear," Brian started. "I can get it to you by end of day tomorrow."

"Same," Claire chimed in. "I can get supplies at the lab, swing by Brian's, and make a drop-off at your house by dinnertime."

"Great!" Brian exclaimed, delight leaking from his skin as he sat back in his chair. "We can grab dinner and meet Lil at the shore before she gets out, then we can head to my place to listen to the recordings, and-"

"We'll meet at Nan's," Lil said, cutting him off. "I'll call when I'm on my way."

"Well," Claire smiled, looking around the table. "This is coming together nicely."

"Mmm," Lil offered, her thoughts already drifting, concerned she might be taking on more than she should. Again, she reminded herself of the incinerated mammoth, though that had been with Gunnar, for Magnus. This was for Claire, really, who she wholly trusted. Brian, though… There was something about him that made her uneasy, perhaps his eagerness, maybe something more.

Gathering the empty plates and cups, she stood, said her goodbyes, exchanged some banter with Todd, and headed off home to the water, to what dreams would come next.

6.

Saltwater lapping at her neck and ears, Lil spotted Brian on shore.

His head snapped in her direction as she exited the ocean, her long hair blending with the black of the wetsuit and the night beyond, only the moonlight reflected along her silhouette suggesting she was more than a face floating toward him.

As she emerged, Brian noted the utility belt with pouches and pockets, then the absence of tanks, mask, and snorkel.

Lil's eyes had been on him from the moment they were clear enough to see, but it wasn't until she became uncomfortably close that she spoke.

"Brian," she said, her voice calm, but firm. "I told you I would meet you at Nan's."

He looked away, then back. "Yes, but curiosity about your process got the best of me. Claire and I took separate vehicles and, well, it *is* unusual for-"

"You need to respect my boundaries if you want my help."

Brian looked uncomfortable, which was warranted. "Understood."

Is it though? She thought. "You have a cooler in your truck?"

"Yes"

"I obtained samples, recordings, and gossip," she said, pulling out several glass tubes, a recording device, and a small plastic container from her belt. "I'll meet you over at Nan's."

He stared, mouth slightly open. It wouldn't be right to call it a *blank* stare, as he clearly had so many questions.

He inhaled a little bit, but no words yet.

"Brian." She prompted.

"I... Lil, I'd really prefer to discuss this now and head to the lab directly with the samples. I can text Claire, she won't mind if I go ahead. It's a long drive and... This is... This is amazing. Where are your tanks? Do you even have *goggles?*"

The wind picked up, waves waking, hitting harder against the rocks, moon suddenly obstructed.

"I'll meet you at Nan's, Brian."

He turned to go with her as she walked past, the hair on his neck rising, stopping him where he stood. With an inaudible exhale, Brian tried to reason with the adrenaline coursing through him, set off by some animal notion he wasn't consciously privy to. whatever had spiked his adrenaline. As a man of science, Brian didn't like the idea of being intimidated by the unknown, but as a man who'd once been stalked by a cougar on a hike... He stopped following her all the same. Instead, he stood there, watching her disappear over the rocks, through the trees, and back into the darkness. As she faded, so too did the self-preserving instinct that had been triggered in him.

Alone again, he took the path to his truck, aware of his surroundings but with more questions than he thought he'd ever have answers to.

7.

Claire sipped her beer, laughing almost too hard to swallow. "How about that time we were lost and those wolves came," she choked out, "and snuggled you!" To Brian, she explained "I thought we were lost, and then-"

"We were never lost," Lil sighed.

Claire's eyebrows shot up. "I *thought* we were lost. It was very real for me."

"I have never given you cause to question the trust between us, and you should have trusted me when I said we weren't lost. I had to breathe with you for like, ten minutes to calm you down."

Brian looked between the two women, and put his two hands up. "I just want to be clear that what you are *not* disputing is the claim that wolves were snuggled. Because that's what I'm hearing. You two are getting into it about feelings and trust, and can you please address the wolf snuggling?"

Claire laughed harder.

Lil rolled her eyes, a smile peeking through. "It was more of a nuzzle. They came upon us, curious, and I made contact."

The smell of the forest flooded into Lil's mind; its scent embedded in the wolf's fur as she sank her face into it, wet noses of the others brushing against her skin. Dangerously close to pulling her in, pulling her back to something else.

"No one ever sees them," Brian marveled, his presence calling Lil back to the irritating, albeit mildly amusing conversation. "You know that, right? Ever. I don't think anything else in this life can surprise me. Did you hunt together? Share a meal? Paint each other's nails, excuse me, *claws*?"

Lil sipped from her cup, eyes deep and unimpressed. "They don't have thumbs, Brian."

"Thumbs..." He mused. " I still can't believe you got those samples. And all this," he patted his open notebook on the table. "They're learning to hunt from transients, and this pregnancy... It's unbelievable."

"What's *really* unbelievable," Lil paused dramatically to take another sip of her tea. "Is that Claire told you where I'd be coming ashore." She turned to Claire, eyebrows raised. "Betrayal is not a good look on you, Claire."

Lil had released of the bulk of her irritation back at the water, but still needed to acknowledge the trespass with her cousin present.

Claire's shoulders sank, remorse audible. "Lil..." she started, heartfelt, and slow. "I'm so sorry. I really didn't think he would go and *meet* you there."

"Claire was pretty upset," Brian confirmed.

"I was upset too," Lil said, looking right into him with a calm stillness, a stillness so profound, that Brian found it difficult to move.

"Do you remember how upset I was at the shore, Brian?"

Brian nodded with effort, like moving through quicksand.

"You violated my personal space, Brian, but the greater offense was in breaking Claire's trust. Listen, I know that you two will confide in each other, and sometimes I will be the topic of discussion. No matter what you share between you, whether it be about me or anything else, it's vital that you honor the knowledge as a seed entrusted to you. Some knowledge is meant to be scattered: a recipe for a great pie is worth spreading so more people might have the tools to create something delicious. But some seeds, Brian, like the knowledge of how I'm helping with your research, would grow a fruit I don't think you'd enjoy eating."

She held him there, his eyes with hers, until Todd approached wearing faded jeans and a light grey shirt that read *Tao AF* in darker grey letters. He placed a glass of golden liquid with an ice cube in front of Claire, then a bottle of blonde ale in front of Brian, eyeing him.

"Snitches get stitches, bro, but it's not me you need to worry about." He glanced at Lil, then back to Brian. "You take anything about Lil to the grave, son." Then he looked back to Lil with a smile. "I had no idea what you wanted. Pretty sure tea and a pastry are involved, but I didn't feel like rolling the dice on that tonight."

Lil released Brian's attention, hearing his sigh as she turned to give Todd's hand a squeeze.

"I'll get it. I want to browse, but I'm pretty sure I'll go tart," she smiled. "Have I mentioned how much I love your shirts?"

"Just about every day," Todd said. "And I told you I'd hook you up anytime; I know a guy."

"No way, the shirts are your thing."

"A teenager called me son," Brian whispered, though not quite enough to evade Lil's ears.

"We still hitting the waves tonight?" Todd called back on his way to the counter.

"You know it," she said, putting a hand palm-up on her shoulder

He took a few steps back toward her, slapped his palm down on hers, slowly pulled away. "Nice, I'll text you after I close up."

"You surf out there too?" Brian asked. "At night, with *him*?

"*Him?*" Claire laughed, mocking horror. "Really, Brian, he's like a surrogate brother."

Lil fought through her smile enough to form words. "Yes, Brian, I go surfing with Todd at night on occasion," she said, thinking of how far Todd had come, how far they'd both come. "There's a different feel at night," she continued. "It's the same ocean, same waves, but for many people a feeling of the unknown is enhanced in darkness. The connections to one's daily life can be loosened, trivial threads break, and one can find an awareness of themselves they'd be too distracted to see in the light."

Claire looked down, swirled her golden drink, and took a sip.

"What is that, scotch?" Brian asked.

"When have you known me to drink scotch, Brian?"

Right, Lil thought. *Because you've known each other for so long.*

"It's ginger wine."

Brian made a face of disgust.

"Really? It's refreshing with some grapefruit soda and a sprig of rosemary. Straight up isn't for everyone," she sighed, taking another sip.

Lil's phone vibrated against her chest from within the small bag she wore. She pulled out the device, put it to her ear.

"Gunnar."

"Hey kid, just checking in."

"Any updates on that tea," she asked, trying her best at deterring attention as she added, "or the one who got away…?"

"Magnus has a list, not a peep on the other thing. Demo is on schedule. Sleeping okay?"

"Yeah, last night was uneventful, but I think, hold on."

"Practicing?"

"I…" Lil glanced across the table, thought about her exchange with Brian, his stillness when she'd confronted him. It occurred to her that she had, perhaps, held more than his attention with her eyes… "I'm not sure."

Nan, came to sit down with a drink as Lil stood.

"I'm just getting up for tea and a pastry," Lil said, a content smile lighting her face as she nodded her head toward the counter. Then, into the phone, she whispered, "I think I kept someone from moving just now, like, his body."

Brian watched as Lil walked to the counter. "Does she have any affiliations?" He asked, his voice kept low.

Claire glanced to Nan, Brian following her eyes as he continued. "She's a groundbreaking asset. I don't understand why she isn't spearheading her own research."

"She's done some work at The Orn," Claire offered. "Though I'm not sure what. She was very young."

"Like, undergrad?"

"*Way* undergrad. She was, what, seven? Eight when she started? And she didn't go to college, really. She just jumped right in. I mean, she learned things. Nan homeschooled her."

"Guided," Nan corrected. "I guided her, is more like it."

Brian's face contorted into an expression of familiar confusion.

"I told you, she's brilliant," Claire smirked.

"I don't understand," Brian said. "She should be teaching, conducting research. Great minds can change the world, but she-" He turned to Claire, nodding his head covertly in Nan's direction as he whispered, "Does she know about the animal stuff?"

Nan's face turned deadly serious. "Are you asking Claire if there's something that has somehow escaped me about the girl I raised from a child?"

"Oh no, ma'am, I didn't mean to, well, yes I was asking her. I didn't mean to presume there was something you didn't know; I just didn't want to speak out of turn."

Nan's face softened a little. "I appreciate that you wanted to check with Claire before speaking about one of Lil's more sensitive attributes. I continue to be hopeful that she made the right choice in trusting you with that knowledge." Nan sighed, looking over to the counter where Lil held a cellphone to her ear with one hand, mug in her other, Todd feeding her a cookie.

"It's my understanding that you've taught at the college level," Nan started. "Is that correct?"

"Yes," Brian said with a nod.

"Have you or any colleagues saw need to teach a grizzly bear how to hibernate?" She asked, face straight as death's stare. "Do you know how to hibernate?"

"Well," he began, "there was a study some years back that showed scientists were able to induce hibernation, but bears aren't true hibernators, we call what they do *torpor...*"

"Don't patronize me, Brian."

"No ma'am, I do not know how to hibernate."

"My point, Brian, is that there's nothing the bear needs to know about itself to hibernate. There's nothing to teach the bear in that regard... And there's certainly nothing the bear can teach you about hibernation that would result in you being able to sleep through winter. The bear just lives, and it does so beautifully," she sighed. "And when you try to unnaturally alter the path of a bear, you risk getting your throat ripped out."

Brian's eyes went wide, grip a little tighter on his bottle.

Nan tilted her head, and shrugged. "Perhaps I shouldn't have gone with the bear analogy. What can I say, it's late and I'm feeling whimsical... What I'm mean is, with all the knowledge we have of how everything works, we still need to go to the bees for honey. And while we can learn more about how to predict the weather, we still wait for the rain with our mouths open. Lil is like the bees, and the clouds, Brian. There's nothing to teach or be taught, and if you try to alter her path, well... I stand by what I said about the bear."

"Right," Brian agreed, any traces of fear fading back into curiosity and confidence. "The importance isn't *how* she does it, but what she does with it. I don't mean for her to lecture on how to communicate with orcas. Just, look at how she's helping with my research. Imagine if she could-" He looked at Claire then back to Nan. "Is she capable like this, with other animals? You mentioned wolves... She could do incredible things, Nan..."

"She is living, and *that* is incredible. Have you heard the Zen proverb: *before enlightenment, chop wood carry water, after enlightenment, chop wood carry water?*"

Brian shook his head.

"These tasks are both meditative and necessary for survival. They need doing, whether or not one has achieved enlightenment, prestige, fame, saving the whales, or whatever one is seeking to attain. She's chopping wood and carrying water, Brian, and she is doing it beautifully."

"I'm fortunate to have her help, I can say that much. Just went out and got samples..." He shook his head and turned to Claire. "With *consent*..."

"Just remember," Nan added. "Wild things are of the wild. You cannot force nature's path, and believe me when I tell you Brian, Lil is a force of nature. If you want to learn from her, do it by letting her be what she is."

"There's definitely no alternative there," Claire chuckled.

"Oh, I've learned that lesson," Brian said.

"Well, I'm glad to see you here on the other side of it." Nan replied.

Lil approached with her dragonfly bug mug and half a tart; pastry flakes and cookie crumbs sprinkled down the front of her dress.

Nan raised her eyebrows.

"Oh please," Lil huffed with a smile. "As if I was going to wait to take a bite of that."

"Nor with the cookie, it seems," Nan said, standing to dust the front of Lil's dress before giving her a hug. "I'm going to turn in early and read a book in bed. Todd can close. He'll probably go out after too."

"He's surfing with Lil later," Claire said.

"I knew it. Don't keep the boy up too late. You might run on tea and salt water, but he needs to get some sleep if he's going to make it here by ten in the morning. And making it here at ten doesn't count if I catch him sleeping in the kitchen at ten thirty," she huffed, then laughed a little to herself as she walked away, mumbling, "turning my grey hair white, that one."

"You two should probably get going," Lil said, finishing off her pastry. "That blood isn't going to drive itself to the lab."

"Speaking of labs," Brian hinted… "I heard you spent a little time in the lab yourself…"

Lil rolled her eyes and glared at her cousin. "Really, Claire?"

"It just came up," she shrugged.

"So, what, were you just wandering the halls as a child? Wasn't that weird for the people working there? What did Magnus Orn tell people?"

"I had an escort with me…" Lil said trailed off. "Hey, I'm gonna head out to the orchard for a walk, maybe take a power nap before closing." She dipped down and gave Claire a hug. "Drive safe."

The orchard always had a special feel, the whole place did; the gardens, field, but the orchard… she really wanted to sink her hands in the dirt out there.

"Alright," Claire said, standing and tapping Brian, rousing him from a stupor. "We'll let you know how it goes. Oh! And don't forget, we're going out to see some of Brian's friends play a show at a bar. You should come; it will be fun."

Lil sighed and wrapped her arms around Claire. "No promises. Just remind me."

8.

The orchard was not silent, but rich with the sound of insects and the scent of apples, fresh and fermenting, rising from the ground.

Lil leaned against the base of a tree in a moment of observant stillness. She needed to practice. Gunnar planned to drop by later to assist her in helping explore what she'd done to Brian, but she thought, maybe in the orchard... with no expectations...

She slid her fingers into the soil. She'd grown an apple tree from seed once, with a child's carefree ambition. And she'd grown a garden from a corpse... With a slow steadiness to her breath, Lil reached for that place in herself, the tingle of hope and possibility, the need to reach for fresh air above and depth below. Glancing down carefully as though not to spook anything, Lil saw the sprout poke through the earth, the stalk thicken, the bud burst into a main of yellow that would have made Claire squeak with joy, because dandelions were among her favorite flowers.

Shadow and movement took form before her as a male deer paused, antlers like petrified branches forming his crown. With pupils like enormous tunnels, he stood staring, snorted, but came no further.

"I'm not always hunting," she said smoothly, her arm outstretched, sensing his assessment, caution, curiosity.

The male approached, his crown catching the moonlight as he dipped his head down, then raised it up under her palm. Her fingers slid over his muzzle, his forehead, then between his massive antlers, and around the side of his face. His thoughts were of smells and sounds, his vision different. Acknowledgement. Interest.

Her eyes stayed with his as she twisted loose an apple from the closest branch, an offering. He didn't need her apple; hundreds covered the orchard ground, but he took it from her hand.

Reclining at the base of the tree, she watched the creature ease back into darkness, listening as the rest of the night moved on. Her breath slowed and deepened, body relaxing into the cradle of the earth, becoming lighter.

Gentle stroking along Lil's hair roused her eyes open to tailored black trousers grazing the top of a crouching male's bare feet. A man.

Black trousers and no shoes.

She inhaled heat, cardamom and myrrh blending with the moist earth and apples. Soothing, smoldering. She was so comfortable, so content, but for a wisp of frustration working its way in. She was dreaming. She'd seen his hands carving stone, and now his feet… The thought melted toward her mouth as his fingers continued.

"I like having you in my dreams..." she sighed.

"Being with you this way brings me some peace while I wait," he breathed.

"I'd like to see more of you though. You smell divine," she whispered, turning her face toward his hand

"As do you... like a storm, like rain and the ocean, and apples, like clay, and ferns, and life."

Something moved behind her ear, and then she heard him inhale, breathing her in. She relaxed further into the idea of sharing a part of herself in such an intimate way.

"What are you waiting for?" She asked, slowly replaying his words in her mind.

"For you to wake up," he said. "Lil," he added, with a voice that wasn't his.

"Wake from *what*?"

"Ilati," he sighed, reluctance in his voice.

Fingers slid out from her hair, and whatever fog the dream laid over her lifted, leaving the orchard as she'd found it.

"Lil?"

She exhaled, stood, and found Todd at the edge of the trees, looking slightly nervous.

"I didn't want to bother you, but you left your bag inside with your shoes... and you said to find you after I closed up. Magnus called the shop asking for you, but he said it wasn't urgent.

Lil smiled, seeing that he'd carried her things with him.

Lil checked her phone; Magnus had called her cell as well.

"He said it wasn't urgent?"

Todd nodded, and shrugged. Probably just an update on what had happened up north, the tea, or maybe to ask her again about Iceland...

"I'll call him and see what's going on, but we're still hitting those waves tonight. Gunnar's joining us to work on a project, and it might get weird. Think you can handle it?"

"Depends. Is he bringing candy?"

A little over two hours later, Todd Lounged by the fire in her living room, contentedly folding a caramel wrapper while his hair dried. Lil sat on the couch across from Gunnar, a knife in one of his hands, stone in the other.

"Are you sure?" She asked again, not quite sure how to begin. "I grew a dandelion in the orchard."

85

"You want another caramel?"

Lil rolled her eyes.

"What you did with Brian is different. He's an animal. You need to be able to control this same way as you do your storm stuff, but this might be more important. This kind of thing, it could be noticeable, and that's dangerous."

"I'm not even confident I did anything."

"Yes," Gunnar said, his features softening. "You are. We ran it through several times. Something happened."

"Wish I'd seen it," Todd said, chewing loudly on another caramel.

Gunnar passed his knife over the rectangular stone, sharpening the blade. Repeating the action, he said, "Try to slow me down. Stop me if you can."

She focused on the sound, connecting to it, the movement of his arms, grounded at his shoulders, the sound again, like waves, interrupted by Todd's *chewing. That* she wanted to stop. Her eyes flicked to where he sat by the fire, tone deaf and oblivious to how the noise from his mouth clashed with the soothing rhythm of the knife over stone. *Stone*, she thought, hyper focused on his teeth, his jaw. Stone. Stop.

And the noise stopped. He stopped, not even his eyes able to express the horror he surely felt.

"Shit, shit, shit, *Todd!*" she shouted, springing from the couch, lunging for him, hands on his shoulders. "Gunnar, I don't think he's breathing. "Todd, move, *start!*" She pleaded.

Todd inhaled deep, his body suddenly shifting, adjusting, his eyes wide.

"Dude," he finally said, shifting the caramel still in his mouth.

"I'm so sorry, Todd. I was trying to focus on Gunnar, and al I could think about was your chewing, its not an excuse, there's no excuse, I'm so sorry."

"All good," Todd smiled. "That was kind of epic, and I wouldn't mind if you threw some of that Brian's way."

"I'm not suffocating Brian," she sighed leaning her forehead against Todd's shoulder, still recovering.

The weight of Gunnar's hand rested on her back as he crouched beside her.

"You okay, kid?"

She nodded. "Yeah."

"Good. My turn."

Sitting across from him again, blade over stone, she focused on the solid mass of him, then his arms where they began to deviate from the mountain, followed them down to his hypnotic hands. Slowly, she brought his rhythm to a different time, until the sound stopped altogether.

Fearful, she lifted her eyes to his, unmoving as the rest of him at first.

Then, he smiled.

9.

Lil opened her eyes to the sound of a rhythmic, vibrating noise, her body surrounded by white linens and darkness. She was in bed, the billowy comforter soft and crisp against her skin, night sky twinkling through the skylight. Above the simple wooden headboard, one of her ocean paintings stretched out a scene of still waters. She hadn't set an alarm, and yet…

She reached for her cell, and saw Claire's name.

"Everything ok?" She breathed.

"Were you sleeping?"

"I took a nap. I was planning to go for a swim later, well, now I suppose. What's going on? It sounds loud on your end. Are you at Nan's?"

"No way, I'm at that bar with Brian, remember? I told you about going out to see his friends play. They're *In a Cave of Seeds*? Who? They're in a *Nick Cave* cover band, but they haven't gone on yet. Cancel your swim and come meet us. It will be fun. I'll text you the address."

Lil's first instinct was to groan silently, but she liked music. She played music, but that was alone on the deck with the cello or in the living room with the piano and the back door open. Live music meant people, but it also meant less talking. Have a drink, get lost in some sound, then return home and take that swim.

Lil rolled over in her cloudlike nest, and sighed. "When?"

"Come right now! Just wear what you have on and get here."

"I was sleeping..."

"Ok, so put clothes on, and come now. Wait, Brian wants to know if it was a research swim."

"I've known the ocean long before Brian decided to study it," she said, pausing to look at her phone. "I got the address. I'll see you in an hour or so."

*

The music's volume outside the bar fluctuated as the door swung open and closed. People had gathered at the entrance, but Lil managed to slip in without speaking to any of them, passing through into a different kind of darkness, one of artificial night, night with walls and contrived unknown.

Lil carried a thermos and wore a dress the color of coal with a draping boat neck and very short sleeves, fitted at the hips, hem hitting mid-thigh. She felt the cool of the stone necklace like a beacon against her chest under the fabric where the club's humid air couldn't reach. The scent of sweat, mint, deodorant *on top of* sweat, spilled beer, and whiskey invaded her, clinging to her skin. She'd need to shower or walk directly into the ocean to recover... Closing her eyes, Lil focused on the bass, then, cancelling out the droning noise, she heard Claire's laughter.

The lower level contained a great deal of leather and wood, with a band playing on a low, dimly lit stage down back. Lounge chairs and tables were tucked along either wall, a section of high tables huddled in the middle, and area of standing room by the stage. A long, wooden bar spanned half the wall on the right side.

Weaving through bodies close to the bar, Lil followed the sounds of Claire and Brian carrying on in light conversation, until she was suddenly overcome with a scent like earth and myrrh, cinnamon-dusted sandalwood engulfing her like ether. She braced herself on the back of a chair, trying to remain upright as something warm brushed against her upper arm and shoulder. A current of heat went through from the site of contact and, as it faded, she steadied herself, regaining enough control of her eyes to look around, catching on the man in the chair she'd gripped.

"I don't usually have this effect on women without touching them first," he smiled. "How about I buy you a drink?"

He was good looking, short hair, t-shirt and jeans, clearly interested, but not in a creepy, leering way. Probably very pleasant.

Lil held up a thermos. "I brought my own drink, but thank you, really. I'm meeting friends, so, I'm just going to-"

"Listen, the bartender is a buddy of mine. I'm Greg, by the way. I'll tell him to give you my number if you change your mind. Any chance I can get your name?"

Lil shook her head.

"I'll just tell him to look out for *The Girl with a Thermos*."

Lil smiled and turned, finding Claire just a few feet away, engaged in conversation with Brian and a man Lil didn't recognize, all sitting around at a low table with several empty chairs amongst them. Lil took a moment before announcing herself to size up this new person. He wore a dark blue suit with a darker blue shirt underneath, no tie, and a grey pocket square. His hair was dark, short, and well groomed. Very intentionally put together.

Brian spotted her, then looking her up and down until his eyes caught what she was holding.

"They let you bring that in?"

Claire nudged his arm with hers and laughed, "She probably gave them the old *these are not the droids you're looking for*."

"Claire," Lil snapped, shooting a surprised-turned-stern look. Cutting a sideways glance at the amused stranger, Lil loosened up. He thought Claire was joking. "It's tea..."

"Of course it is, and you probably brought more in your bag too. Hey, where's your bag?"

"I left it in the truck."

Claire got up and gave Lil a hug. "You smell *good*, like propolis; were you at the hives? No, that wouldn't make sense."

"I was sleeping," Lil said as her cousin sat back down.

"So, what about your wallet? And your phone, keys, and all your stuff? I know they're not hiding in that dress."

Lil sat down in one of the empty leather chairs and sighed. Claire was tipsy...

"I don't plan on buying anything in here. You have your phone if Nan calls, and I have the truck key tucked away on my person... I just didn't want to have all the things."

"But you carried in a thermos of tea?"

"*That,* I'm actively using."

"Lil," Claire began, attempting subtlety as she gestured to the man sitting with them, "what if someone wanted to buy you a drink?"

"Then I'm even more fortunate to have brought my own."

Claire sighed, refreshed her smile and waved her hand more deliberately toward the man in question. "Lil, this is our friend JD from the Orn. Well, he's not *from* the Orn, but that's where we know him from..."

Here it comes, Lil thought.

"JD, this is my cousin Lil that I was telling you about," Claire beamed, avoiding Lil's stare.

Claire knew not to set her up. She wouldn't mind meeting new people so much if she didn't have to go through this inevitable dance of politely negating romantic interest. It wasn't even so bad that people were interested, the guy at the bar for example, he was nice. Those with a creeping persistence were the trouble makers.

JD leaned forward as if to engage her, but Lil unscrewed her thermos, and brought the rim to her mouth.

"So, Lil, what do you do?" JD asked, his smile twitching with amusement.

"I drink tea, and you?"

He held up his glass, a quarter full with amber liquid. "Whiskey. What's your blend?"

"Rosehip, apple, cinnamon, and a little chamomile."

"Sounds warm. I'd love to try it."

"We have it all at Nan's," she said, and that was that. *Not too bad.*

"Oh!" Claire exclaimed. "Lil, did you hear about the explosion at Cambridge Bay? The whole research facility went up! Something like eighteen dead, they said."

Eighteen who had been dead *before* the explosion.

Magnus had been in touch with an ingredient list for Amka's tea, several items hard to come by, and one she couldn't identify, but Magnus stated he would procure. He gave updates on Saul and Martine's research and the demolition, but hadn't asked anything more of her in that regard. Lil hadn't told Claire anything about her time in the arctic other than she'd taken the day to run an errand to one of Magnus's private labs up there. She'd wanted to say more, to sink into what she'd felt and done with a hot drink and her cousin, but Magnus had asked her to be discrete. He'd also politely reminded her about the trip to Iceland several times.

"Brand new facility," Brian added, shaking his head. "All the buildings affected; total loss. Tragic."

She sipped of her drink, turning toward the bar as the others continued to discuss the explosion, though she observed JD's eyes in her periphery, that they remained on her.

A rumbling sound built and faded throughout the space, bass from the music, perhaps. She felt it all around her, like distant thunder, but inside the room.

As the sensation passed, Lil continued browsing the room, surveying the guys on stage stepping away from their instruments.

"It's a break," Brian said. "A few of my buddies from university are in the band. They're going to have a couple drinks with us between sets. The one on the right with the sideburns is Howard..."

Lil drifted off while Brian continued to talk. Senses wandering, she picked up the scent she'd noticed upon her arrival, not the bar smell, the one that had been warm, pleasant, dreamy. She closed her eyes and inhaled deep, something like the understory of a dense forest, with a spice that made her neck go soft and her head tilt. She exhaled, took in another long, slow breath, and opened her eyes.

Across the room, in a leather chair in the darkness... Her focus caught on a man who seemed to be filling the entire room, larger somehow than the space he occupied. He turned away just as her eyes found him, tugging on the magnet that had apparently lodged itself inside her.

His hair was long enough to pull back, looked dark, but it could have been the lighting. He had a beard, kempt. He sat across from a blonde man with a similar build: tall, judging from how high their heads were in their chairs, and with wide shoulders. This other man had this hair tucked behind his ears, and looked up at her frequently through his lashes.

The two didn't appear to belong any more than she did, but they didn't seem to be drawing any extra attention to themselves, other than from her. Like predators concealed, they'd somehow managed to shield themselves in plain sight. And they were so *familiar*, she couldn't look away.

A Story in Stone

The blonde nodded to his companion, whose face she couldn't see. She wished he hadn't turned, desperately wanting to get a look at his eyes. Her body began to heat, felt different, then someone moved in front of her, blocking the view. She tried to shift a little to look around.

"This is my buddy Scott I was telling you about," Brian said, referencing the man responsible for the legs in front of her.

"Scott, this is Claire's cousin Lil that I mentioned earlier."

That he mentioned earlier? Lil shot a sharp, severe look at Claire who winced, silently mouthing, *I'm sorry.*

Deep breaths, Lil thought to herself. She took a sip of her tea and, as Brian's friend sat down, she was finally able to see the dark-haired man across the room. Hands gripped his chair, his fingers sinking deep into the leather. The blonde one was looking at the wall, smiling.

Scott interrupted her observation with abysmal timing. "I heard you were an artist," he began, "and you're immensely talented. I love the arts. I work in the history department, European history, with a particular interest in medieval romantic poetry."

Lil reluctantly gave the speaker her attention. His brown hair was short in the back but long in the front, swooping a little. He had stubble, a sleepy smile, and eyes kept partially open, trying to emit a relaxed, perhaps seductive mood.

Brian lit with anticipation and pride, Claire looked nervous, and JD sat back, swirling his drink, eyes on Lil. The corner of his mouth crept up slightly. Lil thought if he were a man of any less control, he'd be sporting a wicked grin.

"Oh, what a coincidence," Lil smiled. "My husband went to school for history when we met, but he changed majors to geophysics and chemistry." She then picked up her thermos with her left hand and took a sip, displaying a gold band that coiled twice around her fourth finger. "He felt the change would lead to something exciting, and more *useful.*" She heard a sudden choking cough, a throat clearing in the distance over the crowd. Lil looked across to the dark-haired man again, his profile in view, clearly showing a smirk. The blonde one had his head down, hair hiding his face.

"He's a volcanologist," Lil said, turning back to Scott. "We were married before he left on his last research expedition. We don't see each other often, but when we do, it's explosive. There's a pun there, what with the volcanology..." she added, taking another sip of tea. "I keep my private life private, Scott. Brian probably didn't know I was seeing anyone, never mind married."

Lil gave Brian a sideways glance, meant to chastise, though he was probably oblivious, what with his wide eyes and slack jaw. Defiantly didn't see that coming. Claire, mouth slightly open, hadn't either.

I did what I had to do to clean up his mess, Lil thought, perhaps speaking with her eyes. While Claire, Brian, and Scott shared a silent exchange, JD, focused on Lil, held his glass up to her, then took a drink. She tipped her thermos toward him, then brought it to her lips. *Cheers.*

While Lil cautiously omitted sharing parts of herself on a regular basis, she rarely encountered a need for outright deception. Having a close, small circle of people she interacted with kept things from becoming complicated that way. Boundaries and trust had long since been established, but Brian was new, and this, she supposed, was part of the learning curve.

Brian finally gathered himself enough to speak.

"Claire! I can't believe you didn't tell me!"

Scott laughed; Claire joined in.

"They're her details to share, plus you and I have been so busy with work it never came up." She raised her eyebrows and leaned over to kiss him on the cheek. "We need more opportunities for these little gems to unfold."

Another band member approached: grey suit, black shirt, short salt and pepper hair, stubble.

"Bill!" Scott called out.

Lil turned to Claire, "Round two? If the first one didn't work out, Brian had a backup waiting?"

Claire grimaced, whispering, "I'm sorry, it was supposed to be just hanging out with friends," then she spoke up, gesturing to their new companion. "This is Bill, he's- "

"He's delighted to make your acquaintance," Bill politely interrupted. "And what is it you do when you're not working with Claire at the herbalist's establishment?"

So, he knew about her as well. Okay then.

"I'm a little bit of everything," she replied.

"The arts," Scott boasted.

"Yes of course…The balance remains then, as I hail from the archeology department," Bill said with regal humor, putting one hand on Brian's shoulder, the other on Scott's. "I exist as a bridge between the hard and the soft sciences."

"I'm hard where it counts," Scott protested.

They all groaned.

"What?" Scott demanded, throwing his arms out in defense, leaning back into his chair. He uncrossed his legs, kicking a foot up and into a martini glass on the low table between them, flipping the glass down toward the floor.

Claire let out a *yip* as everyone's reaction time dragged.

Except Lil's.

Her hand reached, grasping the glass mid-air before it had a chance to shatter. The downward force from the speed of her movement brought her stone pendant tumbling from the neckline of her dress.

"Nice reflexes," Brian said.

"Nice necklace," Bill countered, staring at her chest curiously, then up to her eyes.

Lil broke away from what came close to a stare as Claire spoke up, defensively saying, "I don't usually get martinis. I just wanted the olives, really... Those glasses are so unstable!"

"It was just an accident; a spilled drink you didn't want anyway," Lil smiled back. "Want to share some tea?"

"No," Claire laughed, "I told you; it was mostly about the olives..." Then she held up a beer bottle. "I started in on this before the glass even went over."

Lil's smile widened, but as her gaze scanned away from Claire, she saw JD swirling his drink, looking at her with subtle fascination, and possibly heat. Bill had a curious look on his face, still fixed on her.

"I am fascinated by your choice of beverage," Bill started, "but even more so by that there." Gesturing to the stone hanging from her neck, he continued, "Wherever did you pick *that* up?"

"Oh," Lil looked down, feeling caught off guard. She really didn't care for talking about herself, especially to bar acquaintances... "It's a stone I've had for a long time. I always wear it... It's just sentimental, really."

"But where did you *get* it?" He pressed with excitement.

"Perhaps her volcanologist?" Scott offered.

Lil rolled her eyes, but the comment only fed the fire that was Bill's curiosity.

"She has a volcanologist on staff? You are a wealth of intrigue, Lil."

"Magnus?" Claire asked.

Lil's cousin had inquired about the necklace when they were children, and more than once since. Lil always responded honestly, that she wasn't sure of the story behind it. Of course, in her adulthood, learning of Magnus and his fondness of antiquities and artifacts, Lil could see how Claire might ask such a thing. It was how she'd acquired the ring.

Lil looked up at her cousin and shook her head. Magnus had not gifted her the stone, but he'd certainly noticed it. She remembered the early days at Nan's

97

when she'd first met the old man. They'd been sitting on a bench in the garden, as they often did, silent but for the surrounding sounds, Lil painting in a journal. The necklace was so long on her then; the blue stone cylinder practically rested in her lap. Magnus had respectfully asked if he could examine it, and she'd placed the stone in his hand with the chain still around her neck. As he looked closely with a very *Magnus* twinkle in his eye, he told her the stone was almost as unique as she was, and that was the end of it. Lil suspected he knew more.

Breaking from her memory, Lil returned to where she sat in the bar, the need to answer Claire's question.

"It came from my parents; at least I think it did. I've just always had it, since before I came to live with Nan."

"Lil was adopted," Brian added.

Claire glared at him.

"How delightful… We have a mystery on our hands." Bill looked down at her chest then up to her eyes. "May I," he asked, stretching his fingers out toward her, and waiting.

In answer, she put her hand under the dark blue stone, raising it up away from her body.

A low, animal-like rumble surrounded her again, like a growl she felt vibrating through her, though it was not coming from her, and certainly not Bill. The sound was so low it was almost inaudible through the droning chatter and loud music, but it was there, in her core and through her bones.

"Could you?" Bill asked, handing his phone to Lil with the flashlight activated.

She took the device, shining it down at the necklace.

"Lapis lazuli," he murmured, slowly twisting the cylinder. "You must have taken a good look at the carvings. We've got what looks like a sun with eight points, and those little circles around it are eleven planets… I've seen this before, but different." He twisted the stone. "Two figures, male and female from the waist up, but fish tails from the waist down. Those squiggling lines below are water. I'm not sure about the other marks around them…" He continued twisting the stone. "We have a male and female in this last section, but with legs and wings. Their hands are together, holding a tree. It's challenging to know exactly what is going on. The stone is worn, and it's the impression that is meant to be read." He pulled his gaze from stone to Lil, who'd found herself unexpectedly interested in what he had to say. Somehow, he was able to open a piece of her past she'd not uncovered, and the idea of knowing more had drawn her in.

"This is… quite old," he continued. "Ancient near east old. Mesopotamia. Unless it's a replica, of course. Either way. Cylinder seals are like stamps. They were used to make literal impressions." His eyebrows rose. "What we need is some clay." He turned to Scott and asked, "Do you think they have a stocked kitchen? With flour and salt?" Then he turned to Lil, explaining, "We could make a quick salt dough if they have the supplies. We'd just need flour, salt, and oil." He turned to Scott, then to JD and Brian. "Shall we head to the bar and ask?"

Brian looked skeptical. "This is a bar, not a bakery, Bill."

"And don't you have to go back and finish your music?" Claire Added.

"We don't need to do this here," Lil sighed, reluctantly speaking up. "I have clay at home. I'll just check it out when I get back."

"Yes, of course," Bill said, "but then *I* wouldn't get to see the impression."

Scott stood and smirked at Brian, "I'm definitely interested in uncovering more of Lil's secrets."

"More?" Bill questioned. "What did I miss?"

Brian rolled his eyes, but it was Scott who couldn't resist answering.

"Oh, it was nothing really," he teased. "Only, it seems to have been unknown to Brian that Lil is married to an adventuring volcanologist." Turning to Lil, he said, "While I was disappointed to find you romantically unavailable, and I'm not saying I've given up, this has been an unexpected pleasure. When we get back, with or without our dough, I want to hear more about these little details Brian has somehow overlooked. Perhaps Claire has a prosthetic limb? A house on an island in the South Pacific? Talk amongst yourselves," he laughed, heading to the bar.

Brian shook his head, releasing a chuckle. "I really don't know how I missed out on it."

Bill patted him on the shoulder. "We all miss things. Well, some of us," he teased. "Come on, we'd better get to the bar before I have to go on again. Howard went out back to call his wife. That'll only buy us so much time."

JD placed his empty glass on the table and stood, flashed a quick glance toward Lil, then took out a tin of mints. "I need to check in with work. Lil," he said as she looked up to meet his eyes. "If you find your thermos empty, it would be my pleasure to buy you a drink worthy of occupying it when I come back."

She allowed a small nod, and a smile with it.

"Work? It's the middle of the night." Claire said.

"The family business is global, Claire. I'm always on the clock."

After a quick wink, he turned and headed down back.

Lil thought of Magnus, always flying off someplace, yet answering his phone when she called, no matter where he was or what time it happened to be.

"Drinks and dough!" Bill shouted, as he, Scott, and Brian moved further away, into the crowd of standing bodies.

Claire spun in her chair to face Lil.

"Where did you get that ring?" She blurted out.

"At an auction I went to with Magnus and Gunnar. It was in Norway about a year ago, we met up with his friend Malcom."

Claire paused a moment. "It always struck me as odd, your friendship with Magnus. He's so... Well, he hardly says anything. Don't get me wrong, he's kind, and brilliant, and always gives me latitude with my research. He's asked me to do more at the Orn, in fact, but... he's always been so quiet, and *old.*"

Lil smiled. "He's family at this point. And I consider the selective use of his voice to be one of his finest qualities. We can be present in each other's company and not speak for long periods of time, and it's not uncomfortable. He doesn't need to make noise... Unless he's in one of his talkative moods, then there's no stopping him," Lil chuckled before shooting a reprimanding glance at Claire. "And before I forget, which I wouldn't have... I don't appreciate the set up. Way, *way* out of bounds. We've been over this."

Brian, making slow progress through the crowd, turned back briefly as Bill and Scott kept on toward the bar.

"So, you're really married?" he asked.

"No," the two women answered in unison.

Brian shook his head and continued to the bar as Lil's mind drifted to the mystery man across the room.

Her focus landed on him, and this time his head turned toward her. Their eyes met, and her breath caught, an electric current shoot out from her heart. He stood, holding her gaze, his stature impressive, his suit dark, and his eyes piercing into her.

I know you, she thought.

"Lil, Lil your fingers," Claire panicked.

Lil couldn't break from the connection that sent a warm glow pooling inside her. As he took a step in her direction, she raised a hand to her heart, feeling it speed up both within her chest and at the tips of her fingers.

His eyes widened, the blonde man setting a hand on his shoulder.

Someone passed in front of Lil, blocking her view again. She stretched her neck long, trying to see around, but there were too many people in between.

She could have sworn she'd seen a light in his hands.

"Lil, it's like St. Elmo's fire on your flipping arms," Claire panicked. "You need to make it stop."

The impact of Brian's coat hitting her chest startled Lil into turning, but when she looked back, the dark-haired man was no longer there, the blonde gone as well.

"Did you see that guy across the room?" Lil asked. "He was coming over, then you threw a coat at me, and he vanished."

"Maybe he was coming over because your arms were having *electrical issues*, but no I didn't see him."

"This is serious, Claire," she said, breathing deep through her nose. "I can still smell him. Can you smell that?"

"Are you asking if I can smell a person who was not near us, and has left?"

Lil tossed the coat aside and examined herself. "My arms are fine."

She scanned the room again, unable to see him anywhere.

"I should get going."

"Your arms are fine *now*," Claire pushed, "but something happened, and we're circling back to it at some point. You're really leaving? What if the guys come back with dough? "

"They're not going to make salt dough in the bar's kitchen, Claire. And honestly, I just want to get back home. My mind just isn't here right now."

The necklace revelation wasn't something she'd planned on. She'd had it her whole life, of course she'd noticed the markings, but why hadn't she thought to press her stone into something to see the images more clearly?

She briefly brought her hand up, tucking the cylinder back under her clothes. Magnus would have an idea of what the necklace was, she'd sensed it before. Even if he didn't, as a man who frequented the auctioning of antiquities, he'd know better than most how to find out. He was leaving the following morning, though, and she didn't want to wake him over it. She'd have to pick his brain when he returned from Iceland.

Lil picked up a cocktail napkin off the table. "Pen?" she asked.

Without thinking, Claire reached into her bag and pulled out three for Lil to choose from.

"It's the recipe for the tea I'm drinking," Lil explained, writing quickly. "Could you pass it on to JD?"

Claire's eyes widened.

Lil knew she wasn't easy on her cousin when it came to meeting new people. Bill was benign, kind, and while he had useful information, she just didn't care for the immediate closeness and talking, the quickness of depth. Scott was a problem, but JD was quiet. He seemed to be waiting, something either pensive or lurking within him, either way, he hadn't been offensive. He was certainly more tolerable than Brian.

"He's comfortable with his own silence," Lil shrugged. "I don't mind him."

"I'll guard your recipe while you sneak out," Claire started, wrapping her arms around Lil. "Call if you need anything. I'm at The Orn tomorrow, I know it's a Saturday, but it's just for a few hours in the morning. I'll see you Sunday though. Did I tell you I'm bringing Brian to the kids' tea party next week?" She smiled. "I'm thinking of dragging him to sunrise yoga."

"You think he'll be up for that?"

"Hey, if he can get up early for the orcas, he can get up early for yoga," she laughed. "And I really am sorry about Brian and Scott. I didn't think it would get weird, and I didn't know he told the guys so much about you. We were all hanging out beforehand, maybe he said something when I went to the bathroom. I'll give Brian a stern talking-to later."

"I have faith in your justice," Lil smiled. "He does have boundary issues, though."

"That he does," Claire sighed. "But everyone has quirks. He gets blinded by work and a compulsion to do what he thinks is right, whether it's for the whales or setting up a friend. Could be worse things wrong with him, I suppose," she shrugged. "He's certainly backed off a bit after that night he crashed your swim, though."

"If he hadn't learned after that, I'd be worried Claire, for both of you," she said, tightening their hug. "See you Sunday."

They parted, and Lil walked off through the crowd, up the steps, wishing she felt something looming behind her, but it wasn't there. The unknown in the room had vanished, leaving only contrived darkness and provided her with nothing she needed.

Cool air rushed over her skin as she opened the door, and she continued into it, into the air and the night.

10.

Lil held the lump of clay in her hand, cool, moist, smelling of earth. She'd not kept track of how long she stood in the kitchen, staring at it, but eventually she wrapped it in a damp cloth and left it on the counter.

I'll press the stone later, she told herself, not yet ready.

She'd expected a few hours of music, drinking, and a little overstimulation at the bar. She'd not bargained for thoughts stirred, following her home.

Lil leaned against the counter, half a mug of chamomile beside her, kettle cold.

Maybe a swim, she thought, knowing very well what she was doing She felt foolish for it, but nevertheless, she stripped off her dress and strode to the back door, pausing just long enough to grab a couple empty jars.

An hour or so later, Lil returned, refreshed and relaxed. She'd put on the kettle and started pouring ocean water into a bowl at her work table.

Her phone buzzed on the counter.

Claire had left her a voicemail, several text messages, and a video. The still image displayed Claire with Brian and his friends at the bar.

Lil rolled her eyes and pressed play.

"Lil. Lil! You can't be sleeping. Are you swimming?"

"Why would she be swimming?" Scott interrupted.

"Shhh! Lil! Lil, Bill wanted me to-"

"And Scott!"

"Bill and Scott wanted me to call you but you didn't answer, so I texted and they want to see the stamp! From your necklace! Did you stamp it? Howard is here too; you didn't meet him. He's back there texting his wife. Her name is Sharon and they have a little boy, Levi, he's three years old and- Oh my *gosh*, Scott, do *not* grab at my phone like a *child*. Brian! Lil call me back or send a pic and call me or text. Ok, bye!"

Lil chuckled a little as she emptied her mug and refilled, steam rising as she set more chamomile to steep. She eyed the bundle of clay on the counter, then looked back to the work table, bowl of salt water waiting. She could hardly avoid something that'd been hanging around her neck since childhood.

Clothes first, she decided. *Then I'll get to work.*

With dry undergarments, a cozy top, and a mug of chamomile waiting, Lil worked the cool clay in her hands as she walked around the room, massaging and digging her thumbs in, thinking about the man from the bar. He'd been more than familiar, stood staring at her, all the particles of her body reacting. He'd looked at her, then his hand. And while she could have been assigning something to him that wasn't there, a play of light, she'd felt it herself as well. Claire had seen something.

Dipping her fingertips in the bowl of ocean on the worktable, Lil moistened the clay disc in her hands, leaned against one of the living room chairs, eyes lingering on the cold fireplace.

A fire might be nice, she thought, finding another task to assist in her delay.

She knelt at the hearth, twisted old newspaper into a structure with small sticks and bark, then crossed a couple logs over. Lil savored the sulfur scent pinching her nostrils after the match struck.

Settling in on the couch, she leaned forward, examining the flattened clay. Before giving herself time to think it over much more, she grasped the stone dangling from her neck, pressed it into the left side of the moist earth, and with slow, gentle pressure, rolled the cylinder.

Lil let out a long, slow breath, and wiped the stone off on her shirt.

It was all there.

The drawings she had grown up seeing bits of, etched around her dark blue stone, were laid out in front of her, in a four-centimeter square.

Bill had said the star in the upper left-hand corner was the sun, the eleven tiny circles around it planets. This celestial corner took up little more than a square centimeter, the rest of the imprint separated into a left half and a right half. On the left, a male and a female, absent clothing, had fish tales from the waist down, surrounded by wave lines. Curved lines flowed out from the male's hands as well. The right half of imprint had contained a male and the female, but with legs, and wings. They faced each other, hands stretched toward one another, supporting the roots of a tree, its branches reaching almost to the top of the imprint. In both the left and the right images, lines sprouted from the bodies at various intervals: five lines from the head, longer at the middle and shorter as they went around. *Such detail for something so small,* she thought.

Lil let her fingers run over the clay, gently, as not to disturb the integrity of the impression. She wanted to feel it, to be closer to it, something that had rested against her skin, that she knew so little about.

With a deep breath, she looked to the fire, tears creeping into her eyes, as she wondered about her parents, thoughts lingering in the void of knowledge. Was this their treasure? A token of love from one parent to the other? Maybe one had been an archeologist, like Bill, leaving her with an artifact from their life's work.

She reclined, placed a hand over the stone at her chest, and closed her eyes. Crackling fire and ocean waves continuing around her.

Maybe her mother accompanied her father on digs, perhaps the other way around. Maybe Lil had gone too, as a baby, before her time with Nan... She felt a memory forming, from when she'd been small, of large arms and strong hands placing the seal around her neck.

Lil's body drifted with waves of water, then, when she became aware again of the fire, she took a deep breath, and let it out. The room smelled warm from the burning wood, but there was something else in the air, something more than fire and clay...

Her eyes felt slow, somewhere between awake and asleep, but she opened them enough to see him sitting in the chair across from her. Holding her mug in his hand, firelight dancing across him, he just casually existed not more than two meters away, a look of contentment as he watched her, close enough for Lil to see his eyes. They were brown in the center like deep earth, fading to a ring of shaded evergreen.

A warmth flushed through her, heart beating strong, but without panic.

"The tea must be cold," she whispered.

"It was," he said, steam wafting up toward him as he took a sip.

She'd had that cup to her lips before dozing off, her mouth where his was.

"This is a dream," she said.

"Something like that."

Something like that.

Lil wondered if there was a scale on which to measure the reality of a thing. *Dreams are as real as waking life,* she thought, *though only the dreamers are truly present.* Had she enlisted him to become the face of the man she'd dreamt of, the one in the orchard, the one carving a cup from stone? Had anyone else actually seen him in the bar, other than her? Could she have put him in the bar as well? It was possible. More likely, though, he'd been there, a stranger, and she'd applied his face to a presence which needed one, further personifying the smell from upstairs in the barn.

"I've felt you before," she began.

"You have felt me always."

Her truth in his words.

"Why did you leave the bar?"

"Timing," he sighed. "It's becoming... *difficult* to maintain distance, but we agreed I would wait until you wake." He looked deep in thought, eyes turned toward the depths of the fire. He took a deep breath, exhaled, and, drawn to his rising chest, Lil caught a glimpse of something familiar.

His sleeves were rolled up, at least the two top buttons of his shirt undone, and there, in the open space over his sternum, rested a cylindrical stone so dark it could have been black.

But Lil knew it was a deep blue.

Bringing a palm to her chest, she found her necklace intact and resting against her skin. When her eyes flicked up to his, he was waiting.

"You've discovered your seal," he said.

"I've had it for as long as I can remember..." Her voice trailed off as she watched him lean forward. His fingers grazed the top of the clay, as she had done, reverence in his touch.

"Our story," he breathed.

He stood, took a step toward the fireplace. Crouching down, he reached beneath the flames, and extracted a handful of blackened wood. Meeting her curious eyes, he moved to the table behind him, seawater sizzling as he sank his fist into the bowl she'd left waiting.

Lil watched his hand rise from the steaming vessel, liquid trickling down his raised arm as he worked the coal into a paste; the effect hypnotic.

Subtle grin on his face, he said, "One needs to be comfortable with heat, for success in a field like volcanology..."

Lil felt herself blush. He'd heard.

She looked down at her finger for the ring, but it was gone. She'd taken it off when she'd arrived home.

"I find everything about you endearing, wit included."

He came close, crouching before her, his eyes never leaving hers as he took the stone from around his neck into his blacked palm. He glanced down to his raised forearm then back to her, signaling for her to watch. Reluctantly, she broke his gaze to look down, witnessing as he rolled the stone slowly over his skin.

The black markings told a story, as her clay did.

The celestial corner to the left were there, the man and the woman with wings and the tiny lines around their bodies. They supported a fruit tree in their hands, or it grew from them. The winged man appeared at the upper part of the next etching, reaching down for a woman reaching up, both surrounded by little lines, but she had no wings.

Three slim panels followed, separated from each other with a line running from top to bottom. In the first, a man with wings stood with a shorter, smaller, long-haired person, lines present but absent wings. He had something in his hand she couldn't make out. The next panel displayed the winged man with a wingless woman, both with the lines around them. In the last panel, a man stood with a woman, both with wings, lines jutting out from their bodies, wave lines under their feet, and a tree.

Our story, he'd said.

Lil became slow again, losing focus. She felt a pull in herself, like being drawn out and fading, distracted by something she couldn't put her finger on.

She looked around for the cause, and his eyes widened, working to catch hers again.

A sound like thunder rumbled from his chest, hypnotic, then there was another noise, separate from him. Lil heard a pulsing vibration, one she recognized, but couldn't quite remember.

His hand met her face, providing warmth where her cheek was cradled, sending a flood of heat moving through her as his eyes held hers.

"Stay," he pleaded with a whisper.

She leaned into his hand, closing her eyes, breathing the smell of his skin mixed with the scent of coal and fire. She heard the rumble in his chest, like the purr of a great contented beast. The sound surrounded her, and then there was a deep growl, followed by that buzzing again...

Lil leaned in further, burrowing into him, feeling his hand slide down her face, then she opened her eyes, and he was gone.

Disoriented and deflated, Lil sat up and looked around, then down at her phone buzzing on the table. Claire. Lil had missed another three calls, and her cousin was already trying again.

Lil could run on very little sleep, but Claire would need caffeine and sunglasses in the morning.

Reluctantly, Lil accepted the video call.

As the feed came through, Claire scrunched up her nose, blurting, "What's all over your face?"

"What?"

Lil looked down at the phone, studied her image in the upper corner of the screen. Five black streaks ran into a giant smudge on her cheek. Her hand went up, touching the marks, leaving coal on her fingertips.

Lil's heart galloped as she looked to the empty mug on the other side of the coffee table, then to the roaring fire. How many logs had she put on? Her eyes

111

darted around the room and over to the kitchen. There was no one else with her. It had been a dream.

Something like that, he'd said, the thought echoing through her mind in his voice.

"I... I lit a fire in the fireplace-" she stammered.

"Did you stamp it?" Scott interrupted.

Claire's head whipped to the side. "Scott, so help me... If you interrupt *one* more time... Brian, handle your friend please."

The image on the phone moved around as the phone was jostled. She saw JD speaking with Brian just behind her cousin.

Claire let out a frustrated breath and continued as part of Bill's head appeared on the screen.

"So, I called nearly fifty times, Lil," Claire continued. "And yes, there is alcohol involved, but you always pick up, and I got worried. Are you okay?"

Good question.

"I went for a swim and saw the messages when I got back in."

Bill's face turned, mouthing *a swim?* Then Brian whispered, "The ocean... No, I'm not kidding... I'm not getting into it. She says she's married."

JD's eyes flicked between the two men, then over Claire's shoulder, to Lil.

"So, you just got back in?" Claire asked.

"Oh, no, I lit a fire and fell asleep on the couch thinking about my necklace. And I did roll it in clay," she said, switching the camera's' view to show the coffee table instead of her face.

The clay was there, imprinted.

Bill's face come into view on his end as he took hold of Claire's phone.

"Oh my," he breathed. " Can you rotate and move in closer, please? Wonderful." He paused a moment. "It's so nice to see the whole story."

"What if," Lil started. "What if there was another seal? Are the necklaces ever made in pairs, for stories that continue on?"

Bill's head tilted slightly. "Do you have another?"

She didn't respond.

"Lil?"

She flipped the screen's image back to her face and propped it on the table so she didn't have to hold it.

"Yes?"

"Do you have another seal?"

What could she say? *No, but I had a dream that a guy from the bar was in my house wearing one...* Maybe?

"I had a dream after I rolled out the stone... Sometimes my artwork has an effect on my dreams. Brian told you I painted..."

She needed time to think it over, run some ideas by Claire, if she could just get her alone. Lil could talk it through with Nan or Magnus too, or Gunnar. She should have called him over before she started with the clay, but would she still have had that dream?

"I'd really like to work on this with you," Bill started. "The guys and I are staying in the area two more nights. If you send a screenshot, I could do some research and contact a friend of mine. The ancient near east is his jam. We studied together as undergrads, then he did some work in Iran, went on to get more into conservation. He works at the MFA in Boston."

Boston...

Lil rested her head in her hands, hair falling forward, eyes closed. Magnus would be stopping in Boston for a few days before Iceland...

After the dream she'd just had, combined with the more tangible phenomena she'd been producing... she felt something close, but just out of reach. And for what felt like the first time, she found herself fueled with a sense of longing, needing to know more about what hung from around her neck, more about herself.

She hadn't *needed* to before, but now… Magnus was right, some part of her was waking, and this was part of it. Some part of her wanted this piece of her puzzle investigated, so much so that she's started working on it in her dreams, apparently.

"Is your friend in Boston awake now?" she asked.

"I imagine he would, what with the time difference."

"I know it's inconvenient, but would you mind calling him?"

"*Now?*" Bill asked, giving Lil time to protest. She didn't. "This night competes only with itself as the most remarkable experience I've had in a long time," he said. "I'll try texting… Claire."

"Lil," Her cousin started, repossessing the phone. "What's going on?"

"Brian is safe to drive, right? Because if not I'm getting in my truck right now."

"Lil, seriously."

"Magnus is leaving in the morning… for Boston."

"I thought he was going to Iceland?"

"Can we just switch to audio?" The video feed ended, and Lil brought the phone to her ear. "He's taking a detour to Boston for a few days; putting some face time in with the bio-med folks there and visiting Mira's brother." She waited for Claire to connect the dots, but her cousin hadn't been listening to Bill too closely it seemed. "Bill offered to put me in touch with a friend of his, some type of near east artifact specialist… he works at a museum in Boston. Do you mind going in to Nan's in the morning?"

Claire managed to still herself, pushing aside the alcohol and the frenzy.

"Of course, I'll go to Nan's, but Lil, the bit in the bar, Bill, the quest for clay… That was all fun, but… this has never been something you bothered with before."

Lil closed her eyes. "There's been more, dreams, but more things happening when I'm awake as well. The favor for Magnus, I manifested some things, I'm not on speaker, am I?"

"No, of course not."

"I need to sink into this necklace thing for a moment."

"Could you ask Nan again? When's the last time you spoke with her about it?"

"As a child, when I first arrived… then again when I was about ten. She said the necklace and poetry book were left with me when I came, that the book seemed to be a source of calm for me, and speculated the necklace, somehow, did the same."

"The poetry does help," Claire said.

"It does."

"Do you ever take the necklace off?"

"No."

"Better not test it then. So, was it something Bill said?"

Lil leaned into the softness of the couch, glancing at the fire, then to the bowl of salt water, wondering if she'd find coal sediment settling down at the bottom…

"I was sleeping on the couch when you called. A man appeared here with me in the dream, explaining the seal. He had a necklace too, but it was a little different. He rolled it out on his arm so I could see."

"Was it the guy who smells like the barn, the one in the cup dream?"

"Yes, and I forgot to tell you, I had another one in the orchard, he was there, but I only saw his legs, but-"

"And tonight?" Her cousin interrupted excitedly. "Did you see his face?"

115

"Claire… He looked like the man from the bar. He was *right* here. It was important to him that I understand the story engraved in the stones. I think my mind is trying to work out what they are… compelling me to learn more. And while the brain is a remarkable thing, I think I need more information from sources outside myself." Lil sighed and closed her eyes. "I wish you were here, just you."

"Me too," Claire lamented. "So, you'd fly out first thing in the morning? The guys had wanted to coordinate a brunch."

"Wait, what?" Brian interrupted in the background. "Where? How long will she be gone?"

"Brian…" Claire warned. He was undoubtedly concerned for his research, which Lil had no intention of providing additional help with.

"Lil hold on, I'm passing you off to Bill."

"He's on my phone," Bill started, out of breath but full of enthusiasm. "I have Sami on the other ear, told him about how we met at the bar, the necklace, what I saw. He's *very* interested in getting in contact with you."

"Is he available tomorrow evening?"

"He can take your call right now, if you'd like."

"I have a friend flying to Boston in a few hours. I'm fairly certain I can join him."

"In a few… can you *do* that? Don't you need more time, to prepare… Tickets and all that?"

"Private jet. Is your friend available tomorrow?"

There was a long pause before Bill spoke. "Yeah, give me a minute."

"Lil?" Claire said.

"If it's a go, do me a favor and text me with the contact info for this guy Bill's talking to, okay? I'll message Todd to bring a couple friends to Nan's tomorrow, I'm sure you'll be in no shape to put too many hours in."

116

"Sure, okay, here's Bill again."

"Lil, he's available. His name is Sami Hanna. He says you should meet him at the museum, that would be best, good lighting and resources, but also because his parents are staying with him, so his place is a bit crowded."

"Wonderful. Thanks, Bill. You can give Sami's contact information to Claire, and please tell him I'll be in touch when I land sometime in the evening. Also, please thank him for being flexible enough to meet so last minute. I'll text after I confirm the flight with Magnus."

"Wait, Magnus *Orn?*"

Lil hung up the phone.

It almost seemed too much, too soon to be in the air again after all she'd been through recently, but after what she had learned in the bar, her dream, the pull to know more was undeniable.

She had another call to make.

Though texting seemed less disruptive, Lil knew he would prefer her voice.

"Are we having trouble sleeping?" Magnus answered, sounding tired, a touch of concern behind his humor.

"I'm interested in joining you later this morning, if the offer is still open."

"Gunnar will pick you up at five o'clock, which doesn't give you much time. Do we need to delay?"

"Well, I have the two steamer trunks to organize my outfits into, the makeup needs sorting, and all these shoes…"

Magnus released an amused chuckle. "I'll see you on the plane, dear."

11.

Lil had been ready when Gunnar arrived, waiting on the back deck with a bag and two thermoses. She quirked the corner of her lip up at the sight of him strolling through the uninterrupted morning song. Maybe the birds sensed the calm in her and took their cue thusly, or maybe it was their own awareness of his belonging, either way, they didn't stop chattering when he came through.

Lil had noticed the phenomena as a child when he'd come and pick her up from Nan's. The creatures would acknowledge him, and continue on as they were with naught but a brief pause. And he knew where to find her always, whether in the woods or at the house. He had a sense about what trees to walk between, what doors to knock on. A sense of what she needed.

"Have you had enough rest?" He asked.

"Probably not," she signed, knowing he heard the weight in it.

"I've got a box of cigars and a liter of bourbon in the truck to help you unwind," He said, turning to walk back around the house.

Wait, what?

Then he glanced back at her, confirming with his eyes the intentional absurdity of what he'd suggested. "I made caramels. Let's go."

Lil's face melted into an easy smile as she followed. *Candy and a touch of humor*, she thought, considering how few people saw the side of Gunnar that made her laugh.

*

The jet was as she remembered: white leather, taupe rug, bathroom and kitchenette somewhere down the end.

Magnus sat at a small table with an empty chair facing him, Lil in a spacious seat across the aisle, blanket on her lap and thermos by her side. Gunnar sat in one of two adjacent seats, reading Twenty Thousand Leagues Under the Sea.

"Now that we're in the air," Magnus began, "is it safe to discuss the reason for your last-minute change of plans?"

Lil caught Gunnar look up, a brief assessment before returning to his book.

She'd anticipated Magnus's question. He'd not given in over the phone, or upon greeting her, having wanted to provide their discussion with the uninterrupted devotion it deserved.

"I met Claire at a bar last night. She was with friends, one of them an archeologist. He saw my necklace, became interested, and I allowed him to take a closer look. I politely brushed it off his interest, initially, but my curiosity came through, even in my subconscious. When I went home, I pressed the stone into clay and looked at the imprinted images for the first time, then fell asleep and dreamed of seeing a second seal. It was *similar*, but..."

Magnus suddenly looked startled, going still as his eyes grew wide.

Lil paused briefly at his reaction, then continued as he regained his composure. "Clearly I want to pursue finding out more," she continued. "And that need seeped into my dreams. Bill, the guy from the bar I mentioned, he has a colleague who works for the Museum of Fine Arts in Boston. I thought it was a coincidence too fortuitous not to take advantage, so, here we are, in the air and on our way."

"I can think of at least ten more useful resources off the top of my head," Magnus said, fingers laced together around his overlapping knees, thumbs raised in emphasis. "The British museum, the Ashmolean at Oxford, several private collectors… *Me*. I know you meant no offense, Lily, but, really. You didn't think to ask me? I'm more than a businessman; I know a thing or two about artifacts…"

"I know," she sighed, tipping her head back against her seat. "The stone, the *cylinder seal*, hasn't been something I sought to explore until now. I mean, I asked Nan, but she didn't know and I let it alone. I hadn't come to you before this moment because I had no previous desire to pursue things further. And I *did* contact you as soon as curiosity burrowed in, though it was to coordinate travel, and I hardly think it would have been an appropriate time for an in-depth discussion on the necklace or your affiliations. Please don't feel like I've overlooked you as a resource, Magnus. I value you more than you can know, though I'm sure you have some idea," she smiled affectionately. "And I know you have some idea about this necklace, too. I remember you inspecting it when I was a child, you got that look you get."

"So I did," he trailed off, almost whispering as he continued, pulling his thoughts from the ether. "The timeline is not always as we suspect, is it. And what we know, not always ours to share. Sometimes we must come to see that we are here but to witness as the seed sown takes root… as buds unfold to blossoms, and blossoms to fruit."

Though not out of character, Magnus's commentary had become so esoteric, it could've only been intended for himself.

With renewed clarity, he said, "I'm not sure how much of the story we are meant to know. I think my role here is as it has been, not to interpret or unveil, but to facilitate and guide you on this journey of discovery. So, was the young man in the bar able to enlighten you when he examined the piece?" He asked with returning amusement.

"I'm sure his education touched upon the Near East, but it isn't his area of expertise. He was fascinated nonetheless."

Magnus nodded with subtlety, divided between being present and receding into his thoughts.

Lil knew the feeling well.

"He was wise to suspect the importance of what rests around your neck. Deficient as he was, his judgement proved sound in that regard."

Lil managed an internal eye roll before Magnus continued.

"I might be able to facilitate some guidance," he went on, tapping the screen of his phone, and putting it to his ear. "David," he smiled. "Magnus. Yes, of course. We are in the air enroute, though I have two additional companions with me. No, no," he shook his head slightly. "The Boston apartment should still be adequate. We'd planned to continue on to Iceland afterwards, however, with the school's approval… I'd like permission to bring two guests with me for a visit to The Arboretum, to make use of the archives. Gunnar, my grandnephew and recent alumnus… Yes, quite well. Indispensable. The other guest is a young woman I've known since her childhood, and very much like my own daughter…" There was a pause during which Magnus smiled and shook his head. "I'm afraid nothing will turn up if you do, and that's by design. She is very private. Indeed. I'm aware this is highly irregular. We're scheduled to be in Boston until Tuesday morning, but there is some flexibility. I understand and would expect nothing less… Likewise, always a pleasure, David. I look forward to hearing from you."

"That was David Williamson," Magnus said, tucking his phone away. "He works for the school Gunnar and I both attended as younger men. I'm sure you gathered the purpose for the call. We'll have to wait and see if my request is

121

approved. They're private and protective, but unlimited in their generosity when it comes to members. They keep properties internationally for faculty, students, and alum use, accompanying guests too, of course. I usually stay in the Boston apartment or with Martin when I visit."

"That's Mira's brother?"

"Yes. He is a retired internist. I came to know him while attending university in Boston, as I did Mira."

"You met at school?" Lil had heard different versions of Magnus and Mira's story in the past, though the truth of it remained the same. It was the song of their spark and, while Lil had not felt it in waking life, his stories of Mira were a reminder that such a thing could exist outside of dreaming.

"We met as many do during the excitement of autumn, what with the falling leaves, cooling air, and increased need for things intimate and warm. She studied biology, but minored in art. Had quite the talent for botanical illustration. That woman was fascinated by fungi, and I had no chance of escaping her enthusiasm. That she had her own research team at the Orn was naught to do with her status as my wife, but with her own merit... well, mostly," he smiled, taken by the thought of her.

Lil had become more than familiar with the work of Mira Orn, and never found herself averse to learning more. Older mycologists at the lab sang her praise, telling stories of working alongside her. In addition to her accomplishments in the world of fungi, Lil had grown up with Mira's botanical artwork decorating the walls of Nan's shop, gifts from Magnus's late wife to her dear friend.

When Lil moved into the ocean house, it hadn't been a big to-do as far as heavy lifting. Magnus had softened her up on the idea of residence by first tempting her to paint there. After the paints and clay made their way in, the kiln appeared in the garage with a note. When she finally agreed to move in *officially*, it was more a ceremonial transport of clothing and assemblage of foodstuffs for the fridge rather than the backbreaking rite of passage many go through when transitioning from their childhood home. Nan, of course, stocked the pantry with herbs for tea and helped her to get the sunroom setup as a greenhouse.

Lil remembered filling the kettle at the sink while Magnus and Nan settled in at the counter. She'd looked up and found a rectangular package wrapped in brown paper tied with twine. Having given so much already, Lil wondered what they could have veiled in paper.

Slipping the twine over the corner, she unwrapped the item, revealing a framed watercolor of an apple blossom and several buds having not yet burst forth, fresh green leaves, gentle pink touching white petals. Lil had known whose work it was, though she'd never had the opportunity to meet the woman. *Mira would have wanted you to have this, a piece of Nan's orchard that she painted once, to keep here with you,* he'd said. *She loved Nan like a sister, and would have, I think, loved you like a daughter, as I do.*

With a soft blanket wrapped around her, the mood of the memory, and the sound of Magnus retelling his early years with Mira, Lil found herself dangerously close to a nap.

Magnus's expression transitioned from sweet nostalgia to one of concern.

"Are you rested?" He asked.

"I'll be fine. I brought watercolors, Zen Archery, Chopin."

"Do us a favor, Lily dear, don't read music while in flight."

"I'm not going to fall asleep."

He held her eyes a moment, his silent comment, then reached for his bag. "I have some material that might interest you," he said, handing over a leather-bound book with *Manon I* printed on the spine.

"A friend of mine and fellow collector has an affinity for diaries. He had this one digitally archived and bound. It was written by a young French woman named Manon during the fifteenth century, family very well to do.

"There are the daily entries typical for the time: bullet points regarding errands and tasks performed, food consumed and guests received, a hymn or a poem jotted down. Then," he paused with a subtle mischievousness about him. "There are the occasional, *unusual* entries that increase in frequency as one reads."

He was baiting her.

She indulged him.

"Unusual in what way?"

"Manon had a rebellious spirit, and a knack for healing as well as social justice, it seems. I shouldn't... I should just let you read it yourself but I'm so tempted... I must," he grinned.

Magnus was charming when amused, wearing a youthful giddiness that became infectious. *How many people have shared in his joy when he is delighted so*, she wondered, then thought of Nan and Magnus together, baking and taking walks.

"There's a young man," he began. "He had been attempting to court Manon, but he is a scoundrel. Manon initially finds him distasteful, but when she discovers he has assaulted one of the servants, she shows interest in him… Manon and the unsavory fellow are out having a picnic on the grounds and, *Oh*, but the way it's written. Here, let me find it."

While Magnus flipped through pages, Lil turned to Gunnar, silently observing. He raised an eyebrow, also curious.

"Here we are," Magnus announced. "She writes: *I selected from the garden a lovely arrangement of belled flowers I knew well. Long stems with hanging blossoms in pink, purple, and white. I laid them down in the center of the blanket he had set the food upon. I insisted he try the strawberry preserves I'd chosen for his enjoyment, adding that I had picked the berries myself. He offered me the first bite, but I relayed my distaste for the fruit, admitting I had*

124

brought the delight especially for him. He found this confession most agreeable, and consumed an exceptional amount.

Not much time passed before he began to show signs of discomfort. I inquired as to the manor of his sudden illness, but he had been rendered unable to speak. I thought to run for help, but did not wish to leave him alone, staying with him as his body quieted, and was breathing no more.

My screams called attention to the matter.

I was rushed away from the scene, but not before stumbling over the jar of preserves, knocking it off the blanket. The remains were contaminated with dirt such that no one else would be able to take part. It brought me comfort to know that the last taste on his lips was something so beautifully crafted, and solely his."

Magnus exhaled softly, as not to disturb the passage while it settled.

"How beautifully woven that was," Lil said with approval, still picturing the picnic spread in the garden, hearing the insects, birds, sun on her arms.

Manon had left the flowers she'd used to poison him on the blanket. She'd documented it all evasively enough, but hadn't resisted altogether; writing for her own amusement.

"I thought you'd enjoy her," he said, offering the book again. "I don't have to ask if you can read French, but the penmanship can take some getting used to."

Lil smoothed her hands over the leather. The binding was new but it still evoked some sense of appreciation for the work inside.

"Thank you, Magnus."

She tucked the book between her thigh and the chair, took a sip from her near empty thermos.

"What have you brought to drink?" He asked.

"Apple, rose, a little cardamom. Thank you again for the list, the ingredients for Amka's tea. Some of the ingredients will take some work obtaining. Good

125

thing I know a guy," she smiled, thinking of the words Todd often spoke. "I brought some for you to try. Hey, how's Tom doing?"

"He's well; taking some time with family before going back to work, elsewhere of course."

"I heard about the *explosion* from Claire. Do you think it was enough?"

"They leveled it," he said with a nod. "Now what's this about tea?"

Ever the collector of rare things.

"It's... *unique.*" She knew his ears would perk up at that. "Subtle, earthy, floral; familiar but also unlike anything I've had. It must be the lichen. She said they all drink it up there and, like any recipe passed on, they all have their own little twist on it; a pinch of this or that. She also said she sends it with Tom whenever he visits home."

From the look on his face, Magnus was traveling rapidly between thoughts. Just for a moment, then his eyes returned from that distant place, locking with hers.

"Everyone at the site who was unaffected by the illness drinks this tea, including Tom," he stated.

Lil nodded. Magnus had expressed hope that there'd be dietary or genetic factors providing resistance; something that could be studied, replicated.

"And you have it with you?"

She nodded again, "Yes... I brought half; the rest is at the house."

"Good," he sighed. "With your permission, I'd like to have Claire pick it up from your house and take a look. I'll email her instructions now and read her in fully by phone later. I'll reach out to Tom for a thorough examination of the ingredients and assistance with acquiring more. When Claire has taken a closer look, we'll send what she's got to Saul and Martine. And if it's not too much trouble, I'd like to take a sample from the portion you brought along and drop it off with my people in Boston. They won't know the application, but it won't hurt to have more than one team on this, given the implications. We have things contained now, but Pandora's Box *has* been opened. We'll do what we can to find a means of countering the pathogen before it surfaces somewhere else."

"Of course."

"We won't need to sacrifice all of your supply in the name of science," he added playfully. "We should have enough for at least a cup or two left over…"

"At the *very* least," she smiled. "Any ideas on who the other guy was, the one Amka said was first on the scene up there?"

"Not a clue, and I've had my feelers out. I'm hopeful that, given the time gone by, we would have heard something by now if there'd been a *situation*, though the business from Cambridge Bay has been kept quiet. We can't know for sure…"

A smooth, grinding sound began, wet, familiar, and accompanied by a look of annoyance on Magnus's face. He turned toward Gunnar, who paused the knife on its passage over wet stone.

Lil loved that sound, of knives being sharpened, like slow waves rolling in and out over the shore.

"Really, Gunnar? You start that and you'll send her to sleep, warm blanket or not."

Gunnar smirked as Magnus turned back.

"Now, the tea, dear… should we try a cup?"

"It might be worth waiting until we've landed and settled in."

"Wise beyond your years, Lily dear. The Boston apartment has a lovely courtyard patio, perfect for savoring something delightful."

As Magus got to work on his laptop, Lil leaned down, gathering her travel paints, dabbling in pinks, purples, greens, and blues, depicting irises and foxglove. Working shades of fading blue and song onto the page, Lil looked up briefly to see Magnus close his laptop and stretch.

"I'll just put my feet up briefly," he said, heading toward the couch at the other end of the plane. Gunnar glanced at their companion in acknowledgement before returning to his novel, and Lil got back to work rendering experience in paint, letting it seep into the cotton.

Finished, Lil put her brush down. Page still wet, she knelt on the floor beside Magnus, watching his eyes flutter slightly beneath their lids.

She wasn't sure if the effects would be the same, what with Magnus having not been exposed to the painting while *falling* asleep, but it felt right to leave it with him. She placed the sketchbook open at his side and stood as Gunnar looked up from his book. She rested a hand on his shoulder, just a moment less than lingering, and walked back to her seat, feeling his eyes on her as she settled back into her nest with Manon I.

The book was filled with script in various shades of faded ink sweeping evenly across each page. The style was different than Lil was used to, but it didn't take her long to decode the text.

Spring has brought rain to the garden, mud to my skirts, joy to us both.

Mother had a deck of cards painted. They arrived today. We spent a great deal of time marveling at the images. Ladies Isabel and Collette, who joined us for tea, also took in the works with great enjoyment. We were almost reluctant to put the cards to use.

Several entries went on this way, with brief descriptions of weather and events, the embroidery of her dress and so forth, peppered with bold little comments here and there. Pleasant enough, but Lil had gone in knowing Manon's writing would develop, or so Magnus had reported.

Mother invited the ladies for cards again, this time for an attempt at play. Mother was curious to see if I'd have a knack for them. It seems she is always conflicted as to whether I should dazzle or quiet myself. I'd much prefer the latter, as it affords me more freedom.

Sweet Marie came to me today, asking for help with her father. His feet have swollen, as if someone had filled them with water. The use of one's own hands can call attention, so I advised that he avoid consuming anything salted. I brewed for her a tincture of Dandelion, instructing her in the how to produce this herself, with a tincture being preferable to tea, as to avoid additional intake of water. I am thankful for all that Aline taught me during my stolen time with her in the kitchen. Though she's been here since I was born, she's as youthful as she is talented with baking. Estienne must surely miss her cooking.

I've taken to wearing mother's pearls around my wrist as a bracelet. She insists it wouldn't clutter my neck to wear them along with the pendant, but it feels odd to have them both there.

I've learned that my dear brother is coming home to visit. I have missed him so. It was always Estienne who came to ease my fear when tremors shook the house. He is on the right path for a brave man, but I will be glad to have him here.

I played a wonderful game of find the object today. Unfortunately, my bracelet caught on the finger of Aline's daughter, young Marie. Pearls scattered everywhere. Marie was devastated and a little frightened that mother would be upset. How quickly I turned her fear into joy. I issued cookies to all the servants' children and informed them that they needed to eat their treats slowly so I would have time to hide their treasure. It took me no more than twenty minutes to hide the pearls that had fallen. As I write, twenty-six of the thirty pearls have been found, and I let the children keep their prizes. They have yet to locate the one on the frame in the foyer, the one tucked in with the eggs in the kitchen, the one threaded and hanging from a needle with the sewing, and the last in the smaller fountain with the statue of the fish. I slipped that one into a fish's mouth, and I dare say I think it will be the last found, if at all.

My dear Estienne has returned, and will stay for several days. I observed as he approached on horseback alongside his fair-haired friend, the largest man I've ever seen. It was clear from a distance that he wasn't large from gluttony, but from the use of his body. The exchange we had upon their arrival was overwhelmingly familiar, like two brothers came home this day, rather than one.

Went riding with Estienne. His friend remained absent, as did Cendres. The cat tends to follow Estienne and I into the woods, however, he has been so taken with my brother's friend that it was just the two of us sparring at the stream... Estienne claims I strike with a quickness lacking in most of his men... We ate, drank, laughed, and wet our feet. With such strength as he has, Estienne was not able to keep his feet in the frigid stream as long as mine, remarking that the contest was not fair. Like flowing ice, so clear and true was the water, that I took a pebble from beneath it and let the ink swallow it upon my return to the pen, that my thoughts should flow so on paper.

Gunnar was the closest thing Lil had to Estienne, she supposed. She didn't have any formal martial arts training, training in *anything* she supposed, but she did have the advantage of an innate self-defense response. It wasn't likely Manon could have stormed her way out of a confrontation, or frozen an adversary in place, potentially suffocating them... or caused them to catch fire. Those talents of hers were difficult to control, and could result in collateral damage. Practice. Gunnar helped her some, but she'd been reluctant... Lil floated back to Manon's scenery. A pleasant spring afternoon, the water still crisp, insects not yet humming, but the sound of rippling water murmured, lulling as it passed between light and shadow.

Something brushed against her hair, her face, then rested where her neck met her shoulder, warm and heavy. She opened her eyes to see Gunnar crouching in front of her. She'd been...

"Sorry, kid."

She'd fallen asleep.

The blanket still surrounded her, but the diary was in Gunnar's hand.

Magnus's laptop remained closed on the nearby table; Gunnar's undersea adventure novel resting beside it without a bookmark.

"Any new developments on the Nautilus?" She asked, in part, if she was honest, to avoid talking about herself.

"Professor Aronnax has catalogued many sea creatures... Had to close the book before I ended up like you," he smirked.

Gunnar shifted so she could see over his large shoulder, tilting his head in reference to the silver haired man lying on the couch.

"Magnus is still resting his eyes," he said.

"And you're on security detail."

Lil knew they both cared for her, but there was some heaviness about being thought of as something volatile that needed to be handled lest it explode.

He nodded with understanding, and there was comfort in the gesture.

"Last night I slept little, if at all," she started. "This thing with the necklace, it's left me restless within myself. I need sleep to refresh, but I can't do it here, and we'll be busy with transition when we arrive, then we'll be at the museum shortly after, and who knows where my thoughts will be once I've met with our contact there..."

"When you are ready to sleep, I'll see to it that you rest well. For now, though... we keep you awake." He tilted his head toward her bag, and said, "What leaves can we heat up?"

"Mint will be good."

"Let's go then," he said, unwrapping her cocoon. "You could use some time away from this blanket."

With her thermos refreshed, Lil settled in to continue with Manon I, while Gunnar played sudoku in the seat across from her. Magnus eventually woke, returning her sketchbook with thanks and a kiss on the cheek.

As the plane slowed on the tarmac, Magnus moved toward the cockpit for a word with the pilot, and Lil felt a buzzing from her bag. Her phone. Claire.

"Lil! Did you make it?" Her cousin asked.

"We *just* touched down," she smiled. The timing was surprisingly accurate. Her cousin was likely worried an accidental dream might have triggered a tornado. "Things ok back at home?"

"Nan had me lead yoga, which sounded dreadful, but was just what I needed. And I should be thanking you for giving me a solid excuse to miss brunch with Brian and company..."

"I understand completely." The thought of a follow up with that crowd sounded incredibly unpleasant. The collective undoubtably had a multitude of questions they'd have asked with little to no regard for her feelings. The idea alone was stressful.

"I got Magnus's email and just left your house with the tea; now I'm headed into the Orn."

"Todd running the shop solo?"

"No, he's got his friends, Kerry and Duncan with him. More on the way later."

"Give him a big hug for me. I should go," she smiled, glancing Gunnar. "I'll get in touch later on."

"Sounds good, love you."

"Love you too."

Lil tucked her phone away. "That was Claire," she said.

"I know."

Lil quirked up an eyebrow. "It could have been Nan…"

"I know when you're speaking with your cousin," Gunnar replied. "Your face is like summer solstice."

She felt it too, the infectious brightness Claire had.

"How have you never met her?" She asked.

"I saw her once, from a distance."

Interesting. Lil hadn't gone to the Orn on days when Claire stayed with them in her youth, she and Gunnar never crossing paths.

132

"Her parents delayed picking her up," Lil said, suddenly recalling the morning. "They'd attended a conference; came for her Monday instead of Sunday. I ran to you from the field after saying goodbye to Claire when they arrived. She was still out there with them in the lavender."

Gunnar nodded, gathering their things. "Come," he said. "We can remember another time, after the long night ahead."

12.

Twilight added a veil of rose to the granite steps and iconic columns of the museum's entrance. The archer, though, remained bronze. This shirtless man, a statue, knelt down with a longbow in his left hand, his right elbow pulled back, fingers empty by his shoulder, having just released a projectile.

Left eye dominant, she thought.

Imagining her body in the same position, Lil felt moist ground against her knee, the surrounding smell of the damp earth, the musk of the animal she'd been waiting for. She was patient, gathering potential, the eventual release of energy seamless.

Her aim was true. It always was.

A weight on her shoulder pulled her back, grounding her. Gunnar's hand.

Lil opened her eyes to the blushing grey of the steps, the stillness of the archer and the pronghorn to her right. The front legs of the deer had raised up, neck arched back as it stood forever frozen, receiving the arrow.

"You were hunting," he said, both soft and heavy.

She nodded, still clearing herself from the depth of the forest.

Lil had napped before the bar the previous night, and then briefly after, but she wasn't rested. She'd not been able to sleep on the plane per the established safety protocol, overkill as it was, and time didn't allow for it after their arrival

Spending longer stretches awake than most was not uncommon for her, but, standing outside the museum, she felt the full weight of the day and the burden of her thoughts. When tired she was perhaps more vulnerable to being less guarded, leaving her particularly thankful for her companion, for the cool evening air.

Gunnar squeezed Lil's shoulder before handing her his phone, the name *Sami Hanna* on the screen.

She let out a breath and hit send.

With the phone to her ear, she turned left, then twisted right, pulling her brows together as she took in the other sculptures further down on each side.

"Hello? Lil?"

"Yes."

"Fantastic. Have you arrived?"

"Yes.

"At which entrance?"

Lil looked left and right again. "The one flanked by large infant heads. One asleep, one awake."

"Baby heads. That'd be the Fenway. Got it."

About five minutes later, a man exited the museum doors carrying a small, round tin. He paused at the top of the steps, patrons trickling around him. He wore a deep blue shirt with a pattern of little white flecks on it. The shirt was tucked into dark blue jeans belted in chestnut brown.

He spotted her, and smiled. "You must be Lil," he greeted, still descending the stone steps as she and Gunnar approached.

Placing the tin in his left hand, Sami extended his right. "Pleasure to meet you, I'm Sami Hanna." Releasing Lil's hand, he glanced up at Gunnar with a curious grin. "Sorry for the delay, I had to bribe the guards," he joked. "Bill told me the trip was very last minute. Do you come out this way often?"

"I've not been to the MFA before," she said, curt but friendly.

Lil briefly brought her hand up to where her necklace rested beneath the fabric of her dress, pressing the stone against her skin. She was already planning to share what felt like too much, though still felt it necessary.

"I was only expecting Lil," Sami said, opening the tin he'd been cradling. "But I have more than enough."

Gunnar unapologetically eyed the contents, raising a brow at what appeared to be cookies, mounded in shape with two distinct decorative patterns pressed into them.

"The round ones with the circles, have a date filling," Sami explained. "The oblong, oval shaped ones with the lines are pistachio. Either way, you should pass if you have a nut allergy."

Gunnar silently selected a date filled cookie.

The muscles of his face not involved in chewing relaxed, his fingers hovering just in front of his mouth, holding what had not yet been consumed. He turned what could have been one last bite into two, savoring. Opening his satisfied eyes and rolling them toward Lil, he titled his head at the tin in invitation.

"Did you make these, Mr. Hanna?" Lil asked.

"Oh no, call me Sami, please. I confess, it was my wife who made the ma'moul, but she was making them anyway. My parents are in town and staying with us..."

Lil watched Sami as he, too, took a sample from the tin, one of the rounder ones, and brought it to his mouth, then extended the tin toward her.

Whispering under her breath about the likelihood of butter, Lil cautiously reached in, hand hovering over an oblong cookie. With the corner of her eye, she caught the subtle tick of Gunnar's head to the side, and she moved to select the date filled alternative she had observed him eating. He was right; it would be the safest option.

With a sigh, she closed her eyes, her thoughts drifting.

"These taste like nostalgia," Lil whispered between bites.

Sami smiled. "They taste like my childhood."

Lil made a mental note of mentioning the treats to Nan. Better yet, she'd try to make them herself.

"What is used to make the decorative shapes?" She asked. "A press or a stamp?"

"Come," Sami said, closing the tin and gesturing for them to join him in walking up the stairs. "It's a wooden mold. Traditionally, a different mold is used for each of the three fillings: date, pistachio, and walnut." He held open the first of two glass doors for his guests to pass through, Gunnar opening the second. "They're available in specialty stores, but you can get anything online now."

Sami gave a wave as they bypassed the ticket counter to where a seated woman scanned the tickets of a couple ahead of them.

"Carol," he greeted. "These are the two Canadian colleagues I mentioned."

"Mmmhmm," she smirked, glancing up at Gunnar, then Lil. "If you keep coming by with that tin, you can bring as many *colleagues* through as you like."

"*Carol*," he said, mocking offense. "Are you questioning their credentials?"

"Head on in, and give my thanks to Imani for the cookies," she winked.

The three walked down a curved hallway, then turned into a vast open room where a large area had been sectioned off, arranged with tables and chairs as a cafe. Sami paused at the entrance to the space, once again extending the now open tin.

"Pistachio or date? You'll have to finish them before we reach the glass doors on the other side, but it shouldn't be a problem," he smiled.

Perhaps noticing the hesitation of his guests, Sami reached in and selected one of the oblong cookies, raising his eyes to meet theirs as he did so.

Gunnar took a pistachio cookie, then Lil did the same, though she waited for Gunnar to process a few bites before she started in on hers.

Their selections were, as Sami predicted: gone before they reached the other side of the room,

Lil finishing hers midway as she looked upward, eyeing the green glass sculpture that spanned floor to ceiling. It looked like an enormous, fluorescent aloe plant and reminded her of something she couldn't quite put her finger on.

"The Chihuly," Sami smiled.

Turning right, they passed through two sets of glass doors into another smaller room where there seemed to be a change in pressure, a difference in the way the air smelled. Lil was met by a stone statue of an Egyptian man in the center of the room, bits of it supplemented with plaster. To the right wall, detailed stone carvings told of a different time in a language she shouldn't have understood.

They walked straight through another set of doors, turning again and again. Lil's eyes passed over jars, jewelry, carvings, all manner of things laid out to distract as they moved along, finally settling on a glass case housing a great many small stone cylinders.

"The seals are displayed with their impressions made in clay, so we can see the full image," he started. "Because the shape of the artifact itself is a cylinder, we can only see one angle at a time, *however*... We recently acquired a 360-degree camera. One of my projects is the cataloging of our cylinder seals so we can see the flattened image of the stone itself, in addition to a clay impression."

Lil leaned in, examining everything laid out before her. Some of the imprints were of lines and shapes, others had names and words, animals, and people. *Our story,* she thought. There were so many stories there, little figures acting out scenes from long ago. The dates listed for the artifacts spanned thousands of years. So much could happen in such a length of time. How could something like this be *her* story? Maybe it was not the carving that was hers, but the way it had come to her, the journey.

Sami glanced down to Lil's chest where the necklace rested under her dress, then back up to her eyes.

"I thought you might benefit from seeing some of our collection here, what we have on display, before we really dig in. Take a moment, see the different stones used. Notice the sizes, shapes, different styles of imagery. I have a few in the lab I've selected for us to take a closer look at, but I also felt it valuable to be here, surrounded by these objects from the place and time we are thinking about."

Lil wasn't sure what she expected to happen, but she felt no connection to the other stones. Yes, she had a general feeling of curiosity, a hint of something that bordered on familiar, but these were the stories of others.

Perhaps she'd hoped for an explanation of some kind as to where her stone had come from, where her parents might have obtained it, and why, a hint as to what made her different.

"Who would these have belonged to?" Lil asked. "There seems to be a variety of stones, images, and dates of origin." She pictured wet charcoal smeared across a wide forearm, could smell the saltwater and char, that earthy, spicy heat. Her hand went to her chest again, stone pressing against her skin. "For what purpose?"

"Seals were often worn as pendants," Sami began, "such as what you have on now, or pinned to the clothing. The object brought power to the wearer. As an amulet, a seal could function to evoke protection, fertility, and good fortune. Even as a purely decorative piece, it would still bring social power to the wearer by way of displaying their status. Cylinder seals were also used as a signature representing the identity of the owner, affording power in trade, power to wield authority, sealing rooms, goods, legal documentation. To be seen wearing such a thing would visually convey the status, and therefore the power, of the wearer."

"As excited as I am to share this room with you," Sami continued, "I'm much *more* excited to get into the lab space. Come, we can take a closer look at a few carvings that aren't on display, and examine the one you've traveled so far to understand."

Through more halls and doors, Lil felt the way one might while going through old boxes in a basement, pulled by the thread of connection to pieces of what once was, of loved ones gone. Perhaps that feeling was what motivated many to become historians and curators; to investigate such things, to dive deep.

"I've set some seals out with corresponding clay impressions," Sami said upon their arrival. "I also took the liberty of leaving some fresh clay rolled, should you become inclined to make an impression of the seal you brought with you."

Sami walked around the table where a large tray housed several cylinder seals, each paired with its impressions in what looked like long jewelry boxes. He'd positioned a rectangular slab of glass on the table as well, about twenty centimeters in length. A rolling pin lay off to the side with a paintbrush, small bag of clay, and a long, skinny strip of wood and rubber about the same length as the glass.

"This one is in the geometric style," Sami said, referencing a stone with diamond latticework. "It was thought to be used more for decoration than for leaving a mark of authority in government or trade. These two here," he continued, moving on to where the next seals laid close together. "These are Neo Assyrian, but the glazed ceramic piece is in the linear style. You can see an archer, who may or may not be a king, shooting a horned animal. The chalcedony stone is of two men conquering a winged creature with the head of a man. Both are thought to be from six hundred to eight hundred BCE, though the styles are so different. What they have in common is the theme of strength, virility, power. Most likely worn to display social status and used to leave a signature of authority."

He moved along the table, pointing out the details of the remaining stones.

"Sumerian, Early dynastic, limestone, with a plant and animal theme going on. These horned creatures are facing each other, and a bird, presumably an eagle there. It's thought to be from three thousand to twenty-three hundred BCE. This last one is an old Babylonian Hematite piece thought to be from about nineteen to sixteen hundred BCE. A presentation scene with a god, goddess, king, and other males praying. The presentation style was common during this period, often with someone offering something, a sacrifice or prayer, to gods or goddesses. Obviously wearing perpetual worship of the deities was thought to bring good fortune," He smiled, leaning back against the table. "I was hoping I wouldn't need to ask, but may I take a look?"

He eyed her hand as it pressed against the stone hanging beneath her dress, as she fished for the seal by its chain and it rested in her palm, outstretched toward him.

He paused briefly, asking permission, before gently placing his hands under hers, allowing her to release the tethered stone to him.

Gunnar's hand met the small of her back as he moved closer, a solid presence, a breathing mountain.

Sami kept his eyes fixed while reaching off to the side, retrieving a peculiar pair of glasses. They had protruding microscopic lenses mounted over each eye.

"Tele loupes," he said, putting them on, then he took a long, deep breath as he inspected the seal, his exhale the only sound in the room until he began to whisper.

"Based on the chipping I've observed around the drill hole, and some of the details from the tool used to make the circular markings of the planets and the fruit on the tree... I do believe this could have been constructed Before Current Era."

His expression of reverence morphed into that of a man who was troubled as he lifted his lenses away, and looked up at her.

"How long have you had this piece?" He asked, closing his eyes a moment before continuing. "I ask because I've not seen this item before, nor have I heard of it, but a seal like this... if not recently recovered, it should have been documented."

He looked concerned, and Lil found that to be worrisome, that there could be something wrong with it, or with her. Would he try to take it? Gunnar's hand pressed into her, the rhythm of his breath intentionally becoming more audible, a sound for her to lean into.

"I've had it as far as I can remember," she said. "And that's over twenty years."

Sami let out a sigh that hinted relief, though he still held some burden. "When the United States invaded Iraq in 2003, the Iraq museum was pillaged in the chaos, and many archeological treasures were stolen, lost. The museum had some seven thousand cylinder seals at the time." He shook his head. "You would have been a child then, already in possession of this remarkable specimen. Forgive me, but I had to ask. Oftentimes when artifacts have a veiled history, there is forgery, theft, or some other such darkness involved... And there is plenty of mystery here," he said playfully, smile returning to his face. "Perhaps we could find out more."

Lil felt the corners of her lips turn up at Sami's renewed enthusiasm, and she gave a tentative nod, ready for more, ready to satisfy the need creeping into her dreams.

"I've let this go a long time," she started. "I've been comfortable not knowing, but I'm ready now." Lil felt a sense of truth and awe as she spoke, which were beautiful emotions, but often the trigger for an outward manifestation that would require explanation in mixed company. The rising feeling in her blood and bones transferred to her skin as a gently tingle, followed by a hum in the air, a sound on the cusp of catching light.

Gunnar inhaled sharp and turned his body between hers and Sami's, speaking for the first time since they'd entered the room.

"Water," He said, handing her a small steel bottle, then whispered, "Like a mountain stream, cool, and slow over stone."

Lil took in his words with the liquid, both carrying calm through her.

"Thank you," She said, one hand offering the bottle back to him, the other resting on his chest. "You always know when I'm thirsty."

Gunnar transitioned again to Lil's side, and Sami came into view again, puzzled, but not uncomfortably so.

"Do you mind," Sami started, "and I don't want to offend, but how *did* you come into possession of the seal? Were your parents diggers? Private collectors?"

"My parents died tragically, and I was adopted," Lil began matter-of-factly. I don't know who they are or what they did. They could have been fur traders, school teachers, assassins, grocers, or doctors. I know as little about them as you do now. I came to live with my guardian, Nan, when I was about five years old." She pressed her hand over the stone. "This was around my neck when I arrived, and it's been with me ever since."

"Please forgive me," Sami whispered, face stricken. "I didn't mean to bring up something as devastating as the death of your parents."

"It's ok," she said with honesty. Discovering her parents were deceased could be uncomfortable for people. They didn't know how to respond properly, as if there were some ritual of condolence they needed to work through, but the details were unclear.

"Their mystery is one I'm content not to solve just yet. The stone, on the other hand…" she hinted with an attempt at returning them all to a less somber state.

"Yes," Sami beamed from his chair, wheeling back slightly from the force of his excitement, hands splayed out in the air. Lil half expected to see fireworks shoot out from them.

"Let's begin with time. When it comes to dating an item, should you want to do such a thing, there are several useful things we can look at. The first is context. Was the object found in a sealed room? What was it surrounded by? How deep into the earth? With the stone you've brought in, we don't have much context other than your neck and your story, which don't reveal much.

"Another tool is analytical chemistry. The seal, if it had been used as such, would have residue from the substances it has been pressed in over the course of its existence. The trouble with this is, well, Bill has already told me that you've pressed it into clay recently. I don't fault you for this, but it might be challenging and time consuming to go this route. And seeing how comfortable you are wearing it, I'm willing to bet it's been through a lot."

Lil nodded. He was correct there; she never took it off.

"The X-ray and the electron microscope could prove useful. While I can't pinpoint an exact year, this technology can help us to better understand what tools were used to fashion your treasure. And, of course, there's the imagery the carving presents. As you've seen, some seals have text, some have geometric shapes and patterns, some have animals, humanoid figures interacting. If we see soft drink logos and automobiles, we can assume this is not a BCE artifact," he smiled. "Although, assumptions can be dangerous."

Gunnar reached for the water bottle, turning his body in front of hers again. Bringing his mouth close to Lil's ear. "Whatever its origin," he whispered, "the stone has found its way to your body. It has meaning and value regardless of price at auction."

Lil took a sip and nodded, holding the stone in her fingers, thumb smoothing over it. With a deep breath and a pulse of determination, she said, "I'd like to start with the clay."

After brief instruction, Lil rolled her seal along the flattened streak of grey.

"Wonderful," Sami breathed. "Even pressure... Yes, well done," he smiled reverently.

Lil tucked her necklace back beneath her dress, feeling it drop cold against her skin. Pendulum restrained, she leaned back over the table with Gunnar and Sami to inspect her work, eager for the analysis she'd flown across a continent for.

"Okay," Sami started. "From left to right we have the eight-pointed sun and eleven planets in the upper corner here. It's amazing what observations of our solar system were made so long ago, before the known invention of the telescope. Here we have a male and female with fishtails instead of legs, both unclothed. These curved lines represent the water they're swimming in. The short lines emanating from their bodies could be light or power. Curvy lines coming from his hands are water. Now, as we move to the right we see, once again, a male and female figure, lines emanating from them, both with legs, but there are wings present now. The figures are facing each other, hands almost touching, a tree in their hands with roots dangling down, fruit on its branches."

Sami concluded his narration and leaned back in his chair.

"The style seems old Babylonian, but I'm not sure..." he sighed. "I'm familiar with the tailed figures, water from hands, the celestial details, the tree... It's not a presentation, not a conflict or display of power, like a contest. There is *definitely* a fertility motif here, what with the water coming from the male, and the growing of the fruit-bearing tree between them. I mentioned before, that seals could function as amulets. This could have been worn to evoke reproductive power."

"The power to create," Lil said, her voice trailing off, thoughts picking up speed. *The power to create…* Wasn't that the essence of what made her different? Making things happen?

Gunnar leaned down toward her ear. "Do you ever take it off?"

She lifted her eyes to his and shook her head.

"The power to *create*, exactly," Sami said. "The fertile waters have been thought of as male in some mythologies, particularly the ones we're thinking about in association with your seal. The water coming from him is seen in depictions of Enki, a Sumerian god of fertility, fresh water, wisdom, creation, healing. The male on your seal is bearded, though typically Enki would have been seen with a domed helmet-like crown."

Lil looked down at her stone once more. No crown. And *he* was a fertility god, not the woman.

"Tiamat and Apsu were primordial creator beings," Sami went on. "He was associated with fresh water and she with salt water. Sometimes she's depicted as a sea creature. She's said to embody both chaos and creation. But," he sighed again, "I'm just not sure. There are elements I'm familiar with, but others not, and pieces I'd expect to be present that are not. Either way, my bet is this was a fertility amulet." He glanced at his watch and grumbled, "I'd like to phone a colleague at the British Museum, but I'm certain he'll be sleeping. Perhaps first thing tomorrow we could meet again and conference him in."

"It's also," Sami continued, looking at the impression with a thoughtful eye. "I mean… water, light, male and female, fruit bearing tree. It's a bit of a creation story in itself, isn't it?"

146

"A story..." Lil said, thinking back to her dream. "So, in a way, one could call that *our* story. As in, the story of all of us, rather than the story of, say, just two people?"

"One could say that, I suppose. What are you thinking?"

"Oh, it's nothing, just the words, *our story*, had come to mind...What if a seal was made to go with this one, to continue the story? Do seals ever go in pairs? It would be unusual for a person to have two, right?"

Sami considered her words, then, cautiously, he said, "Bill mentioned a second seal. Can you tell me a bit about that?"

"I saw the second seal Bill mentioned in a dream after we met, after I pressed my stone in clay. The one in my dream had the same figures, I think, but..." she closed her eyes, picturing the image. "Do you have paper and a pencil? I could draw the impression."

"Of course."

Lil quickly got to work, first sketching out the space of the wide rectangle, omitting the magnificent forearm it had been laid on top of. From left to right she recreated the sun and planets, the man and the woman, both with wings, then the winged man up high, as if in flight, reaching down to a woman without wings as she reached up to him, detailed lines coming away from their bodies...

"And the color of the second stone was...?" Sami whispered as she continued her work.

"Like mine," she said, drawing the winged man with a child sized person, then the winged man beside an adult sized female, and finally, next to a winged woman, all of the figures having those detailed lines emanating from them. She added the waves underfoot, tree at the end.

Sami hovered over the completed drawing, glancing between the dream impression and that of the necklace she wore.

"The celestial elements are there, and the tree. The male figure is the same." He looked back and forth between the two, then leaned back in his chair. "I'm going to need more time with this."

Not likely, she thought.

"It does seem like a continuation of this story," he went on. "The same figures appear... Perhaps your mind did the heavy lifting of creating what should come next, playing with the new symbols you've recently acquired. Though this stone has been with you your whole life, as you said, it is only just recently that the details took hold of your interest. Another possibility is that you may have seen this other seal as a child, and are bringing your memory to the surface through dreaming."

She'd suspected as much.

"Symbols are important," he continued. "And what are dreams but a collection of symbols manifesting not just visually, but with sound, smell, emotion, every facet of our senses working to create something meaningful in a way that is so tailored to ourselves we often don't even understand the complexity of it. And we're the ones creating these dreams," he laughed. "It gets me every time. We are quite amazing," he sighed.

"So, what do we know now," Lil asked. "I have powerful dreams, and maybe have a fertility amulet?

I believe so," Sami nodded. "The seal you're wearing was likely a fertility amulet and, upon initial outer exam, I'd say it's BCE, but I need to spend more time to dial it in. I would be *very* excited to investigate further with you," he went on. "Chipping around the drill hole, as I mentioned, can be an indicator of ancient authenticity. We can easily run an X-ray to examine the drill hole. Authentic seals have been drilled from both ends, so there can be an interruption in the center where the two meet and an irregular profile. Drill holes will have random concentric anomalies in the outer portion of the bore from the abrasive slurry used."

The stone was really old, but no help in the discovery of who her parents were, how, or why she got the necklace in the first place. Not ideal, but not a loss. A fertility invoking amulet made sense if there was a connection to her abilities, but she'd need to test for correlation later.

Do I need to know more? Lil asked herself.

She looked at the clay, knowing the imprint would harden, a piece of her left behind, and this left her unsettled. She didn't like the idea of someone having a piece of her, whether blood, stone, or clay. It wouldn't be enough. Sami would want more, and any further information he managed to glean would not outweigh the unwanted attention she'd receive. He already wanted to involve colleagues...

"Sami," she said, pulling his attention from her drawing. "We came right after our flight without grabbing something, and those delicious cookies could only do so much to make a dent in our hunger. Would it be ok to take a break and get a bite to eat?"

"Of course. If you're looking to get some fresh air, there's a bakery right down the street. They close at eight so you'd want to get going on that soon. I'm not sure what you prefer for delivery options, but there's a great Thai place close by with a vegetarian menu if that's your thing. The tamarind tofu is good. If you like spicy, I recommend the larb tofu. I brought Carol enough ma'moul to smuggle a dog in, never mind some takeout," he laughed. Shouldn't be more than twenty minutes."

Gunnar produced a granola bar from one of his pockets, handing it to Lil.

"For the interim," he said.

Lil took the bar, but Sami held up a hand.

"I'm a little particular about food in this area…" He said, starting for the door. "Let's head down to the Café with the Chihuly. When we get back, I'd like to use the new camera I mentioned, to create a flat image of the entire stone. Then I can just send the image to some colleagues."

Lil felt Gunnar lingering at the table as she followed Sami. With a glance, she saw him crush the clay imprint she'd made, then old fold her drawing into his pocket, leaving no trace of her behind.

Lil paused down the hall, caught by something she'd missed on their way in. To her right, just before a set of glass doors, a mesh dress hung like a beaded net on a dress form. The beads, whatever they were made of, in hues of blue and bone.

Lil closed her eyes and felt the weight of the mesh over her body as though she were wearing it; cold against her flesh. She lost focus for a moment, chilled air moving over her skin where the beaded mesh left much of her exposed. Though the air was cool, warmth radiated from within her. She felt on the cusp of something, anticipating, and whatever it was, she wanted it wholly. Then felt it. Something. Someone. She felt their heat against her first, then fingers grazing over the garment, a palm, a large thumb hooking through one of the open diamonds of the netlike weave. A sudden downward movement and loss of weight accompanied the sound of beads crashing to the stone floor, echoing inside her. She was left with a flood of emotions; relief, suspense, excitement, love.

Lil startled at the weight of arms around her. Opening her eyes, she saw the dress intact in its case before her, the floor free of beads. Back in the hall, air shifted, lifting the ends of her hair, a persistent tremor underfoot. She'd been waiting for something, and it had been so close, reaching out to her. The loss of the memory or the dream, leaving it too soon, was devastating.

Gunnar's body surrounded hers, drawing her eyes upward.

"Not hunting," he whispered, voice low and concerned.

She shook her head, still getting her bearings.

"Do you feel that? Sami asked, alarmed. "These rooms have temperature control," he added, then stopped, holding up his hand. Another rush of air swept up at her.

Sami's eyes widened, "Do you feel that vibration? I'm so sorry but I need to go. Call me when you return." He moved swiftly down the hall, cellphone to his ear.

Lil leaned against Gunnar as soon as Sami's back turned.

Breathe in, breathe out.

Where had she gone? The room had been stone.

She needed to get outside, but outside was so far.

Breathe in, breathe out.

Lil registered the unwrapping of something, a caramel in Gunnar's hand, the taste in her mouth, sweet, smoky, and-

"Lavender," he said, smelling the wrapper. "There's maple and a few rose ones in the bag too. Deep breaths, kid."

With an arm still around her, Gunnar led them through a series of glass doors and into the room with the giant green glass statue. Sitting on a bench, Lil's heart rate slowed, and she leaned against him; the wide space that went up at least three stories not feeling quite as closed in.

Any vibration she'd initiated had passed, but the Chihuly still swayed, testing the strength of the cables tethering it to the ceiling. She was tired, and didn't think it would go down but...

"I can probably keep it from hitting us," she began, "but it could get weird, so, if it falls, it might be best if you intervene."

"It wouldn't be the first time I rescued you from kelp," he said smoothly.

151

"*That's* what it looks like," she smiled, then closed her eyes and sighed. "Those caramels, though, she said, looking up to him. "Thank you."

He studied her for a moment, his dark eyes moving subtly as he glanced at the different parts of her face, landing at her eyes with palpable sincerity. He nodded, and rubbed her back before looking away.

She wasn't sure when it became more than a job for him. For her, it had been that first day in Nan's garden.

*

Unexpected rainfall coated the granite steps, and though the downpour was letting up, thunder still cracked as Lil and Gunnar exited the museum.

He met her eyes, his voice a low whisper with an undercurrent of disbelief, though he still asked the question.

"You?"

Lil shrugged and shook her head. Sometimes rain was just rain.

They passed the bronze hunter, then the wide-eyed infant head. Their plan had been to call the car, but the promise of pastry made for a compelling detour. After shaking the foundation of the museum, Lil needed more than fresh air, but the fresh air was a start.

Wet clung to everything, elongating lights and adding something to the sounds of their feet, of tires on asphalt. There was something else, a feeling like something was with her, watching, *close*. Slowing her steps but not wanting to draw attention, she scanned her periphery, searching, finding only cars, buildings, pedestrians.

"Something is off," she began softly. "I think we need to get inside."

Gunnar put one hand on Lil's lower back, picking up the pace.

"Do you think…" she whispered. "If the stone is somehow connected with what I can do, and someone else knew… *Could* someone else know? It wouldn't be impossible, right?"

"No more impossible than you, kid."

It was true, she supposed, that in a world where she existed, there wasn't much that could be written off as unlikely. The thousands of years since her necklace had been created would be enough time for knowledge to have spread about the seal. The stone had only been hers for twenty-five years at most, who knows what lives it could have been tangled in before, or who might try to lay claim to it.

Gunnar's hand stayed on her back as their pace increased. He maintained contact until the door to the bakery opened, and she smelled something reminiscent of Nan's shop.

They were the only ones in there.

"The driver is on his way," Gunnar said, tucking a phone back into his pocket. "What did you feel outside?"

Lil shook her head. "I'm not sure. I felt *watched*."

"We are well lit here, well seen," he said, guiding her toward the counter. "You might be visible, but if someone was following you, they'd be foolish to attempt anything in this space. So now we eat pastries, and slip out when the car arrives."

Allowing herself the momentary illusion of disconnect that the bakery provided, Lil let go of what happened in the museum, what she felt on the street. With Gunnar just behind her, she approached the counter and focused on the menu.

"Chocolate mousse," she sighed. *Or a cinnamon rose. Claire would love that ginger apple turnover,* she thought.

"What can I get for you?" asked the young man behind the counter.

"Oh, I definitely need another minute," she smiled.

"Take your time."

Lil did just that, absently swaying to the song overhead as she browsed her options. The music was old, something worth slow dancing to over generations. There was a dreamy quality about it, lulling her such that she didn't notice the few wisps of light falling like flurries from above. Without glancing back, Lil raised her arm, meeting Gunnars hand with hers so he could assist in a slow twirl, then the resumption of their previous stance. A ground shaking tremor followed, however, and she met Gunnar's waiting eyes, brows pushed together with concern.

"You?" He asked.

"No."

The door opened then, and a new customer entered: tall, broad, shaved head slick with rain and reflected light. His expression was playful, but with an undercurrent of ferocity. When his amber eyes met hers, something clicked inside, and time seemed to slow. She felt an overwhelming sense of recognition, her blood humming, but why? There was something, something *vitally* important that she could almost taste, something just out of reach, and the impossibility of connecting to whatever it was began to build in her. As Lil's emotions undulated, the lights above wavered, dimming almost completely for a moment. The pause allowed her to see that the stranger's eyes were lit from the inside, almost glowing.

Flickering glass bulbs began to strain as their light intensified. Gunnar's hand came to her shoulder, and his chest against her back in attempt to decrease her racing heart. She was beginning to feel the speed of what was happening, spiraling out of control. If she didn't calm herself something could break, someone could get hurt. What she really needed to do was look away, but she couldn't.

By some miracle, the man at the door closed his eyes and, for a moment, things were still. Her breathing slowed, in and out, and the lighting returned to a normal glow.

What was that?

Her eyes flicked over to the young man behind the counter, who seemed oblivious to anything other than how cool the light show had been. Releasing her tension with a sigh, Lil eased back into Gunnar, and returned her gaze to the man still standing at the door.

Then the stranger's eyes flew open, rings of flame around his pupil boring right into her.

Lil gasped, triggering an explosion of white light in a flash; shattered bulbs raining glass and powder down.

A shout came from behind the counter as Gunnar hunched over her, a shield against the falling debris. Through the cave of his body, she saw the descending particles sparkling in what light remained. Though born of destruction, there was an ethereal quality about it.

"You ok?" asked the employee behind the counter. Without waiting for an answer, he shouted, "Vee! I need an assist out front!"

Another man, slightly older, came out from the kitchen and stood still, eyes wide, surveying the damaged lights and fallen glass.

"They all just broke," the kid said.

"Good *god*... You guys okay?" Vee asked.

Lil nodded, and Gunnar brushed off his arms where some glass and powder rested.

"Hey buddy, you mind flipping the sign on the door?" Vee called out to the obliging stranger. "Thanks."

Lil heard footsteps behind her. And though he was clearly walking toward the counter, it felt like the stranger was coming for her, like he hadn't entered the shop for the baked goods, but because she'd been there. Her mind went to the conversation she'd had with Gunnar outside. She'd felt targeted, followed. Ludicrous, obviously, but still her hand rose up and rested on her chest, adding another layer between her stone and the newcomer with fire in his eyes.

"I am *so* sorry for whatever just happened out here," Vee continued from behind the counter. "Are you all ok? Everything encased should be fine if you'd like to take something to go; on us. I can't guarantee the bags didn't get glassed though, best to avoid those."

After a silent moment passed, Gunnar gave her shoulder a squeeze, and she realized the man behind the counter was waiting for her order.

"I'm still looking," she whispered. "You go ahead."

Amber eyes found hers as she turned, now only a meter away, and working over her in what felt like an inspection. Was he checking her for damage, or the necklace?

"Two croissants," he said to the man across the counter, though his attention remained on Lil, unwavering.

"Plain?"

"Yes, but... are those... are those pistachio? Okay, two plain croissants, and the two pistachio," he grinned, then turned back to Lil. "Shame about glass getting on the bags. I'd have loaded up. It's been a while since I've hauled a bag of pastry. Story for another day," he added, leaning his forearms against the freshly wiped counter, closing his unsettling eyes. His nostrils flared as he inhaled deep, and she couldn't blame him. The warm smell was something one could easily get lost in, were the conditions right.

He seemed to linger when his lungs filled, his mouth resting gently in the sweetest smile, nostalgia wafting off of him and into her heart. She wanted to reach out, but kept her hand cautiously on her chest, watching his expression change ever so slightly. His brows pushed together, one eye pinching more than the other as if he were questioning something. His lip quirked as he looked to Gunnar, his smile transitioning back into the amused playfulness she'd seen on him when he'd entered. It put her at ease a little for some reason, watching the silent exchange between the stranger and her friend.

Lil's eyes drifted down to the powder and debris on the man's shoulder.

"I'm sorry about the glass," she offered. "If it had gotten in your eyes…"

"Please don't apologize," he whispered. "It was out of your control."

Flaky pastries were passed to him, interrupting. She felt his hesitation, that he wanted to do or say something more.

"I move around quite a bit," he said, before taking a bite, then speaking while chewing. "It's exciting, but there are comforts I miss. This is an experience I have gone without for far too long. A feeling like home."

He winked, flourishing his partially eaten croissant at the darkened ceiling where the lights no longer functioned.

"I appreciate a good pastry as well," Gunnar commented, much to Lil's surprise.

"I'm sure you do. There's a new place in Melbourne," the stranger said. "The atmosphere is a little *clinical*, but the product is quite good… It's lacking that small café feel, though, somewhere touched by generations of hands." He took another bite and stared at her for a moment, seeming lost in thought. Then, with another heavy breath, he grinned, and began to walk away.

"The cinnamon rose," he called out as he passed into the night. "Or both. You have two hands."

Lil took a sharp inhale as the door closed, the air shifting through to bring in the scent of something familiar from outside. With the change in lighting, she could better see through the glass.

"There's someone else out there," she breathed. "I think it's…"

The second figure seemed somehow even taller than the amber eyed man beside him, shoulders wide, details unclear, but... It looked like the dark-haired man from the bar, from her dream. The idea was absurd, but...

No more impossible than you, kid.

Using all her strength, she pulled her focus from the window and looked up to her companion, who undoubtedly saw the fear in her eyes.

Then she turned back, and the men were gone.

13.

Lil pushed the courtyard door gently closed behind her, two mugs of Amka's tea in her hands. The October sky and fieldstone floor welcomed her, as did the relaxed state of her friends in the early morning light.

The Boston brownstone had a patio off the back of the lower level, but exposure to the neighboring buildings left it lacking. The brick walls of the courtyard space on the upper level, however, were tall enough to provide privacy; more than satisfactory for tea.

Though the apartment was reserved for transient use, it was maintained to have the feel of a well-loved home. Several long strands of copper bells hung from the walls, which must have produced a lovely sound under falling rain. Ivy cascaded from hanging planters, and huge pots of herbs had been stationed around the space, their fragrance and familiarity refreshing.

Gunnar sat to Lil's right as she entered, reclining in one of two chairs, his long legs stretched out, book in one hand and mug in the other. Beside him, an apple and a knife rested on a low table, an empty chair waiting for her on the other side.

The apartment had two large studies and an extensive collection of books. Gunnar had selected *Around the World in Eighty Days* the night before when they'd finally made it home from the museum, an appropriate follow up to his reading material on the plane ride over.

A Story in Stone

Magnus, who was both a night owl and early bird at times, had left a note in the kitchen the night before, indicating he was feeling inclined toward the latter, and would they please join him in taking some fresh air upstairs in the morning. He also informed them in writing that he had heard from the school. A visit would be permitted, details to be discussed later.

As she and Gunnar had parted to go into their separate rooms for bed the night before, Gunnar claimed, somehow, that he wasn't tired. "I expect I'll be up reading for some time," he'd said. "Should you become unsettled by your dreams, you won't be left to them alone."

Though one of Lil's paintings hung in the townhouse, it was not in her room, and she'd not thought to look for the watercolor work she'd done on the plane, or attempted another. Instead, she lied in bed, drawing focus to her breath, when a familiar sound washed over her. Through the walls and the darkness, a blade passed through water and over stone. She knew whose hand held the knife, who guided the ebb and the flow like a seductive metronome calling her body from chaos to keep time. Like feathers on air, waking life fluttered from her, falling not into ocean waves, but into the echoes of another rhythm, leaving Lil soothed as she drifted peacefully to sleep.

The smell of ginger pulled her gently back into the morning, something Gunnar had infused in his drink. He looked up, nodded, then turned back to the tale of Phineas Fogg.

Magnus was there in shades of grey: white collared shirt, light grey sweater, dark grey wool trousers and, of course, his beard. He sat a little left of center at a small table opposite an empty chair, reading a newspaper. A cup and saucer sat in front of him beside a plate of biscuits, scones, and fruit.

"I've not decided if I should let you settle in before asking how things went at the museum," he said.

He truly can't contain himself, she thought, lips quirking up into a smile.

161

Lil left the mug of Amka's tea in front of him, continued to the chair over by Gunnar and, upon seating, decided not to make Magnus wait.

"Sami showed us the cylinder seals in the collection on display, then took us to his lab where we looked at a few that he'd selected."

"Mmmm..." he hummed, sipping the hot tea. "And did he unlock for you the great mysteries of civilization?"

Magnus was still brooding over not been consulted first about her seal. He wasn't petty, nor did he linger with such nonsense as grudges, but he wouldn't turn down an opportunity to deflate something he felt didn't elevate on its own merits.

"Sami examined my seal. I did an impression with it in clay, and drew a likeness of the other seal that I dreamed about. He believes it to be dated sometime BCE, and was *very* interested in investigating further with his equipment... Wanted to send images to colleagues."

Magnus raised eyebrows, concerned, silently asking her to continue.

"We took a break for dinner, but never returned to the lab."

The question remaining on his face was obvious.

The subtle sensation of cool water spreading from her chest to her arms was, she suspected, the manifestation of her anxiety blooming. Lil found elaborating on the events that took place after they left the lab daunting, but not because she feared disclosure, or being judged. To say she trusted Magnus would be an understatement. She was hesitant to further explore that moment for fear of prompting another inconvenient event.

She and Gunnar had spoken little after returning from the bakery. No good would have come of it given how exhausted and incident prone she'd been, so they existed comfortably in each other's company with few words. Lil knew he would wait for her to initiate discussing what she'd experienced with the beaded dress, what triggered her to explode the lights in the bakery, and she just hadn't been ready. Her nerves suggested she still wasn't.

Just start at the beginning, she thought, *step by step, run it through.*

"There was..." she started. "On the way out, we were in the hall and I saw a beaded dress. It reminded me of something I couldn't quite put my finger on. I stopped, I had to, then became lost to my thoughts... It was..." She trailed off, gently feeling herself pulled toward the memory of what happened in the hall, the sound of the beads falling.

Gunnar's steady voice continued for her. "A localized tremor and temperature change occurred in and around the gallery where we stopped. Sami became concerned and excused himself to investigate."

"Was anything left behind?"

"No."

Magnus nodded, sipping at his tea. "Lily, dear, this drink is delightful."

She silently consumed her own, regaining equilibrium.

"Did Sami provide you with his interpretation of the markings?" He went on. "Give you a clue as to his opinion on the function of your piece?"

Lil took a breath in. "It's his opinion that I'm wearing a *fertility* amulet. I was thinking about fertility, as being a power to create... not just through the birth of children, but to create life, say, from the soil, or to create energy. To create wind, waves, or fire..." she added, with eyebrows raised.

Magnus didn't miss a beat.

"You're wondering if your power comes from the stone."

She nodded.

"Your reasoning is sound," he said. "The seal you wear has been a constant. You have no memory of its absence while you've had your moments of creation, correct?"

Lil shook her head, "It's always been here," she said, hand on her chest.

163

"Of course. It's logical then to investigate causality."

"There's something else. I felt like I was being followed on our way back from the museum. We left and went directly to a bakery around the corner, and I had this intense feeling of being watched as we walked. When we got to the counter, a man came in. I was so worked up, I exploded the lights in the shop," she admitted. "Do you think this stone might be something a person would try to come for, if they knew about it?"

There was no doubt; of course they would. The stranger's motivation for entering the bakery couldn't be known for sure, though. Perhaps it had just been the croissants.

Lil thought about relaying the feeling of familiarity she's experienced, and the possibility that the man from the bar was there. Deciding against it, she waited for Magnus to respond.

He sipped Amka's tea, wheels turning.

"First things first," he began. "We need to test your theory. I have plans with Martin again today, and I don't wish to cancel, but I can get us into a secure space at the Boston campus this evening. If you're looking for an outdoor opportunity we can wait until we've reached the Iceland property. It's coastal, and quite secluded. If we receive permission to visit the school it would delay things, although worth it to stop there. The school is remote as well, however, might not be an appropriate venue for an experiment. There are the children to consider, and I wouldn't want to overstep. As far as others taking an interest in what you have around your neck, it's an undoubtable possibility. The first thing we need to do, though, is test your theory."

Lil felt the subtle drain of disappointment. She hadn't thought of herself as impatient, but why did they need to wait? She didn't need equipment, just her necklace, or lack thereof.

"I can do this here," she said, soft and clear. "This morning. There's no need to put it off."

"The delay is not a matter of *avoidance,* Lily dear, it's taking the time to set things up properly, to account for potential problems that may arise, prevent risking exposure. This isn't the ocean, a room at one of my facilities, or an expanse in the arctic. Are you confident in your ability to maintain safety?"

"I'm calm. You are both here, I'm drinking tea, and this sweater is extremely cozy," she smiled, sliding a hand over her shirt. "I think with safety, the key is for me to stop if I get frustrated. My biggest challenge is control in the setting of escalating emotions, and I have you two here to help with that. I grew a dandelion the other day and immobilized Gunnar. *Yes,* I stopped Todd from breathing accidentally but, my point is, I don't need to create a storm or an explosion to test our theory."

Gunnar's teeth removed a chunk of apple, the sound crisp and tart as the fruit.

Glancing at the open core, Lil got an idea. "Life starts small," she said. "Perhaps I can too."

"Indeed," Magnus affirmed, grinning like a child. "It seems there's potential for a rather exciting start to the day."

Gunnar stilled, looking down at what had been only food moments before. His thumb drifted toward the casing, drawing closer to the exposed seed. Lil watched as he pressed into the small, brown treasure, sliding it out along the moist fruit. With the remains of the apple down on the table, he held the seed between his glistening thumb and forefinger. His other hand, empty, extended toward her.

Lil kept contact with his eyes as she removed the necklace from her body. She pooled the chain in Gunnar's open palm, rested the stone on top, then watched his fingers close over the etched images. His other hand came across the space between them, damp as he pressed the seed against her skin. She looked from the tiny gift, to the stone, as his thumb smoothed over the carvings, then back up to his eyes, poised to meet hers.

"Okay, kid?"

Lil nodded, aware of an absence. She reasoned it might only be the weight of the missing seal itself she felt. It wasn't as though something had been removed from inside her, just shifted mass.

Refocusing her attention on the tiny universe of potential she held, Lil felt the life resting in her palm, waiting, waiting to grow into a tree capable of producing fruit, of bearing thousands and thousands more seeds capable of nourishing and growing indefinitely. She remembered the apple tree between Nan's and the barn, remembered her curiosity as a child.

She sighed, hand squeezing gently around the little brown teardrop.

Focus.

Eyes closed, Lil remained aware of Gunnar and Magnus. They maintained proximity as to offer support, but politely allowed her the privacy she needed to attempt her process, whatever that meant. It had always been emotion driven for her, but not forced. The things that made her different resulted from strong emotion or unspoken curiosity. She'd grown a dandelion in the orchard, a tiny garden from a dead man in the lab unintentionally. Surely, she could get a sprout to grow at minimum.

She heard a page turn to her left, then every sound and sensation seemed to distract her like an itchy sweater, every fiber setting off a response.

Lil sighed again, louder, lifting her heals and pressing her toes into the cold stone floor. Cold, but not uncomfortable. She was too aware her audience, the sound of that newspaper, of the way her chair felt.

Opening her eyes, she stood up and paced the courtyard, inspecting the sounds and smells of the small space. She hoped the movement of her body would be enough to wash out everything else. Why wasn't anything *happening?*

Maybe she was thinking about her task too much, or maybe nothing sprouted because the stone was in Gunnar's hand, instead of around her neck...

Lil opened her palm to examine the seed: still contained, still waiting.

This wouldn't have been the right place for you to grow anyway, she thought.

She placed the seed down on the table beside Gunnar and settled back into her chair. Letting her right arm slide down toward the large pot of rosemary, she dipped her fingers into the dirt, pushed her hand in deeper until she was alone there, with the roots. The orchestral hum of the earth below Nan's garden didn't exist within the terra-cotta. The mood of the soil was different. Rosemary stayed all through the year in Nan's garden, but it would be too cold during winter on the brownstone's patio. Perhaps caretakers brought the pot in during the winter. Lil wondered, as she reached out to the roots, if the plant had ever blossomed. With a need to communicate the pleasure of flowering, she projected the hope of going to seed, the hope of new life.

Lil inhaled deep, the scent of rosemary reaching her with increased strength and a desire to become *more*. She imagined petals quivering under the movement of a pollinator, tempted to make it so.

In and out, Lil's thoughts shifted to her breath, and then to the prospect of her tea getting cold. As she opened her eyes, she saw Magnus and Gunnar, both staring at her hand, then she looked down as she retracted it from the dirt. No, it was not her hand they were transfixed by. It was more likely the purple flowers blooming on the rosemary plant towering over her.

"Not the stone then," she whispered.

14.

"I agree that it's unnecessary, however…" Magnus sighed, twisting to look back at Lil from the driver's seat, expression sympathetic. "I gave my word to David that it would be done."

Lil nodded and closed her eyes, allowing Gunnar to tie the scarf around her like a blindfold.

"Two hours?" She asked. The drive would be long behind the fabric mask, and she was tired.

"Two or three," Gunnar replied, his hands gliding over her neck as he pulled away. "It's slow going at the end but you'll have your sight back by then."

Lil jolted at the sudden sensation of her seat vibrating, felt Gunnar shift beside her.

"Claire," he said.

The phone brushed against her ear, her fingers passing over Gunnar's as she took hold of it.

"Lil?"

"You have a knack for calling right around touchdown, though you're a little late this time… We're in the car. Everything okay?"

Lil wanted the conversation to be as normal as possible but, speaking on the phone while blindfolded, she was aware of the oddity.

"Oh, thank goodness, you've landed," Claire said. "Where are you?"

"A Scandinavian day trip," Lil started, not wanting to reveal she was being driven to a remote, undisclosed location, but not wanting to lie, either. "Heading to one of Magnus's favorite libraries, then off to his Iceland home. Just a day trip. I'll let you know when we board again so you can time your next call," she smiled.

"There's one more thing," Claire began, a thread of concern in her voice. "I've got it covered, but Sami has been asking for you. He's called Bill saying your number is no longer working. So, Bill has been calling Brian... You can see where this is going. Brian has been after me for your contact information. I refused. I even changed your name in my phone to *The Barn*."

There was no phone in the barn, but Brian didn't know that, and Claire believed so strongly he'd go through her phone without permission that she'd changed Lil's name. The idea was disconcerting. Why had Claire not mentioned this situation when Lil had called her last? She likely didn't want her thinking it over on the flight.

"If you can't trust him with your phone, Claire…"

"I know… I saw him yesterday but won't again until next weekend. I'm busy with this lichen thing for Magnus." She gave a stressful little laugh. "Todd and Duncan have really stepped up at Nan's, handful of others, the usual suspects."

"That kid always shows up."

"Right? So, this time away from Brian, it will give he and I some time to breathe. JD asked me to pass along his thanks for the tea recipe. He can be hard to read, but I think he's into you."

He wasn't someone she'd want to see often, but if he was present now and then socially in a small group, she'd be comfortable with that.

"Let's not read into things." Lil said. "And *don't* encourage him, Claire."

"*You* may have encouraged him with the recipe," she countered.

"Honestly, Claire… It was a friendly gesture. We had a pleasant time in a group together, don't turn something that works into something that won't."

"Okay, okay… I promise to cool it with the matchmaking aspirations, though it would probably work out well for you because he travels for work and isn't around a lot… you'd have space."

"Claire… just let it be what it is."

"*Okay*, I'll leave it alone."

"I do appreciate the thoughtfulness. Your heart is never in the wrong place."

Lil could feel Claire's warmth through the phone.

"One last thing, I promise" Claire started. "Was there… We read about a *seismic event* in Boston… "

"It was me," Lil sighed. "Everything is fine, and I'll tell you the whole story when I get home. It was a long flight; gonna try to rest in the car. It must be getting late where you are, huh?"

"Yeah, I'm still in the office, but I've got a couch in here. I'm already lying down," she said with a breathy laugh. "Call before you fly again, okay? No matter how late it is."

"You got it. Sweet dreams, love you."

"Love you."

Lil felt the phone slide from her fingers, then Gunnar's hand moving past her neck to her shoulder, gently pulsing her toward him, encouraging her to recline into him.

She leaned in, accepting his silent invitation. With his body supporting her head, it wasn't long before the sounds of the vehicle were replaced by those in her mind.

Some three hours later, Lil opened her eyes slowly, anticipating uncomfortable brightening as the blindfold slid from her face. Instead, she was met by light filtered through the forest, further softened by mist clinging to the in-between of it all. Evergreens and birch stood like ghosts bowing over the trail before them, lining the dirt road so narrow that if another vehicle were to approach, one would need to pull off into the ferns and moss to let the other pass.

She rolled the window down and breathed the moist and the green deep through her nostrils, pulling in the rich, damp scent she'd imagined through the glass. They were all there, and then some: earth, mud, stone, the sweetness of the ferns, the cool pinch of the evergreens, the dankness of decomposition making fertile the ground for new life.

As the forest opened up, their dirt path became a long driveway. In the center of the circular drive stood an apple tree that must have been several hundred years old. Beyond the tree, what looked like an English manor house of extraordinary size came into view, three stories of gray and tan stones. The narrow drive looped in front of the structure, and turned off toward a large, modern looking garage made of glass and wood with four bays and an asymmetrical roof sloping low on one side.

There were almost no words. Almost.

"It's beautiful," she whispered.

Gunnar released a sigh.

"Indeed," Magnus agreed.

She knew they'd both have fond memories of the place, and hoped for herself to get a taste of its essence, to know, if only a fragment, what it meant to the two most important, if not only, men in her life. *Todd*, she amended to herself. She couldn't forget Todd.

As they neared the circle, Magnus steered off toward the garage, opening up Lil's view of the main house The modern addition to the side and rear appeared very much in the style of the garage they approached.

"We're only permitted a day visit, so we won't spend our time touring the grounds, but you can see a glimpse of how spectacular it is. That addition there

171

is the library and data center, natural light just *pours* in the windows. The older books and manuscripts are in an environmentally regulated sub-level, of course. There's another of the newer additions on the other side with a kitchen and dining area."

They parked by the garage and, as they exited, Lil caught sight of an orchard behind the building where a group of roughly thirty children practiced what looked like tai chi chuan.

And Magnus had teased about morning yoga at Nan's...

A man stood waiting out front wearing brown trousers, sweater, and a blazer, all in shades of coffee and espresso, save for the white collar peeking out from under the sweater. His hair was a few centimeters long, and it wasn't until they were a several yards apart that she could see the sandy color was about half filled in with grey.

Magnus paused his steps and turned to stand in front of Lil, smoothing his hands down the fitted sleeves of her sweater dress. It laid over her like a thin coating of deep green moss, hitting just at the knee. Without touching the stone cylinder seal, Magnus lifted it by the chain and dropped it beneath the fabric of her neckline, then kissed her on the cheek, and turned back to face the man who strolled toward them. *Interesting.*

"David," Magnus greeted with a smile, his expression genuine.

David's grin widened. "Magnus, Gunnar, and this must be Lil?"

Magnus shook David's hand, then the two transitioned into a warm hug. With one arm still around the man, Magnus said, "Forgive me, David, yes. Allow me to introduce my friend, Lil. Lily dear, this is David. One could call him headmaster, but it's hard to give a title to what David does here at The Arboretum."

The Arboretum. Magnus hadn't mentioned the school's name, only referring to it thus far by its function. No, he might have said it on the phone when they'd first boarded the plane to Boston. She stood surrounded by trees, and supposed that could be the origin of the school's name, perhaps the orchard in the back. Or, maybe it spoke to the legacy nature of the school, its students like branches.

Lil released a smile and waved, hoping to deflect an invitation to shake hands.

David nodded, perceptive and non-judgmental.

"A pleasure, Lil. I've heard little about you, but the words spoken were captivating. And thank you for agreeing to be blindfolded during transport. It does seem a dated method of security, but it's non-invasive, and I dare say it adds to the mystery of the place."

"You have apple trees," Lil observed, eyes drifting to the aging beauty not too far from where they stood.

"Yes, an orchard and a few more, scattered about a stone wall behind the school."

"We grow apples back home, and lavender."

David nodded his face pleasant and knowing. "We grow a great many things here."

"I thought it best if you move right to the library," David continued as they entered the front doors. "Exploration of the grounds at this time would be disruptive to the students' practice. Focus is part of training, however, the presence of someone not affiliated with the school might be too distracting for some."

Several pairs of boots had been clustered under benches built into either side of the entryway. Lil relaxed as her feet moved over the worn stone floor, imagining the absence of her shoes, feeling the cool surface under her, the connection between her body and something formed so long ago. She fell into geological time for a moment, her body on autopilot until Gunnar reached down to give her hand a brief squeeze.

Passing through another set of wood and glass doors, they entered a foyer of sorts, lit by a great deal of natural light streaming in. The same stone floor continued, working its way up into a large fireplace with a massive, faded wood beam for a mantle. A wide staircase to the left of the fireplace led up to somewhere, and to the right, a long, bright hallway terminated in mystery. A set of glass and wood doors on either side of her let more light in, and through the door on the left, a bit of movement as well. A young boy peeked his head through the doorway, blonde hair flashing gold with subtle hints of copper in the light. He couldn't have been more than nine years old.

"You've come to talk about what has kept you from movement," David said, addressing the boy softly. "And I suspect it has something to do with the bandage on your hand, yes?"

The boy's face held no fear, and in David's voice there was no criticism, no suspicion nor accusation. With a warm feeling, Lil was reminded of how Magnus had interacted with her when they'd first met, and since.

The boy moved from the doorway toward David, stirring the air around him, wafting a familiar scent toward Lil. She thought of Nan's bedroom, the cedar chest where she kept some of Grampa Pat's things. Among the treasured possessions were two flannel shirts, two thick sweaters, and a quilt. Grampa Pat had been a big man, so when Nan put one of his sweaters on, it hung low like a dress. Lil remembered the feel of the thick wool when Nan pulled her in for a hug. Lil would sink in to the embrace, inhaling the scent of cedar mingling with Nan's lavender and whatever she'd been baking. The boy had a similar smell, like the cedar chest and a warm kitchen.

When he reached David, he caught sight of Lil, and drew in a gasp.

"Hamish," David said, gentle and cautious. "You're not in movement." Both an observation and an invitation, reorienting the young visitor, refocusing his attention away from Lil.

174

"I saw her," Hamish said in a low voice, flicking his honey-colored eyes toward Lil then back to David. "From the *kitchen*," he added with even more of a whisper.

"I see."

Crouching down, David put his ear to the boy's mouth to receive his words. The whispers were too quiet for most, but Lil's hearing was exceptional.

"I saw gardens and the ocean, and she was there. I don't know when she's from but they always take her."

Take her? Lil's heart thumped a little. Looking to her companions, she saw from their calm expressions they'd not heard that piece.

"Slow down and breathe, Hamish," David whispered. "Can you change what you saw this time?"

The boy shook his head. "I don't know how it happens. Some of it was from before, but some of it was from... not yet."

"Will she be safe?"

From before? Safe? Lil looked to Gunnar and Magnus again, her heart picking up speed, eyes questioning. They didn't seem to hear any of what was being said and, therefore, weren't sharing in her alarm, but Gunnar had caught her expression. Puzzled, he took her hand, giving her a squeeze of reassurance.

"This time," the boy whispered. "Her aim is flawless, and she's fast, and she's so *good* Master David. She's kind, and the children love her, and the dragonflies, and she smells heavenly."

"Slowly, Hamish."

"But they keep coming..." The boy's voice became shaky. "They always do, and they always try to take her. And I saw her with-"

The hairs on Lil's arms began to rise up.

"We'll talk more on it later, Hamish."

Always?

175

David looked gravely concerned as he hugged the boy, steeling himself before releasing their connection.

David eased back from the embrace, and Hamish wiped his eyes. No longer whispering, David said, "Later this afternoon or after dinner, I'll make time to sit and we'll work through it. Right now, we should get you to movement. Class will help to ease your mind. I'm glad you came to me, but that wasn't the only reason, was it?"

Hamish looked down to his bandaged hand.

"I dropped a knife. I was in the kitchen when I saw... I grabbed the blade before I could think whether or not I should."

David lifted the gauze to examine the boy's work.

"This wound is fresh?" David asked.

Hamish nodded. "Just now, in the kitchen. It was really deep... made a bit of a mess."

"It's healing *remarkably* fast, and the suturing is superb Hamish, well done. I'll walk you to your movement session, but please check in with Marissa afterwards. She'll be in the greenhouse. You've done a more than adequate job, but I'd like her made aware so she can monitor the wound's progress. I dare say we can probably remove the sutures by end of day at the rate things are going. Oh, and do knock if Marissa doesn't come out straightaway; she may have a guest visiting."

Hamish nodded as David placed a hand on the boy's shoulder and turned back toward Lil. He lingered a moment at her eyes before the boy interrupted.

"Gunnar!" Hamish smiled.

Gunnar stepped forward and mussed the boy's hair before crouching to give him a hug. Leaning back, Gunnar pulled something out of his pocket, offering it to the child. Hamish unwrapped the candy, his smile growing as he made an effort to chew the caramel.

"Settling in alright?" Gunner asked.

Hamish nodded; teeth fused with sugar.

"I spoke with Auntie Bri yesterday. She might need more than one call from you, Hamish… Sometimes our grown-ups take a little longer to adjust than we do," he winked.

Hamish smiled and nodded again.

"Head to class. I'll catch up later if I can."

"I'll leave you to find the archives on your own," David said, ushering the boy toward the other doorway. "I know there's no need for me to guide you, Magnus. You've been down there more than I have over the past thirty years. I'd like a word afterwards, though, in private, if we might. When you're through with your research, of course. I'll look for you in the tea room."

"You know me too well," Magnus chuckled.

"I'm expecting Remmond to make an appearance sometime today," David continued. "When that will be… your guess is as good as mine. I suspect he's arrived and spending some time in the greenhouse," he smiled. "I've not spoken to him in just under a week, so your visit should be a surprise, though I'm sure he'd love the opportunity to see you all. You know, he's hinted at retirement. It may be just a couple years before his replacement steps in."

And just like that, they were having a normal conversation… after a boy Lil had never met came to talk with a man she'd never met about some recurrent grave danger. And she was *quite* sure it was of her they spoke... Processing this while maintaining a sense of calm took nearly all her strength.

"Was Remmond not involved in determining Lil's approval?" Magnus asked.

"I reached out, but communication with Remmond can be sporadic. The council has decision making leeway in his absence with time sensitive issues and an otherwise unanimous ruling."

"I see," Magnus said. "I still remember when Gunnar was recruited by Master Remmond. I've met him only a few times since." Turning to Lil, he added, "I was recruited by Master Artturi, who was followed by Master Azemi, Remmond's predecessor. Go on ahead with the boy, David. We'll catch up a little later."

Lil flashed Gunnar a look of expectation as David left them.

"He's my cousin," Gunnar offered. "His mother was my mom's sister. Hamish was orphaned young, and our Auntie Bri has raised him since. I assisted with his recruitment and orientation to the school."

"Magnus," Lil said tentatively as they moved into the hallway. "I overheard what Hamish told David. The boy said he saw me. He mentioned danger, and my being *taken*, but that I would be ok this time..."

Magnus paused briefly but, to his credit, continued pace.

"There are many with intuition," he began. "But genuine ability to see is extremely rare in my experience. There was a student here before my time who had dreams of a predictive nature. We are a legacy school, and these things can run in families. Do you share any of the traits found in that of your young relation, Gunnar?"

"Intuition of a sort."

"Were there any with sight during your time at school here? True sight?"

Gunnar gave a silent shake of his head, looking forward as they continued on down the hall.

"If you were truly in danger, Lily, David would say something. Oftentimes young people with this trait need help working through what they see, support in understanding what they can and can't change. You know how dreams can be, dear. Don't let what you heard weigh you down."

There was wisdom in his advice, not unusual from Magnus. She knew better than most the toll that dreams and visions could take.

178

Lil didn't doubt the boy had seen her, but what he saw, the context, remained unclear. Magnus had faith in David's judgement, and she had faith in Magnus.

Moving through the library doors, Lil found herself unable to focus as the three-story room flooded her with light. Windows lined the walls, and through them she saw the orchard, a rock wall dappled with stone cairns here and there, gardens, a greenhouse, and a large group of children moving in unison through tai chi. The expanse of the school's grounds stretched until a wall of trees held firm to the mystery beyond... And a woman. A woman with loosely braided auburn hair stood just outside the greenhouse with a large, blonde man. Lil's view was of his back, but she could see his hand on the woman's cheek. *Remmond*, she wondered.

The upper levels of the library existed only as rings around the room, leaving the center open to a ceiling with large, exposed beams. From the beams hung seven long ropes holding white woven nest-like hammocks.

Rows of bookshelves, comfortable seating, and private desks occupied the rest of the main floor space, shelves lining what she could see of the upper levels.

Magnus and Gunner proceeded to walk her toward a curved stairway off to the left. Instead of up, they walked around the stairs to a door with a keypad where Magnus entered a code, revealing steps that spiraled down to another door. Entering the sub level came with a change in atmosphere that reminded her of those sections of the museum where ancient items were displayed.

"It's kept under thirty-five percent relative humidity and fairly cool, though I'm probably the only one of us who'll suffer from the temperature, what with my old bones," Magnus smirked. "I've spent many evenings in this room, after the renovations of course. When I was a student here, the archives were kept in another location."

Book stands were available by the entryway, but, "gloves?" Lil asked.

"No, contrary to popular belief, white gloves are not the standard of practice. Impedes dexterity. Lessons are given before students are permitted to handle originals."

Knowing exactly where to find what he was looking for, he walked among the shelves and pulled three boxes and three books before returning to one of the three tables available.

"Much like the diary you read on the plane, many of the older works have been digitally archived. The book-bound copies are available alongside the originals, which are kept in these boxes, so the reader can be with the work at length without putting a strain on it."

Magnus slid the box across to her, the book beside it. The cover and Spine were simply labeled, *1-262*. Lil took a breath before opening what appeared to be a notebook. The first page was warn, yellowing with brown stains and fingerprints, the handwriting peculiar: backward script, written right to left. The page had been dated, September 15, 1507.

She remembered something about backward script like that...

"*Magnus.*"

A trace of something cool raced through her blood, her heart tentatively picking up pace as he reached out and turned several pages quickly, offering only a brief glimpse of the notes, schematics, and sketches contained, until he stopped.

Releasing a slow breath, Magnus turned one more page, and drew his hands back, leaving the book open for Lil to process.

Gunnar leaned in close behind her; one hand braced on the table to her left, the other on her right shoulder. Air entered him audibly as he took in the images left in silverpoint and ink.

What Lil saw on the left page would have been remarkable on its own, had she not glanced to the right... where two people had been sketched sitting at a table with the artist, who remained unseen. An open notebook laid on a table had been sketched, a hand holding a pen. To the upper left, a woman's body leaned over the table toward someone directly across from her. The woman's head hadn't been drawn, fading out after the neck, though the image was so close to the top edge there would have been no room. Her hands were delicately entwined with another, masculine set. Seeing their faces wasn't necessary to detect the love between them. Large forearms trailed off at the right. Suspended above them, the artist sketched a cylinder seal hanging from a necklace. Its twin, though not identical, dangled down from the woman.

The artist depicted his notebook in the drawing, open to the page he'd been sketching, scribbled words appearing on the small rendering of the left-hand page. On the right, he'd drawn a tiny reproduction of the man and woman at the table, this one shifted slightly downward, that their roughly drawn faces could be included.

Lil looked to the bottom left of the page to sketch of the couple's hands, then to the right of the bottom of the page, where her heart began pounding harder. It was as if the artist had sketched the imprint of both her seal and the one from her dream, both there, detailed in pen and ink.

She'd not seen the other imprint outside of her head except by her own hand at the museum.

This representation was a little over five hundred years old.

Her breath stilled, the sensation of electric ice flowing out through her center and down her limbs, the five-hundred-year-old drawing of her necklace gripping Lil like a frozen hand.

"Why do they have this here?" She whispered.

The air around them changed in temperature, a breeze raising Lil's hair, threatening to flip the page her hand firmly pressed.

"Why do they have this?" She repeated softly. "Why isn't this book with his other works?"

She didn't give Magnus long enough to answer before continuing, one hand resting at the stone over her chest. "You've known since you first saw this around my neck, and you didn't explain... Why didn't you say something? *Anything?*"

Lil felt overwhelmed twice over. Once at the existence of the image, knowing its origin, mystified as to its significance. The second blow came from knowing Magnus had been aware of what waited in the archives, had known since she was a child.

Third. The second seal was not only a dream. It had been drawn in ink on paper, five hundred years prior, and rested on the table before her.

Too many thoughts.

Another gust swept at her hair, followed by a rush of heat pulsing out over her skin, ice inside her, flowing through her, pushing outward.

Magnus flashed a calm but firm look.

"The materials in this room are very old, Lily, requiring consistent low temperature and humidity. Remember your breathing."

The intensity of her frustration became further compounded by the idea that she couldn't fully express herself. She found it infuriating that her *special circumstances* required her to mute the full spectrum of her emotions, when others could rage, grieve, weep... but if she let go, if she let it build, the room could be destroyed, possibly the floor above. She was escalating and, as justified as her emotions were, the archives weren't the right place to explore them. Once she got started, though, there was a sense of momentum...

"Lily, dear... *Breathe.*"

Gunnar began slowly tapping his middle finger against the wooden table, a metronome cuing her breathing to keep time.

She closed her eyes, imagining the vibration of wood resonate through her.

In, two, three, four, hold, two, three, four, out, two, three, four, hold, two, three...

Breathe in, breathe out.

Breathe in, breathe out.

Stillness.

Lil opened her eyes, feeling Gunnar's hand fold over hers, seeing his head nudge toward the door.

"I should have better prepared you," Magnus said, voice heavy with remorse. "To surprise you was a foolish self-indulgence. The tea room," he continued. "I'll be in the tea room when you're ready."

Lil climbed the stairs with Gunnar at her side, his arm around her, guiding her through from the library. She moved swiftly, pausing only a moment at the sight of the empty hammocks swaying like the Chihuly.

The rest of the journey became a blur of hallways, rooms, and thoughts until they arrived in a modest kitchen where windows let in light over a counter with a large, double farmhouse sink. On the opposite side of the room, more counter space with potted herbs, an oven, stove, and fridge. A large butcher-block island grounded the center of the space, a rack of copper pots and pans hanging overhead. Toward the back, a simple wooden table with six chairs, and behind it, a large cast iron stove burned, a stack of wood to the side.

The dated room struck her as odd, given Magnus had mentioned a more modern addition.

"The old kitchen," Gunnar explained. "Feels more like home."

Lil agreed, the room had a familiar coziness about it. She thought of Nan's, which sent more than the fire's warmth through her, and with it a twinge of longing to return to where she was most comfortable.

Gunnar moved slowly about the room, perhaps touching upon memories of his own, but she knew he was both giving her space and making himself available.

He had a way of knowing what she needed.

"It's a lot," she sighed.

"The museum, the bakery, the archives… Before. Your dreams."

Lil nodded.

Gunnar leaned down toward her, rested his cheek atop her head, and breathed in deep, rubbing her back. They stood like that for an extended moment, in comfortable silence without the unnecessary gilding of words that would have only taken up space.

Leaning back just far enough to make eye contact, his mouth transitioned into a subtle smile.

Then he broke away and moved toward the table, to the large bowls with tea towels covering their contents. Lifting a corner, his lips curled up further, pleased with discovery he'd made.

"Scones."

Lil approached and leaned in, breathing the scent of vanilla and lemon.

"We have to bring one to Magnus."

"Two," he replied, moving to the drawers to retrieve a towel, then a small basket from one of the cabinets.

"Magnus was recruited by Artturi, told me stories about him," Gunnar began, placing a towel in the new basket. "Magnus said Artturi would return for visits and bake with the students, and so baking in the small kitchen became a tradition, continued on while I was here. A small group of us always found our way to this space." He said, placing four scones like eggs in a nest, one by one into the basket, folding the ends of the towel over the precious cargo. "I started to experiment with making candies when I was about twelve."

184

"Your caramels are a gateway to the soul, Gunnar," she said, remembering the last time one melted in her mouth, feeling herself melt a little as well. A smile crept up on her as she thought of Magnus and the butter, wondered if he knew how many caramels she'd eaten over the years.

Gunnar approached the fridge and pulled out a small, clear jar with a light, burnt orange colored substance inside.

"Cloudberry jam?" She asked.

He nodded.

"I think I'll enjoy the scones as they are this time, but I'm making a mental note to ask Magnus about bringing some back with us."

He put the jar back in the fridge and walked toward her, extending a hand to rub her upper back lightly as they exited the kitchen, his touch, the stories, and the place of comfort leaving her thankful and refreshed.

The walk from the kitchen was slower than her journey there, allowing her to take in her surroundings: the artwork, architecture, the flooring, the ambiance. She looked forward to what the tea room might be like, and to how delighted Magnus would be with the scones. The weight of the basket in her hand fueled Lil's optimism, until her thoughts were disrupted by the sudden sensation that the skin over her entire body had become awake. It wasn't a tingling, or heat, but just a sense that her body was responding to something, prompting an anticipatory alertness.

They turned a corner, and came upon David, casually speaking with a much taller man. Her view was of his broad back and blonde hair that reached just past his shoulders: the man she'd seen earlier by the greenhouse. The stranger paused suddenly, ticked his head slightly to the side, and, flared his nostrils.

David's smile widened; the conversation he'd been having silenced as the blonde man turned fully, and Lil's heart nearly stopped. She knew that face. He'd been in the bar with her just two nights prior, on *Vancouver Island*...

It had to be him, the light haired one who she'd had a decent view of while desperately trying to see the face of his companion. Even if she were to question the accuracy of her memory, her body sang with recognition, and his eyes went wide, brows drawn upward. He had a look of hope and longing that transitioned to fear, then a calm stillness braced with formality.

Lil latched onto Gunnar's hand, squeezing tight. In her periphery she saw his face turn toward her with concern, and wondered if David or the stranger sensed how uneasy she was. Lil got the feeling the blonde man was steadying himself as well, but why? And why was he at the school?

"As foretold, here he comes," David announced with a smile. "I informed Remmond of your visit just now, Gunnar, and here you are."

"You look well," the blonde man whispered, still looking at Lil. Adjusting to face her companion, he continued with a strong, clear voice. "I am pleased to see you, Gunnar, it's been years."

Remmond smiled, reaching out and grasping Gunnar's free hand. "You were preparing for a transition to faculty the last time I saw you."

Lil stood a meter away from this *Remmond*, as if they were unknown to each other, though the connection between them was staggering, hanging in the air. Could no one else feel it?

"Indeed, but Magnus pulled me for an assignment with him, one that has become long term."

Remmond had no intention of revealing they'd seen each other just a few nights prior on the other side of the world, but she knew it was him.

He suddenly took on a distant look, as though he were distracted by or listening to something. She scanned his ears for a Bluetooth, but saw none. His eyes glanced down; she followed them to where her hand met Gunnar's.

Lil heard a growling noise that sounded as though it came from inside her own head. She let a gasp slip and, while it appeared to go unnoticed by Gunnar and David, the blonde man inhaled sharply.

Flames in the fireplace flared, to which David chuckled, "The wind must have a sense of humor today."

Gunnar tightened his hold on Lil's hand.

"Sorry," she whispered to him, before raising her voice to the man she had questions for.

"Who was with you in the bar?" She asked, eliciting a quirk of curiosity from David, stillness in Gunnar, and the return of emotion to the blonde man's face; longing and amusement.

"A brother of sorts."

"Why did he leave?"

"It was time for us to go."

"Why were you there?"

"Curiosity, and you?"

She had been curious as well, she supposed; curious to see if she would have a good time, if she'd be able to sink into the music, converse freely.

"We were both *there*..." she said, as if to spell out that he had not answered her question. "And now we are both *here*."

"The profound nature of that coincidence is not lost on me," he trailed off, drifting again, distracted. Glancing back up, he turned to Gunnar. "I heard Magnus travels with you. I'd very much like a word with him before you head home. You must be off to meet him," He added, eyeing the baked goods Lil was holding in her other hand. "He does like scones, if memory serves."

"I bake for him often," Lil said with a gentle, creeping smile. "I made him bring his own butter to my house the other day." Laughter bubbled up a little as she continued. "And he did, wrapped in parchment." She sighed, feeling as

187

though she were catching up with family, then she remembered where she was, who with, and saw that the blonde man appeared to be hanging on her words.

"It was good to see you," he said, his face softening. Turning again to Gunnar he added. "I'll be along later to find Magnus. You go ahead."

Gunnar nodded. "Master Remmond. David."

The two men would certainly have something to talk about with their privacy restored.

Lil said nothing, but looked each man in the eye before turning to leave, maneuvering about Gunnar to maintain the connection of their hands.

Once in the hallway, Lil registered about three steps before Gunnar pulled her into his body, whispering one command: "Breathe."

In and out.

She would have to explain the bar, seeing them, the glowing, and the way the dark-haired man had looked at her. The blonde had been with him. He knew. Had *he* seen her glowing? Did he know about the archives? Had he seen those drawings? Is that why he was at the school? Was that why he was at the *bar*? Was the dark-haired man at the Arboretum as well?

Lil felt the hair lifting and floating about her head, tendrils rising off her shoulders.

"Breathe."

In and out.

His left hand was against the small of her back, his entire right forearm flat on her spine with that hand around the base of her neck. She was secure, she was stone, she was still, she was the mountain.

In and out.

In and out.

Stillness.

"Are you able to move? We should brief Magnus."

188

She let out a sigh, nodding against his chest.

Gunnar loosened his grip and, keeping one hand on her back, walked beside her as they headed for a room she knew not the location of.

"It's just here," he said, guiding her through the doorway.

A large stone fireplace occupied the center of the sun-lit space. Large iron arms hung over the hearth, three of them with kettles, one hovering over the flames. Cream walls between large glass windows encased the room on three sides, the exception being the innermost wall connecting to the hallway. Large plank flooring ran under beautifully woven rugs, the chairs and couches inviting but absent of occupancy, save for Magnus, sipping from a porcelain cup.

He sat on one couch facing another with a low table between. His face brightened upon seeing Lil and Gunnar's arrival, then grew concerned as he read their expressions. He had, no doubt, expected her to be recovered from the archives. None of them could have predicted what had unfolded during her return from the kitchen. Not even Gunnar knew fully what had occurred, nor did Lil for that matter.

Magnus sat on edge in silence, eyes darting between them as he waited to be informed, waiting to know what had happened, for something surely had.

Lil placed the pastries on the table, breathing deep, letting the air out as she set them down. With a somber look to the old man, she said, "Forgive me Magnus, I cannot sit."

"You are in need of fresh air," he observed, desperate for knowledge, his need to soothe her more urgent.

"And water," she added.

Magnus reached for a glass, but Lil shook her head. That wasn't what she meant.

"No. I've been idle too long with my body while my thoughts have run. I need to join them. I've been cramped in cars, and planes, and buildings. I need to move; I need to *swim*." She closed her eyes. If she'd had wings, she would have broken through that giant window, taking to the sky from where she stood. She'd have soared to the ocean, diving down with feathers tucked firmly behind her as she breached the surface.

She needed to get out of there.

A rhythmic tapping surrounded them, rain on the glass. Lil opened her eyes to see Magnus and Gunnar exchange silent understanding.

"You know your way to the lake?" Magnus asked.

Gunnar tilted his head, as if insulted by the question.

"The children are in greenhouse or indoor study until lunch. The path should be vacant but best not to use it. I advise that you move slowly until you are beyond the trees. This is a school with an understanding of the extraordinary, but I don't want you alarming anyone. Meet me back here when you've had the time you need. If more than two hours pass, I'll make my way down to you."

Gunnar moved quickly, guiding Lil back to a large mud room. It was similar to the front entrance in that they went through a set of doors to get in, built in benches on either side. The major difference was the presence of so many jackets, boots. A second set of doors led outside, but there was also a single wooden door in the wall by one of the benches. Her eyes lingered on it.

"A tunnel that comes up into the greenhouse," he said. "There are branches that lead to other outbuildings. Convenient in winter."

Lil nodded as they continued outside, where the turbulent cloud cover mirrored what she felt within herself.

"Breathe," he instructed. "The scent of the outdoors is strong here."

She inhaled deep through her nose, a sense of calm and anticipation growing as they moved toward the trees.

"When it's safe to run, I'll keep pace to give you direction. When you can smell water, take what speed you feel necessary. I won't lose you."

She nodded, the tree line growing closer.

Breathe in, breathe out.

Fir trees and birch; Lil had barely passed their branches when she felt the weight of her restraint lifted.

She took off running.

Gunnar remained beside her, somehow maintaining pace slightly ahead as she wove effortlessly through the trees, springing over moss covered logs, rocks, places where the earth dipped down.

Soon, the smell of the forest began to change. The lake. It couldn't have been more than half a kilometer from where they were. Eventually the green before her transitioned to lighter shades of grey until the trees gave way to large rocks dropping off before still water.

Lil paused long enough to pull the dress over her head and slip off her boots before leaping into the fresh water, ice cold and thoroughly invigorating, vaguely registering a nearby crack of thunder as she descended.

Lil floated on her back facing the muted sky, feeling the bite of air on her skin where she broke the surface. Her arms made gentle ripples, mist hanging above. She'd needed this.

Lulled by the sensation of floating between water and air, Lil drifted into the place between waking and sleep. As her thoughts slowed in peace, the scent of moss, apples, and some warm spice bloomed over her. She felt fingers trail up from the tips of her own, over her palms, under her arms, her neck and through her hair. Her mind and the water worked together, their languid attention maintaining her state of tranquil contentment.

When Lil felt as though someone hovered over her, their warm breath on her skin above the surface, she opened her eyes slowly to the light, seeing the sun had revealed itself. She smiled, plunged deep, and swam to shore.

A Story in Stone

She found her dress neatly folded by her boots on a rock not too far from where Gunnar reclined. She pulled the soft fabric on over her wet undergarments, extracting her hair from the neckline and twisting out the bulk of the water.

"I lost time in the water," she said, boots in hand, not yet ready to encase her feet. "It feels like we should be seeing Magnus soon."

Gunnar nodded, a look of curious concern passing quickly over him. "He should already be here."

Light footsteps did little to disturb their surroundings as Gunnar and Lil moved at a relaxed pace through trees and birdsong. Though reluctant to use her voice while surrounded by such beautiful sound, Lil took the moment to speak.

"I saw your Remmond a few nights ago, back home. That night at the bar when I was with Claire. He was *watching* me, Gunnar."

His brows furrowed.

The birds, unoffended by their voices, persisted with soothing chatter.

"I don't know what it was," she continued, "and I don't know why it happened, but I felt him on our way back from the kitchen before we even turned the corner, and you saw his face. You heard what he said. He acknowledged that he saw me, but he was evasive."

Gunnar nodded, and she continued.

"He was with someone at the bar, a dark-haired man that I reacted so strongly to... When we looked at each other, my arms lit up. The same dark-haired man was in my dream that night. He wore a necklace in the dream, the one I drew at the museum. The likeness of both stones was in the five-hundred-year-old notebook we saw just now in the archives," she sighed. "I thought the incident at the bar was an anomaly, but then to see the blonde one here... *Here*, Gunnar, in a place so secretive I had to be blindfolded enroute. I don't want to jump to conclusions, not that I even know what they would be, but there's obviously

192

more than a coincidence at work. And I could have sworn I saw the dark-haired man outside the bakery with that bald-headed stranger as well. I'd felt watched just before that. Followed."

"Your instincts are accurate."

"I should tell Magnus."

"Agreed."

When the forest gave way to the open grounds of the school, Lil saw what had been keeping their old friend.

Magnus stood with his back to her, shaded by a large tree beside a rock wall. Cairns of various sizes balanced along the stone spine, small monuments of serenity. He was speaking to Remmond, whose eyes locked onto hers the moment she looked at him, like he'd been waiting for her to emerge.

Strengthened by the by the tranquility she found under the water's strange hands, Lil did not pause. Her stride stayed long, and her free hand did not reach out for her companion, though she was thankful for his presence beside her.

Magnus's attention remained held, he did not turn as the space between them diminished. Remmond's chest expanded fully, nares widening, and Lil had the oddest feeling that he was breathing her in. She knew she had more than the fresh scent of the forest on her, that the overpowering and unexplained scent of smoldering resin clung to her with the lake water.

She watched him exhale with a look of relief that gave way to amusement as she closed the distance, never dropping his gaze.

She'd just been about to reach her arm out when Magnus, suddenly released from what he had been saying, startled at seeing her.

"I'm relieved to see the sun making an appearance." Remmond said, Magnus still in a pleasant moment of bewilderment. "Light catches on the water left behind."

She wasn't sure if he meant the passing rain or the lake water saturating her hair.

His eyes flicked down to her feet, then back up to her face, his expression warm with an affectionate smile, but there was something about it, like he could read her cards in a game she didn't know she was playing. Lil wasn't quite sure what to make of it, but she was certain there was no malice there; he was devoid of ill intention.

"I was floating in the lake," she started. "I managed to drift off a bit, possibly for over an hour… Then I felt this warmth over me, but when I opened my eyes, it seemed to be the sunlight seeping through the clouds. I came out smelling *divine*," she sighed. "It reminds me of something back home." She trailed off, remembering the scent of the barn, then she stilled, recognizing she was again falling into this sense of being uncharacteristically familiar with the blonde stranger.

She found herself both suspicious and at ease.

"There does seem to be something clinging to you that wasn't there when we last spoke. Must have been something in the water," he smiled, then lifted his blonde brows and said, "You're hungry. You were on your way with scones earlier but you haven't eaten."

Lil shook her head. "No, we were on our way to meet Magnus but then..."

"You needed some air."

"Yes."

"Perhaps the lake needed you as much as you needed the swim."

She realized then that they'd been the only ones talking, and he hadn't commented on the oddity of her taking an early October swim, or that she'd returned barefoot and damp.

"Gunnar," he said, "It was good of you to take her to the lake, but she needs food as well as water."

Gunnar nodded.

"Magnus," the blonde man continued. "It's been wonderful catching up, but I must be going. I'll have some food sent to the tea room, please make sure she eats." Then to Lil, he said, "This time with you has been an unexpected pleasure." And, with a slight nod that felt like a bow, Remmond walked off toward the nearest door.

Sure enough, when they arrived back in the tea room, plates of fruit and baked goods waited on a table, a boy and girl, both in their early teens by the look of it, there to welcome them.

"We need to get back to preparing for lunch. Do you need anything else before we go?"

"No, this will do nicely, thank you, dear," Magnus smiled.

With her mug sipped halfway down, and a second scone initiated, Lil leaned back into the warmth of a soft couch. Gunnar sat on the other end, Magnus across from them, describing what happened on his end when she'd left earlier.

"It was the strangest thing, and you won't hear those words from me often, given what I experience regularly with you," he smirked. Lil rolled her eyes but smiled as he continued. "Enroute to meet you, I hadn't waited long, but I was concerned. I thought, even if you weren't ready to return, we could spend some time at the lake and talk there. No sooner did I step out onto the grass, did Remmond intercept me with conversation."

Unusually convenient, she supposed. If Magnus hadn't been caught by Remmond, he would have made his way to the lake and interrupted her aquatic reverie.

"Oh, and I had a word with David," Magnus continued, face slightly somber. "The boy, Hamish, did have a vision of you, Lily, and David found some of the details to be concerning. It seems there was or will be an abduction attempt of some sort. The boy was confident that you will thwart the effort, but it was unclear to David if it was an isolated incident. The boy was overloaded with imagery and felt like he was seeing more than one occurrence, perhaps something that had already happened. He was rather overwhelmed. Sight is not uncommon for Hamish, but it was an uncommon presentation for the boy, I'm told. David spoke to the him a little more when they were alone together. Hamish described a dragon waiting for you to sleep, a dragon's arm, or *in* a dragon's arms, I'm not sure. He also mentioned a man with golden hair, says they play stones together, so who's to say what it means. David needs more time with the boy, but these things can't be rushed or pressured, especially with children."

"So, possible danger, but not *grave* danger, at *this* time," Lil said dryly before taking another sip. "Oh, and dragons. I'll just keep an eye open for the Great Lizards of Vancouver Island when I sleep next."

She joked, if she was honest with herself, to ease her own tension. The possibility of being abducted was the perfect addition to her belief that she was perhaps being followed.

"Nonsense," Magnus scoffed with a touch of humor. "Gunnar and I will protect you from the beasts. You could stay with Nan of course, but I fear for what might happen to the dragons with that woman on watch."

"I'm not losing my independence over this, Magnus."

"Of course not."

"On the bright side," she said, raising her brows. "I overheard Hamish compliment my aim, and he said I smelled good."

"He didn't need a vision to tell him the latter, you were in the room," he chuckled, putting his mug down.

Magnus gave her an assessing look, doing his best not to offend, but he was checking her over.

"I'm ok, Magnus. And," she sighed, "And I think we should go to the archives again. The swim was thorough, we've had our fill of fruit and pastries, and I need to see those images. I need to know more about what's down there, and I need to tell you what else happened at the bar the other night."

"An unveiling for us both, then. I won't make a fuss by apologizing repeatedly, but know in my heart..."

"I know your heart, Magnus," she said with softness, taking an apple slice as she stood. "Come on, let's go."

Once in the archives, Magnus quickly went to work, retrieving the boxes and books that accompanied them. With the materials on the table, Lil placed a hand on his, meeting his eyes as he looked up from the first book.

"You accept me fully, for who I am," she started. "For all of whatever that means. I accept and love you for who you are, too, Magnus. You've never done anything to cause me sadness, intentional or inadvertent. You're not thoughtless, and I've never known you to do something without reason."

He placed his other hand on top of hers, squeezing, eyes holding liquid while his lips crept up at their corners.

"I won't apologize for my response earlier," she went on. "But I will say that I'll try to do better, and that I continue to feel fortunate to have you in my life."

His hand raised to her cheek, a tear slipping to meet it.

"A little sprinkle should go unnoticed. It was overcast when we came earlier, and what with the downpour at tea..." he chuckled.

"Before you open another book, I need to share what happened at the bar the other night. I couldn't have fathomed it would follow me here, outside of my own thoughts," she said, sitting across from him at the table, Gunnar silent at the door.

"The bar was crowded. I noticed two men across the room, and they noticed me. One was Remmond. We met upstairs on our way back from the kitchen.

When I asked if it was him, he acknowledged he'd been at the bar, but was evasive about his reason, blaming coincidence for our chance meeting at both locations. He said the other man was *a brother of sorts*."

Magnus's appeared pensive.

"Both Gunnar and I live in the area," he offered. "It's possible he was checking in, but neither one of us heard from him. Gunnar?"

He shook his head once.

"Hmmm."

"He recruits students, yes?" Lil asked. "Do you think one of my parents could have had some connection through their lineage to the school? Is it too far-fetched to think Remmond may have been investigating my family line? The necklace is connected to this place, the drawings are right here."

"Nothing is too far-fetched I suppose, with not every generation presenting a student, and you having been orphaned. Perhaps the man he was with will be taking on his role as recruiter." He paused a moment. "I find it odd that Remmond or his protégé would not have made contact. And I would think he'd have reached out to me as an alumnus who is as close to you as family."

The fingers of his right hand absently worked his well-trimmed beard, wheels turning.

"The man with Remmond at the bar," Lil went on. "His back was mostly turned to me, but I felt compelled to see his face. Finally, we both stood across the room from each other, and Magnus, I have never felt as connected to another living thing as I was then. Claire saw my arms begin to glow, and I could have sworn I saw light at his fingers. And there was a smell. Claire thought I was losing it, but I know I smelled something different and I thought maybe-"

"What did he look like?" Magnus asked, apparently on the verge of something.

"Tall, broad, muscular. Dark hair, long enough to pull back. He had a beard, and I think he may have been outside the bakery after the museum when I exploded the lights. The stranger he was with then had amber eyes and a shaved head. I felt like-"

Magnus looked as though he'd ingested a paralytic, blood draining from his face; eyes widened slightly. The changes were subtle, but shocking.

"Do you know him?" She slowly asked.

He seemed not to hear her question, then his eyes found hers. "The dark haired one," he started, "did he speak to you?"

"Not at the bar, perhaps not at all. I went home after, had a swim, and pressed my seal into clay for the first time. Then, I fell asleep by the fire and woke in a dream. The man from the bar was there with me, with a necklace like mine. His matched the other in that sketchbook you showed me," she said, nodding her head toward one of the closed books on the table.

Magnus looked as though he couldn't breathe, his face capturing that lingering instant when one realizes their airway has been obstructed by a bit of food.

"Magnus..." she whispered, not wanting to startle, but to ease him back. "Magnus, do you know him?"

He looked at her with awe, wonder, and a hint of sadness. His disorientation faded, but whatever had shaken him was not gone.

"I'm at a loss for verse or metaphor," he sighed, his lips forming a tender smile.

A unique situation indeed, to have her friend befuddled so. Lil relaxed her shoulders, her breath easing, thankful for his recovery.

"Would you like to keep going with the archive materials?" She asked.

"I think so, yes," he nodded. "Forgive me for my reaction; there are just so many pieces to put together. This one, I think," he said, patting one of the boxes and selecting a tall, slender book from beside it.

She was not familiar with the work.

"Shennong Bencaojing, or The Divine Farmer's Material Medica," he said, turning the thin pages carefully as he spoke. "From the fifth century, and the earliest copy that I know of. The original was said to be from about two hundred years prior to this replica, and is thought to no longer to exist. There have been other reproductions; of course, none living outside these walls have seen this copy. The modern illustrations don't include this detail."

He turned the pages to a depiction of two men, one with an arm outstretched as if handing the other a plant. The first man wore a necklace with an oblong pendant, but the ink drawings were highly stylized and the details of it unclear.

"You don't think that's my necklace, do you?" The book was from China, the necklace allegedly from the ancient Near East, and the sketch she'd seen in the artist's journal was from fifteenth century Europe. "There are no details. It could be made of any stone; it could be a vial."

It was probably stone, but *hers*?

Magnus turned the pages until he reached an illustration of the man and the farmer, but there was also a woman present. She stood, holding hands with the man, her other hand outstretched to the farmer. In her palm was what looked like a tiny tree bearing fruit, its roots hanging down. Around her neck hung a necklace, the same shape as the man's. With no further detail of the necklaces, their presence alone she could have passed off, but the imagery... the scene they were presented in, the tree growing from her, it was too similar to what the seal presented, the man and the woman, fertility, the fruit bearing tree. If the necklaces were the ones from the sketchbook... how did her parent's get one of them? Why?

"What do you think it means, Magnus?"

"I truly believe it is not my place to say."

She reached for the sketchbook they'd looked through earlier, the one he'd surprised her with. The two necklaces were there, the two seals. No wonder she'd pulled that man into her dreams and had him wear the other seal; she must have seen the other during her forgotten childhood, her brain pushing her to find it. And her parents must have known the seal's legacy, divulged some sense of the importance to her. If she'd seen the other stone, that would mean her parents had possessed both. What had become of the other?

"They knew you were special," Gunnar said from his post by the door. "Worthy of wearing it."

"One thing we might take away from this," Magnus began, "is that your seal has had an incredible, meaningful journey… that stones last a very, very long time, and this one's story is not over."

*

Unpaved ground crunched under the tires of their vehicle, the grey and green of trees and ferns surrounding them. Lil thought about the school, how Magnus had gone on to form a company that not only boasted a global presence, influencing humanity's pathway through innovation in energy, biology, medicine. Gunnar had apparently been on track to teach but was then pulled into service as what, her body guard? Personal attendant? Did he regret his path? He didn't seem to. What did other alumni go on to do? David was an alumnus, had become headmaster.

"Did Remmond go to school with either of you?" She asked. "I suppose he's too young to have gone with you, Magnus, and too old if he recruited you, Gunnar, though he looks like he could be your age. How old *is* he?"

"I cannot speak to the manner of Remmond's education," Magnus said, "but it was not with us. His is the only position not filled by alum. Traditionally it has been this way, though I'm not sure why. The recruiter has a position on the council and sole authority in choosing his own replacement. They often have a strong relationship with their students, act as a bridge between families and the school. Where David remains here, Remmond is constantly moving from one place to the next. He has a modest home here, not a ten minute walk down a fork in the dirt road we passed some ways back. I'm sure he comes and goes at all hours, what with flight schedules. And as for how old he is, I wouldn't dare ask, but he seems to age well, keeps fit."

He *was* in excellent shape. Nan certainly would have remarked on it.

Remmond came and went, but David and the other faculty… They never really left, she supposed.

"What do other alumni do for work? Are there others like you, Magnus, out there changing the world?"

"Oh, we're quite private about that, as you can imagine."

"And the faculty are always alumni, with the exception of recruitment. Do you think they, David for example, do you think he would have liked something different? Don't misunderstand me, please, the school is heavenly. There's something like home about it, save for its distance to the ocean, but I just wonder if..." *How to word it?* "Do you think there's a part of him that wants to explore, climb mountains, create something magnificent?" The more she spoke, the more she thought about herself, swimming in the ocean by her home, working at Nan's, molding clay and pushing paint. She was content, or she had been. Maybe it was the same for David, content where he was, conducting small miracles, as she did.

"We all play a vital part in something," Magnus began. "Think of the human body. Many parts are not meant to leave it: blood, lymph, our hearts. To maintain the body's functioning so that it, *as a whole,* can do magnificent things, they stay where they are. We send out satellites, as words, as ideas, the way we touch others in our lives, build with our hands. David serves in a way that is right for him, right for the world. He is content and we are thankful."

Lil felt the vehicle slow to a crawl as Magnus turned toward her. "What I do is important, yes, and people know my name. What David does is of equal significance. He is important, as is Gunnar... As are you, Lily."

As the vehicle began to move again, Lil took a breath with her body, within herself.

"I think I should head home," she whispered.

"If you need to unwind, come to the Iceland house," Magnus offered. "It's breathtaking and secluded, just what you need. I'll be entertaining some colleagues, but they'll be in a separate, professional building on the compound, so you'd avoid them altogether. We have the space, and you need practice, Lily."

She knew what he meant, and he was right, but she also felt a pull toward home.

It had been good for her to get out and investigate, to *awaken*, but in some respects, she was still the same. She wanted to swim, to walk the orchard, the fields, to enter Nan's shop and breathe in deep. Nothing she'd learned had changed the core of who she was.

"You're right," she said. "I just feel like I need to be *home*. I can practice in small ways while you're away, then we can discuss the Orn, and larger spaces, when you get back."

The vehicle came to a stop, Magnus twisting to catch her eyes again.

"Very well," he nodded, "but the flight will be long. The plane will drop me in Iceland. I'll have the chopper come for me and you'll go on home from there. Are you certain?"

Lil nodded as strong hands reached up and gently tied a scarf over her eyes, then Gunnar's voice rose from the darkness, low and steady.

"I'll make sure she's safe."

15.

With arms and legs wrapped around billowing peaks of white fluff, Lil opened her eyes. To one side of her bed, the fireplace was quiet; to the other side, evening crept in above the ocean. Gunnar had driven them straight from the plane and insisted on staying, to which she'd made no protest. She hadn't been allowed to sleep on the plane, and he'd stayed awake to keep watch. Flight after flight, neither of them rested with the exception of refueling, and a nap she'd had in the car. Then he'd escorted her up to her room with assurance he'd do a walk-through of the entire house before closing his eyes.

Taking a moment more to sink into her pillow, Lil reviewed the messages on her phone. Claire had written; planned on coming over that evening. Todd texted as well, wanting to surf later. Claire would probably stay until she was ready to fall asleep, which would be about eight o'clock if she'd been at Nan's since yoga. Todd would come by late, after he closed the shop.

Lil padded down the stairs, following the scent of apples and ginger to the kitchen where she found Gunnar drinking spiced cider.

"How'd you sleep?" She asked while he poured her a cup from a pot, still warm.

"Like a sloth," he smiled. "The fire did flare at one point; so loud it woke me. I know quite a bit about many things, but not chimneys. Wouldn't hurt to have Magnus get someone in to take a look."

Lil managed a nod, almost lost to the taste of the cider. He'd steeped cinnamon, ginger root, and star anise in there. Pleasant.

"I know you probably have things you need to get done," she said, "but my cousin Claire is coming over in a bit. You're welcome to stay."

"No, I'll take a quick shower then head over to my place, hit the grocery store, touch base with the guys over at Magnus's."

Lil nodded again, taking another long, slow sip.

"I'd like to come by afterwards, though. Wouldn't be until nine or ten, but with what happened in Boston and the things Hamish said… I'd be more comfortable staying a few nights. Late, but I figure you'll be up. If you're asleep though, and the door is locked…"

"I'll be up. Todd is coming by to do some surfing. And if the door is ever locked, Gunnar…"

"Go around back. If that's locked, get creative."

*

"You're going to miss Gunnar again," Lil said, leaning her back against the arm of the sofa. She curled her legs, letting Claire tuck the tips of her cold feet under her shins. "He's coming over later," she continued, pulling the blanket over them. "Todd wants to surf, and Gunnar's going to stay the night.

Claire raised her eyebrows.

Lil leveled a bored stare. "It's not like that and you know it."

"A lot can happen on a weekend trip…"

No truer words.

"How are things going with Brian?" Lil asked.

"Great," Claire laughed. "I haven't seen him."

"Well, that's a little ominous…"

"No," Claire sighed. "Well, I mean, we've both been busy. Magnus had me stop everything I've working on for this lichen project. We need to get something to Saul and Martine as soon as possible. It's rather exciting, really, though not nearly as exciting as your experience with the mammoth! I'm so proud of you for trying after what happened in the lab. So much of what you do is unintentional, beautiful, Lil, but unintentional, or at least not consciously intentional. I think a part of you means for things to happen, and you're just not wholly connected somehow? But to have made the detour to the site of the mammoth, to try like that, and with people there… I'm so proud of you for that. I mean, you make waves intentionally, but that's for fun, there's no pressure."

"I know! I know…" Lil laughed with a little shake of her head. "I've literally said the same thing about the waves."

"And if you hadn't gone for it, we wouldn't have the lichen from Amka's tea."

"And you wouldn't be living your best life working overtime and sleeping at the lab. Things are really ok with Brian?"

"Things are fine, I'll see him this weekend," she said, gesturing with her hand as if waving it off. "You're back at Nan's to give Todd and his friends time to take a breath, though the experience has been good for them. Todd really stepped up."

"Love that kid."

"So, what *happened*? You filled me in on the arctic stuff; I need Boston details."

"We went to the museum first. Sami, our contact there, estimated my necklace to be thousands of years old, maybe a fertility amulet of some kind. So, when we were leaving, we passed a beaded dress, no fabric, just a mesh of beads, and I had this daydream or a vision? It was like I was somewhere else, but I don't know where it was or who I was with, but I was wearing a beaded dress."

"The dress you passed?"

Lil nodded. "Though it couldn't have been the same dress. The one I wore was torn and the beads scattered everywhere. It was overwhelming, the realness of it, and..."

"The little seismic event," Claire smiled.

"Yeah." Lil couldn't help but to smile a little herself; the moment had passed after all. What else could she do? "I don't think anything was damaged, but Claire... They have a glass sculpture that goes from floor to ceiling, and I watched it sway, wondering when the suspension cables would give..."

"Oh, your reflexes would have kicked in," her cousin said, pulling her feet out from between Lil's shins. "How are your legs so warm? My toes are already toasty."

"I just run hot," Lil smiled.

"Ok, so what happened next? You guys got out of there?"

Lil nodded. "Yeah, and I felt like we were being followed. Felt it in my bones, Claire. And I wondered if, with the necklace being so old, and me having different *abilities*... I wondered if it wasn't too far-fetched that there might be a connection to what I can do, and the necklace. And if there was a connection, would it be something someone else might know about, and try to come after."

"Oh my god."

"I can do things without it, we ran a test, so that theory is out, but I still think the necklace has a history. There could be other's out there who know of it, want it for themselves. People steal ordinary things all the time, artwork, cars."

"No wonder Gunnar wants to stay over again. Did you see who was following you?"

"No, this was, well, I was panicking a little because of the context. We had just come from the museum where I caused an earthquake while trying to figure out my necklace. I was primed for fear, and so was Gunnar. He's usually calm as stone but we quickened our steps and ended up in a bakery."

"Ohhhh, I bet you missed Nan's so bad."

"Of course I did," she said, then proceeded to skim through the bakery and patio incidents. When it came time to talk about what happened at the school, Lil stuck with a restricted truth about where she'd been.

Walking back from the kitchen with refreshed mugs steaming, Claire wrinkled her nose, pulling her eyebrows together.

"He *blindfolded* you?"

"Mmmhmm."

"It must have been a very exclusive library," she said as Lil arranged the blanket again, Claire tucking her toes into the warm space beneath her cousin's calves. "I thought he would have had a bit more trust, though."

"He does, and I trust him, Claire, that's why I allowed the blindfold. I won't give details out of respect, but I can say it was beautiful there." She didn't think she should mention Hamish, as he was a student. It felt a little too private, and a story not entirely hers to tell. "There were archives, documents so old we handled copies as not to damage the originals, but the originals were there. You know the kind of people Magnus has access to; the exclusivity…" She sighed. "I held a Da Vinci notebook. It contained a sketch of my necklace, and a second one…"

Claire's jaw had been slowly lowering since the mention of the Italian artist. Lil took a sip of her drink, watching her cousin's mouth close, transitioning from shock to consideration.

"The details were clear enough to identify the stone as yours?"

"With just a two-dimensional rendering of a three-dimensional object, I couldn't be sure, but what was depicted in the sketchbook looked like at least one angle of my stone, and also… the impressions of both seals were rendered. It was as if the artist had seen the clay impression of both my necklace and the one in my head."

"Your dream, from before you left," Claire whispered. "What could it mean, though? And more importantly, what does it mean to *you?*"

Lil had wondered the same thing when leaving the school.

"Maybe I'm meant to find the other stone. Maybe, in some way, it's calling out for me from deep in the earth, buried under a mystery or around some man's neck. Maybe the necklaces have something to do with my family that I don't understand, because why would I? Whatever the story, when we left the archives, I began thinking about what you just asked, what this all means to *me...*" she trailed off. "I believe I've, quite literally, been experiencing a wakeup call."

"From yourself," Claire added.

"Yes," Lil smiled, a little laugh in her voice. "From myself. And aren't I waking? I'm going to try doing little things here and there, the equivalent of stretching exercises I suppose. Work my way up. I think the key is releasing this energy or whatever it is before it gets built up, maybe? And, I mean, I could have gone to Iceland with Magnus, really cut loose, but... Outside of my dreams, this is the closest to a sense of home I can imagine. Here, with you and Nan, Gunnar and Todd, Magnus, the shop and the ocean. I can find comfort anywhere there's life, salt, or stone, but there's something to be said for Nan's warmth and the smell of her kitchen, Todd's antics, Gunnar's strength, your toes under my leg. For as much as I have always felt a piece missing, I know comfort here."

"And so, you came home."

"And so, I came home."

16.

"You really don't need to bring your own cribbage board, Joan. We have one over on the books and games shelf," Lil said, melting back into her usual routine at the shop.

Things had returned to normal, with the exception of her *practicing*, which seemed to be working, since her dreams had been refreshingly common: salt water, song, damp earth, warm breath behind her ear. She'd been successfully enhancing plants in her greenhouse, and started a fire outside on the rocks, twice, with Gunnar standing by. He'd stayed at her house the first few nights since they got back, but, feeling more confident in her safety, and with zero dragons noted, he planned to start sleeping at his own place again.

"Oh, I know sweetie, but then I would need to get a smaller purse, and I'm too old for that," Joan laughed, her companion, Audrey, joining in.

"Suit yourselves, ladies. A pot of Earl Grey with lavender, rye muffin for you Joan, and a maple scone for Audrey. I'll be back in just a few minutes."

Lil walked behind the counter to prepare their order as the landline rang.

"Nan's," She answered.

"Hey Lil!" Claire beamed. "I'm at the Orn with Brian, and we ran into JD, which is odd because it's the weekend, but we were thinking about swinging by to see you. How's it looking over there?"

Lil knew her cousin hadn't seen Brian until that morning, but things must have gone well. She sounded like sunshine and mint leaves.

"Not too busy. The Cribbage Ladies are in, Suit Guy, and a couple who left their baby at home with the grandmother. They have both their phones on the table, checking for updates," she smiled.

"I really wish Joan would stop lugging that cribbage board in her purse. Who carries a *stone* cribbage board around?"

"She'll never stop."

After ending the call, Lil got to work preparing orders, then settled herself back behind the counter with a few books, chamomile tea, and a tart.

*

Lil's eyes brightened at the sight of her cousin's smile, her favorite green cardigan coming through the door. Then she saw both Brian *and* JD following her in.

Lil sighed. Claire had agreed days ago that Brian wouldn't bring up Bill or Sami, and Lil hoped he would stick to his promise.

She put her book down, held firm to her mug.

JD eyeballed her choice of reading material.

"Inventionen und Sinfonien?" He asked, raising his brows suggestively, then, with a pull on the corner of his mouth he added, "mit fingerzätsen…"

Lil rolled her eyes.

"You read German," he said.

"As do you, it seems."

"Lil's good with languages," Claire responded.

"It's music."

JD looked down at the spine of another book. "Zen in der Kunst des Bogenschießens? That's not music." His playfulness calmed to genuine intrigue. "Are you an archer?"

"She could read a book written in whale if there was someone to write it," Brian said, saving her from having to respond to JD, though his comment was less than helpful...

Claire froze, shooting daggers with her eyes. "Brian, can I talk to you outside for a minute?"

Claire hooked her arm through his, *encouraging* him outside.

"I noticed you're not wearing your wedding ring," JD said once the other two had left.

"Oh, I'm-"

"Not interested," he finished, to her relief. "It's ok, I understand. I wear a smile on the job. I'm friendly and meet a lot of new people, many of them female. Sometimes they can get the wrong idea. Sometimes the idea is *very* right," he smirked, "but not often. When things line up, it's with the understanding that it's a transient interaction. Besides," he added with a touch more seriousness, "there's something to be said for waiting... for permanence. I don't mind it. I find it exciting, rather like hunting of a different sort."

Lil gave a subtle nod of her head. "Your understanding is appreciated."

"I'll say this though," he chuckled, "I've never been closer to making a career change to volcanology,"

She couldn't help but let a laugh slip.

"I'd have plenty of work if I did; the Andes are on fire right now."

Lil flashed a puzzled look. She knew the Andes were part of the ring of fire, many active...

213

A Story in Stone

"Eleven devastating eruptions just yesterday; three in Colombia, two in Ecuador, another two in Peru and four in Chile. Several in Indonesia as well, Java and Sumatra. Devastating," he added, rocking on his heels as he looked over the menu. "Claire has, rather firmly, instructed Brian not to discuss or inquire about your trip to Boston… But she's made no such request of me."

Why did he have to bring that up? Things were just starting to feel close to comfortable, aside from talk of natural disasters.

"I'd really rather not," she said.

"Allow me one question," he pleaded. "How was the in-flight entertainment?"

Puzzled and relieved, she tilted her head with a smile. "Reading material and hot beverages were provided."

"Sounds cozy. I'm feeling relaxed just thinking about it."

Indeed. Lil wondered how much of the museum event she could have avoided if only she'd been able to sleep on the plane…. Perhaps not. One can't know.

"Circling back to hot beverages," JD said, looking at the menu while mocking a forlorn expression. "When we met last, you brought a *thermos*…"

She felt her heart rate pick up a little.

"I arranged for the items on the list to be brought to my place before I returned from the bar that night."

Where did he even get the ingredients that late?

"The balance of flavors was exquisite," he continued, with an intensity that almost made her feel uneasy. Looking back to her from the beverage options, he asked, "When will I have an opportunity to provide *you* with a drink?"

"I can't make any promises," she said, "but I'd be willing to let you attempt choosing what I put in my next cup. See anything up there you think I'd like?"

JD looked to the menu then coyly back. "I think the secret is right here."

He leaned against the counter and dragged her mug over to himself slowly. *Don't you dare put your mouth on it*, she thought.

He peaked in and inhaled. "Chamomile, and who am I to interfere with a relaxing afternoon? Though, if I might make a suggestion, you could add some mint. I am partial to mint myself."

"Chamo-mint happens to be a staple in my brew rotation."

"Chamo-mint," he chuckled. "I like that. And if I were to see you again during the evening, socially, with friends of course, what kind of drink might you like then?"

Claire and Brian re-entered the shop, Brian sheepish and Claire ready to move on from whatever had happened out there.

"I enjoy tea... sometimes cider. I've been known to drink tap water. Where is this going?" Lil asked, feeling she didn't need to explain anything else.

"I didn't mean to put you on the spot, I just noticed what you weren't *drinking* when we were out at a bar, and I wanted to politely ask if you were opposed to alcohol, but now we have an audience. I apologize for that."

"Lil's metabolism does not a cheap date make," Claire posed with a teasing look. "We got into Nan's port once to test it; took about two and a half bottles to get Lil's cheeks pink. She got *real* silly, and-"

"I think that's enough, Claire..." Lil said.

Claire was brazened enough to roll her eyes and smirk. Brian knew too much about her already, much to Lil's disappointment. He didn't need to know how much it took to get her drunk.

"I don't care for the taste enough to put in the effort," Lil explained. "Don't get me wrong, the warmth is nice, and sipping is fine, but if I'm drinking for taste and warmth, I'll stick with teas, and right now I'm going with chamo-mint."

"I'll have a tart and hot cider with ginger and cinnamon," Claire smiled. "What do you guys want?

"I saw matcha on the menu," JD started. "Do you use sweetened powder?"

"No," Claire replied, scrunching her face.

"Perfect. I'd love a matcha, and also a spearmint tea, if it's not too much trouble."

"Can't do just one cup at a time?" Claire teased.

"The matcha goes down quick; otherwise, sediment forms at the bottom of the bowl. The mint won't have a chance to cool before I get to it, trust me," he winked, then perused the pastries a little longer before flirtatiously announcing that he'd *always had a weakness for tarts.*

Brian seemed reluctant to speak up, ego still bruised after being taken outside. He meant well, at least; Lil was fairly certain of that. He wanted to save the whales for goodness' sake.

She gave a little sigh, figuring he'd suffered enough. Claire had probably given him a good talking to out there.

"How about you, Brian?" Lil asked. "Coffee?" She looked closer at him for a moment, looking in. "How about I make you a hot chocolate, dark, with a little almond extract?"

His eyes lit like a child's.

Claire let go of whatever weight she'd carried within her, adding, "We have those oatmeal cookies without raisins, too. You guys go grab a seat. I'll help Lil get everything together and we'll be over."

"I have news," Claire whispered as JD and Brian walked away. "And it's juicy."

"Todd and Kerry?"

"*No…*" Claire smiled, rolling her eyes. "My friend Ajay used to work at Manipal in India but now he's with the National Institute of Virology. There's some stuff that went down in his lab with this emerging virus, it's like Nipah, from fruit bats, and it's catching like wildfire in Southeast Asia. Kind of a big deal. So, things are getting chaotic and guess who Ajay sees: A six-foot three guy with hair like mine and no lab coat."

Lil froze with what would be Brian's mug in her hand. Eyes wide, her mind went to one person: Amka. *"The arctic guy,"* she whispered.

Claire nodded. "The arctic guy."

"Do you think? Both Arctic Guy and this person your friend saw were tall and blond, but it's not like they had blue skin and a tail. The height and hair color could be incidental. Ajay doesn't know about what happened up North, does he?"

"Only what the media put out about Cambridge Bay. He took notice of the guy because of a story his girlfriend Wendy told him a couple weeks ago…" Claire raised her eyebrows and paused for affect, which was successful only in trying Lil's patience.

"So, Wendy is out in the field working with bats. They're remote, like in the jungle, and there's some local kids coming out of a cave, but they aren't alone. This tall blonde guy comes out with them, and he's charismatic. He says hello, but Wendy said the whole thing felt odd. No gear, not a bead of sweat on him."

"Have you told Magnus?"

"This morning with my update on the lichen," she nodded. "And it's *definitely* the lichen in that tea. I'm just working on isolating secondary metabolites, and honestly, that the treatment grows in the area where the pathogen was found isn't lost on me. Reminds me of how jewelweed and stinging nettle are often found growing close together. Nature blows my mind." Claire paused, releasing a controlled breath. "It's so exciting Lil, I just… I wish I was up there with Saul and Martine. We'd get so much more done if I was there."

Lil smiled, pouring hot water over leaves while Claire plated the pastries. Her cousin was fearless and brilliant, and it brought Lil joy to see her finding a thread of passion. She deserved sparks anywhere she could find them.

"So," JD began as Lil sat down, "is this a typical Saturday afternoon here, or is it slow for you guys?"

Claire shrugged. "It's usually like this, give or take, unless we have an event going on. It can get going after dinner time. Right now, it's just Mr. Lee playing chess with his son, the Cribbage Ladies, and Suit Guy. Cribbage Ladies are Saturday regulars but the others are in the give and take category."

"Cribbage Ladies and Suit Guy?"

"Well, he's not in a suit *now*. He comes in about four out of five days during the business week. Says his office is too busy, has three young kids at home. Coming in helps him to get some work done before he gets to the office where perpetual meetings keep him from being productive. His boss is into it because Suit Guy gets things done, and his wife is into it because he's usually home early."

"And now I know way too much about Suit Guy," Brian joked, tearing into his cookie.

JD raised his eyebrows. "I respect his company's outlook on performance. In my business, it's about loyalty and showing up when and, for travelers like me, *where* it counts. The time in between is my own so long as I produce results. It's certainly not about being in your cube every day like a caged animal. I might have an idea in the middle of the night, or need to fly out on the spot. I stay flexible." He downed the last of his green drink and placed the bowl to the side. "Be flexible, get creative, get things done: everyone's happy."

"I know you work for your family, but I don't think I've ever asked you about them," Claire began. "Do you have any siblings?"

"Two brothers."

"Do they work with you?"

"It's a big business. Jonah," he smiled to himself and sighed. "He's an academic machine. I'd say you remind me of him, Claire, but you're too human. Then there's Daniel, the Golden Child... I'm sure every family has one. Daniel could compete in an Iron Man competition, beat me at chess, build a laser, make a gourmet dinner, and rescue a kitten from a tree, all before sunset. He's unreal," he said, pausing to take a drink from his spearmint. "They both work for the company, but not with me directly. Almost all the cousins as well, in some capacity."

"Big family, huh? I didn't have a siblings or cousins until Lil. You can't imagine how happy I was when she came along," Claire smiled. "How's your matcha?"

"Superb, and finished, thank you." He answered before turning to Lil with a look that, outwardly, seemed very friendly.

"Now Lil, it has come to my attention that you are an artist. These," he gestured to the paintings surrounding them on the shop walls, "are your work?"

She nodded silently, sipping her chamo-mint. She wasn't sure how he was going to play it, but she felt where he was going.

"As you know, my job requires that I travel quite a bit internationally, and I always have my eye open for original pieces."

"Please don't take offense, JD, but I don't do much work for others, and I'd never do a corporate sale. It's just not something I'd consider, but I am flattered by your interest. My work is *very* personal, and this place is very personal. It's the only public space you'll find my paintings."

"I'm disappointed, but completely understand. If you change your mind, anytime, just call. And I do mean anytime… Always on the clock," he smiled. Now," he sipped his tea and looked around the table, refocusing. "I'm in for one more day, unless plans change. What are you all up to tomorrow? Care to keep me company?"

"We'll be here from sunrise until almost dinner time," Claire said, already exhausted by their schedule.

"All of you? Do tell, it sounds like a party. Am I invited?"

"Yes and no," Claire laughed.

Brian spoke up, explaining, "They do sunrise yoga here every day, apparently. Claire is leading tomorrow and I've agreed to come along. I repeat: *sunrise*. But then, wait for it, I'm helping put on a *fairy tea party* for a group of children."

Brian and JD began laughing, then Lil relinquished a chuckle as Claire protested.

"Hey, it's not bad! It's a magical time actually. We dress up, the children dress up."

"Dress up?" JD lifted an eyebrow to Brian.

"I won't be in costume..."

"So, you should wrap up by early dinner time. Want to get together for a bite after?"

Brian and Claire looked at each other. Brian shrugged. "Sure, but we'll have to play the time by ear a little."

"How about you, Lil? You in?"

"You'll have to count me out on this next one. I'll be here helping Nan with a little cleanup. Todd can't do all the work."

"How about after?"

"I need to make it an early night. I'm hunting Monday and will be up long before the sun. Even I need to put in a few hours of sleep now and then."

220

Lil felt herself getting a little too familiar. JD really didn't need to know that she hunted or required little sleep, though many people could claim both, she supposed.

"You *are* an archer," he said, like he'd won a prize and learned a secret all at once.

Lil spotted Joan and Audrey weaving their way through the tables toward her. *Oh, thank goodness,* she thought, grateful for the interruption that the Cribbage Ladies would provide. Letting herself focus in on their conversation, she couldn't help but smile internally.

"A roast chicken," Joan said.

"Sounds good," Audrey shot back. "Are you stuffing it?"

"The chicken? No, I'm making mashed potatoes. And I've got my starter bubbling for bread tomorrow to go with the chicken soup."

"You'll boil the bones?"

"Of course, I'll boil the bones."

"I'm having pasta tonight. I'm not sure what kind, but I know what I'm having tomorrow."

"What's that?"

"Your soup!"

They both laughed.

After all their years together, the two women still maintained separate homes, though it was to Lil's understanding that they spent most of their time together, at one place or the other.

"Don't you get up now," Joan said as she approached. "We left the money on the table. You sit and enjoy your friends. Claire, good to see you dear."

Joan pointed to Brian behind his back and raised her eyebrows; not subtle in the slightest.

Claire nodded.

221

Joan winked; she and Audrey giggling as they walked out the door.

"Those two are a hoot," Claire said, smiling as they left.

JD was still gazing at Lil, deep in thought.

Lil turned, open eyes pleading when she saw Nan make her way out of the kitchen. Nan gave a slight nod, fussed behind the counter for a minute, then scooted to the table with a mug, stainless-steel chain draped over the rim.

She put her hand on Lil's back and whispered, "It needs to steep a bit but its here." Then she looked up and said, "Hello there, I'm Nan."

"Oh, I'm sorry," Claire blurted out. "Nan, this is our friend JD, he works all over the place but he's at the Orn sometimes. He introduced me to Brian, actually. JD, this is Nan."

"Nan, a pleasure," he said, standing with an extended hand. "I've heard so much about you, and of this gem here." His other hand outstretched to reference what appeared to be the surrounding space, though his eyes lingered on Lil. "A treasure well-guarded. And I wouldn't have had the opportunity had it not been for Brian and Claire."

He sat back down under Nan's assessment.

"You all met at the Orn. I know what Claire does there," Nan said, "but what is it that you do?"

"I am the face," he said, flourishing with his hand. "I travel globally representing the family business. There are older versions of me, for those who require a different feel. Someday I'll be the old version, and I expect one of my cousins, nieces, or nephews will replace me. It's been that way for generations. Now these tarts," he said, playfully changing the subject. "I've always had a weakness for tarts, but these are heaven."

Nan inhaled, relinquishing a smirk. The man was a charmer, she'd have to award him that. And Nan had no doubt noticed that he was obviously fit under that suit. No wonder his company kept him as their *face*, or whatever it was.

222

"Thank you, I bake most of the pastries myself, though Todd and the girls have been taking on more and more."

"I heard a little about what they're taking on tomorrow... Brian mentioned something about buying a pair of tights."

"I'm *not* wearing tights..."

They all shared a good laugh at his expense.

"I'll ask Brian and Claire to fill me in at dinner afterwards. And I expect pictures." JD stood again and continued. "But now, I must depart." Brian made to protest, but JD kept on. "No really, I have an ongoing project for work that needs tinkering, and I should put the time in. Work hard, play hard, right? Lil, you can still change your mind if you wrap up early tomorrow. Nan," out went his hand again to shake hers, giving her shoulder a squeeze with the other, "a pleasure."

Lil took a sip of the Chamomile and lavender Nan had brought, while Brian and Claire debated the merits of sunrise yoga. As JD walked out the door, Nan tracked his path with her eyes.

Leaning into Lil's ear, she whispered, "Watch out for that one."

17.

Just before dawn, through light cool as the air, Claire looked out over the lavender fields shrouded in mist. Soft footsteps approached where she sat perched on a bench. Nan.

"Ginger mint," she said, handing Claire of two steaming mugs.

The old woman wore a lilac shirt with a thick, dark grey knitted wrap, jeans, some type of grey, slip-on wool shoe, and silver earrings dangling clusters of little purple stones.

"I left Brian inside," Nan sighed as she sat. "He wanted to get one coffee down, then come out with the second..."

"I swear he gets up early. We just had a late night, and today's going to be a marathon."

Settling in with her tea, Claire looked out somewhere beyond the fields and released a weighted breath. She'd had a bit on her mind, and it didn't get much better than Nan when it came to getting things off your chest.

"I know it's sort of an unspoken rule that we don't talk about Lil, or, well, we talk about her, but... You know what I mean."

Nan, sensing her granddaughter wasn't done, held off on speaking.

"Ok, so, Brian and I are on similar paths. We have differences of opinion on some *major* issues, and things are rocky at times, like now, sort of, but we could grow together, as partners, hypothetically. I've been thinking of Lil lately, and, maybe what sparked it was Brian and his experience when Lil started helping him with his research. He couldn't shake what happened that night he waited for her to come out of the ocean. He's talked about it repeatedly, trying to work out what happened, how it made him feel. He said when she emerged it was like something out of a myth or a dream, awe inspiring but equally unsettling. I mean, you know how she can be, how she *is*," Claire corrected, then took a sip of her tea. "Brian said he hadn't been afraid like that in years. For me, though, growing up with her, I just adapted to who she was, and it's normal, like people who have cats."

Nan raised a brow.

"If you and I walked into that kitchen," Claire said, pointing behind her to the shop, "and there were cats in there, on the counter, napping on top of the fridge, we would freak *out*. But if we were cat people, it would be no big deal to wake up with one of those furry guys wrapped around our head or strung across our necks, leaving little dead birds and mice offerings as tribute," she smiled. "We're not cat people though, we're Lil people. And hearing the perspective of someone who *isn't* a Lil person describe his personal experience with her, I guess it just had me thinking a little more, in a different way."

Another sigh escaped; big thoughts, big feelings, big breaths. Shaking her head, Claire said, "Nan, There's something heartbreaking about her otherworldliness."

Footsteps sounded as the first two women attending sunrise yoga trickled toward them. Claire and Nan nodded as they passed, then shared a moment of silence before Claire began again.

"I've tried to set her up before. She is *firm* about being uninterested, but I'm holding on to this hope that she might find a connection with someone. I still gently encourage, but nothing like a *setup*. Last week, before her trip, Lil came for a night out at the bar with Brian and some of his friends… Brian was a little liberal with sharing information."

Nan shot her a look of tentative alarm.

"Nothing off book, but his intention was clearly for her to hit it off with one of the guys. It was an entertaining *disaster*," she laughed. "But, you know, I was beginning to think it might be possible. One of Brian's friends is an archeologist and they seemed to get along. He spoke with her on the phone later that night, really wanted to spend more time with her, but it's a no on her end. And yesterday, she met with us and our friend JD, who was also at the bar that night. She wasn't too abrasive with him, and he seemed to be interested in her, maybe subtly fascinated but not in an ogling, moonstruck kind of way. She even left a recipe for a tea she'd been drinking so he could make it himself at home. And he *did*…"

"I don't want to step out of place," Claire went on, "but, I wanted to just ask you if there's something I should know. I'm completely in the dark about what her life was like *before*. She always said she didn't remember, but..."

A handful more women passed by, silent but for their footsteps.

"I'm aware that sometimes," Claire whispered, "if someone had been hurt when they were young, it can be hard to have relationships, like *dating*, so I didn't know if... Maybe I should just quit while I'm ahead, although I'm not sure I still am..." she trailed off.

Nan shook her head slowly with a knowing smile, "We're family, and you're asking from a place of love." She reached out and gave the Claire's back a little rub between the shoulder blades before speaking again. "Lil had an unusual childhood, with more heartache than one should bear at *any* age, but she's not experienced the hurt I think you're alluding to," Nan said before draining her cup. "It would take someone very particular to be a match for Lil, and I think she just hasn't met what suits her..." She reached down and put a hand on Claire's wrist. "Things of the sea belong to the sea, dear, and of the air to the air," she paused, "and of dreams, to dreams... Lil is a blessing, but there is both hope and worry in my heart for her." She gave Claire a squeeze, let out a cleansing breath and smiled. "She certainly has us though, doesn't she?"

Pensive and still, they sat content in their thoughts and togetherness until the crunching of Brian's feet sounded.

As he sat, Claire stood.

"You can still join," she said, nodding toward the women stretching in the distance. "You might need to lose the khakis though."

"The khakis stay. You go have fun," he said, holding up his mug to her as she turned and headed to the field.

"I was glad to hear you'll be assisting us in putting on the tea party," Nan started. "I was even more pleased to see you here so bright and early. I suppose it's not quite bright yet though, is it." She eyed his hooded sweatshirt and tan pants. "Might need to get you into something a little more festive… for the kids."

He glanced down at himself. Certainly, she hadn't expected him in formal wear or Peter Pan tights… He had a blazer in the car if need be… It wasn't his ideal way to spend a weekend, but it wasn't terrible. He and Claire had spent some time apart, and it hadn't been terrible, in his opinion. He'd accomplished quite a bit at work, though it was an inconvenient time for Lil to step away. He'd been reluctant to push things. She'd seemed uninterested in getting serious about research, which, as far as he was concerned, bordered on abhorrent given her abilities. She could make big changes in the world, and he wasn't even sure the extent of what she was capable. He could understand her desire to just *exist*, but, what about the obligation to the greater-good? Could she communicate with bacteria? Algae? Could she coerce a disease into stopping its affliction of a person? Lil could save lives, of that he was sure. He had a list of new objectives he'd worked on while she was gone, and now that she was back…

"So," Nan exhaled slowly, "what do you make of all this?"

"To say this place is special would be an understatement."

Brian shifted his attention to the grounds, the beehives at the far edge of the field, then to Claire, facing eleven people who stood spaced out between the lavender, three to a row except one in the middle with just two. From the field to the surrounding maple trees, and then to the dense fog of the apple orchard, Brian couldn't see Lil anywhere.

"Let's start in mountain pose," Claire said, leading the group in reaching their hands up. "Inhale deep from the earth, bringing your arms up. Feel the mist rising around you as it rejoins the sky. Exhale and fold down, let your arms hang, your fingers dangle…"

He watched Claire, his thoughts drifting to the woman he'd dated previously. Tracey had been a yoga instructor and dance teacher who did much of her work in the evenings, and liked to drop in at his office during the day. She'd wanted to be a part of what he was doing, he suspected, because she wasn't fulfilled by what *she* was doing. He'd tried to accommodate her, but it ultimately pulled him from his work, felt a lot like letting a toddler *help* make dinner. He had nephews and had seen what meal preparation with a three-year-old looked like. Having Tracey *help out* wasn't as messy, but it wasn't productive, or good for their relationship. Claire, though, had her own ongoing research, work that followed her home like his did. She was someone who he could share breakthroughs with and read grant proposals to. It wasn't *romantic*, but it's what made for a good partner.

Shifting shadows in the orchard behind Claire caught his eye, then, like an apparition, Lil emerged from the mist.

"And return to mountain pose," Claire said, advancing to the empty space in the middle row. Four rows of three faced Lil as she stood where Claire had been. She brought her arms out into the mountain pose of the others, and then they all moved as one. With no words spoken, the thirteen folded, lifted, lunged. They worked through the movements as if it were a rehearsed dance.

"Have you eaten," Nan asked as she stood. "Come on in and I'll make us some oatmeal. The oats take a while to cook," she said with a wink. "But waiting provides a solid excuse to have a pastry, and hold a good book while you close your eyes."

18.

"After the sugar dissolves, we'll add the lavender and blueberries," Claire instructed Brian, his hand vigorously stirring ingredients into a heated pot.

"So," Brian began, "I wanted to ask you about-"

"You wanted to ask me about the blueberries?" Claire teased, retrieving a giant bag from the freezer. "Two scoops."

"It's not terrible having Brian around," Nan whispered to Lil, both observing from a distance in the shop's kitchen. "Good to see what he's made of. It's taking me some time to size him up."

"He fits with Claire, but I would've liked more of a spark for her. And I don't think we need to whisper," Lil quietly added. "They're the type that gets focused on a project and can't be torn away. We could light firecrackers at the front counter and those two wouldn't notice."

"We probably *should* set off firecrackers, or bang on something to wake up Todd out there. I think he's nodding off again. Todd!"

Todd, who had been leaning over his hands and obviously napping, stood up fast, widening his eyes as she approached.

"Yes, ma'am."

"Todd, I want you to go with Brian and bring three, no, four of the wooden tables from the barn to the field. Set them under the big sugar maple, all in a row for now, we'll rearrange them when we go out to set the tables in a bit."

Todd nodded and yawned.

"You have *got* to wake up, Todd," Nan scolded.

"I know," he whined. "But I worked last night, and I'm back this morning so early."

"Did you go out after work last night?"

"I met up with friends."

"Head over to the barn, Todd. Let the sunshine wake you on the way. I'll send Brian over."

"Yes, Ma'am," he said on his way.

I love that boy, but I swear he's turning my grey hair white," Nan sighed. Then, putting her arm around Lil, she leaned in, and said, "Let's make some scones for the little fairies."

*

Claire eventually went with Brian out to the field, leaving Lil and Nan to make shortbread and scones in the kitchen.

Nan brushed floured hands on her linen pinafore, the one with the blueberry stains at the hem. She always wore it, even with the remains of The Great Blueberry Incident that had also colored a bit of the apron Lil had at home. Lil thought the result rather beautiful, the faded pink and indigo river swelling on one side of the fabric.

"I had a nice talk with Claire before yoga today," Nan began, her fingers working shortbread dough into a pan as she continued. "She and I sat for a bit while Brian lingered inside, priming himself with coffee."

Lil stretched an honest smile as she started in on the scones. "They do have something in common, maybe not with coffee, but with relentlessness in their work. It's good they're making time for other things, though, like today, and going out to the bar last week." Lil paused, stopping with her dough for a moment as she went on. "I thought there would be something different for her, but they seem content."

"Indeed..." Nan sighed. "Should I do any round cookies or just stick to the shortbread pans?"

"Pans."

"So, I understand poor Brian tried to introduce you to a friend... hoping for the blossom of romance."

Lil tilted her head back and made a grunting noise of comical frustration. If only Nan knew the half of it.

"Don't you worry, Claire will set him straight. But I think she's worried about you a little, in the same way that I have found myself worried for you."

Lil felt very much caught off guard, to be in Nan's kitchen, the ovens warm, her hands working dough. It qualified as sanctuary, not a place of sudden, penetrating conversation. Or perhaps it was the ideal setting.

Though a little warning would have been nice...

"Nan, I'm strong, independent, and I have you. I have Claire. I'm fine. I'll be fine."

It was her hope to just shake off the topic and get back to baking.

"You're independent and strong, but you're also soft, and your heart is deep. I won't be here forever, and Claire could move on with, well, with *someone*. She told me she's having dinner with Brian after the fairy party." She gave Lil a sideways look.

"They're having dinner with JD."

"The three of them, hmm?"

Lil felt Nan's love, but it wasn't quite enough to wash away the discomfort of being ambushed.

232

A Story in Stone

"I'm the last person to tell a woman that she needs a partner; please know that's not what this is. But I won't discredit how profound it is to find a deep connection with someone, a connection you feel it in the soul of yourself. I don't think it is wrong to want that for you. Do *you* want it though? Would being in love fulfill something for you, or is it... do you already feel so much, that what you have could be enough? I want to respect what makes you different, but I don't want to neglect something as precious as this… Help me to know how you feel, Lil. I worry for you."

"It's as if I already am," she sighed. "In dreams, and during waking life, I feel a connectedness to something, separate from the earth, or the ocean. Something I feel almost homesick, or nostalgic for. A deep love that has been there as long as I can remember, and there's nothing else that resembles it."

Lil paused and thought hard about how to continue, took another deep breath, let it out slow. "If you were hungry, Nan, and I offered you a Twinkie, you might turn your head... but if you were hungry enough, *really* hungry, you would eat it. If you were starving and I offered you a stone, though, would you eat that? Of course not, because it's not even food." Lil's hands had stopped working dough at this point, her breath unsteady. "It's not that I don't hunger, Nan, it's that I've only found stones in that regard. Somehow, I eat differently than everyone else, and there's no food for me here."

The liquid in Lil's eyes swelled, breath quivered.

"Don't you dare drop one tear into those scones," Nan affectionately scolded, her arms pulling Lil into a warm hug. With remnants of dough still on her hands, Lil clutched the back of Nan's pinafore, sighed, and let the saltwater seep safely onto her apron.

"Deep breaths, my girl," Nan whispered. "Let's keep the sky blue for our little fairies today." Nan rocked them from side to side a bit, patting Lil's back. "We need some alone time, just us. I've been meaning to talk with you about when you were little, when you came to me, but now isn't the time. We have far too much work to do today. A picnic out in the orchard tomorrow? Oh, you'll be hunting. Maybe when you finish up? Tuesday or Wednesday? Whenever you get back let's make some time. Claire's been busy working on something for Magnus, but Todd can have his friends come over and help out."

"It's a date," Lil sniffled, pulling away to look at Nan, drying her eyes with her sleeve. "I've had questions too, about my necklace... and I have a *lot* to share about my adventure with Gunnar and Magnus. The dreams have been getting intense. The things... happening. We haven't had time for an update. And Nan, I do love you. I would never want you to think, I mean, with what I said about stones..."

"I know, sweetie. There's more than one type of love." Nan took a shortbread pan up in her hands. "Now, let's get these goodies in the oven."

In no time at all the lemonade had been chilled, tea brewed, and the kitchen smelled like heaven.

*

Outside, small wooden tables had been set together as one under the big sugar maple. An oat-colored runner ran the length of the surface with sliced tree trunk discs of varying sizes supporting the serve-ware. Potted rosemary and lavender had been arranged aside tiered stands holding vanilla scones and shortbread, sliced fruit and vegetables. Four teapots offered different teas, each with a butterfly motif that matched tea cups and saucers at each setting. A large glass drink dispenser with a spigot held lavender blueberry lemonade at the end of the table, and little bells hung from the branches above, tinkling in the air as a breeze swayed through.

Another couple of tables had been set not too far away, providing a place for caretakers to indulge in refreshments of their own, giving the young fairies a sense of separateness and importance.

As the children arrived, they were given a pair of wings to slip on over their shoulders then escorted through the garden by Nan and her humble assistant, Brian. His khakis had proved sufficient; his shirt, however, had been replaced with a long sleeved, white linen blouse that laced up the chest. Nan insisted it was unisex.

Brian looked up as he approached the sugar maple, feeling slightly more comfortable in his lace up shirt as he spotted Claire. She'd changed. Blonde hair hung down over the cap sleeves of the dress she wore, both fluttering around her shoulders. The gentle fabric flowed to her knees in gentle shades of pastel green, accented by yellow butterfly wings with glittering golden details that complimented the bracelets jingling on her wrists, the beads on her sandals. She spread a huge smile, her cheeks and eyes dusted with shimmering gold powder. She caught his eye and waved, both to Brian and the kids as they approached, then she crouched down to child-level and introduced herself.

Brian meandered over to the parents' table and, glancing back to see Lil coming around the maple tree as if from some secret door. Her brown hair gently curled down her back. The deep blue fabric of her dress was covered in a second layer of a sheer, white, gauzy material flowing down to cover her bare feet like mist hovering over dark water. Her white wings were of the same sheer material as Claire's, with silver and gold details.

Brian looked closer at her face. She didn't have gold powder dusting her cheeks as Claire did, but there was something luminous about her skin. Was it always like that?

Lil crouched down and, as she raised an arm, a flit of movement started around her. A dragonfly landed on her shoulder, then another on her hand as she brought it up to the face of the closest child. Wide eyes, open mouths, and wonder looked on as a third, then a fourth dragonfly landed, tiny insect legs tickled her skin, and there was definitely one in her hair. One after another, more flew in, then they began to land on the children.

Giggles, gasps, and awe followed.

Lil inhaled the surrounding smells and sounds; the droning chatter of the adults several yards away, the birds carrying on with conversations of their own, insects moving about, Claire identifying the dragonflies on the children.

"These bright red ones are Cardinal Meadow Hawks, and oh, Sarah, that's a Blue Dasher. It's a little late in the season but, oh, Four Spotted Skimmer there. There's a pond nearby, and that's super important for these dragonflies. Can anyone take a guess as to why that is?"

"For drinking?" Suggested the girl with the short brown hair.

"Don't they have their babies near the water?" Asked another girl, this one with freckles and orange wings.

"Good answers! Many lifeforms require water, but dragonflies use water for more than just drinking. They lay their eggs in it. The larvae that hatch from the eggs can live in the water for years before transitioning to their adult dragonfly form. Pretty fascinating, huh? Oh look, Paddle Tail Darner, and another Meadow Hawk!"

Lil closed her eyes and sent a thought out around her, swiftly followed by subtle breeze. When she opened her eyes, all the dragonflies took flight at once, scattering. The children cheered, following the paths of the insects as best they could. Then, when they'd lost sight of them, their gaze returned to Lil, who'd sprouted a mysterious smile.

Raising her eyebrows, she whispered to their waiting ears, "Tea time."

*

Bellies full and feet restless, the children began wilting at the table while parents shuffled around, gathering their things.

236

Without words, Lil walked away from her chair, toward the rows of lavender, her unspoken invitation calling the children to follow. Lil's pace began to quicken. She clutched the material of her dress, raised it a bit, and then, glancing behind her with a mischievous grin, she took off running through one of the rows. The wind rushed through, elevating her hair and dress as they trailed behind her. Pure joy filled her as the children roared with laughter, spreading their arms out and taking off at speeds that threatened, unsuccessfully, to trip up their feet.

They wove through the lavender, inhaling the intoxicating scent that wafted from the field and, eventually, Lil rounded them back to their waiting parents.

After a collective release of breath as their guests departed, Claire smirked as she bumped Brian's shoulder.

"Nice shirt."

"Nan said it was unisex!" Brian cried out, his cheeks flaming as Lil and Claire laughed.

"Oh please," Nan said dryly. "Everything is unisex; men and women can wear whatever they like." She looked over her shoulder toward the garden and beyond. "Well," she sighed, "it's clean up time, though we should probably check on Todd first. He's been alone in the shop for the past couple hours."

Nan and Lil headed in, Claire and Brian lingering behind with a slower pace.

"You know," Caire started, tugging on his shirt. "There's something a little bit pirate, a little bit medieval, but also a little bit-"

He interrupted her by placing his index finger over her lips. "Not one more word unless it's to compliment my masculinity or ask me what beer I want when we head in."

"Blonde Ale?"

"I'm going to need at least four... and I want to talk to you about something."

Claire paused her steps, holding him back. "Talk about what?"

"Nothing bad, just an idea I've been working on," he smiled, rubbing his hands briskly over her shoulders as if to warm her up or prepare her for something. "Ok, hear me out," he started. "Lil's assistance with my research has been nothing short of miraculous. I... My team and I, are in the beginning stages of putting something together with BBC for a film focusing on-"

"A film? Like a documentary? Oh my *goodness*, Brian, that's fantastic!"

"Right? I hope Lil feels the same way. She can be so uptight about her work and being around other people, which is crazy because she works at Nan's, serving people drinks and food."

"Wait, you don't mean for *Lil* to be involved in the film?"

"She's integral to our communication with the Orca, and she could be playing a much bigger part worldwide if she could overcome her insecurities. What if she could cure cancer, Claire? Would you let her live out her life here, tucked away at Nan's shop, making mugs and paintings? She might not be the cure for actual cancer, but could be for a metaphorical cancer, for environmental issues that threaten life as we know it. What if there isn't anyone else like her, for hundreds of years? What if it's too late then?"

"Brain, it has to be her choice. You cannot spring something like this on someone. It's not right."

"I think with the right kind of encouragement she would agree to it. You've been coddling her here for too long. She evolved for a reason, Claire. Nature provided her to itself, for a reason. The documentary could be a first step for Lil in accepting her potential, the obligation of it."

He linked as arm with hers, moving forward, toward the shop.

"Brian," she sighed. "I'm sure you remember how upset she was when you met her at the shore that day. You can't try to force her into this. It... it would be unwise."

"Right, that's why I'm talking with her about the film *ahead* of time. And I'm hoping you'll help."

They found Lil with Nan, peaking at Todd in the kitchen. Nan had tasked him with washing dishes from the lunch crowd if there was a lull... And he was currently sound asleep, resting on the counter next to the sink with his head on his arm. He looked like he was about ready to fall in.

"I should just send him upstairs to take a nap, poor thing," Nan whispered. "But not before I teach him a lesson, or at least have a laugh at his expense. You're never too old for good, clean fun."

Nan took a wooden spoon from the counter, then looked over her shoulder with a devious smile as she grabbed a saucepan and wailed on it.

CLANG, CLANG, CLANG!

Todd's eyes bulged open in panic, his arms swinging out to protect him from god knew what. As his left arm swept, it took the clean cups, plates, and bowls with it, sending them crashing to the floor. Todd's expression moved from fear to confusion, rounding back to fear again when he put together what had happened.

Nan, Lil, Claire, and Brian all stared in silence.

Todd's vocal cords failed all attempts at sound.

"Todd, this was an accident," Nan started, then, reluctantly, said, "though I may have played a part in it... Let's start picking up the big chunks and we'll sweep the rest. Girls, don't come in until you've got your shoes back on." She walked over and gave him a firm rub on the back. "It's ok, Todd."

He finally let out a deep breath before inhaling what seemed to be twice as much. "Nan, I'm so sorry. I fell asleep again and I shouldn't have gone out last night. I'm so, *so* sorry. And Lil, your cups."

"Don't sweat it, Todd. I have tons back home, and it will give me an excuse to make more. It's like therapy, really." She shot a concerned look to Nan, then again to Todd. "Did any of those cups have a dragonfly stamped into it?"

"No," Nan said, "I believe your bug mug is safe."

"Todd, you're forgiven," Lil said with renewed assurance. "I'll head back to my place and load up a box; I can easily replace what's broken here.

"Brian and I will stick around and help with cleanup," Claire offered. "We have plenty of time before we meet up with JD."

19.

Hours later and well into dusk, Lil returned to Nan's with a box of replacement ceramics. She bounced up the wooden steps to the porch as a short-haired man passed her on his way down. He smelled like grease and Altoids.

She entered, scanning the collective of drinking and smiling guests at almost every table, Brian delivering scones to a couple playing chess. Nan chuckled down back with a few surf school friends of Todd, Kerry and Duncan among them. When Nan looked up and caught Lil's eye, she held up a finger, silently saying, *I'll be right there.*

Lil set her box of stoneware creations down on the counter and looked into Todd's worried eyes. "Don't sweat it. Things break, okay? You're family."

"Thanks Lil," he said with a relieved smile, one that showed his youth.

"Give these a rinse before you use them. And, do you mind getting some tea started for me? I know you're busy but I thought I'd have something hot before I get going." She closed her eyes and inhaled. "Chamomile mint."

"I got you. One chamo-mint coming up."

"I am so glad you are here," Nan said upon approach. "We started filling up. A few of the fortunate got what wasn't broken, but you can see what the others are drinking from. It doesn't feel right using paper plates and cups. Todd," she called, peaking around through the doorway of the kitchen. "When you're done with that, I'd like you to get four hot ciders ready to go for Kerry and the boys, they're heading out. And thank them again for helping."

Nan put her hand on Lil's shoulder, guiding her. "Come on, there's an empty table. Let's sit for a moment. I need to talk to you."

Lil counted fifteen patrons, not including Todd's friends. It was a lot for Nan on a night when they'd all been up since before sunrise without a break, and most of the mugs broken. Lil had only planned on dropping the box off and calling it a night, and Claire and Brian had plans with JD, should have been long gone already.

"Where's Claire?" Lil asked.

"I got a bit nervous when we started bustling, so I sent her over to the barn to check for extra supplies. I know we have some of her insect ceramics over there somewhere," she chuckled. "I'd have sent Brian, but he doesn't know where anything is. Oh, here he comes."

When Brian sat down, Nan turned back to Lil with a look of discrete seriousness.

"There was a man in here asking about your paintings."

"...And how did that go?"

JD had inquired the day before, but it had been a while since a customer asked about the work with anything more than passing curiosity. Occasionally, serious buyers or dealers came through, though Lil never sold, and Nan never gave out her information. Most had accepted her disinterest as a welcome mystery and went on their way, but a few had been uncomfortably persistent. She credited them for their determination, but they could become intolerably intrusive.

"Well, he came in and ordered a black coffee, then walked around the back drinking it while he looked at your work. Eventually he sat down. He had short, silver hair, late sixties maybe, *very* fit... his shirt sleeves clung to the arms nicely, and I could see from his neck muscles that-"

"Do you need me to get you a napkin, Nan? For the drool?"

"Nobody's drooling. I'm just being detailed, and recognized that he puts the work in. Anyways, more people were coming into the shop and things got busy. I was down by a back table when he asked if I worked here. I said yes, and then he asked if I knew the artist who did the paintings. I said yes, and we left it at that, *initially*. He went on to say they were very calming, that he would be interested in having a piece commissioned for his home, and could I please share the artist's contact information."

Nan and Lil looked at each other for a silent moment.

Brian's eyes shifted between them. "That's good, right? You said yesterday that you don't do corporate commissions, and this guy said it's for his house."

Lil shook her head, feeling a flicker of annoyance until she read the sincerity on his face. "It's a nice thought, Brian, really, but I've found that my quality of life is better when there are fewer complications. I can count on one hand the number of people I've painted for, and that works for me."

"It just seems like you have a lot to offer the world and maybe this could be a good way to start, something small." He shifted and looked back to Nan, "Did you give him her number?"

"Of *course* she didn't..." Lil sighed.

"No, I didn't. I told him my granddaughter was the artist and I would never give her information to a strange man without her permission. He asked if you ever come in, and would you be in later or tomorrow. I said tomorrow you'd be out hunting and told him he could just leave his number with Todd over at the counter and you may or may not be in touch."

Todd set down Lil's mug, then turned to Nan. "There was a guy with short blonde hair who came up to the counter just before Lil got back. Said he wanted to drop off his number for your granddaughter. I told him she was out at the barn getting some plates and cups and stuff, and she'd be back in soon if he wanted to wait, but he just left."

Nan's eyes grew wide.

Lil felt her skin tingle, the sensation of something cool pouring out from her chest and down her arms. She got up and pushed her chair aside in one quick movement, nearly knocking her mug over, then paused, as if listening for something.

Brian moved to rise but Nan put her hand on his shoulder, gently advising him to sit back down.

"Stay here," Lil cautioned, moving swiftly for the door, then erupting onto the porch where she broke into a run. With her left arm out, she gripped the railing and leapt over the edge, a river of long, dark hair flowing behind her as she jumped into the garden.

She could smell him, grease and Altoids.

Light leaked out from the barn windows. She could hear Claire's shaking voice in the distance, but not from inside. They were around the back. Lil listened as she ran over flowers and through herbs, to the gravel path, toward the words echoing in her ears.

"She said her granddaughter did the paintings, and the kid said this is where you'd be, but you're blonde, and short. You're supposed to be different."

The man's voice was oily, charged with assumed power.

"You don't seem right," he continued. "How old are you?"

"I told you, my name is Claire, and those aren't even my paintings. I don't know what this has to do with anything. Please move aside." She was scared but holding on, just barely.

Footsteps swift and light, Lil rounded the corner of the barn unheard. A man leaned in toward Claire, her back against the building. He looked to be in his early thirties, of average height, dressed in dark jeans and a grey shirt. Claire's arms were wrapped around a large box like it was grounding her to reality, keeping her hands from shaking. Lil wondered how things would have looked if Claire hadn't had the box. The man probably would have felt her cousin's foot connect with his face.

Lil had mere moments to decide if she would attack or question him. She could choose both, but if he was too severely injured, he might find it difficult to speak.

Claire turned, relief and warning in her eyes upon seeing Lil.

The man followed with a look of surprise and intrigue, absent any display of fear. That would change, of course.

"Claire," Lil looked into her eyes with a fierce but gentle authority, "Head in. Let Nan and Brian know you're ok. Wait for me there."

"I'm not leaving you out here with this, this *psycho*," Claire seethed at the stranger. "Who questions people about art like this? What the hell is wrong with you? I have a box of ceramics I could have dropped!" Her priorities were skewed, but adrenaline can jumble things.

Lil let a smile creep to one side of her mouth, a breeze playing at tendrils of her hair, something building in the air, a mounting charge. She liked when Claire got scrappy, though, she didn't care for the current circumstances.

"I'm not concerned with your *arts and crafts*," the man said, stepping toward Lil. "I am, however, interested in speaking with *you*."

He stalked toward her with what one might call a crazy look in his eyes. He was daft, Lil realized, missing something that provided healthy fear to those who had their faculties in-tact.

Claire's hand rose behind him. She held a large, thick mug, which she brought down hard on the side of his head.

He stumbled but didn't fall.

"It's stoneware!" Claire shouted.

"Well, that was unexpected," Lil huffed with a smile.

But the fun stopped when he turned on Claire.

Lil's hair whipped around as rain began to fall. A low rumble sounded all around them, then a series of flashes lit the patch of garden where they stood. Wisps of lightning threaded up from the ground beside them, crackling, then then a boom sounded as bolt came down from the sky beside the stranger.

Claire jumped, struck not by electricity but by fear. It had been too close.

Another loud crack came from behind her, the flash throwing their shadows across the side of the barn.

With one hand pressed to the bleeding wound on his head, the man stared at Lil, perhaps beyond her.

Knowing what she'd done to Brian, what she'd practiced with Todd and Gunnar... Some sense of instinct took over, and she managed to fix the stranger where he stood.

Rain and blood dripped down his face and neck. Panic in his eyes accompanied by a lack of mobility let Lil know she'd been successful in denying him access to his skeletal muscles, but the change in color and lack of chest movement indicated she might need to dial things back as his diaphragm had paused as well.

With the renewal of his breath, Lil relaxed, and the wisps of ground lightening receded. She planned to release what muscles were necessary for him to speak, and begin her interrogation, but a smell came through the rain and wet soil; smoldering and spicy. The scent was like digging through moss, through the fertile ground and cool water to the warm center of the earth and sinking in as it wrapped its arms around her. She knew on her skin and in her blood that someone was there, behind her in the orchard.

She turned and stepped away, toward the feeling calling to her.

"Lil!" Claire cried out.

That scent, through the trees and the rain, like apples and embers.

"Lil!"

She twisted back toward her cousin, shaking off the trance, her focus broken. The stranger brought a hand to his ear, his shouting unintelligible as he ran around the barn.

Claire seemed more shaken than when Lil had first arrived.

"You ok?" Lil asked.

"Your skin, it did that electric light thing. It was all over you."

Lil looked down at her arms. They seemed normal, though she had felt charged up, then she got distracted, and-

"Did that guy have an earpiece?" She asked.

"A what?" Claire squinted. "Like comms? He was grilling me about your paintings, thought I'd done them. Can we not talk about this out here?"

The rain had stopped, but wanting to get back in was understandable.

"You're right," Lil conceded. "We should get inside."

"Where are you going?" Claire hollered.

Lil didn't realize she'd starting walking, not toward the shop, but toward the trees.

"I thought I saw something…" she said. "Did you see something over there? Smell anything…?"

"I saw a creepy jackass over by the barn not too long ago. He smelled like mints and bad choices, and I'd like to get out of the darkness."

"Daylight is just a deceptive veil of photons," Lil sighed as the shop drew near. "It's all the same: the lavender, the orchard, the barn. When the light leaves us, we have a heightened sense of the unknown, and that's what we are afraid of. The unknown is there though, like the lavender, and the orchard, and the barn.

The unknown is always there, like the universe looming on the other side of our atmosphere."

Claire looked up to the heavens, then back at Lil, unsettled.

Lil took a deep breath, trying hard to remain in the moment, to be there on the path to Nan's, with Claire. She was almost envious of the box in her cousin's arms, of its grounding weight, of the distraction a task provided.

"I'm sure they're worried," Claire said, climbing the steps.

"I'm surprised Todd hasn't run out with the bat."

The warmth and familiarity of the shop welcomed them, Nan behind the counter, her hand resting on the shop phone. Todd and Brian stood in front of the counter, making their best effort at discretion, though Todd held a bat in his hand and Brian looked both thoroughly shaken and suddenly relieved.

An undercurrent of tension thrummed in the shop. The folks down back were engrossed in whatever they'd had going on when Lil abruptly left, but those who sat closer to the entrance were glancing her way, no doubt noticing that she and Claire were wet on a night with no expected rain.

Claire, sharp as ever, began to limp as she waved to the four older patrons sitting closest to the front. The Lunds: Mary Ellen and her husband Phillip, his brother Jon and Jon's wife, Sue. The Lund brothers played all manner of string instruments and used to *jam* with Claire's dad when he came into town, bringing their music to Nan's shop on occasion.

"You know, I went and twisted my ankle out there," Claire said laughing at herself as she hobbled onward.

"And still insisted on carrying the box once I got out there," Lil scolded, taking the burden out of her cousin's hands.

Brian's arms went around Claire, and they all headed for the kitchen where Lil set the box down, sharing a look of concern with Nan, then smirking at Todd.

"I knew you'd have that bat," she smiled.

"She wouldn't let me out!"

"You would have had my back though," Lil said, her arms enveloping him.

"You know I would. I had to find this thing in a *closet*. It needs to stay behind the counter," he said with authority, setting the weapon down.

"Why don't you take it there now," Nan instructed. "And stay out there in case our customers need something."

"I should be here for the debriefing," he protested.

Nan rolled her eyes. "This isn't the intelligence service, Todd. Go on out there and give us a moment."

"You know what I mean, Nan. I need to be here. I'm a part of this."

She gave him a stern look and he let out a huff before returning to the counter with his bat.

"What the hell happened out there," Nan whispered. "I heard thunder, and you're both soaked."

Lil turned around to confirm Claire and Brian were still in a prolonged embrace. She could hear Claire's voice, so much steadier now, telling him what occurred.

"There was a man," Lil started, leaning in toward Nan. "I'm guessing the one Todd talked to. He thought Claire had done the paintings and was interrogating her out by the barn, but he didn't seem like the dealer type. He's someone that gets sent to acquire something regardless of what the thing is, and knows not to return without it. And I'm pretty sure he had an earpiece," she sighed. "Maybe he works for a collector like Magnus, someone with enough money to throw an earpiece in his man on the ground?"

Lil thought back to what Hamish had said about dragonflies and the children. Could this guy behind the barn... could he have been trying to *take* her? If anyone's aim had been true, it was Claire's with that mug.

"Honestly though," Lil continued. "Who else comes in here aside from locals, and those passing through that have heard of the shop by word of mouth. And even those we don't know usually have someone we've met with them. Why would he be here?"

Nan's lips drained of color. "Did you get any information from him?"

"We scared him off," she said with a gloriously devious smile as Claire and Brian approached. "He couldn't handle Claire's scrap."

Nan eyed Lil. "Are you sure it wasn't the sudden change in weather he couldn't handle? We're not done talking..."

Brian's arm remained at Claire's shoulder, hers around his waist.

"Well, I think this is as good a time as any for a cup of chai," she said. "How about I make a double batch and we just sit and breathe for a minute?"

In the extended pause, Lil looked to Nan, who seemed lost in thought.

"Why chai?" Brian asked.

"It's a recipe Nan always kept by the phone in the house and here in the shop," Claire explained. "I didn't really notice it until I was seven or eight, when Lil came. Any time there was something scary or a storm, we'd have chai, and sing the recipe together when we made it, well, not *sing* really; it was more like reciting like a poem. It's posted out front by the phone, under the lavender illustration."

"Wait," Brian spoke up. "Has anyone called the police yet?"

Nan shook her head slowly. "No, I don't think we need to take it that far."

"We handle things internally," Todd added, returning to the kitchen.

"Todd..."

"What?"

Claire sighed, "I hit him pretty hard with a mug."

They all turned to Claire, and Todd put up a hand to collect a high five before they walked back out to the front of the shop together. Todd went around gathering empties from a few tables.

Things started to quiet, the mood of the place shifting as customers left.

"Self-defense," Brian offered to Claire as a couple came up to the counter. She got them two beers, an oatmeal cookie, and a croissant.

"You two should get going," Nan said, placing a hand on Claire's shoulder. "You're all fired up now but any moment you're going to crash. Might be nice to get where you're going so you can have a rest."

"Do you want to stay at my place?" Lil offered.

"No, I'm staying at Brian's after we meet up with JD; we're *so* late. I'm going to make it a short day at the lab tomorrow, then back here with Brian to meet Nan for dinner. You should come."

"I'm hunting tomorrow. Depending on when I get back, I can try to make it. I'll call, but don't wait for me. Need me to stay on to help clean up?"

"No, I have Todd, and the place seems to be settling down. Once these folks finish up, I'll turn in and let him close up."

"He's got to be exhausted."

"He wasn't up for yoga this morning, and he's had a nap. Not to mention he's the youngest of us all. He'll do just fine, and we'll call in a couple of the kids to help in the morning. Speaking of yoga, I'll be running it myself tomorrow," huffed, putting up a hand. "Don't feel sorry for me, it's not like I have to drive here. Let me walk you out before Todd can put up a stink."

"Fair enough."

They walked out to the porch and down the steps, pausing for a hug goodbye.

"You're so beautiful, in here," Nan said, resting her hand on Lil's chest, drawing up memories and conversations due. "Calm as a cradle, ruthless as a storm. We still need to have a talk," she continued. "Tuesday? Lunch? Or if you make it to dinner tomorrow you could stay over after. Just think about it."

Lil Leaned in for another a warm hug. Nan smelled like Lavender, vanilla, and the shop. It was a smell that was as close to home as anything in waking life could be, aside from rain, damp earth, and the room above the barn.

20.

Salt water dripped from Lil's skin and hair. Waves lapped at her legs, her feet passing over stone as she emerged from the ocean. She'd gone straight in the front door and right out the back upon returning from Nan's, ready to leave the night she'd had behind in the water.

As she walked up the shore, something bright stood out among the black and grey of the rocks and shadows: a cairn of stones with some type of pine cone balanced on top. She couldn't tell what type, but it was young, oozing sap, and wasn't from one of her trees.

A cairn she didn't remember building, but she hadn't remembered the stone cup either. Had she dreamed it into existence while out in the water?

Lil scooped up the cone, brought it inside, made a cup of tea, and went upstairs. Her bedroom was much like the living room, with a wall of glass and a balcony overlooking the ocean, and a stone fireplace with a mantle. Her bed, situated against a wall between the ocean and the fireplace, had a simple, reclaimed wood frame with one of her paintings hanging over it.

Lil set the mystery-cone down on the mantle in her room, her palm sticky from the sap at the base of her fingers. Cupping her hand to her nose, she inhaled, the scent crisp, woody, and eye opening.

After rinsing off in the shower, she crawled beneath the puffy blankets of her bed. Still drained from the events of the evening, she just draped her wet hair off to the side, thinking she'd be out before the dampness of her pillow become bothersome.

The man behind the barn puzzled her, the intensity of pursuit by someone she'd never before met. How could a stranger be so focused on her? The man was obviously working for someone determined, who wouldn't take no for an answer. Determined, perhaps, to take her. What kind of employer would send a guy with an earpiece to intimidate and possibly abduct an artist he was interested in? *Who would do that for art*, she thought. *Not art. A necklace.*

And she *knew* someone had been in the orchard.

She'd be awake all night if she kept up that line of thinking.

At risk for racing thoughts keeping her awake, Lil glanced over to the glass wall. Feeling the ocean beyond, she sighed, got up, wrapped a robe around herself, and headed out to the balcony lounger to clear her thoughts.

*

Like a somnolent metronome, the waves below lulled her, cradled her, rocking her slowly. She felt herself lifting, the sensation of her robe sliding down to the cushion beneath her as she floated away. A warm ripple moved over her head and through her steaming hair until it was dry. The ocean faded into the distance, and her body settled into a cloud.

With a foggy sense of time, Lil couldn't determine if she was entering a dream or waking from one. The fire crackled and she was warm, cocooned in a heady scent that made her eyes roll before she opened them.

A hand moved slowly up her back. It felt good, this hand, unobstructed by clothing, moving freely over her skin. It occurred to her then, that she had no shirt on, and she was dreaming of the man from the bar. She wanted to open her eyes, but hesitated for fear that she'd wake.

254

"Open them," a low voice purred, so close she could feel the warmth from his mouth feathering over her ear.

Lil found her lids heavy, lifting them as much as she could manage.

He was still there, head propped up by his hand, hovering over her, closely.

"You were in the orchard," she said. "I could smell you."

She felt tired, which made very little sense as far as she was concerned, given that she was sleeping.

"And I you," he replied, low and deep, inhaling slowly, closing his eyes, a man savoring a memory like some forbidden delight melting on his tongue. "I saw the wind playing at your rain-soaked hair. You immobilized that peon effortlessly, so he would stay still while you turned for me…" Fingers trailed up the back of her neck as he leaned into the space below her ear and inhaled, his lips just brushing against her skin. "Magnificent."

"He ran," she said with difficulty focusing. *Is this what pheromones do*, she wondered. Her mind briefly managing to return to her previous thought before being derailed again. "I still don't know who he was."

She felt a glowing light pooling in her. Opening her eyes again she saw it reflected on him.

"He is an extension of something larger beginning to unfold. I have remained as separate from you as I could, so not to draw attention while you wake… Waiting for you to remember, and the *wait*," he sighed. "It appears, though, that you are in the early stages of being discovered. The bright side being that I no longer feel it necessary to keep my distance.

This is a lot to take in.

"Indeed, You need to wake up, then I'll explain, and you will remember."

Remember?

His hand traveled down her back, scooping under her, pulling her body toward his, the ease of the intimacy overwhelming.

Glancing down at the vanishing space between them, she saw the necklace he wore, and her mind began to pick up speed.

"I haven't dreamed of you since you showed me this," she whispered, recalling the way his muscular forearm dripped with darkened sea water. "I thought it was where my power came from," she confessed. "Though I put that theory to bed when I enhanced a potted plant without it on."

He smiled with soft amusement. "Your abilities now are but a fraction of what you are capable, and they do not come from an object." His fingers gently combed against her scalp as he inhaled from her hair. "I meant it when I said it was our story. Into your stone I carved a promise to return what you have forgotten. And into mine, a reminder that I will always find you."

She lifted her palm to his cheek. He felt so real.

"I am," he murmured, emitting a deep sound that morphed into a growl. Closing his eyes, he turned his face into her palm, inhaled, then suddenly his eyes shot open, his hand gripping hers.

"Cedar," he concluded, though the gears in his head still appeared feverishly at work.

She felt him like he was inside her own mind, asking a question she couldn't hear.

"It's from a pine cone, a *cedar* cone, I suppose," she said. "I showered but, it's so sticky. Some must have stayed on my hand. I don't feel it there, though." She ran her thumb over her palm, searching for a tacky patch she couldn't find. "I found it on a cairn, brought it in and left it over on the mantle. Just be careful about the sap."

He was by the fire in an instant, the hot glow undulating over his skin. His movement stilled as his gaze landed on the object in question, then his eyes flicked to hers, asking what was not said.

"I found the cone tonight after swimming. It was just sitting on a pile of balanced rocks at the shore as if someone had placed it there. I've been finding things and I don't know where they come from, like a stone cup the other day. I think I dream them, make them somehow."

"I didn't leave this," he growled.

He'd left the cup, though, had been the one crafting it in her dream.

"Cedar," he huffed, confirming something to himself.

She hadn't put it there, nor had he. The house had been unlocked while she was swimming, and the person who left it knew she was swimming. Had they been watching her? Maybe they were afraid of getting caught inside? And what would they leave a *cone* for? Was the sap medicinal?

"It was my attention they sought. Contact with you would have been unwise... Even the proximity of the rocks was bold, telling of urgency. The *messenger*," he paused, "has not reached out to me in quite some time."

He gripped the mantle, his fingers digging in, a rumble forming, whether from air or earth, Lil wasn't sure.

"Why didn't they just call you?" She mumbled.

He released a breathy chuckle, his smile captivating.

"It certainly would have been quicker."

Her heart sank slightly. She liked these dreams with him, but they had to end, as all dreams do.

"I'm not leaving that here," he announced, eyeing the specimen on the mantle. "I'll need to wrap it."

"You could take a cloth from the bathroom, or there's clothes that need to go in the wash- "

"I'll not have something of *yours* smelling of *that*."

She let out the tiniest gasp, just a short inhale, at the sight of his chest in the firelight as he removed his shirt.

"Each departure is more difficult," he grumbled. "This will be the last."

Her eyes were too heavy to remain open, so they didn't, and she sank back into the surrounding cloud. Later, upon waking, she found the cedar cone to be missing, the cairn no longer at the shore.

21.

Lil's pulled her truck down Magnus's long driveway at about half passed three in the morning, parking in front of the custom timber frame home, perfectly nestled in the forest.

She wore black fitted pants that were durable, but allowed movement. Over them she had olive green gaiters, hiking boots, a fitted olive shirt, her hair in a long braid. Once outside the truck, she slipped on the straps of the pack frame, fastened the chest and waist belt. There was no pack, just the frame, belt outfitted with pouches.

Bow and quiver in hand, she approached a man who stood waiting.

"Gunnar," she smiled. "You're always here when I'm here," she quietly teased, his presence unsurprising.

He nodded, the corner of his lips hinting upward with warmth. "By design," he said, voice low and slow, like a bear whispering.

"Nothing else pulling you away?"

"Nothing else catches the eye."

He slid a hand through the open front of his jacket, the widening space of this outer layer revealing the black shirt sculpted to his chest, and a shoulder holster. As his arm retreated, his hand emerged, extended toward her.

She maintained eye contact as his palm opened, then, finally, she glanced down at what looked like a tiny candy wrapped in brown waxed paper, twisted on both sides.

Her eyes flicked back to his as she accepted the gift, unwrapped it in silence, then put it in her mouth. Her tongue moved over the caramel, soft from having rested against his body. With a sigh, she closed her eyes. There were no words, she just nodded slowly.

"A hint of Grapefruit," he said.

"Please don't stop making these."

"If I'm here when you return, I'll give you another."

"If I'm not back by nightfall, call Nan's. Or, Magnus I suppose; he can call Nan."

"I spoke to my cousin again." Hamish... "He's been dreaming about that golden haired man for years, says he's a lot like David, kind. *Playing stones* is when they make little towers; larger rocks stacked under pebbles."

Like the ones she'd seen on the rock wall at his school, like the one on the shore outside her home...

"It helps to have someone to talk to," she said. "About the dreams."

Gunnar nodded.

Clever boy, dreaming up his own therapist. She had dream man of her own, stones and all.

"I think he saw me with the children at Nan's party," Lil continued on a lighter note. "Let's hope what he says about my aim holds."

Gunnar reached down somewhere on his person. Lil had hoped for more candy, but reluctantly took the satellite phone he offered.

"He gives me one every time," she sighed. "And he knows I won't turn it on."

"But he knows you'll have it with you, and so do I."

She nodded, put a hand on his arm, then walked off toward the tree line.

About a kilometer in, Lil stopped to listen, and to inhale the scent of the forest, the damp leaves underfoot; rotting remains. Water trickled in the distance to her left, further still the call of a barred owl cried out. Great, unfolding wings moved through trees, swooping suddenly as the bird came to rest on her shoulder.

The animal shifted on its feet, talons squeezing as it settled in. Lil turned slightly to acknowledge the owl, who expressed reverence, curiosity, and an intention to stay with her for the time being. With acceptance, Lil faced forward again, continuing on while keeping the sound of water to her left. After another half kilometer, she paused again, crouching down to examine fresh deer sign. After evaluating her surroundings, she decided to hunker down and blend in.

Sitting at the base of a tree, she nocked an arrow, and closed her eyes. Talons tightened once again on her shoulder, followed by a push as her companion lifted off. Movement of air and feathers faded, and she drifted into a brief sleep.

The song of the dawn chorus eased Lil from her slumber and into the blue light of early morning. She flexed the fingers on her left hand, rubbed her thumb along the bow's grip, tightened her hold, and observed.

He walked slowly, coming in from her right. She could hear the damp moss and leaves under his hooves, smell decomposing plant matter mixing with the musk from his body. Lil had become one with her surroundings, the rhythm of the trees muting her heartbeat and slowed breath. He acknowledged no threat.

The deer passed in front of her, robust build, antlers branching wide, then he paused, head down, to inspect something. The broadside shot he offered was the most effective she could have asked for, allowing her to collapse both lungs, render an efficient death.

With a smooth motion, Lil raised the bow with her left hand. Her right pulled the tight string back until the little ring fixed to it rested at the corner of her mouth, her thumb and fingers grounded to her jaw. When her eyes brought the site just behind the animal's shoulder, she relaxed her forearm and allowed the bowstring to break through her three fingers, propelling the arrow swiftly into the animal.

Her aim was true.

He skidded and tore through the trees, his body becoming lost as the crashing sounds of his movement faded. An almost silence followed, and then the slow trickling of noises as birds and other creatures began using their voices again.

After a drink and a snack, Lil retrieved her arrow, finding frothy blood at the site, a good sign that the lungs had been punctured and the transition would be quick. Another fifteen minutes or so passed as she followed the blood trail and chaos to his felled body. He was no longer taking breath but had not yet left. Lil wasn't sure how she knew this, only that she did.

She knelt down beside the hair and bone, still inhabited, then put her bow to the side, hands on her knees. Slowly passing her gaze from his face to his tail, she laid a blanket over his body. The covering had not been woven of fiber or water, but of something unseen she called from herself. Once she felt him pass cleanly through, she knew he'd moved on.

As she positioned the body of the animal to be field dressed, Lil heard a swooping sound, and turned to see an owl had landed on a rotting tree stump close by. The same barred owl had returned to her, unsettled. Lil leaned in toward the bird, and made a connection, seeing what happened through its eyes. Two men were in the woods, and they didn't belong. They had scoped rifles and were dressed like hunters, one with a black knit hat, both in camouflage...

No one else hunted Magnus's land.

Did you see their faces? She asked.

The one with short, flat grey hair, had both a rifle and a side arm. He looked to be in his late fifties or early sixties, very fit. The other had a small knit hat with thin blonde hair poking out, probably in his early thirties. He had bruising coming down from his temple where Claire had hit him with a mug.

Lil's heart began to race, finding no coincidence in their presence at her location, the man who'd smelled of Altoids and the older one Nan had maybe objectified... Hadn't Hamish suggested there would be more than one attempt to take her? The boy had said the outcome couldn't be changed, or was it that *he* couldn't change the outcome? He also said she wasn't in grave danger.

She didn't care for the distraction that knowing had caused. There was nothing useful in it.

Thank you.

As the owl flew off in the direction of the murmuring stream, Lil took a moment to slow her heart and her breathing. She reconnected with the trees, moss, the deep smell of the earth rising up from under her. She felt the weight of the knife in her hand, and made her first cut.

The heart, liver, and kidneys, she placed in a waxed canvas pouch. The remaining entrails, she moved to a pile by a rotted tree trunk, a welcome meal for scavengers. Lil wiped her hands onto the dense moss, removing the bulk of the blood, then rolled the animal to her pack frame. She'd been about to slip the straps over her shoulders when the sound of the owl's call came through the trees, and she froze.

The intruders were close.

Approaching the site where she'd left the entrails, Lil set her pack frame down, and nocked an arrow. She walked about twenty paces, turned, got down on her right knee, and leaned her left side against a tree. She raised her bow, sited in her pack, then released the tension on the string, and lowered her bow back down. Breathing in slowly, she felt a stillness in herself that had spread across the forest floor and up into the trees.

We sit together, the mountain and me, until only the mountain remains.

Breathe in, Breathe out.

Cautious footsteps sounded; their attempted stealth ineffective. They didn't belong.

Two men halted at her pack. Rifles in hand, they inspected the remains of the deer and surveyed the area.

"It's fresh," the older man said.

Lil recognized the firearm Altoids Man held, but the older guy had a gun with an odd, thin stock. It was greenish. She found herself puzzled, then suddenly it clicked, and she knew. A tranquilizer gun. Were they wildlife management? Not likely, with Altoids having strong-armed Claire the night before.

A low vibration resonated, either from or around her. It spread out and hung in the air between the trees, up through their roots, up through the legs of the men standing by her harvested deer.

"Do you feel that?" Altoids asked.

"She's here. Alone."

"How do you know she's alone?"

"If she wasn't, we'd already be dead."

Eyes frantic, they scanned the forest. The older man seemed to have more control, but Altoids had a touch of panic about him.

Lil rose from her position; arrow nocked, string back, bead on Altoid's neck. It was possible they had protective gear on under their clothes, and she didn't want to take chances.

Both men startled. Altoids raised his gun, but the older one put his hand over the barrel and pushed it down, his eyes on her, lip curving up at one corner.

"We meet again," he said.

No, it was Altoids she'd met the night before, not the grey-hair.

"We have an opportunity for you," Grey continued. "My name is John, and this is my colleague, Andrew. We're here on behalf of an organization that wishes to assist you in reaching your potential."

An undulating rumble rose from underground.

"How do you know me?" She asked, her voice strong, resonant.

She felt them before they arrived; the five, no, seven wolves in shades of grey and brown moving through the trees.

"We've come to know about you… over time." John started. "It seems like you're still a bit in the dark about that."

A soft, warm body brushed against her hip where an eighth wolf stood beside her. Lil was confident she could handle this on her own, but their support and strength invigorated her.

"You've been off the map for a while," John continued, his voice remarkably steady given the animals clustering around her. "Some things that correlated with your *unique qualities* came to our attention recently… So here we are."

And with a tranquilizer gun. The *audacity*.

A small burst of energy rippled off of her, knocking the men back a step. One of the wolves moved forward, flashing teeth. Andrew swiveled toward the animal, bringing the scope of his rifle to his eye.

His arms dropped before he was able to sight her in, knees buckling, energy draining rapidly. Blood came in strong spirits from both the entry and exit

266

wound made by the broadhead Lil had sent through. She had a fresh arrow nocked and sited on John before he had a chance to turn his head.

"Others will come, Lilith. *My* people want to cultivate what you have, but the others-"

Her arrow loosed as the ground heaved beneath him. One of his feet came up as his shoulders went back, the blade's edge slicing his neck as he went down. The wolves were on him before his head hit the moss; first at his bloodied neck, next at his upper arm. Skin tore, arteries opened. His scream quieted quickly though, once he was no longer able to pass air.

Lil lowered her bow and put her hand to the animal beside her, fingers sinking into dense hair and fur. They walked together, approaching the others until a calm passed over them, and eight pairs of eyes turned toward her.

"Thank you," she whispered.

One of the wolves, stained pink and red, stalked toward her. She crouched allowing him to nuzzle her chest, neck, and cheeks, painting her skin with blood.

The rest of the pack stared at her a moment longer, then all returned to the trees, leaving her alone with the two bodies and a racing heart.

She reached down for the sat phone, powered it on, and dialed Magnus.

"Lily, what's wrong." He answered.

"I'm a couple kilometers in from your place. Two men came for me; must have come in from the road and tracked me somehow. They were looking for me at Nan's last night. And Magnus, I don't know what Hamish was thinking when he said there was no grave danger, because they were both armed. One of them had a tranqu' gun. They were trying to *collect* me… bring me back with them…"

"I have your coordinates; I'm sending some men to escort you out."

"No, I can make it out, there's just somewhat of a mess here. Someone will need to clean things up; the scavengers will take some, but there will be bones, clothes…"

"You've neutralized them, then?"

"Yes, Magnus, I shot one and the wolves took the other down when my arrow missed its mark."

"You missed?"

"The arrow went where I told it to go, but there was a *disturbance,* and the target stumbled."

"Leave everything as it is. Touch nothing. My people are already on their way out to your location. You don't have to wait for them, but contact me when you get to the house. I'd like for you to stay, if you would. It's the safest option until we know more about what happened."

"I need to be home; to rest, breathe, to swim, I don't know."

"Your uncertainty is disconcerting, Lily. I really feel it's best for you to stay."

"I'll text when I get to my truck. This phone stays on until I get there."

"Very well, dear. Stay safe."

Birdsong had resumed. The deep smell of the earth remained, stream trickled in the distance, and there were two dead men on the uprooted ground in front of her. Lil left the scene as it was, taking with her only what she'd brought in and the blacktail she harvested.

The journey out was uneventful, save for her thoughts. She tried to let the meditation of the walk, the load she carried, and thoughts of the work ahead calm her, but as she emerged from the tree line, so did a knowing of things to come.

Crushed stone crunched under her feet as she moved toward her truck. She caught Gunnar's eye but continued on, releasing the weight of her pack into the bed. Opening the back door, she stowed her gear and sent a quick text to Magnus.

When she closed the door, Gunnar was there.

"Long shift?" She asked.

"I slept this morning."

Magnus had likely called Gunnar and notified him of the situation, though he did seem to have an uncanny awareness of what she needed, that she needed anything at all.

With Gunnar there, something in her strength eased, and she began feeling unsettled, bordering on frantic as her mind slipped to what had happened. She'd managed to stay distracted while hiking out...

"I have to get the deer home," she started. "There's a family I promised the meat to, and I need to shower." If she focused on the tasks she had to perform, she could reign herself in.

His hand went behind her neck, bringing her head to rest on his chest. Stubble passed over her head, catching her hair as he whispered, "Slow down, kid."

Lil closed her eyes and calmed her breathing, felt the solid wall of him around her; safe, familiar. She heard a crinkling noise, then, "Open."

Her tongue slid over the caramel, a breath and a sound slipping from her. She'd needed him, the mountain of him.

A door to the house opened a ways off. Footsteps approached, and Lil lifted her head to see another of Magnus's men approaching, handing something to Gunnar.

Wet warmth smoothed over her face and neck as he wiped the blood away. When the bulk of it had been cleaned, he passed the cloth to Lil so she could get her hands.

"I had him run in and grab a washcloth as soon as I saw you coming out," he explained.

"I still need a shower," she whispered.

"Do it here."

"Did Magnus tell you what happened?"

"Yes. We'll take care of it."

"I'm not sure how much can be taken care of."

"We can take care of *you*, if you stay."

She looked up at his face, his strong jaw, concerned eyes.

"Let me see you home, at least. If you're okay to drive, I'll follow, check the house, and be on my way if that's what you want."

She nodded, managing a weak smile. "Thank you."

22.

The shower had been hot, and necessary. While the cold didn't negatively affect her, she still appreciated steaming water pouring over her skin. It was her hope that the unease she felt would liquefy and run down the drain, out to sea... but it was not so. The encounter in the forest rested heavy enough that its weight, while not unbearable, maintained her attention.

Gunnar had followed her home as promised, a gesture that helped to partially ease both their minds. She had no trouble sleeping while he remained in the house, still, she encouraged him to go, though not until he'd checked the property, had a cup of tea and a snack. The scones took fifteen minutes to bake and no more than five to whip together, enough time to ease them both into a sense of comfort. When they finished their tea, Gunnar headed out to hang the deer in her workshop before returning to Magnus's. Once he was gone, Lil threw her clothes in the washer and headed upstairs to the bathroom where unexpected rain clouds muted evening through the bathroom skylight.

She showered, then dressed in soft clothes: a slate tank top with a light grey, wide necked shirt and slate pants.

She padded down to the kitchen, and straight onto the couch for a nap, because sleep would help. Sleep, then maybe a swim.

A Story in Stone

Closing her eyes, Lil let her focus drift away, carried by breath and waves into a dream.

*

The four-year-old girl sat with her mother on the deck of their sailboat, surrounded by teak and mahogany, a cool afternoon and a warm sweater. The boat rocked gently, chilled air fluttering long brown hair around her pale face. She scanned her mother's deep brown skin and dark eyes, wondering.

"You said DNA is like a map two parents make so the baby knows how to grow," she started. "I know I was inside you, so how come I look so different?"

"Your soul is very strong, Lilu," her mother replied, "and had its own idea of how the map should be. We are so blessed that you chose us to be your guides in this life, to love you, snuggle you, to listen to your dreams of sea creatures and flying with the birds. And while I love your creations, I am thankful we didn't bring any clay or play dough on this boat because sometimes..."

The girl gave a knowing smirk as her mother continued.

"Sometimes the clay and the play dough end up on the floor... and embedded in your clothes... and stuck to my socks!" Her mother pounced, planting rapid kisses on the girl's face, neck, arms, and back as they laughed together.

Her father came up from below deck with two steaming mugs and a smile that reached his dark, almond eyes. "What's all this commotion up here? I thought it was wind-down time. I brought some nap-facilitating tea, and there may have been biscuits, but now I'm not so sure..."

"Biscuits!" The girl shouted.

Her father gave her a pretend serious look, then she whisper-shouted, "Biscuits!"

A Story in Stone

He set the mugs down on the table, sat across from his wife and daughter, and scratched his beard. "Oh right, the biscuits..."

Finally, he pulled the small bag of treats from his pocket.

"So, Lilu," her dad began. "What are some of our calm-down tools?"

"Chamomile and lavender, the rhythm of the ocean, my heartbeat and breath, poetry."

"Let's hear a poem then," he smiled softly.

The little girl inhaled slow and released, took a sip of her tea, and then spoke. "The birds have vanished from the sky, now the last cloud drains away. We sit together, the mountain and me, until only the mountain remains."

"And who wrote it?"

"It's a translation of Zazen on Ching-t'ing Mountain, by Li Po."

"How does it make you feel?"

"He's just being there, and he is quiet. His thoughts are quiet, and he fades into the stillness." She looked out to the ocean, feeling herself sitting on the mountain, clouds drifting away and her thoughts with them. "I feel calm and still, and a part of the things around me. I feel a part of the mountain. I am still, but if I wake, I will wake the mountain too."

With a solemn face her dad looked right into her, and said, "You don't ever need to be afraid if you wake the mountain. You are in control."

She exhaled slowly out her nose and, while she felt on the cusp of being overwhelmed, her father's confidence was reassuring.

"Thanks dad," she smiled.

"Lilu," her mom said. "Why don't you take the rest of your tea down below deck and read a bit until you fall asleep? I think it's just about time for naps."

One biscuit later, the little girl made her way down the steps.

The girl's mother reached across the table, taking her husband's hand. "Sometimes, I'm just so in awe of her... then I find a crayon in the dryer."

They laughed together; it had happened more than once.

Sam got up and sat next to his wife. "I brought up more than biscuits and tea, Nora." He pulled out a crossword puzzle book and pencil. "We still have a few more to go before we get to the medium ones."

Leaning into each other, they puzzled, cursing the book for using absurd clues. The wind picked up, gradually at first, then rapidly the sky darkened as grey clouds grew out of nowhere.

They both stood, Nora heading for the stairs as she shouted, "Get to the helm in case I can't wake her fast enough."

She took the steps quickly and bent over her daughter's restless body, sliding firm hands over her shoulder, her back.

"Wake up, Lilu. Come on, Sweetie."

Frightened eyes sprang open. "Mumma, they're coming."

"Shhh. Calm, Lilu, find the calm."

"They're coming fast. I think I'm taken."

"Let's go up and talk to Daddy. Calm, Lilu. Calm your heart and your breathing. Use your tools."

A Story in Stone

Lilu breathed, clouds paler as they ascended.

Her father eased his grip at the helm, concern darkening his face as the girl retold her dream.

"They must have tracked us," he said, grunting with frustration, rubbing a hand in his hair and over his face. "I should have committed to no electronics."

Nora looked out to the horizon, then back to the boat. "What can we do right now to improve our situation? We could call for the coast guard, or use the sat' phone and call the number. What do you think they would send? A boat? Helicopter?"

Sam put an arm around Nora and Lilu, pulling them both in. Face buried in his wife's neck, he whispered, "Sat phone. Make the call."

Below deck, Nora punched in the list of numbers she'd memorized.

"Ringing," she said, then, "No answer, just a tone. Should I try the coast guard?"

Boat rocking, eyes searching the surrounding horizon. And then they saw it, an incoming boat moving fast, as Lilu said it would.

"An MRCC," Sam said from behind binoculars. "Three mounted guns."

The sky blackened once more, clouds growing into one another until only lightning illuminated the boat coming toward them over mountains of darkness. Soon, they were unable to see the vessel at all; the waves too high.

Lilu slid across the deck as the ocean collected into a massive swell. Thunder cracked with another flash of lightening, then the incoming boat tumbled and vanished. The wave's crest scraped the clouds above as an enormous set of wings swooped from above the mast. In a turbulent moment, Lilu saw feathers and light so white it looked blue.

She was airborne, and then there was darkness.

23.

Windshield wipers on high speed, Claire wished she could drive faster, but the rain had picked up since she'd left Nan's and she couldn't afford recklessness. Pulling in the driveway, Claire felt some relief upon seeing Lil's vehicle, but it came with an awareness of the potential burden she faced, what she might find.

She raised the hood of her jacket, exited the jeep, and ran through the turbulent darkness. Grasping the loop of the knocker, she rapped hard on the front door. With no answer, she tried the knob. Locked. She jogged over to the garage Lil called her workshop, not locked, and entered.

Rain pounded on the roof as she caught her breath, echoing through the high ceiling and down into the dark room.

"Lil?"

No response, just the relentless pattering of the rain and crashing waves. She'd hoped to see a deer hanging, or some evidence Lil had returned from her hunt successful, something more than the truck in the driveway. But the space was empty.

Claire approached one of the deep freezers, slowly lifting the lid. Antlers trailed down to frosted, lifeless eyes. She didn't frequent Lil's freezers, but hoped the head was fresh, that her cousin was home.

Claire needed to find her.

Making her way through the back door, Claire spotted something down on the rocks: Lil, wearing a dark tank top and underwear, sitting in half lotus pose, spray from the waves flying onto her as she meditated.

"Lil!"

Lil turned her head, rose, and walked up the rocks over to Claire. As if there wasn't a wall of falling water between them, she asked, "What are you doing here?"

Wind whipped rain and surf hard at Claires face as she shouted, "Inside!"

Lil nodded, and they started up to the deck. Once inside, Lil stripped off her shirt and continued past the kitchen and down the hall.

Claire hung her saturated jacket by the door, slid off her rain boots, and peeled off her wet socks and jeans. After tossing them in the dryer, she headed to the kitchen.

"I'm making us chai!"

She put a medium saucepan on the stove and added a cup of water, whispering the recipe as she gathered the ingredients from the pantry. Star anise, cinnamon, cloves, black pepper, cardamom and ginger all went in, simmered. Eventually, she turned off the heat, adding the tea, maple, and almond milk.

Lil emerged from the hallway wearing a light grey, wide neck shirt, her pants soft, slate grey.

"It smells so good in here," she said, holding out a pair of sweats for Claire.

"These are *really* soft," her cousin purred, pulling the pants on. "What are they *made* of?"

"Cotton and cashmere; it's like wearing a warm cloud. I thought you were having dinner with Nan and Brian tonight."

"Well," Claire started, straining their tea into two mugs. "You weren't answering your phone, and rain wasn't forecasted for today... We became concerned when the sky turned *ferocious*." Claire raised her eyebrows and paused for effect. "Brian is still at Nan's."

Lil inhaled deep from the mug of warm spice, then drank. Rich warmth spread into her, a comfort, but there were places it didn't reach.

"I need to speak to Nan," she whispered. "There were some details I had forgotten about, from when I came to live with her." She took another sip and met Claire's eyes. "I saw that guy who cornered you out by the barn. He was in the woods this morning with another man, both armed. I shot and killed him. They're both dead. Magnus is taking care of it."

Claire only managed a blank stare, so Lil continued. "They were trying to recruit me into some organization or something. They had guns. One of them was a tranquilizer gun, Claire. They wouldn't have taken no for an answer, so I didn't bother with hearing what they had to say."

"Lil, I don't... This is unbelievable. I mean, I *believe* you, but Lil, we need to call Nan," Claire sputtered, shaking her head. "No, I should just drive us over there."

"I'm really teetering on the edge," Lil said, her voice almost too calm. "I think I should stay, and maybe take another hot shower, or go for a swim. I just need to settle, get centered."

"A *swim*? It's too rough out there, even for you. *Please*, come back to Nan's with me. I'll drive. Whatever you've been doing, Lil, it's not working."

"I was fine, but then I had a dream, a memory from before Nan. It set things off again, so I went down to the rocks."

Her cellphone buzzed.

"Magnus?" Lil answered.

"How are you doing, dear?"

"I hit a rough patch, but Claire's here now."

"I see. I'd like for you to head to my home until I have more information on our *situation*. We are still looking into what happened... And have yet to identify the men or locate their point of entry."

Who were they and how did they find her? Why? *How?* It was about more than artwork, she was certain of that. People didn't retrieve artists from the woods with tranquilizer guns. Maybe something she'd done at the Orn? She hadn't been there in years though. The necklace? Had they been following her in Boston?

"How could they have known where I was? Who I *am?*" She whispered.

"Oh, several possibilities where location is concerned... It didn't seem like there was a tracker on you, otherwise they could have just taken you at home, who knows, maybe they didn't *want* to take you at home. I'm not clear on why that would be the case. It would have been much simpler than hunting you down in the forest, though perhaps they thought they would somehow have the upper hand? They would have expected you to be armed though. Either way, to have found you the way they did, there could have been a tracker or they could have had a thermal drone. Knowing the area you'd be in, it wouldn't have taken too long."

"They could find me again, Magnus. Could I go to Nan's? I can't go there, can I?"

She closed her eyes, heart racing. She could keep them safe if she was there, but if she went, wouldn't she be leading danger to her family? What if they showed up anyway and she *wasn't* there?

Claire approached, mouthed, "What's going on?"

"What can I do?" Lil whispered, shaking her head. "Magnus..." She cut off and handed the phone to Claire. Closing her eyes, wiping the moisture that had formed there, Lil walked outside.

"Magnus?" Claire demanded. "Magnus, what's going on?"

"What's going on is Lily's life has been threatened, and I believe she is not safe at her home. You need to leave. I've offered my residence, and there's always the Orn, but the more likely choice she'll agree to is Nan's."

Claire looked outside. "Oh god, Magnus."

"Do you need me to send a car?"

She stared out the glass door to where Lil had crouched on the deck, rain pouring over her.

"Claire! Do I need to send a car?"

"I have my jeep. I need to call Nan."

"I'm sending one of my men, Gunnar. You may need help getting her out of the house, and they have a bond. I'll make contact with an updated plan, but you are to call me when you depart so I can breathe."

He hung up.

Claire put Lil's phone down and dialed Nan from her own.

"Did you find her?" Nan answered, breathy and panicked.

"She's here, but it's not good, Nan. The men who came to the shop last night found her in the woods, tried to take her or something, and she killed them. Magnus knows. It's serious. He said he wants us to head to your place until we hear back from him, but she's *freaking out* on the deck." Claire looked out through the glass again and took in a sharp breath. "Her skin is getting a wispy light over it."

"Do you remember the recipe for chai?"

"Yeah, I just made some, but it's not working."

"I need you to listen to me, Claire. The recipe is a phone number. I want you to hang up and dial it."

"What?"

"The numbers in the recipe, in the order I taught you, are a phone number. I was told to dial it if there was ever an emergency with Lil. Call it now, Claire. I'm hanging up."

The call dropped and Claire took a deep breath as she stared down at the phone. Whispering the recipe, again, she began entering the number:

One cup water

Two star anise pods

Three cinnamon sticks

Five tsp rooibos tea

Five cardamom pods, they should be green

She paused and looked back out to Lil. She was rising up from her crouched position, soft wisps of electric light flowing over her skin like a glowing mist.

Five slices ginger, to add some spice

One tsp black pepper corns, because heat is nice

She looked back up. Lil was walking down to the rocks again. Claire held the phone in her hand, approaching the glass to keep her cousin in sight. Lil stood on a large, flat rock, looking out into the darkness.

Five cloves, whole not ground

Simmer it, simmer it, simmer it down

With only two numbers left, Claire looked back up. Lil's hands were slowly rising from her side. There was a loud crack as a flash surrounded the rock, and then… Who the hell was *that*?

24.

Lil crouched on the deck under falling rain. Light from the house hovered behind her, darkness and the movement of the waves in front. The storm seemed to have a mind of its own or, rather, it had no mind. It was only emotion. She couldn't protect them like this; couldn't keep her family safe. She'd been practicing her whole life only to feel she couldn't control anything.

She needed to get closer to the water.

Rising up, Lil stood, walked across the deck and down the rocks. She noticed the soft electric charge hovering around her as she moved, bouncing off the moisture in the air. And then she heard a whisper as if spoken within her own mind: *I'm coming*. With those words, came the comforting promise of calm, easing her enough to feel the connection with her surroundings. She began to see the storm as a song she had composed, and her instrument sang.

With a resounding crack, all the cells of her body became at once aware of him. *Him*, there, suddenly beside her.

His dark hair was somewhat long, long enough to tie back, and his eyes… His eyes were deep green surrounding a dark, earthy core, like moss in an old growth forest.

Taking a tentative step toward him, Lil reached up to his face, blue light wafting around them. Her fingertips grazed over his mouth. He was out on the rocks with her, tangible, not some dream to be pulled from.

His hand met her hair as he brought his face toward her, breathing in deep. With his head resting against hers, he let out an enormous sigh, releasing air that needed to be displaced that he might inhale again, to take in more of her. Lil knew, because she felt herself doing the same.

"How?" She whispered. "How is this not a dream?"

His scent was like the deep woods in a downpour; rich and intoxicating. Her fingers slid into his beard, just long enough for her to grip. Leaning into the hand on her neck, she burrowed her face behind his ear, finding warmth to how he smelled, like myrrh and cardamom.

"I've always been here," he whispered. "Since before there was a beginning. Before water, before light, I was with you."

The rainfall slowed; large, infrequent drops hitting the air around them.

"I *know* you," she whispered.

"And I know you."

She had so many questions but, for the moment, Lil just felt compelled to continue breathing, taking him into her, feeling him close, against her skin.

A Story in Stone

A distant banging noise called both their heads to turn up toward the deck where Claire stood, pounding her palm against one of the glass windows. Seeing that she finally had their attention, Claire put her arms out in a full body expression that screamed, *What in the hell is going on?*

"Claire," Lil whispered. "We were just about to leave, but I became overwhelmed and came out for some air... There's a lot happening right now, it might not be safe here."

He slid his hands across her shoulders to her neck. Pulling her toward him again, he whispered so close his lips brushed her ear, "There will be time for you to share everything, and for me to do the same."

"You were at the bar the other night. I felt you there, and I swear I could *smell* you. But then you were gone." *What happened?*

"Reluctantly, I found it was not the right time for us."

"*Remmond!*" The name flew out of her mouth as the thought entered her mind. "He was at the bar with you! I saw him days later at a school across the planet. Explain *that*."

"I was *incensed* by his proximity to you, and I was careless in my reaction."

The roar in her ears, from *inside* her.

"Though I was thankful," he went on, "for the opportunity to join you in the lake."

It hadn't been the sun alone. Somehow she'd known.

Claire's banging restarted at the glass door. Lil turned to see her cousin frantic and understandably annoyed, given she was out on the rocks with an unknown man after having just thwarted an abduction attempt in the forest.

"I have to explain who you are," Lil sighed, "but I don't have an explanation. And the dreams? Was that real, I mean, real for more than just me; were you there too?" She looked around, then back to his eyes. "How did you get here?" She placed her palm over his white collared shirt, felt the stone resting beneath. Shaking her head subtly as if shaking something away, she asked, "Who *are* you?"

"I am here, that's all she needs to know, and she can see that for herself." He let his eyes close, inhaling again from Lil's hair. "There is a great deal to be done now, things you need to remember, and for that we should be alone. We can go anywhere you're most comfortable, but you'll want to speak with her first, yes?"

Lil nodded. That she would go with him wasn't a question. An undeniable trust existed; though she didn't understand it.

Lil led them toward the house. She sensed him behind her, but the separation was uncomfortable.

"I'm not leaving you," he said. "I'll just be out on the deck."

Lil smiled, warmth blooming. Having him visible to someone other than herself was almost beyond comprehension.

Scowling, Claire opened the glass door, glaring over Lil's shoulder, presumably at the man chuckling under his breath outside.

"None of this is funny," Claire grumbled, closing the door, glaring at Lil expectantly and with dwindling patience.

"You want to say something," Lil said cautiously.

"Well," Claire began, and like a flood, the words and emotions poured from her. "There are people hunting you, apparently, and you start losing it, understandably, and so there's a storm... Magnus wants you out of here, but I couldn't get you to leave because you were out on the porch glowing. Nan gave me some cryptic instructions with an emergency number to call," she said, holding up the phone in her hand. "And I was dialing, but the next thing I know you're out there, engaged in some sort of electrified *necking* with a *stranger!*"

Claire was panting, exasperated as they moved into the kitchen, though Lil thought her cousin's reaction appropriate given the events she'd recapped.

"I don't think he's a stranger," Lil whispered. "Claire, he's the guy from the bar."

"Barn smell guy," Claire gasped, eyes wide. "*Dream* guy?"

Lil nodded, then heard his voice, deep and calm.

"There's no need to call the number Nan gave you," he said.

The women turned as he closed the door behind him, his movements smooth, yet Lil felt the impact of each step as he neared. Able to see his whole body now that she wasn't buried in his eyes and neck, she noticed the dark suit he wore over a white shirt. Was that a pocket square?

"I was at an event," he said, unbuttoning his jacket as he approached the kitchen island and placed the garment across the back of a chair. After rolling up his sleeves, he set his hands on Lil's hips, looked into her eyes, and said, "I need to speak with you at length, alone. Would you be more comfortable here, or would you rather go to Nan's so you can feel secure about your family's safety?"

Claire huffed, but said nothing.

"I should probably change," Lil said, looking down at her wet clothes.

"Are you cold?" He asked, with a knowing turn at the corner of his lip.

"No," she breathed.

"Of course not," he whispered, his hand stroking down to her leg. "Go ahead and change."

"You might be Dream Guy," Claire said to him, her frustration resurfacing. "But I am her *cousin;* and we are in the middle of a crisis that did not stop because of your sudden oceanside arrival."

"I'm not competing with you over who knows Lil better," he said, his voice calm, but firm. "And you are correct, there is a crisis. Something is happening which goes beyond you, beyond the atmosphere you've become safe in, and until her body stops drawing breath, I will not be leaving. Let's avoid this conflict and move on."

"Who even *are* you?"

"I am here."

"A name?"

"Call me Lu."

"Lu," Lil repeated. "I remember this name, from a dream or a song from long ago; like a memory on the other side of a veil."

He came so close; his eyelashes grazed her cheek. "My name is the sound of your breath," he whispered. "Others have been spoken over time, and I respond to them when convenient, but the vibration from your making, that was my first and only true name."

Lil felt sheer fabric layers fluttering over the universe that remained covered inside her. His words, the air from his mouth, they stirred something.

"Claire," she began, "I'll meet you at Nan's. We can follow you to there in my truck. I'll be right behind you."

"Do you feel safe though?" Claire asked, nodding toward Lu. "My brain says this doesn't add up, but it *feels*... it feels right somehow. Really, do you trust him to be alone together if I go? You're hardly defenseless, but I'll never forgive myself, and neither will Nan-"

"Yes." There was no hesitation.

"Then pack a bag," Claire said. "Tea, sketchbook, clothes, whatever you can pack in five minutes. I'll call Magnus from my jeep with an update, but I expect you to be *right* behind me. Five minutes." She let out a breath, letting the fear in her eyes show. "He was so scared Lil, and I am too."

"Go. I'll be five minutes behind."

Claire looked hesitant, but before she could protest further, Lil felt a brief rumble in Lu's chest. He went deadly still, seeming to be somewhere else for a moment before relaxing.

There was a knock at the door.

"Hey, kid," a familiar voice said from outside. "Heard you might need a hand. I'm going to try the door to see if it's open. If it is, I'm coming in. If it's locked, I'll try around back before I get creative."

She slid from Lu, passing Claire on her way to unbolt the door. When it had been cracked enough for him to move through, Gunnar pulled her into a secure hug, letting out a sigh of relief uncharacteristically vulnerable for him.

Lil turned in Gunnar's arms to assure Claire and Lu she was ok being touched by a man who was a stranger to them. Lu had a curious look on his face, and Claire… Did she *blush*?

One arm still around Lil; Gunnar used the other to pull a small, white paper bag from his jacket. She reached in, retrieving a piece of crystalized ginger.

"The others are candied grapefruit peels?" She asked.

He nodded. "The blonde is your cousin."

Lil nodded.

The corner of his mouth crept up into a smile as he continued his assessment. "Him. He looks like he wants to gut me, and could do it without moving. He's not adept at throwing knives by any chance?"

"You can call him *Lu*… and I suspect he's adept at everything," Lil mused.

"I don't doubt it," he said, focusing his eyes on hers, rubbing her shoulders. "Magnus gave me a need-to-know rundown of the situation, and I need to get you in my vehicle. Claire can ride with us or take her jeep, whatever you're comfortable with." He ticked his head toward Lu. "Is he with your cousin?"

"He's with me"

That sparked Gunnar's curiosity. *Really?* His eyes asked.

Lil nodded.

"No one with your cousin, then," he whispered.

"And you said nothing catches your eye..." She teased.

"I keep my eyes open to what the sun shines on."
"There's more than one of us out there then," Lil said, smile bright.
He pulled a candied peel from the bag and popped it in his mouth. "The sun doesn't shine on you kid; you make your own light. It's different."

Lil let his words sink in. The sun did shine on Claire, and it brought Lil a spark of joy to know Gunnar could see it. Their enchanted moment didn't last long, though, urgency surrounded them all, and an obligation hung in her workshop.

"I still have the deer out there," she sighed. "I should have just handled it before I showered, but-"

"Meat is in the freezer. Write down the address of the family and I'll deliver it myself if it means getting you moving."

Lil found herself momentarily speechless, and incredibly thankful.

"Lil and I will arrive at Nan's about five minutes or so after Claire," Lu said. "You're welcome to join us after your delivery."

Gunnar eyed him, trying to read the stranger's intentions, to gauge Lil's safety, but before he could respond, Lu spoke again.

"Message your employer and tell him of my presence here. Use my name, and describe this," he said, dipping his finger beneath the chain around his neck, and pulling a dangling stone out from under his shirt. A carved stone, that Lil and

Gunnar had seen sketched on centuries old paper, that she'd seen in her dreams. "Ask for reassurance of her safety, and you will receive it from him."

Gunnar, ever calm, was motionless save for his tightening grip on Lil.

"He's with me," she said, looking up at the dark eyes fixated on Lu's necklace and gently patting his chest. "Call Magnus."

Gunnar nodded and began entering a message into his phone.

"Lil," Claire said timidly, tapping at her own chest to reference the stone Lu wore.

Lil nodded, feeling the weight of what hung around her neck.

It wasn't a dream, she thought.

"Of course not," Lu answered, as if he had read her mind. She wouldn't put it past him. He'd been in her dreams, apparently, knew how to find her, knew…

"How do you know Magnus?" Lil asked. "From Remmond?"

Her unanswered question was followed by Gunnar's vibrating phone. He read the message silently, then looked up at Lu. Pausing to shake off the confusion, Gunnar looked back down at Lil.

"I'll make the delivery," He started. "Check in with Magnus. I'll see you at Nan's when I've finished."

Trust wasn't easy to come by with Gunnar, not where Lil's safety was concerned. It must have been some message Magnus had sent.

"Thank you," she said, her words heavy, reaching far. Then she smirked, and turned to her cousin. "Claire, would you give Gunnar a hand with the venison before you take off?"

Gunnar's face was almost blank. Almost. Lil saw the tiniest curl to the corner of his lips on one side.

Claire quickly closed the distance between them, wrapping her arms around Lil as Gunnar stepped back. "Have you ever had this many people in your house at one time?" She smiled.

Lil shook her head, eyes starting to fill.

"Turn off the dryer before you leave," Claire went on. "I don't think you're supposed to have a dryer running if you're not home; fire hazard or something."

Lil felt Claire's wet cheek on the side of her face, her own eyes leaking as well.

"Don't you get started," Claire laughed, wiping her eyes. "It *just* stopped raining."

"I'll see you at Nan's," Lil sniffed. "I'll be right behind you."

Claire grabbed her soaked jacket from beside the back door. Passing Lu upon return, her expression became quite serious.

"Lil is a brilliant mystery," she began. "Don't you *dare* underestimate her. She's also vulnerable, and if you hurt her body or try to tarnish her beautiful mysteriousness in any way, you will have the wrath of her family, and an international whatever Magnus is to deal with, not to mention Lil herself, who is a *tempest*. There will *literally* be earthquakes."

He chuckled at first but, to Claire's shock, his face became a map of sincerity as he reached for her shoulder.

"I hear you," he said, his voice calm, and low, and directed into her heart. "She is safe and I'm thankful that she has you. You appear formidable in your own right."

Claire nodded, letting loose a smile with a leftover sigh. "I've been known to wield stoneware with fury."

Lil laughed, leaned in for another hug with her cousin, and whispered, "Thank you."

"I'd like to say *anytime*, but please let's not do this again. I'm way too stressed out, and I'm sure Nan is gripping Brian's hand tight enough to break fingers. Todd is probably pacing with that bat, and it's doubtful his behavior will help Brian feel any safer. I'm half tempted to call Nan and have her send Brian home before I get back. He's really not cut out for all this."

"Nan… Can you call her? If I call her there will be too many questions. I can do questions when I see her, but not right now."

"Of course. See you soon. Love you."

Lil gave Claire one last squeeze. "Love you."

Claire nodded, and met Gunnar as he opened the front door with one hand, his other holding out a white bag toward her. She peeked inside and pulled out one of the ginger pieces.

"Stoneware fury?" Gunnar asked as they walked out. If Claire was able to glow the way Lil did, she would have surely lit the night on their way to the workshop.

Lil's hair began lifting slowly, followed by the sensation of breath on the back of her neck, a hand on her waist.

"Your friend that guards you, he is perceptive."

"I've known him almost my whole life," she said. "He works for Magnus, who you seem to know already. Magnus let me work in his lab when I was a kid as long as Gunnar was there with me. It evolved into errands, trips. He was with me at the school, by the lake. He was a student there. We have a great deal of trust between us. Gunnar has seen me when... during times that were challenging. I'm different from other people, and he's seen me when I've been different, when I've... Well, you saw the rain, and Claire wasn't joking about earthquakes. I'm sure you saw the light on my skin outside, but it was on you as well... was that from me?"

She felt his lips brush the skin between her shoulders, echoing throughout the rest of her.

"Mmmmm. You are about twenty minutes from Nan's by vehicle?" He asked.

"About twenty, twenty-five minutes, yes."

He released the cascade of her hair as she turned to face him.

"We have about twenty minutes then, and you really don't need to put too much in a bag. I can bring us back here any time, quickly, but it will be comforting to have some essentials, a change of clothing."

She looked down to the stone against his chest. The sketchbook had been some five hundred years old, the Chinese book older still. In her dream, he said that he'd *made* them…

"I carved them long ago," his deep voice rumbled. "That you might wear a piece of our story, even if you don't remember it."

"A promise to return what was forgotten…" she whispered, remembering what he'd once said. "A reminder that you would find me… *always*."

He'd *made* them. The stones told the story she was unable to remember; their story.

Nan's, they needed to get to Nan's.

"I should…" she starts, and Lu smiled.

"Go ahead," he said. "I'm not going anywhere."

Lil took a deep breath and continued down the hall, up the stairs to her room. What was going on? With each step she tried to put the pieces together.

He'd been in the bar, and in her dreams. Claire said she'd seen Lil become electric… Lil recalled inhaling his scent upon arrival, then stumbling into a stranger's barstool. He himself said he'd been in the lake with her somehow.

My true name is the sound of your breath. Who says that? And why did it seem *true*?

She peeled off her wet clothes, gathered new underwear, spares for the bag.

He'd been watching her before the bar, he must have. He'd known she'd be there. What else had he known? How long had he been watching?

Lil found another pair of those soft pants and put them in her bag, another sweater, pair of leggings, a top: in the bag they went. She grabbed a comfy, t-shirt dress, *and this too*, she thought, grabbing a black long-sleeved top. Stretchy and cotton, the garment fitted snug to her form, but the back was a crossover wrap style that left almost her entire back exposed. She loved the way air moved over her skin when she wore it.

Scanning her room, Lil saw the ragged book of Zen poems by the bed and placed it in her pack. Should she bring her favorite mug? No, she wasn't leaving forever, besides, Nan would have plenty.

She looked down at herself. Undergarments and a necklace. Right. She needed clothes on her body, not just in the bag.

Lil pulled on a dress with a v neck and draping short sleeves, cotton, form fitting, comfortable. After taking a few steps toward the open door, she looked down again, groaned, and rolled her eyes. Right. Shoes. She slipped into her dark leather boots and tucked a pair of flats in her bag, threw in a few more essentials.

The smell of apples wafted down the hall, with notes of rose and cinnamon. As she rounded the corner, a warm smile spread from her heart to her face.

The kitchen was clean. All of Claire's efforts with the chai had been put away, Lu standing there at the counter, in Lil's apron, straining fresh tea into a thermos.

"Apple with rose, pomegranate, and a little cinnamon," he said. Then, when Lil raised her eyebrows, delighted as she gave the apron a once-over, he shrugged. Reaching behind, he untied the strings, pulled the garment off, brought it up toward his face and inhaled.

"Smells like you," he smiled.

Lil stood there, warm cheeks and warm heart, watching as he screwed the top on a thermos, and handed her a round cup made of stone.

"You…" She said, fragrant steam reaching her chin. "You left that here."

He nodded once.

She remembered another dream, of hands grinding into rock, talk of someone drinking… She thought it had prompted her to manifest the cup, but it had been him.

"You made it."

"I made it for you," he said. "The scent of the ocean is still there, through the tea, in the stone."

Lil drank, eyes on Lu until they closed. He'd left some part of himself for her to find. He'd been in her home, knew where she was. Why hadn't he stayed?

Lil felt heat from more than the drink moving through her, eyes almost heavy as she breathed him in over the tea. His hand settled on her arm, moved up to her shoulder, then down, slowly, his thumb passing the inside of her elbow, her wrist. He took the stone cup from her hand, drank the remaining liquid, and placed it on the island.

"Do you feel like this to other people," she breathed, humming with electric potential.

"No."

"I've never experienced this with another person. I didn't think it was possible."

"With another, it isn't," he said, examining her face. "Explaining it is always delicate, challenging, and can be hard for you, for both of us, especially when you've not yet woken." He rubbed his hands up from her wrists to her shoulders, up her neck and under her hair.

She leaned in, smelling the skin on his arm, closing her eyes. "You say that like you've done it before..." she whispered. She'd heard him say that, that she needed to wake. She thought she was, with her abilities escalating, though the dreams... the dreams had been him.

"I'll explain everything, but we need more time. Once at Nan's, you'll be reassured that your family is safe, we can rest and be alone. Unless you'd like to stay here?"

"No. I want Nan to see that I'm okay; to be there in case there's any trouble."

He still didn't know about the woods, the men she'd encountered there...

"I didn't tell you," she sighed. There was so much he didn't know.

"Later," he nodded.

Lil sighed again, slid from him, and switched off the dryer.

"I just need to grab my travel paints. I have little palette that opens and closes like a book. Two watercolor pens fit in there; they have brush tips and hold water inside." She realized she was rambling a bit, which wasn't like her. "I have trouble with sleep sometimes," she added, selecting what she needed from a shelf in her living room. "Not the dreams you're in, but other, *unsettling* ones.

People dying, chaos. I had one earlier where I was little girl on a boat with my parents. There was a storm. We all drowned, I think."

Lu was very still as she spoke, as though no air passed through him while he listened.

"It helps me," she continued, placing the items in her bag, "having the ocean near, or to paint it. It's like my memory from the experience goes in the painting and then seeps into my dreams, soothing me. I've helped other people with them too," she smiled. "Magnus is nearly dependent on them."

Lu stalked toward her slowly, as not to disturb her vulnerability.

She wanted his closeness, her heart speeding up as he approached. When the space between them decreased such that he could reach out and touch her, he gently took the bag from her hands, placed the empty stone cup and thermos inside, then put the strap over his shoulder. Resting his hand on her chest, the time between her heart beats lengthened, her breath easing.

"Soon, you'll have a better understanding of why you are sought after," he said, voice calm and smooth. "What has been done to keep you safe, and what work there is yet to do."

His body moved closer, a hand sliding into her hair, followed by his face, leaning in. As she renewed her sense of his smell, she heard his inhale, and knew he was doing the same.

His hand moved down to hers as he guided her to the back door.

"Lights off?"

She nodded.

They made their way down to the rocks where they'd met, and his arms went around her, tight. Her hands went up to his neck, and his breath to her ear.

"You didn't drive here," she whispered.

"No."

25.

The roaring around her was like the ocean surf in a great storm.

Followed by stillness.

This period of transition lasted only an instant, but time stretched. In that calm silence, Lil felt weightless, felt more space between the particles of her self, more of *him* drifting into her. Then the crashing waves returned in her ears, only to disappear once more, the roar replaced by the sounds of Nan's orchard.

Lu's arms remained around her and, as her eyes adjusted, she saw his left hand outstretch to catch an apple, several others falling to the ground.

"There are vibrations with this type of movement, sounds like thunder," he said, then took a bite of the apple and closed his eyes. "I remember my first taste of apple, the lineage of seeds that brought us here, to this fruit."

He opened his eyes, moss and earth-colored windows into the darkness, into the forever before, forever after.

"Do you remember the first time you tasted an apple?" He asked.

She moved a hand from his chest to his shoulder, then down his arm to the fruit he held, brought his hand to her mouth. Breathing in the sweetness of the exposed flesh tangled with the smell of his skin, she sank her teeth in and closed her eyes.

Memories crept, then rushed into her, fragmented.

A Story in Stone

She picked apples with Nan, baked tarts. Todd caught Claire as she slipped on apple peels in the kitchen, they all laughed. Pressing her cheek against bark in the orchard, she listened, reaching for something. Running through trees in the mist before dawn. She was a child, holding a seed, covering it with dirt in Nan's garden, sinking into the dirt with it. Then her hands were no longer a child's, two hands held hers, covered in earth. Lu. They were planting, swimming in the ocean. Life blossomed in her breath and at her fingertips, knowledge, all of it. She ran through fruit trees, but not Nan's. She planted, but had mixed blood with the soil to form a new seed.

Lil's eyes flashed open.

"We were together," she whispered. "I was a child, but I was grown before that. I'm not sure I understand what I just saw. Was it a metaphor for something? Like a dream?"

"We planted a garden together," he said. "And it was beautiful. But then we were asked to plant a very different seed. We, who knew everything, did not see what would come next."

Interrupted by footsteps, they turned to see Nan, Claire, and Brian through the apple trees.

Nan gasped when she saw them. Hand hovering over her mouth, she stopped short, then crept slowly forward. Tears blooming in her eyes, she went not to Lil, but to Lu.

"It's been at least twenty years," she whispered hesitantly.

Lil's released him, confusion settling in.

"Your body isn't a day older," Nan marveled, putting her hands on his face. "Claire tried to describe what happened at Lil's, and when she said your name I, well... I hoped."

"I knew you would keep her safe," he whispered. "Thank you."

A pang shot through Lil's chest.

"Me," she interrupted. "You mean me, I'm the one that Nan kept safe. You knew I was here the whole time? You two know each other?" She looked between Lu and the old woman, confused and agitated, waiting for a response.

Nan looked from Lu to Lil. "Sweetie," she sighed. "He's the one who brought you here."

Brian and Claire's mouths dropped open simultaneously. Brian's eyes darted around, Claire's focus steady on Lil.

The unsettling stillness was short-lived.

Leaves rustled, wind sweeping up the ends of Lil's hair. Looking into Lu's waiting eyes, she said, "You *left* me here."

Lu stood observant as Nan stepped forward, expression worried. "Lil, honey, slow down. Let's go inside, have some tea and talk it over."

The wind became fierce, carrying leaves through the air, wet and sticking to their clothes.

"Are you trying to *calm me?*" Lil asked, furious. Lu had acted like he'd *just* found her weeks ago, that the timing hadn't been right... but he'd known she was at Nan's the whole time, her whole *life*. And Nan knew. Nan knew someone understood her story; knew who she was and why she felt so damn different. Why had he left her? Nan was loving, and wonderful, but why did he *leave?*

"Lil," he said, his voice resonant and soothing. "I told you, this can be delicate and challenging."

"Yes, *that* you told me."

She wanted to lean into his voice. She wanted to lean into him and just rest, but she was too livid, couldn't let go. She needed space.

Something rumbled, the sky or the ground.

"I'm going to take a walk," she said, her voice too calm. "You can stay here and catch up with *Nan*."

"I left before out of necessity, but that time has passed, and I won't leave you again. I'll be here when you are ready, but we will speak, and you *will* remember."

The rattling leaves quieted, the furious writhing of Lil's hair slowing until her tresses rested against her body. Taking a step forward, she walked past Lu, more than half hoping he'd reach out and touch her skin, that she might permit herself to stop, to stay.

Just a few minutes, she told herself. *Just a few minutes to take a breath.*

She continued beyond him, her family, the trees, and the garden, until she found herself in the room above the barn. Weary, she collapsed on the bed.

Digging her face into the blankets, Lil curled up, took a deep muffled breath and exhaled. Through the building liquid in her eyes, she looked out the balcony to the clearing sky. Spreading her limbs wide, Lil envisioned the roof ceiling absent, night blanketing her.

I am the mountain, she thought. *I am the sky.*

Deep breath, in and out.

Lu said he'd brought her to Nan's for safety, but *why?* Why did he know her as a child? And his cryptic answers about always knowing her… what *was* that?

His smell clung to her. Bringing a palm to her face, Lil inhaled the remaining scent of apple and Lu.

Do you remember the first time you tasted an apple? His voice echoed in her memory. *I've always been here… before there was a beginning. Before water, before light…* His words in her mind and his scent overwhelmed her.

Before light, she thought, seeing his face with her eyes closed, seeing herself with him, swimming in darkness, powerful and undulating in the water.

The sound of footsteps and Nan's breath called Lil back to where her body rested in real time.

With a steaming mug, of course, Nan took the last step and stood waiting, shoulders heavy and eyes tired.

"It's been a long day, hasn't it?" Nan sighed.

"Yeah," Lil managed with a wet laugh and a sniffle.

The bed sank under the old woman's small fame, then familiar fingers began combing through Lil's hair.

"I made you some tea."

Lil took a deep breath in through her runny nose peeked into the cup.

"Chai. You had enough time to make this?"

"Oh, please... We've had a pot going since Claire walked through the door. As you can imagine, *walking* does not accurately describe how she entered the house."

Lil curled to put an arm around the old woman, placing her head in her lap. That she'd caused an ache in Nan's heart weighed heavy.

"I'm sorry," Lil whispered into Nan's sweater. "I know I hurt your feelings, and I'm sorry. I'm upset that he left me, and I don't understand why he did, or who he even is, but I'm glad to have you in my life. I love you, and couldn't possibly want to take any of it back. I can't know what my life would have been like otherwise, but I have known love here because of you."

"I'm thankful for you every day," Nan said, stroking her hair. "I don't know how you came to be in this world, but I know the world is better for it. I'm better for it." With the faintest hint of a break in her voice, she said, "I think it's time I told you the story."

26.

"It was about twenty-six years ago," Nan started. "I was hiking a trail to the shore where we'd scattered Grampa Pat's ashes three years prior. The weather had been pleasant when I started off, but the sky darkened suddenly, angry with rain and thunder. When the trees opened to the shore, I saw a young man out there on the beach. He was distraught, shouting out to the ocean and up into the rain, as if the sky had wronged him. The turmoil rippling off of him was... it was just heart wrenching.

"I made my way down the rocks, through the downpour, and I did what any mother would do. I gave him a hug. He slumped over, sobbed into my shoulder. This big man was so broken. I asked what was hurting him, and when he calmed enough to speak, he told me he'd just lost his wife. My heart ached for his loss, and I explained about Grampa Pat, but to be so young...

"Thinking our meeting serendipitous, I asked if he'd like to walk back to my car, and he was so inclined. We went quite a ways in silence, then he asked about Grampa Pat. I talked a bit, then asked the young man about his wife. He described her as having been with him always, that her loss left him with a disorienting sense of homesickness.

"When we got to my car I asked if he'd driven out this way. He said no and, well, I felt compelled to continue our conversation. He welcomed my invitation to accompany me back to the shop. We drank tea, walked the garden, the field, and I showed him where I planned to plant the apple orchard." Nan smiled, raising her eyebrows, rubbing Lil's leg for emphasis.

"To my surprise and delight, I'd found myself a skilled arborist who, it turned out, was looking for a change and a distraction."

Nan sighed and looked around the room, hand still resting on Lil's leg. "Lu stayed here, in this room. It wasn't a bedroom at the time, but he made quick work of the renovations. Couldn't have been more than a day before it was habitable."

"The bed smells like him," Lil whispered.

"You came up here *constantly* as a child. Even now, like a moth to the proverbial flame, but I just-"

"He planted the orchard?"

"Yes. I'd planned to go to a nursery for trees, but he insisted he just needed seeds, so we went apple picking. Can you imagine?" She smiled. "I thought he was insane, that it would take far too long and we should just get the baby trees, but I indulged him. We went out to an orchard, picked a variety of apples, and kept the seeds from the ones we liked best. Those were the ones he planted."

Nan's thoughts drifted to the rain that night, that it still rained when he'd gone out with the little jars of seeds in the morning. She'd offered to help, but he'd declined, said the work would bring a sense of therapeutic nostalgia he preferred to be experience in solitude. She'd watched him from the garden, though, as he knelt down on the wet ground, his hands sinking into the earth up to his wrists. The clouds cleared, sun shining on back of his damp t-shirt. From his submerged hands sprouted a seedling, roughly a meter tall. He removed himself slowly, carefully patting the mud before moving to the site of the next tree. She wasn't sure how long it took him to finish, but it wasn't yet lunch when he walked through the door of the shop with clean clothes and washed hands. Nan accompanied him out to the orchard, astonished to find rows of trees, hundreds of them. *This isn't the first time I've grown trees from seed,* he'd said. *You want to ask how, but I won't tell you, and this not knowing will be an understanding between us.*

As Nan steeped in her thoughts, Lil found herself longing to have known Lu then, almost jealous of the time Nan had spent with him. She thought of Lu planting the seeds, feeling the soil in her own hands.

"From seed?" Lil asked. "They must have taken a while to grow..."

She knew, though, from Nan's description, and from her own experience. When she was little, she'd wanted to grow her own tree. She'd settled down in the garden among the mint and lemon balm, eating an apple from the orchard. After digging a modest hole, she'd taken a deep bite into the core, picked open the seed chamber, and shook one out into her hand. Closing her fingers around it, she wished life into it, that it would grow big and strong and beautiful. She dropped the little brown seed into the hole and carefully covered it up, resting her hands on top, sending warmth to it. Her seedling appeared the next day.

"The trees were three meters by sunrise," Nan continued. "Covered in flowers a few days later, flowers that turned to fruit." The old woman ran her fingers gently through Lil's hair. "You have the same power in you, Lil: creation, life. Whatever it is, you have it. I've seen it."

Lil closed her eyes, sorting through a flood of memories while trying to steady her breaths, focus on the fingers threading through her hair.

"Why did he leave?" Lil asked. "I don't remember him living here when I was little." She let out a big sigh, and continued. "I have such detailed memories from my whole life here, even as a child, but it's like parts are foggy. And Lu is so familiar, but only from memories, like dreams. I had a dream of my parents on a boat, and people were coming for us. I caused a storm and then I was underwater but... I think his smell was there on the ship, before things went black."

"He stayed on here for about eight or nine months, then he had to go. Said he'd found someone very important to him, needed to go to them, and wasn't sure he'd ever be back. Years passed, but we did see each other again... He returned about five years later, with a little girl." Nan paused as Lil turned and met her eyes. "He came back with you."

The stillness was so thorough, Lil thought her heart had stopped.

"I woke to a loud sound in the middle of the night," Nan said. "It was gone when my eyes opened, then I heard a light knocking on the door. When I got downstairs, Lu was standing there. He'd let himself in, and he was holding you, your tired head on his shoulder. He followed me to one of the guest bedrooms, and when he put you down in the bed, my heart ached. I saw his profound concern. I thought he was your father, but he told me your parents had died. When he released you from his arms, I saw how painful it was for him to let go of you, like he wasn't sure he'd hold you again, and it hurt him deeply somehow. Then he told me why he'd come…

"He had all the adoption paperwork. *Everything.* I was worried, of course, what with child trafficking. What if you'd had family looking for you? I'd known Lu for less than a year, but in that time, I found him to be sincere, deep, caring. Yes, he was mysterious, but not deceptive, or with malicious intention. I trusted him, and I still do. So, while there were unanswered questions about your origin, I agreed to take you as my family, and I don't believe there's anything that could make me regret my decision."

"What did I have to say about it all?" Lil asked. "Was I sad? Did I want to stay with him? Did he want to stay with *me*?"

"You were in a deep sleep, sweetie."

"And he just *left* me with you?" Lil demanded. "He didn't wake me up? He didn't say goodbye? Did he say *anything*?" She paused, angered for what fear the little girl must have felt, the sense of abandonment, but when she reached back to her beginning, Lil found the tension in her chest eased.

"I don't remember being afraid," she said. "I knew I was safe, that I was supposed to be with you."

"I didn't sleep a wink that first night, for wanting to be there when you woke. I put the poetry book he left on the nightstand, and some lavender." Nan smiled and shook her head. "No, not a wink all night, but when dawn crept through the window, I must have nodded off in the chair. I woke to your sweet voice and your little hand on my knee. You told me that I felt kind, that everything would be ok, and then you asked if I knew how to make scones," Nan laughed. They both did.

"He said you were special, *gifted*, and that you would be connected to nature in a way that was beautiful but frightening at times. He said with you being a child, you'd need someone patient and loving, someone calm to help you stay grounded. I asked what I should tell you, what I should tell people, my family and friends, when I suddenly had a child in my care. Things like that wouldn't go unnoticed around here, and I'm not one to make up stories," she sighed. "He said to tell what truth I knew: that your parent's died tragically, and their only contact was a mutual friend who was unable to take you at the time. There was a lot of speculation circulating around after your arrival, of course. Some guessed your parents lived off grid up north and fell to nature in the form of snow, bear, or illness."

"You told me not to believe anything I heard," Lil whispered with a chuckle. "Because no one knew as much as you did, and you didn't know much more than you'd already told me."

"That's right," Nan smiled. "But I did know more, and for that I'm sorry, though I think it was for the best. Lu said you'd be sought after for your gifts. Said that the death of your parents wasn't an accident, and there were people looking for you. He conveyed that, while it would be a risk for me if they discovered you here, I was the best chance for you to stay safe. He gave me a number to call, if there was ever an emergency. The other night, with the man asking about your artwork, and the other one harassing Claire... It was the first time I considered dialing, but I hesitated."

"The boat in my dream earlier tonight... There were men with guns coming for us; for me and my parents."

"He didn't mention the boat, but given what I know now, it's entirely possible your dream was a memory."

"I don't understand why he didn't tell me any of this. Why didn't he tell me about my parents? Why don't I *remember* them? Why did he leave me? And if he's not one of my parents, who *is* he?"

"These are good questions, and you have a right to answers, but I'm not the one who can give them to you. Maybe an uncle or a cousin? You do share rather unusual traits."

Lil could smell him around her, on the bed, on her hands, felt echoes of the electric glow over her skin, the sensation of drifting into his words.

"He doesn't feel like an uncle or a cousin," she sighed. "I am connected to him in a way I can't effectively explain with words. Not just emotionally, but, on my skin, and in my blood. We were both *glowing*, Nan. He feels like home... In a different way than you are my home."

"Talk to him," Nan pressed. Then, inspecting Lil with the eye of a seasoned parent, she asked, "When's the last time you ate?"

"Hunting snacks?" Lil winced.

Nan shook her head. "Unusual day or not, you *must* take better care of yourself. I put together a tray of chicken pot pie to eat with Claire and Brian. With all that's been going on I didn't get around to putting it in the oven earlier, but it's baking now over at the house. Claire and Brian are there, Todd's closing up the shop. I don't know where Lu is, but I'll send him over if I see him. When I left, he was walking alone through the orchard, but I have no doubt he'll make his way in eventually, if you let him. You two need to find your way together so we can move on with our lives, plot our next steps so we can all stay safe."

Lil nodded into Nan's chest as the old woman's arms came around her again. She had so much to think about, but the idea of family, food, and familiarity soothed.

The need for fresh air pulled Lil toward the balcony after Nan left... And maybe she wanted to see if she could spot Lu.

Searching the darkness, Lil found the rain had gone, but the earth was still damp. It smelled good, but he wasn't there. Disappointed, figuring she should go down to find him since she had been the one who'd left.

She turned to go back in, then she felt it, the sudden feeling of something behind her, something other than the shop, the orchard, or the universe. She felt *him*.

She rotated her body out to the night and stepped back, continuing into the room as she took in the full scope of him. Bare-chested but for the necklace that mirrored hers, Lu came into view not from below, but from above.

The span of his wings massive.

He glided down and stood before her on the balcony with what looked like his shirt and coat in the bend of his arm, the bag she'd forgotten in his hand. His wings folded up behind him, then back into the nothingness they came from, Lil watching in awe.

"You have no shirt on," she whispered. "And you have wings."

He laid his shirt and coat on the bed and rested her pack next to them before stalking toward her.

"I didn't want the fabric ripping."

"Have you always had them?"

313

"Always," He replied.

Lost for words, she stared at him, heart drumming as he moved in closer.

"You don't question my transporting us from the ocean to the orchard in the blink of an eye, but the wings?"

"Why didn't you *transport* in here the same way?"

"Things can shake. Its best outdoors."

"Why the wings?"

"Because they're beautiful," he breathed. "And it feels good."

His smell combined with the night air, his proximity, distracting her.

Lil leaned into his hand as it came up her neck, slid to the side of her face. "You built the balcony, didn't you," she asked. "Was it so you could come and go this way at night?"

"Yes."

"Nan said it only took you a day to build it."

"So it did."

"A gardener and a carpenter, planting orchards and building balconies in just one day."

"They say the earth took only six, or haven't you heard that rumor. And it seems I'm not the only one adept at planting trees..."

"I need to know how I know you," she whispered, feeling as though she was losing her mind. "We need to talk about us."

"I thought we were."

She inhaled sharply as his hands went under her thighs, scooping her up, her legs encircling his waist. "You said you'd help me remember something lost."

Pressing her back against the barn boards, he brought his mouth to her ear. "I need to *tell* you the story of who you are, before I show you."

27.

He set her down on the edge of the bed, then slowly slid the boots off her feet. Then, crouching barefoot before her, looked into her eyes, and began.

"I've told you this story over one hundred times; hoping each would be the last. The process can be overwhelming, but I'm here with you, and Nan is just across the garden making dinner with your family."

Relax, she thought, but with the looming nature of his speech, and his use of the word *hundred*, Lil found herself apprehensive. Another cup of tea would have helped; the ritual warmth of it flowing into her, the steam on her face.

"Lie down and take a few breaths," he suggested.

Hundreds, she repeated behind closed eyes. He took a few steps away, a brief wave of anxiety passing through Lil over his absence, until she heard pouring liquid, and opened her eyes. From the thermos in his hand, hot tea flowed into the stone cup. He put his lips to the rim, took a sip, and brought the vessel to her. Crouching by the bedside once more placed what she had silently asked for into her hands.

Leaning in, he cupped her cheek as she drank, the contact warmer than the tea.

Slowly he slid his hand down her neck, then back to himself.

"I want to acknowledge that your family is real," he said.

As her eyes moved from the depths of the steam to his, Lil considered the puzzled look she must have had on her face. Of course they were *real*.

"Nan, Claire, and your parents before; that love is authentic, and the connection has value. They've wiped tears, provided comfort, laughed with you. They are your family, but one that will occupy a fragment of breath in the scope of your existence. I mean not to dwarf their importance, but to put things in perspective. It can be challenging to think of existing in time that spans beyond life on earth. With numbers that large, meaning can get lost, but time does not go away, neither before nor after the human lifespan."

She felt him looking at her, into her. His hand went to hers where it rested on the bed, and he smiled. "We came here billions of years ago, sowing seeds of life, as is our way. When we returned, the oceans were so beautiful. We swam for a time, watching our seeds grow, evolve into new lifeforms. Then, it was decided we would create something new. We were to build an orchard."

The orchard. We. *The royal we?*

"We," He whispered. "You and I."

She set the cup down, glanced back into his eyes, and nodded once for him to continue.

"We were to create a new species, one capable of regarding itself, of tending to the place we built. Our seeds would have *evolved* into such a creature, but the command was given."

"Who decided this?" she asked. "And how could I have been there… I remember being a child."

"There were ten of us, eleven I suppose, but you and I count as one: unique in being a pair. The ten of us facilitate creation," he said, pausing to inhale, closing his eyes. "There is a *guiding entity* not counted among the ten." His face looked pained as he continued. "For this new species, you did what only you were capable of… And one male subject was created in the new way, a reflection of the forms we favor for ourselves." He shook his head. "But this new animal was to be shorter lived, vulnerable, as other animals were. The only one of his kind, he was not compatible with other, similar species that had already evolved here, and a choice was made... A choice you and I were not a part of, a choice that led to dissent, and the dissolution of the ten."

She strained for a memory that barely came, of an orchard that wasn't Nan's.

"It's important that I lay the framework of the story. You're more able to receive your memories this way."

Lil nodded, and he continued.

"It was...*decided*..." he said bitterly, "that you were to pair with the subject, to jumpstart and strengthen the species."

The tears forming in his eyes matched her own.

Lil inhaled a sharp breath, a gust of wind building, blowing through the open balcony door, through her hair. "Why, why weren't seeds used in the *new way* you mentioned, like what was done for the male?"

"There was nothing standard about what we did where this endeavor was concerned. Even after all this time, I'm torn between questioning what happened and moving forward."

"The pairing... Did... Did I...?"

"No, you certainly did not."

Lu leaned in, massaging his thumbs into her palms as he continued. "The creature came to you, as was his instinct as a male. You didn't fault him for this, as he knew nothing, nor did you engage, physically. You were irate, as was I, and several others. Most of us were not made aware until after the match was attempted. You could have facilitated a much cleaner set had you been asked to do so from the beginning, by forming the pair *together*. Instead, given your failure to pair with the creature, the others were forced to do what should have been done to start with, though they're far inferior in this capacity. They made alterations to his marrow to create a female of the same species. And this imperfect formation was not the first failure. These new creatures were different than the other animals, required guidance where the others had instinct, but no help had been given to them. We returned after the fallout and taught creatures how to grow food from seed, how to hunt when necessary, to make shelter, clothe themselves for protection. We gave them the choice to leave the garden, and the tools to do so."

"These creatures," Lil started, already knowing...

"Humans."

"And the garden was..."

"Yes, that garden."

She looked down, one of her hands on the stone around her neck, eyes once again locking with his. "The creation story."

He nodded. "Your defiance, by not mating with the creature, resulted in a reduction of numbers for the ten. You and I left, along with several others: Remi, from the bar and the school, Uri you met with a shower of glass as I watched from the street. Az still longs to see you. He and Uri had been affectionately jealous of your unexpected encounter with Remi at the school. Remi has been made to retell the details of his experience countless times, as has Uri with the bakery. The others, you must understand, while the connection isn't the same as what you and I share, it's love, and they miss you."

She remembered the sense of knowing, of unexplainable familiarity.

"As you can imagine, leaving a group as unique as ours was challenging. We left the ten, but there was a complication. For your defiance, you were afflicted with mortality, though your youth and longevity remain intact. Initially, you lived for hundreds and hundreds of years, unaffected. Eventually, as the human population grew, so did their stories, mythology, and their fear. You were basking in the glory of the moon, sharing a dream with me while I swam when they beheaded you."

Lil's hand flew to her mouth as she gasped, then she brought it up to rest on his cheek. Tears in her eyes, rain pattering the floor by the open balcony door, her heart was breaking for him.

"What did you do?" She asked, hesitantly.

"I killed them all," he said, still and remorseless, with fire in his eyes. "I could have suffocated them from a distance, taken their breath, or stopped their hearts... but instead, I shredded them with my claws and teeth. The extended death I provided left an imprint of fear in their souls as they slipped through my fingers. I've seen to it that they continue on with this terror, haunted by the echoes of their choices. None escaped, though I did allow two to live for a time after that day, that they could tell others their story."

"Lu... she hesitated. "Your name..."

"I told you my true name, but there have been others."

"*Lucifer,*" she whispered.

"That is one of them. And Lilith was one of yours. It seems to have made an impression, as you return to it often."

Her mind reeling, Lil tried to hang on to the truth of him, but that name... She knew that name.

"Was I bad? Had I done something? Is that why they..."

Lu closed his eyes, brought her hand to his mouth and inhaled deep from her palm, his lips gliding softly over her skin.

"You were an angel," he whispered. "Life *and* death are part of the balance, and you've been both, but you were never bad. "

"Then *why?*"

"We'd never harmed them. We *created* them... But their fear of the unknown, fear of the powerful, combined with their ignorance… They're not *just*, as the other animals are. They blamed you for the death of their children."

"Why would I kill children?"

"You wouldn't, you didn't. A sick infant died. The mother hid her baby out of shame she'd done something wrong, and fear from the child's father. The illness spread, as did the *disappearances*, and the stories."

Lil felt his pain as her own, and perhaps it was hers too, sadness for the loss of time they could have been together as they once were. She'd died… but then she'd been a child.

"I felt your soul as soon as it returned."

"Returned?"

"Yes. Our connection is unbreakable. I find you every time."

"*Hundreds of times*, you said. There was a before… I came back before. And I died, again... and again." She just couldn't fathom that loss, the cycle of feeling it repeatedly.

"Your soul returned and you were born through a human, though human you are not. Altered by your soul at conception, your DNA reflects nothing of your biological parents. You look the same every time, smell the same." He leaned in, taking a deep breath from her hair, then smirked as he looked to the falling water through the open balcony door. "You bring your depth down as rain and wind the same. You have a different upbringing every time, adding to a universe of memories that make you who you are."

"I've been homesick for you my entire life. If you felt me when I came back, why didn't you find me right away? Why didn't you stay when I was little, when you brought me here?"

"I came before you were born and helped your parents understand the gift they'd been given. They embraced their responsibility, and I watched you from a distance, and in your dreams. You are supremely powerful, but still mortal. You're vulnerable, especially in childhood, and we've been through this enough times to know its best if we have limited interaction as you develop. Our togetherness draws attention..."

"So, I grow up as a normal child?"

"As normal as you can manage. In this life, I rescued you at sea, but your parents perished."

"Why don't I remember them, or anything from before you left me with Nan, or our thousands of years together?"

"More than thousands," he said plainly.

Lil raised her eyebrows for him to continue; only partially amused by his comment. She'd seen flashes recently, the beaded dress at the museum, the dream of her parents.

"Your memories become muted when you are reborn, much of your abilities are dimmed as well, but only for a time. Everything creeps back in eventually, though this cycle has taken an unusually long time."

"And when you brought me to Nan's?"

"My interference. I thought only to give you a fresh start, knowing what was yours would be returned in time."

Lil's breath quickened with the sensation that she was missing something, wasn't whole. She knew in her heart and somewhere deeper that Lu was trustworthy, but still, she felt unsettled by idea that some part of her wasn't hers, that she could be denied access to her own self. Why had he needed to rescue her, though, in the first place?

"Why were the men in boats coming for me?"

"Returning to you already, it seems. Somehow you were found by an organization that has been hunting you for several of your lifetimes. They've seen your unique qualities and wish to use you as a weapon."

The feel of his hand moving over hers, over her wrist and forearm, it quieted her heart before it began to race again.

"When I was hunting..." she began "Two men found me in the woods, but one of them, John, seemed to know me, like we'd met before."

"They'd probably been sent to scout out rumors of your location and told not to take risks. *John*, it seems, did not learn his lesson. His cousin was killed in an attempt to secure you over a quarter century ago. In his rage, young John damaged your body beyond repair. His organization was not pleased, nor was I," he said with a long, dark sigh. "And then there are the Guards of Eden..."

Lil squinted; the name unfamiliar.

"An ancient, self-appointed group of misinformed fanatics who think we're evil and need to be eliminated. There are those among them with visions and predictive dreams, though it has not always been this way. In the early years, we lived long among the people in between attacks, but at some point, the *Guards* began knowing where you'd be. As you can imagine, the trait is useful to their cause, and they inbreed for it. We've learned through experience and extensive interrogation that they seem to have no knowledge of your whereabouts until exposure to you has occurred. It's then that you begin to appear in their visions. There is another trigger, though... You and I, the explosive nature of our togetherness in waking life has led to your discovery."

"So, we've lived apart."

"So, we've lived apart," he nodded. "But we can only manage for so long. There's either an incidental discovery or your memories begin to return on their own. This cycle has been our longest separation. It has been... trying."

Lil hadn't been aware of what she missed, but she sensed the absence, felt the longing. Where had Lu lived while he waited? And what of the others? Those who'd stayed with her, and those who hadn't?

"What became of the ones who didn't side with us in the garden?"

322

"You won't need to see them. There was a flood once and we, the former ten, worked together, *loosely*. It would not have been as successful without you, and the tactics used to ensure your assistance were unnecessarily brutal. They should have trusted... A story for another time," he sighed.

"A flood..." she said, feeling the storm inside her. "*The* flood?"

"Yes. Death is part of balance, and the humans are not like other animals. They sought to conquer life around them instead of thriving as a part of it, and we saw the path they'd been on. Their imbalance was a threat to what we'd created."

His face had come incredibly close to hers, his warmth sliding along her cheek until his lips reached her ear.

"Our creation," he whispered.

The words resonated with her as sound and fractured memories of the garden, the ocean, the stones they wore and the lives they'd lived.

"You know enough," he said, bracing one of his arms on the bed, his body forming a blanket of comfort over her, the bluish flame of a fire that did not burn ghosting around his skin, and hers.

"Enough, for what?" She asked.

"Enough to remember."

His lips eased against hers, soft pressure, opening. They stayed together as she rolled onto her back, as Lu lowered himself, pressing them into the place where he had slept, and she had wondered, for years.

With a great rush of air, she was in his arms on the balcony. She pulled back from his face, dizzy from the movement, their connection, and the memory of a place beyond words.

"Where are we going?" She gasped.

"Up."

28.

A vibration worked from Lu's chest as his lips moved against Lil's, opening something within her as they rose through the air, and she tumbled into her own mind.

Her hair rested cool down her back, damp from a recent swim. The smell of herbs, flowers, and fresh water scented the air, her pale skin catching streams of light as she walked through the trees. Of the life evolved from what she'd placed in the ground, some forms no longer existed. Others had a great deal of promise. Plants, animals, fungi, and the tiny things, she delighted in them all, for what they were, and for what they would someday become.

Once seeds were planted, the work of gardening began. The others like her lacked the brilliance she had for creating life, but they tended well what grew, each in their own way. Life continued on its own once started, but with the subtle changes a gardener provided, it thrived.

A successful garden required little intervention, but the new creature was the only one of his kind, and needed assistance. His predisposition for curiosity and aptitude for wonderment were promising, though there were concerning signs she hoped could be managed. Lil had taken elements from a being that already walked the earth, and combined them with material from her own kind, forming this new creature that did not evolve through ages into the balance, but came suddenly as an outsider. The fusion was an unprecedented request, but one she obliged, as refusing would have also been unprecedented.

She came upon him observing his own reflection in a pond and, when he became aware of her presence, he rose to his feet and stared. Bipedal, he stood the same height as she, but not as lean, skin not as smooth. The hair on his head fell shaggy, his body unclothed.

After spending his first night alone, he looked at her differently than he had the day before. He looked at her with heat.

His error was unfortunate, but unsurprising given his biology. Lil's form appeared similar to what his female counterpart might have been, had she been allowed to create the pair together.

"Your belief that I intend to couple with you is an understandable mistake," Lil said as she approached.

The animal continued toward her, unaffected by her words.

"He said you are my mate," the creature replied.

He.

Lil ceased her advance, putting a hand out for the animal to stop.

Michael has done something, *she said through her mind, quickly hearing a low, male voice respond.*

Uri just informed me. He was livid.

The ground shook under her feet. Trees swayed, and the creature cowered as Lu stormed out from what appeared to be thin air. His wings flared, eyes wide, like moss growing on rotting wood where hers were an ocean storm. There was no pause in his stride as he approached her, one hand finding its place firmly on her hip, his other sliding up behind her neck, mouth trailing along her jaw.

They were whole when separate, but drawn together no matter the distance. The phenomenon had not existed before them, their unique union so revered that it had been used as a model in the reproductive pathway of many lifeforms. The intensity of their bond could not be replicated, but the pull for two members of a species to join was useful in diversifying genetic material, strengthening or weakening their offspring and species.

Instructions were given for you to breed with the animal, *Lu growled in her mind.* Michael made the assumption that you would object-

He was correct... *she shot back.*

Knowing this, he chose not to inform, but to position you here while tucking the rest of us away, performing unnecessary tasks.

"She has a mate already," Lu instructed. Her beloved was ferocious as he was magnificent, but would not injure the animal unjustly. "The fault is not yours, as you were deceived, but now that you've been corrected, any further trespass will be judged with severity."

The sky boomed, the beating of wings wafting the scent of cedar down toward her. Michael descended, his skin and hair like shimmering sand where sunlight found his body. His golden eyes conveyed he expected an inconvenience, mouth releasing a sigh as his feet touched down.

"Are you not able to see how wrong this is?" Lil began. "Deception is the path of wrongness, Michael. To have omitted your intentions, the intention," she corrected. "This can't be the design that was given. How can you possibly justify this?"

She was hurt by his deceit, troubled that he found it necessary. Though they were remorseless in their pursuit of beauty and balance, it wasn't like their kind to betray each other.

"Your combining with the creature will strengthen its species, and why you were asked to make only one."

Thunder rolled. She wasn't interested in reining anything in.

Michael raised a brow, letting Lil know she'd been heard.

"Combining? Within my body?" She asked with appropriate disgust. "And, am I to stay behind with him, reproducing internally *while the rest of the ten move on?"*

"Don't be foolish. The creature is mortal and will expire at some point. When that time comes, you will rejoin us."

Lu's low growl rumbled through her, a demonstration of unfathomable restraint.

"You certainly wouldn't be tethered to it," Michael added. "Come and go, move about as you do now, though his terrestrial parent species tend to their young extensively. You might find yourself grounded here."

He believes himself to be following the truth, *Lu said.* He cannot be reasoned with.

But he's wrong.

Absolutely, and the others will see it. Uriel has called them together.

"I will not do this, Michael. He should have been made with a partner, though perhaps he shouldn't have been made at all. Given the state of his existence, we can either allow the earth to take him, or I create his mate. Both are less than ideal, but our best solutions considering what has happened thus far."

Feet met ground as the others arrived, encircling her.

A Story in Stone

Az, dark hair and dark eyes, solid as stone. Remi, blonde hair and eyes like ice, pensive. Gabriel thought himself unreadable, but she sensed his discomfort. Uri was incensed, amber eyes like fire. The rest followed, all looking at her, and then to Michael.

"It is my understanding," Remi began, "that you arranged a coupling between one of us and a creature without consent."

"Word was given."

Silence followed his claim, and he allowed it to resonate.

With a look that bordered on compassionate, Michael met Lil's eyes.

"I will only ask once more. Will you do what has been asked?"

His eyes were strong and pleading, weighted with his concern for the balance, his belief that she was misguided.

"No."

"Your defiance has not gone unnoticed," he sighed. "And you're to be reminded it is unacceptable."

Her brows pushed together.

"Vulnerability."

A sliver of cold rushed from her heart to her limbs like water after a thaw. Lu's fingers pulsed heat where they pressed into her body, a reminder of his presence on both sides of her skin.

"Your immortality will be extracted for a time. Nothing else will be altered; you will not age or become ill. Healing will occur at an advanced rate, but should a death blow strike... Your

body will no longer support your soul, and it will move on. Not far though. You will be born, and reborn as the case may be, the way larger creatures are, from a womb."

"Michael..." she whispered.

"This is absurd," Uri snarled.

"It's temporary," Gabriel reasoned. "I will sing."

Lil knew the songs, as they all did, the music embedded in them.

"I will not," Lu rumbled.

"Expected."

"Nor will I," came Uri's voice.

What Michael and the others were attempting could not be done alone. Its complexity required the collective by design. It was meant for the ten, but majority would be enough.

Michael surveyed the members of the circle. Lil followed, meeting each of the others' eyes.

With a face like stone, Az shook his head.

"Word was given?" Cassiel asked. When Michael nodded, Cassiel sighed. "I will sing."

With Raphael, Raz, and Sab in silent agreement, that left just one more.

Remi looked pained. "We have more than ears," he observed when all eyes landed on him. "Did you not feel the possibility of interpretation with this instruction? There must have been room for another way."

"This is the way."

"I will not walk this path with you," Remi concluded.

But Michael had five to join him, and that would be enough.

A sudden stillness fell, not only among those that encircled her, but in the surrounding garden as life paused in awe. Animals had tucked themselves away to observe or hide in what illusion of safety they could find. Trees, grasses, the whole of the plant life appeared as though they were submerged in water. The density of the air hadn't changed, but there was charge, an undulation.

And then, a collective breath was being drawn around her.

As sound is movement and music sound, fine threads of vibration wove through her in a way that was gently invasive, the thrum of the beginning. As their six mouths opened, voices came together, rendering a song that was both beautiful and harrowing.

Lil's body hummed. The pressure of Lu's hands grounded her as a thin veil began to slip from her skin. Instead of being pulled from over the surface, it was as if the invisible substance passed through every part of her insides as it was drawn away.

When the crescendo passed, and the song ceased, Lil sank into Lu, her breath labored.

Michael addressed her as she exhaled, wasting no time in making his next request.

"The animal still needs a mate, as you stated previously. Plant the seed when you've recovered."

The audacity.

Lil turned to the creature where he peaked out from behind a large tree, and she wondered briefly if he would be allowed to remember what he'd witnessed. If denied the recollection, would a story be fashioned to replace what was taken, or would the unexplained absence of his origin remain, perhaps something for his kind to embellish over time?

A Story in Stone

"It would be in your best interest," Michael continued. You'll need one of their offspring to be born into when your body meets its limit, though any milk producing creature large enough to carry you to term would do. I don't anticipate the need will arise for centuries to come, though, you're hardly fragile."

He was right in that assessment. Lil found that when the voices of the six pulled from her, she did not feel hollow. She did not feel weak, or brittle. Her connection to the life surrounding her still surged, the explosive power of her bond with Lu ever present. There was, however, the looming of something, something detectable only in its absence.

Lu's fingers slowly moved from the back of her neck down, passing through her shoulder blades, continuing on as the glow of her skin cast more light under the prolonged contact.

Lil looked to the six who had used their voices together, felt their collective concern and longing, their awareness of the disruption unfolding.

"See where the path you chose has taken you," she whispered ominously.

A building fullness inside her gave way to release as wings erupted from her back. A satisfied rumble from Lu followed as he joined her in the air.

29.

Memories rushed into the vacuum left by the forgotten.

She'd thought it would be like overfilling a balloon, bursting with the overwhelming volume of what she brought into herself, but this was not the case. Instead, Lil found herself to be ever-expanding as the flood flowed in.

"I longed for you," she whispered, tears falling. "I didn't know what you were, but I knew you were missing." The words didn't seem enough, but as she felt him throughout herself, she understood everything.

"I missed you too." An understatement.

As she ascended further into the night sky, Lu pulled her to his chest, holding her firm while some multifaceted explosion occurred inside her. The sensation was warm, electric and glowing, pulling in whatever fuel it needed to grow, coupled with an urge to stretch her arms out wide and flex her back. Cool wind soothed, crisp and flowing over her, then suddenly tugged her away, hard, yanking at her from behind.

Panic surging, she gave a yip and a gasp as something sought to pull her from him, but Lu's fingers pressed firm around her waist, unmoving. She caught his eyes, intense on her, the devilish grin that crept from his mouth. Lil's fear faded to whisps in the air, her curiosity piqued.

"See for yourself," He whispered, warm into her ear, "how beautiful you are." One of his hands stroked up her back, to a part of her she hadn't known was there. "Your whole body is remembering."

Closing her eyes, she saw through his mind what had happened.

Her wings were radiant.

They rivaled his in size, spreading wide, catching and reflecting what light the night offered. As she struggled with the wind seizing the new yet familiar extensions of herself, Lil felt the impossible swell of his heart growing somehow even brighter for her.

"The wind..." she said. "I feel like I don't know what I'm doing, like it will tear me away. Should I just let go?" She looked at him, his wings like a hummingbird's behind him.

"I'm sure your instincts would kick in, but I'm with you. Would you like to try?"

She shook her head. "I don't want to be separate from you yet."

"I'm not ready to release your body either," he smiled. "There will be time for flight training later, Ilati. Go ahead and tuck them away."

"I'm trying but, I-" Lil lurched back as another gust of wind pulled at her. She remembered gliding over water and trees, through mountains. She'd been so agile then, compared to her current state. It was exasperating. "I can't remember how."

One of his arms stayed grounded to her waist, while the other worked up the back of her head.

"You won't fail at this; it's a part of you," he whispered, and she closed her eyes.

The moving air carried away much, but his scent remained strong behind his ear, down his neck.

"Take a deep breath, let yourself relax," he said.

That free hand of his behind her head worked into her hair and trailed over her neck. She leaned into his fingers, flashes of memory projecting in her mind. She saw moments of their togetherness from over lifetimes, a combination of feelings and imagery: fire, movement, water, laughing as they escaped an avalanche they'd triggered.

The back of Lu's hand ran up the inside of her thigh, slowly; not a memory, but some five hundred meters above Nan's garden.

The heat from his hand hit her core like his breath on her neck, eliciting an inhale. The muscles in her arms tightened, leg coiling around his, her wings stretching out.

"Fold them," he said, voice rippling through her like the pulse of his fingers. Her arms began to loosen around his neck, muscles of her wings relaxing.

"Yes..." he continued. "Now bring them into yourself."

By her request or of their own will, feathers and bone dissolved into her back, the rest of her body melting from the inside out.

A primal growl surged from him, vibrating through her. "Are you able to open your eyes?" He asked.

Her mouth opened slightly, hovering over his, unable to raise her eyelids.

"Look through mine," he offered.

Lil's mind flashed to his, and through him she saw light. She saw him looking down at her, through what little space there was between them. She saw his bare chest, his arm trailing down to a hand that disappeared beneath her body. A mist of light surrounded Lu's skin, hers as well. She was luminous, as was the haze of charged particles in orbit around them.

Pausing her breath and tightening around him, Lil rushed back behind her own closed eyes, unable to see the release of light and power shooting out into the night.

Another growl, somehow deeper than vocal cords should allow, moved through him as his mouth found hers. She sighed into him, then gasped as they began to free fall from the sky.

Opening her eyes wide, Lil startled, seeing his wings had stopped and they were plummeting toward the ground. Her relaxed heart sped up again, then she smiled, and her pulse slowed back down. Memories flashed from a time when they free fell over a lake one night. The sky had been so clear, the water so still, it was as if they'd been falling into the stars.

She found his eyes, sharing a moment of deep stillness between them through the rushing air, until his wings shot out to either side, slowing their speed. In an instant, she found her back against an apple tree threatening to uproot from the force of their impact which, given that she wasn't entirely human, was not so much painful as it was invigorating.

"Will we damage the tree?" She breathed, "We could... the room above the barn..."

"Not this time. We'd bring it down."

His hand passed in front of her face to move a lock of hair aside. It was enough to make her eyes roll back and close briefly.

"I need more of you," she sighed.

He planted on hand firmly above her head on the trunk of the tree, his mouth on hers again. With his other hand, he pulled her toward him, that her back could avoid the drag of a rapidly expanding trunk. The tree grew exponentially in height and width, stopping suddenly as he took his palm away.

Both hands behind Lil's thighs, Lu lifted her up against the bark, her legs over his shoulders. With her calves on his back, she realized his wings had receded.

Her mind drifted blissfully to the dream, the memory she had of Lu slowly carving out the stone cup, and she found herself grateful he had an affinity for working with his hands.

He broke contact briefly, cool air moving over her where his mouth had been. His teeth grazed the inside of her thigh and down until a wordless noise escaped her. His shoulders shrugged, his hands supporting her as she slid along his body, mouth meeting his again. He must have finished undressing while she'd been further up the tree, because he was completely uncovered, her dress the only garment remaining between them.

With one fluid swoop, her back met the cool ground, their tongues still dancing. As he lowered, easing into her, she felt the greatest sense of relief; the exhilaration of the building hereafter, and unburdened thankfulness.

"I know," he whispered, lips grazing her ear. "We are often beyond words, as that is where we started."

She twisted, moving him onto his back, his hands sliding up her thighs and under her dress, pausing on her rocking hips before moving up the center of her torso. She tucked her arms in and dipped her head, allowing him to guide the dress off of her.

They slowed a moment, Lil in awe of him as he basked beneath her, illuminated. And then, like salt water over stone, she moved over him, an ocean in a building storm.

Leaning down into him, her fingers curled into moist dirt, catching hold of a root. Lu continued to move with her as she pressed against him. Then the earth rumbled as the tree beside them grew, the widening root expanding in her grip.

"Your hand," he ground out.

But she just couldn't move...

His palm slid down to meet her fingers, streaking mud over her arm on his way. Lil released a breath, her grasp, and a pulse of light and energy out from the center of her, rippling through the orchard and beyond. As her body became fluid, Lu eased her back onto the earth, their bodies still joined, the rumbling beneath thrumming through her. She loved that sound, being engulfed in him from the inside out. She inhaled along his jawline. *That smell,* she thought, her eyes rolling back and closing, then he made that low, growling noise again.

One of her arms went around his back, the other sliding to the ground, fingers curling into the rich earth. In an instant her hands were gathered in his, above her head.

"No roots," he said beside her ear, his lips curving into a smile against her skin. "I think the tree has grown enough."

As the air around them became warmer, a dense mist spread through the orchard, lit by hair-like threads of electricity, igniting suddenly. The glowing web exploded as another burst of energy rushed outward from Lil, accompanied by a great roar, both from Lu and the earth.

As a sense of warmth spread between them, and their bodies shifted, his arm sank on one side.

"Oops," he said, a smile in his voice.

Lil looked over, seeing that the ground had given way beneath his hand to the height of his elbow, forming a fissure that extended about twenty meters in either direction.

Lu eased himself down rolling their bodies so she rested on him. His form molded to hers perfectly, warm under her as the air above cooled, steam rising from their skin.

Extended moments of breath, night, and exploration without words passed. Eventually, Lil's eye's drifted away from Lu's face, to the crack he'd made in the earth, to the massive apple tree towering over them.

A muted laugh escaped her.

Nan can tell people there was an earthquake, but there'll be no explaining that tree, he said in her mind.

Lil chuckled, then paused, turning back to his face, lips unmoving.

That was you in my mind! I can do that too!

His eyebrows pushed together, affectionately questioning her.

Of course, he began with a huff, then smirked. *You'll not remember everything at once. Yes, we can speak to each other this way. Your lips need not move ever, but I do enjoy the sound of your voice through your mouth as well… all of your sounds, really.*

Warmth spread from her chest to her cheeks, remembering.

Twenty-five years, she thought. "For me it was twenty-five years of not knowing… though I felt the pull of you my whole life. You *knew*, and you still kept distance between us. I understand why, but I am in awe that you were able." She felt the rise and fall of his chest, her hand over his heart, bodies entwined. "I don't think I would have had the strength."

"Of course you could… You have the strength to tear down civilizations," he said, his hand stroking her back. "We have done this for many of your lifetimes, the length of some crueler than others. I do what is necessary." She felt him inhale through the strands of her hair as his fingers worked her neck, her scalp. "One of the safest places I've laid your head upon our parting was on Nan's pillow, and it still tore me to do it."

Nan's, she thought.

"The pieces that brought us here… I think there's something special about this place. This time."

She looked away through the darkness, finding the house darker than it should be. How long had she and Lu been out in the orchard?

"I can usually see the light from Nan's at this distance," she started, "but it looks black from here. They wouldn't have all gone to sleep." She propped up on one arm, eyes focused on one window. "There's warmth, like from a candle. She must have the fire going, but I'm not sure it would light the windows…" *How odd.* "You don't think… While we were… You don't think anyone came for me, do you? We'd have heard, or maybe not. I was… I was *very* distracted. I'm not sure I would have noticed a parade of peacocks and elephants through the field," she smiled.

A deep inhale preceded a slight grin on his part. "I anticipated the possibility of a localized loss of electricity."

She was nothing short of intrigued, and her expression masked nothing. *Possible from what?* Her mind reached, drawing a blank.

Lu's eyebrows lifted, as if the answer was obvious. "From our extensive enjoyment of each other. The explosions weren't limited to our internal experience."

Lil inhaled, bringing a hand to her mouth.

"The higher altitude blast isn't likely to have caused interference, but on the ground… That most certainly fried something, though I've not put much thought into how extensive the damage might be."

Lil lowered her hand and cocked her head to the side, resting her palm against his chest.

That does make sense, she thought, quickly putting some figures together, factoring in distance and her location, then the memories rushed in, one from another life… Siberia… She stilled as imagery from the massive fallout flooded her.

No, not like that, Lu said silently, his eyes meeting hers. *Nothing like that happened here.* His hand slid up her back, up her neck, easing her back down to him until she rested her cheek on his shoulder and took a deep breath.

"Siberia was necessary," he assured her.

"I only remember the worst of it…" she sighed. "The rest is slow to come back."

"Some memories will return suddenly, others you will take a while to find; walking through alcoves, rooms, and gardens along the way. It takes time.

Mastery of your abilities takes time as well, as you've felt with the wings, as you've felt throughout your life."

This, she remembered as well. Some things would be like muscle memory, like riding a bike or remembering a language unspoken since one's childhood. Other things would be like learning to walk again.

"Training," she said, remembering this too.

"We'll find a suitable space. I have several locations in mind, where we have worked before, where we can be alone. The others will help when needed, of course.

"The others?" But she knew as she spoke who he meant.

He nodded.

"Remi," she breathed. "Uri… and Az." A pause stretched before Lil gasped, "Uri! Oh, Uri with the fire in his eyes, and you standing outside the bakery while I rained glass on him. He knew *exactly* what pastry I wanted, too. I think he took a shine to Gunnar. And Remi!" Smile bursting, she continued. "Oh, you were so jealous at the school, weren't you? I had no idea it was you growling in my head."

"I was furious. He was there with you, and you holding hands with your guardian… It was too much. Rem did what he could to stall our mutual friend so you and I could spend some time together at the lake; we both needed it. You weren't supposed to be at the school, though I should have suspected it was an option with Magnus toting you around on his plane."

"He never told me about you, and I can understand now why he looked as though he'd seen a ghost upon hearing your description. I told him about seeing Remi with you at the bar, that you were in my dream with the other necklace. You should have seen him. I thought he was going to lose consciousness. He recovered quickly enough; I'd expect nothing less from him." Lil perked up a declaring, "You know Magnus!"

340

Lu chuckled, "I stayed on here nearly a year, it would have been a challenge for us not to have crossed paths. I met Mira as well… she used to sketch and paint in the gardens."

"I have her work in the ocean house."

"Apple blossoms by the pantry," he said with a sigh. "She did that one just before I left."

Lil nodded, her lips brushing his skin as she spoke. "There's something graceful in us all coming together here…"

"Mmm… And as they are your family in this pulse of existence, they are mine as well. We really should go check in with them; they're likely concerned." He smiled, amused with himself. "I saw Nan after she left you above the barn, told her to wrap their phones in foil, get a couple lanterns and the wood stove going. I also advised her not to come out under any circumstances."

Nan must have been out of her mind with concern. And Magnus… Lil pictured the little cellphones wrapped in silver and buzzing across the counter, her loved ones staring at their encased devices, wondering if they should open them or wait it out.

"Magnus is probably in his plane," she said. "Or has his people on their way here."

Lil thought about the man who'd intimidated Claire by the barn, then seeing him again in the woods with the older guy. They'd come for her with *tranquilizers*. When she'd been on that boat as a child, there'd been guns mounted, but it was the storm that ended her parents. She'd been a child with so little control, surrounded above and below by wind and water.

With a pang in her heart, Lil thought of Nan, her family who'd need assistance in protecting themselves if people came looking for her. Their muscle and grit would only go so far, and she would be elsewhere, relearning how to operate her own body. Would they be safe in her absence? Nan wouldn't leave, or maybe she would if both Lil and Magnus could persuade her?

"One of the others will stay here," Lu offered, fingers gently dragging over her back. "Any one of them would do it, the young descendant as well."

"Uri," she said, matter-of-factly. "He's a guardian if there ever was one, and, well…" She smiled as Lu's lips curled up.

"*Pastries,*" they said in unison.

The two of them erupted with laughter, Lu wiping tears from his eyes. Lil flipped through memories of Uri's warrior-like build kneading dough, offering her samples of baked goods that made her limbs loose with pleasure.

"Nan won't want to let him go," Lu chuckled. "He'll be too good for business."

"When we met at the mountain, after Siberia…" Lil said, sly grin still pulling at her mouth. "Remember?"

"Remember? Are you asking if I remember the *duffel bags* of croissants and Danishes he carried with him?"

Lil laughed hard, struggling to gain control enough to speak.

"And so fragrant was his baggage," Lu continued, "That he accidentally transported one of the police dogs pursuing him." Their smiles deflated, Lu's expression sombering. "The Belgian stayed by Uri until she met her end in old age. We've long become familiar with the cycle of passing, but the loss of that dog… It was uniquely hard on him. He will be soothed by more than the pastries here, where our hands have touched the soil. We have grown fruit from it, and Nan has kept its beauty well. All things change, but I do not wish to see this disturbed just yet. Uri is the right choice to guard such a place."

Lil felt the budding of another tear, perhaps the remains from laughter, but more likely from reflecting on the depth of the moment, of lying with Lu in Nan's orchard.

"He can stay above the barn," she said, her fingers playing at Lu's beard. "It's already outfitted with a balcony, so he can stretch his wings at night. But he can't use the bed; it won't smell like you anymore."

"You can smell me directly," he said, leaning for a kiss.

Lil inhaled deeply as he did, relaxing into the movement of his tongue and the reality of his words. She didn't need to escape to take in the scent of an empty bed where no one slept. She didn't need to reach for memories she couldn't recall, or wait until she slept to encounter what engulfed her. Her contentedness was interrupted, though, by the resurfacing knowledge that they'd have to emerge from the trees and make their way to the house.

We will have more than this, he said. *We are stones, a river of time passing over us, though we do not erode. We will have other moments to drink deep from.*

"I'm not sure if I should put this on," Lil said, holding up her dress. "We're so muddy."

"Rain?" He offered.

The vision was lovely but...

"No, I think we've interfered with the sky enough for one night," she sighed, walking beside him through the trees. "Nan has an outdoor shower… mostly for me, really. She put it in after I came here." Lil's mouth drifted into a soft smile as she remembered running through lavender, kicking up dust, digging her toes in as she leaned against an apple tree, creeping barefoot through the garden and in the forest. A twinge of loss swept in, awareness of Lu's absence during those years. "I frequently became covered in dirt and mud..."

Lu paused his steps, and Lil with him, his eyes meeting hers.

"I felt you as much as I could, formless by your side, visiting your dreams, and in a place between."

"You were a comforting presence," she said, squeezing his hand. "Though I didn't know what you were, you felt like home."

They walked unclothed through the garden towards the makeshift shower, garments slung over their arms. From the spigot at the back of the house, one hose snaked up over the wall of a shower enclosure: wood fencing surrounding two wooden pallets over gravel, an old chair under empty hooks by the entrance.

"Not fancy, but it got the job done... kept Nan's house clean," she smiled.

The cold water, rendered Lil crisp and alert. Awake and invigorated, she spread her fingers across Lu's chest, a memory flowing clear into her mind like the streams of icy liquid pouring over him, over her. She remembered a time when everything was blue and white, when they splashed in glacial rivers, running barefoot, carefree through the snow.

"We can go there again," he said, lulling Lil back into the blissful present, both marveling at the miracle of their togetherness. Her hands traveled over his smooth, hard curves, wiping away what earth remained on his skin, while his fingers massaged her scalp, combing through the tangles in her hair, releasing chunks of mud, washing them back down to the wet stone and earth below.

When the water ran clean, and ragged clothes were back on their reluctant bodies, Lil and Lu walked around to the front of the house.

She felt his warmth on her back before his hand found her skin, his finger pushing through one of the tears in her dress. His heat went through her, spreading. Her steps slowed.

"From the tree," he said, explaining the torn fabric "We could go back above the barn for a change of clothes."

They'd paused by the front door, facing each other, Lil's arms making their way around him. Her cheek moved across his as she closed her eyes and breathed in, followed his jaw to the place behind his ear where the hair met his neck. Water could carry mud but there was no force strong enough to wash him away, to mute the part of him that separated into the air and traveled into her.

"We should go in," she breathed.

"There will always be an after, and it will always be us. I have found this to be true throughout our existence, and it will remain so. We can afford a blink to this moment."

Lil felt the softness of his mouth against her neck, and the pull of air he couldn't resist. She felt his arms constrict around her, then she let out a sigh as one arm loosened, and his hand reached for the door.

30.

Lil led the way into Nan's home with Lu close beside her.

An oil lamp flickered in the kitchen down the hall, another to the left in the living room, though it was poor competition for the giant, open fireplace illuminating a pile of small, tin foil bricks on the coffee table.

Nan stood from a reclining chair by the fire. Claire and Brian remained seated on the couch, mouths slightly open, eyes wide. Todd pushed off from a wall beside the entryway, bat in hand, wearing worn jeans and a navy-blue t-shirt that said, *Swell all Day, Swell all Night*. He let out a ragged breath that the room seemed to have been holding collectively, the release echoed by those behind him, waiting as he registered Lu and Lil's entrance.

Placing a free hand over his eyes, Todd took in a deep, damp sniffle through his nose. Still holding the bat, his other arm went out, welcoming Lil into a hug.

"Your breath smells like caramel," she said.

"If you need some, I know a guy."

Lil huffed a little laugh. "You didn't save me one?

"Gunnar left me what was in the bag last time we all hung out. His candy is about the only thing getting me through this nonsense," Todd sighed. "And Nan's cooking," he added under the old woman's glare. "She had us wrapping our phones in foil and getting the lamps going before it started; said we couldn't leave the house 'til you got back. Then, we heard thunder, saw an explosion in the sky, and the lights went out…"

Lil felt the growing weight of guilt sink from her chest into her gut.

"That was us…" She whispered. "I'm so sorry we scared you. We were… *together,* and," she let out a breath, leveling her eyes with his. "Lu is *different*, like the way I'm different… so when we are together, different things can happen, apparently."

Todd took a small step back, arms lowered, eyebrows raised. "Like, *together?*"
She nodded, blushing a little.

Todd's mouth widened into a naughty grin, all teeth, then his expression transitioned to one of tempered seriousness as he looked past Lil to Lu, sizing him up.

Lil felt Lu's amusement and approval, though his face gave away nothing.

Todd offered a shallow nod, then returned his attention to Lil.

Brian, brimming with offended confusion, turned to Claire, whispering, "Did you see that? When you introduced *me* to Todd, I Thought I might not survive with my kneecaps intact. Then *this* guy comes out of *nowhere*, preceding some violent weather and bizarre electromagnetic event, and he gets a nod."

Claire laughed, rubbed his back, and with affectionate condescension, said, "Did Todd hurt your feelings, Brian?"

He wiggled his body, dislodging her hand. "I don't need coddling; I'm just making a point."

Claire rolled her eyes. "Really, Brian… Does that man look like he'd let Todd break his legs?"

Todd set his bat down and nodded toward the kitchen. "We ate already, but I was thinking about having another go. You guys want a plate? Something to drink? There's a pot of chai, a kettle on the wood stove, and, honestly, why do

347

they make kettles like that? The handle gets so hot. I almost burned my hand; it was a nightmare." Raising his eyebrows at Lil, he added, "Not everyone here is fireproof."

"Nan isn't fireproof and she manages fine," Lil countered. "They're called oven mitts. Head in the kitchen, I'll see you in a minute."

Lil rotated her body, torn patches of her garment becoming visible to the others.

"Your dress," Brian announced. "What happened?"

Todd stopped in his tracks, throwing a scolding look over his shoulder. "She was having a good time, is what happened. Don't judge."

Lil's blush intensified, though the color likely went undetected by all except Lu in the low light.

"*Todd*," Claire hissed.

"He needs to check his boundaries," Todd shrugged, carrying on down the hall.

Lil looked back and forth between Claire and Nan, finally whispering, "I don't know which one of you to hug first. Todd was a no-brainer but-"

"Oh my gosh, Lil, hug *Nan*," Claire laughed. "*Go*."

Lil walked into Nan's open embrace, Lu beside her somehow ensnared in her arms as well.

"You must have been worried Nan, I'm so sorry."

"I worried for him, girl, not you," she offered with a tearful laugh.

"I have survived more than you could imagine," Lu whispered. "She brings me back every time."

"I've come to understand," Nan began. "That I don't need to know everything. But I'll accept what you're willing to tell me."

Lu looked into Nan's eyes, gave a single nod, then shifted his gaze to Brian, and back again.

"Why don't we take this into the kitchen," Nan suggested, arms gently corralling them toward the hallway. Claire made to get up but Nan gave a slight shake of her head.

Lu effortlessly tossed something small and black over to Claire. "From Cotopaxi," was all he said as he continued toward the kitchen.

Brian caught the object in a state of shock and confusion.

"Oh, it's a little glass bead," Claire cooed, inspecting the small black sphere in Brian's hand. "I think it will fit on my bracelet."

She Unclasped the chain that carried her malachite bead, threading it on.

"Cotopaxi is a volcano in Ecuador. It's *obsidian*," Brian stated before stammering, "Hey, is that?" He gestured to the hallway then lowered his voice to an exasperated whisper. "Is that the *volcano guy*?"

"Scooped a couple portions into a pan on the wood stove," Todd said from the kitchen table. "Looks like a lot, but I figured Big Guy can eat."

Todd had just about cleaned his plate when Nan suggested he return to the living room.

"Nan." His one-word plea did nothing to soften her seriousness, but her heart had never been hard.

"Take a chocolate croissant with you," she said, transferring one from a tray to a plate. "They're not *Gunnar's candies*, but you seemed to enjoy them all the same earlier. Mind the crumbs."

With Todd placated and absent, Nan prepared tea, plates of pot pie, set the table, sat down and looked them over.

"Spill," she instructed.

"Lil is my wife," Lu said without hesitation.

Nan's mug was halfway to her lips when she froze, but only for a moment, then nodded for him to continue.

"The depth and complexity or our relationship exceeds the term, but it's the best I have to work with. I am immortal. There are a handful of us here, Lil included."

Nan looked to the girl she'd raised, her gaze resting a moment, no doubt wondering how an immortal came to be born and passed off to her as a child.

Lil and Lu briefly recounted their story, Nan's eyes widening with understanding, clearly having been exposed to some version of the garden, however distorted. The woman seemed relatively unfazed as she soaked up their words. But then again, Nan had already met Lu and raised Lil. Emotionally triggered weather, communication with animals, and the rapid growing of trees from seed were all things that had prepared her.

"I've felt the pain of her loss hundreds of times," Lu continued.

"Oh, honey," Nan said, reaching out to place a hand on his.

"Fortunately, I can feel her return as well. Her impending birth prompted my departure from this place those years ago," Lu added, taking a bite of chicken and thus signaling the opportunity for questions and comments.

Nan took a sip of her tea before letting loose the long sigh Lil had been waiting for; the sign that they were still who they'd always been, that the new clothes they were adjusting to still rested over the same skin.

"Well, I'm glad we took this to the kitchen," she started. "Claire would be fine; she grew up seeing bits and pieces of you, Lil. Todd's loyalty is unrestrained, and I'd be lying if I said I wasn't at least a little amused by the way he carries on with Brian…" Nan's eyes took on a more serious look, her tone changing. "I don't want to say I'm worried about Brian, but he shouldn't know more than he already does. Ideally, he'd know less. Unfortunately, that might mean not sharing things entirely with Claire just yet."

"Agreed," Lil said, Lu nodding along.

I could help him to know less… Lu said.

Lil shot him a look of shock that softened with more consideration. *It would be a relief, but Claire might find it in poor taste.*

He tilted his head almost undetectably, glancing back to Nan. "There are entities, both of self-gain and religious motivation, that have become aware of Lil's situation over time. None of them know the truth, how could they, but stories manifest over the ages. The religious folk who hunt Lil, misguided as they are, seek to end her life. They have succeeded, many times. The other category of interested party, are those who seek not to end her, but to use her abilities for their own gain. Their attempts have also resulted in her death."

"They killed my birth parents, from this life," Lil said solemnly. "Lu rescued me…"

"And brought you here," Nan finished, the weight in her heart visible through her eyes.

"The current threat is from the latter," Lu continued. "However, now that she and I are rejoined, it won't be long before the fanatics close in. We need to take some time together, the two of us, away from here, where she can safely sharpen her skills without the need for foil and fire," he added, the undertones of mischief in his smiling eyes sending a rush of heat through Lil.

"Nan," Lil started. "Would you consider closing the shop and going elsewhere, in case trouble surfaces here?"

"They'd have to burn the house down and me with it. I'm not leaving."

"We thought the same," Lu said. "Which is why Lil and I are proposing a friend of ours stay here with you while we're away. We've not discussed it with him yet, but I have no reason to think he'd refuse."

"Gunner?" She asked, turning to Lil.

While Lu maintained a relaxed expression, Lil noticed an amused lift of his lip. "No, a much older friend than that, and I can think of more than one reason he might enjoy his stay."

"His name is Uri," Lil said. "And he has an affinity for baked goods. I don't want to say too much more on that," she smirked. "He can sleep above the barn and help with day to day in the shop."

"How well do you know him?" Nan asked, glancing warily between the two of them.

"I've known him my whole life," Lu said, "and I still trust him."

Nan nodded. "Does he get his hands dirty in the kitchen or is he just a connoisseur of other people's work?"

"There could be flour under his fingernails at this very moment."

"I look forward to meeting him, then," Nan said. "So long as he doesn't step on anyone's toes."

Lil's ear caught the sound of movement outside, increasing in volume: footsteps, one person, firm, determined. *Uri?*

That low rumbling began in Lu's chest before he stood suddenly and vanished down the hall, only to return an instant later, expression relaxed.

"Gunnar," he announced.

The front door opened a few moments later.

"And who's *this* guy?" Brian said from down the hall.

Lil wondered how the mood in the living room would shift now that Gunnar and Claire had met, what with Todd... and Brian present.

She heard Todd and Gunnar embracing, Todd letting him know she was ok.

The pink was just beginning to fade from Claire's cheeks as Lil entered into the living room, but when she looked at her cousin, the blush bloomed all over again.

"Am I the only one Todd doesn't like?" Brian whispered. "They're like old college roommates, except this guy is old enough to be his dad. First it was Lil's volcano guy, who may or may not be her husband, and now whoever the hell this hired gun is. And the kid probably still wants to knee cap me. I save *whales*, Claire. I use *science* to protect the balance of our exploited ecosystem and -"

"Hired *gun*?" She snapped.

"You said he was one of Magnus's men, and he *has* a *holster*. I saw it when he bro-hugged Todd."

"Brian, you've got to relax or get some air. There's too much tension for you to start with this nonsense."

Gunnar's eyes met Lil's as she turned away from the drama on the couch.

"Hey, kid."

She smiled. "How'd it go with the venison?"

"Loading up the truck was nice."

"You're not the only one who had a good time," She grinned, glancing to the couch, then back. "Though, she is sitting with someone else at the moment."

"A spark will burn what's ready to catch."

"There were sparks?" Of course there were.

He nodded, and smiled. It looked good on him, and they both deserved sparks. Sparks, and a big, unrelenting brush fire. With thoughts of Lu, Lil closed her eyes, inhaling him from around herself, thankful he was so close... They had more than a spark. They had a storm that moved oceans, they had falling blissfully in the sky toward star speckled darkness.

Fingers moved up the back of her neck and into her hair as she opened her eyes to his, his smile a nocturne to her soul.

Being in awe of each other, it will never end, will it.

"No," he whispered. "In the eternity that was and what is yet to come, it will not end."

She felt liquid tease her eyes as she brought both hands to his face. She couldn't tell if he was lit from the inside or reflecting her, but a soft radiance grew between them. Under the night sky one might have assumed it was to do with the moon's light on their skin, but in the weakly illuminated darkness of Nan's house, their fading phosphorescent glow was not so easily passed off.

"It's what we are," he said.

As his face brushed against hers, Lil took a slow breath in and out, slowly registering her surroundings. Gunnar and Nan stood beside them. Brian sat on the couch with Claire in some state of shock. Claire. Lil really needed to have a talk with her. Then there was Todd, leaning up against the wall. He flashed a smirk and a wink, then resumed his stoic readiness.

"Speak with your cousin," Lu whispered. "I'll have a word with Gunnar. He missed our talk in the kitchen, but it's my understanding he'd have joined us, had he been here."

Lil nodded.

One hand still trailing resting on Lu, she turned to Gunnar.

"There you go, making your own light," he said.

"Speaking of light," she countered, "I'm going to see if I can coax Claire outside for a breather." She tilted her head and tapped his jacket. "Maybe a couple pieces of ginger could make their way into my hand before I go over there…?"

He reached in and pulled out the bag.

"She hasn't tried the grapefruit," he said. "Take one of each."

"Do you have any caramels?"

"Not tonight."

She nodded, knowing he likely had some, understanding his need to be the one who gave them to her.

"I'm interested in trying one of your ginger candies," Lu said with calm sincerity as he walked with Gunnar to the kitchen. "A very dear friend of mine, who you will have the good fortune of meeting, is both an excellent swordsman and a baker…"

"He wanted you to try both," Lil said, placing the two candies in Claire's hand.

"He just carries candy?" Brian asked. "What grown man does that?" To Lil he added, "And you were lit *up* just now, what-"

"Gunnar makes sweets," Claire interrupted. "And there is just too much going on to get into anything else right now, Brian. I have questions too, but it's just not the time."

Brian was not pleased.

"So, these guys that came after you," he said, changing the subject but not easing up. "Do you know what they wanted?"

Lil looked into Brian with a challenging stare. "No."

"Did they try to explain? Claire said they wanted you to work for them."

"Brian," Claire started, embarrassed that he'd prod her cousin after such a traumatic ordeal. "I think we should let Lil take the lead on what she's comfortable talking about right now."

"All I'm saying is, whatever they need her for is important enough for them to have sought her out in the woods. And she didn't even listen. Instead, both men ended up dead. They risked their *lives* to get her help, and I can think of a few reasons someone might do that."

He held out his hands, ticking off one finger at a time as he listed: "Climate crisis, pandemics, famine, micro plastics, the need for sustainable energy..."

What's wrong? Lu asked, his voice soothing in her mind, apparently sensing her irritation from the kitchen.

Brian.

Hold his breath.

No, she chuckled. *I can't do that...*

Just for a minute. He'll panic, lose consciousness, then rouse with a headache, shame, and fear. Teach him this lesson now, so that he might avoid a harsher lesson in the future.

I'm not sure I can do it safely. I could stop too much.

Just his voluntary movement, then, like you did the other night by the barn. After a pause, Lu continued. *I told Gunnar I'm speaking to you. He asked about Claire and I told him you were going to freeze Brian.* She felt Lu smirking. *Gunnar is amused. He claims you've practiced on him. See? You're more than capable of holding the man still, and you've proven you can do it with minimal risk.*

"Brian, you have *zero* tact," Claire chastised. "You're so preoccupied with her *output.*" Then Claire mocked his voice as she said, *"Is she swimming today? Can you ask if she'd let me swim with her? Can we take samples from Lil? Let's get her in the lab.*" She paused and stared at him before her voice elevated another level, her eyes squinting slightly, "She's a *person*, not a machine, or lab rat. She was *attacked.* This is my *family*, Brian, and you just don't get it. You push too much. Her consent is an obstacle for you, and I feel like you're looking through me at her, not seeing me at all, just a means to a research opportunity.*"

Claire is pretty fired up, Lil said.

I bet Gunnar wouldn't mind seeing that.

Brian looked away from Claire and back at Lil, ignoring her cousin.

"They didn't want to hurt you, right? They were tranquilizer guns?"

Claire shook her head, "I just can't right now."

Todd pushed away from the wall with ferocity, then Lil caught his eyes with a subtle shake of her head. He gave a questioning look, but when she winked, he leaned back against the wall, smiling, waiting.

Go ahead, Lu whispered.

With a sigh, Lil met Claire's eyes reassuringly, and said, "He's going to be fine."

Claire didn't hide her confusion, glancing back at Brian, who sat motionless but for the touch of fear in his eyes. She looked back to Lil, knowing something had happened but not yet clear on what it was.

"I'm helping Brian to take a pause," Lil explained. "He's unable to move, but he's breathing, heart is pumping, and the gears are certainly turning, aren't they?"

Claire inhaled sharply, but said nothing, and if Todd's mirth could light up a room, they all would have needed sunglasses.

"I don't negotiate with terrorists, Brian. There's a line that shouldn't be crossed, and when it is, there's nothing left to talk about. The men in the woods crossed a line." She paused, letting her words sink in before adding, "And you have some thinking to do."

A glowing warmth spread inside her, Lu's love and pride flooding through their bond.

I hope you don't mind, but Gunnar and I have been eavesdropping at the kitchen doorway… A chuckle bubbled in his voice. *I thought I'd have to put my hand over his mouth to silence the sounds of his joy, but he was able to restrain himself,* Lu laughed.

She adored his voice.

I'm pleased to have provided entertainment for the two of you…

She heard his laughter in her head and echoing down the hall, mingled with Gunnar's.

Nan stood, giving Lil a look that suggested she was doing her best to keep a straight face.

"I'm finding myself in need of a beverage," the woman announced. "It's never too soon for another tea. Would you like anything, girls?"

Lil linked arms with Claire and, looking up to Nan with a face no one could refuse, she said, "Chai?"

"I think we could all use another one," Nan sighed. "And I could use something to keep me busy. Todd? Chai?"

He nodded, "Sounds perfect right about now. Need a hand?"

"No, I'll get it. The fewer people fussing in there, the better."

Nan looked to Brian, who remained motionless, then turned her eyes back to Lil.

"Will he be having anything?"

Lil regarded the man frozen on the couch, relinquishing voluntary muscle control back him.

"Brian?" She asked.

Brian, like a child waking from a bad dream, didn't move more than his eyes at first, then, slowly, he swiveled his head to the side. He had things he'd like to say, and more than a few things he'd like to ask, but lingering terror prevented him from going down that road.

With fear of not responding to Lil's question winning the internal battle he'd been waging, Brian said, "I think I need something a little stronger than tea, if I'm being honest."

A little twitchy, he kept rolling his shoulders, testing parts of his body.

"I keep port and ginger wine here. If you want something different, just head down to the shop. Keys are on a hook by the door, the ones with the thistle keychain."

Todd cleared his throat.

Nan rolled her eyes. "There's also a Mr. Zogs *Sex Wax* keychain on there," she said, hitting Todd with a stare. "Todd put it on knowing full well it's too much for my old fingers to get the damn thing off. And *he* won't remove it because he's too amused with himself." Nan turned and walked off down the hall, muttering, "Turning my grey hair white."

"Don't let her fool you," Todd beamed, "She loves it. I've seen her laughing to herself when she reaches for them."

Lil wrapped her arm around Claire and brought her head down on her cousin's shoulder. "Let's go outside for some fresh air. Just us. Even if it's only sitting on the steps."

"I need *exactly* that," Claire sighed.

"Oh, and I'm going to stay in the living room with *Todd?*" Brian huffed. Springing from the couch, he grabbed the Sex Wax keys and headed out the door.

Todd sauntered over to one of the chairs by the fireplace. "I'm not getting involved in whatever that was, but I will say this," he said, leaning over the closest table and settling on a book of crossword puzzles. "You need that guy like you need a stubbed toe."

Lil released an amused snort, and Claire just shrugged, uninterested in making any pleas on Brian's behalf.

*

Though wrapped in one of Nan's sweaters and drinking hot tea, the front steps were cold, and Lil could see Claire shivering.

"Want me to go in and get you the chunky grey blanket?" Lil asked.

Claire shook her head. "No, I think it's mostly nerves."

"Are you ok with what happened with Brian in there? The *pause?*"

Claire nodded. "I knew you'd done something to hold that man by the barn, but it was different seeing it fireside in the living room… on *Brian*. I'm not bothered by it, though it would be a good excuse for my shaking. That, or anything else that's happening: the guy cornering me out by the barn, people being after you, witnessing you freak out on the shore and bringing a storm down on us, Barn-Smell-Dream-Guy coming to your rescue, the same guy who knows Nan somehow and is also obviously in love with you. Magnus is probably *freaking*. All these things could justifiably cause my hands to shake," she said, taking a sip of the chai they'd grown up on. "I think I need to spend some time apart from Brian. I don't know if that means breaking up or just taking some time to think about things. It feels selfish and misplaced to be preoccupied with my relationship status when there are much bigger things happening, but that's where my thoughts are."

Claire had no idea how much Lil needed such a preoccupation in that moment. She found herself soothed by the prospect of discussing anything reminiscent of normalcy. Lil needed the grounding force of the familiar to hold her firm as her universe rapidly expanded, and Claire's relationship, the weather, or Todd's shirt, were all viable options. She wouldn't be held for long, she knew it in her heart and through her being, but she would have that moment, drinking tea on the steps with her cousin.

"I mean, we get along with each other's friends," Claire went on. "He has his own projects he's working on, and he's so passionate about the environment. You should see him out on the boat, how excited he gets about the whales," she laughed, shaking her head. "Is it possible to like the *idea* of being together more than the reality of it? I mean, we make sense on paper, but there's a feeling I didn't even know I was looking for."

"Until you felt it somewhere else?"

Claire nodded silently.

"I don't have much relationship experience," Lil started. *Well, that's not exactly true is it,* she thought. "I don't have *dating* experience, but what I feel with Lu is, well it's… I don't even need to be touching him to feel it."

"You two literally emit light together."

"We do," Lil smiled, cheeks warming.

"He's the one you saw at the bar, and in your dreams. He's *barn smell guy,*" she said. "And he has the necklace from your dream, from those old books. If it were anyone else it would feel absurd to ask, but was he really there, in your dream? At some point I need details. I know I'm not getting all of them, but I'll need *something.*"

"There's a great deal I'm holding back. There just is. For safety, and in the interest of time, and your mind not exploding," Lil chuckled, "I'm only going to say so much right now, and Claire, this isn't for Brian, okay? I need him shut off from new information."

Claire nodded, encouraging Lil to continue.

"The timeline of my life is a little bit... *complicated.* I've known Lu for a very, *very*, long time, and we've always been a pair. There was a time, *before*, so much time..." she trailed off. What to say? How *much* to say? This was *Claire*, who she'd known her almost her whole current life, who'd seen her talk to animals, rain down storms. Through all the years, Claire had an easy trust about her when it came to Lil. She didn't pry, didn't try to use or study her; just accepted what she was, as Nan did, happy to live alongside her.

"Lu has known me for a time beyond lifetimes. He goes on when I die, finds me when I return, and helps trigger my memory," she said. "My whole life I knew something was missing, and it *haunted* me once I'd seen him. Yes, he was really in my dreams. Apparently, we cause a bit of a fuss when we're together," she smirked.

"So, it's complicated," Claire shrugged, sipping her drink.

Lil nodded, smiling at her cousin's understatement.

"We're connected in a way that is, *unique...* that only he and I are capable of."

"Like *glowing* together," Claire asked, suggestively raising her eyebrows.

"You glow in your way, I glow in mine," Lil chuckled. "You blushed the moment Gunnar walked through my door, and don't even deny it," she said, raising her eyebrows. "I saw you. And let me ask this: is there a spark with Brian? You don't need to be a scientist to know that friction leads to heat, but... is there heat without it?"

"I still can't believe we're talking about this right now. People are literally trying to kill you."

"I need to talk about normal things for a few minutes," Lil sighed. "This is helping, trust me… Do what is right for you, but it's my understanding that you should feel something more than *comfortable*. Something like running through a field in the sunshine, or swimming in the ocean in the rain… The feeling will be unique to you, but when you find it, you owe it to yourself to explore it. Life is too precious, too short for you to live without something as magnificent as that spark. You decide what feels right and what doesn't. It's your choice, always."

Slow movement came through the darkness, becoming Brian as the distance closed between them. When he finally reached the steps, he jingled the Sex Wax keys and tossed them to Lil.

"It's been one heck of a night," he said, taking a final swig from his beer bottle. "And I'm sure it's not close to being over, but I'm gonna get going." Turning to Claire, he said, "I know a lot is happening, but it seems like they're handling it, and it might be better if there were fewer of us getting in the way. I really need to take a break from all this and sink my teeth in at work, get an early start tomorrow. Do you want to follow me in your jeep or ride together?"

Lil watched Claire's thumb smooth over the imprints on her mug where Lil had pressed dandelion leaves into the Clay. Claire loved dandelions. The plants weren't weeds in her opinion, they were edible, nutritious, resilient, bright as the sun, and, of course, when in their fluffiest form, carried the irresistible magic of wishes waiting to be blown out into the world. They were the stuff that nostalgia and hope were made of.

"You go ahead," Claire said. "I'm going to stay here tonight. Nan has plenty of room, and I have a change of essentials upstairs."

"Sure," Brian sneered. "I'll head out while you go back in and take more candy from strangers, and Lil continues squandering opportunities to save the planet because she's scared, even though she can *freeze* people, apparently."

A Story in Stone

Claire let out a sigh as Brian turned his back to leave. "Are you alright to drive? You're drinking, and it's late."

Brian raised the empty bottle of ale as he continued walking.

"It was one, and it was *blonde*. I'll think be ok."

31.

Crackling fire and warm conversation drew Lil and Claire back into the sanctuary of the living room. Nan sat beside Gunnar on the couch, Todd in a chair by the fire doing crosswords, and in the other chair, Lu. When his eyes connected with Lil's, a pool of heat ignited, spreading from her chest throughout her insides. Like an imprint, like the feeling of ocean waves over her body long after a swim, she still felt him on her, in her, through her.

"Brian decided to call it an early night," Lil announced, rubbing Claire's back.

"Not complaining," Todd replied, eyes still on his puzzle.

"Well," Nan offered, "it's a little late to say *early* at this point, but I won't fault him for calling it. We're all tired."

Claire tilted her head. "I think more than just the night ended when he left..."

"I see," Nan said, patting the empty space on the couch between her and Gunnar. She picked up a glass tumbler with the other hand, golden liquid within. "Come on and have a drink. Here, finish mine. It's Stone's."

Claire took the ginger wine as she sat down.

Todd made to rise, offering Lil his seat, but she shook her head once with renewed thankfulness that Lu was not a dream. Settling into his lap felt better than sliding into a warm bath after a cold, hard day. Engulfed and content, Lil turned her head just enough to look over at the scene unfolding in the room.

Claire had taken more than a sip of Nan's wine. Gunnar offered her a grapefruit candy, then tossed one at Todd, who caught it with his mouth. The tension had eased. Even with the proverbial storm raging outside, they were together as a family in that moment.

I want to know what you all were laughing at when we walked in," Claire smiled.

"Stories," Nan smirked, turning to Lil. "Catching Lu up on a few memorable moments from your youth."

Warm light illuminated one side of Lu's face; the rest in shadow, but still burning.

"We were discussing how special you are, to all of us," he said with reverence, his thumb massaging her palm.

Somewhere in her periphery Gunnar smiled, mug in hand. "I shared a story about a time when I came to pick you up. You couldn't have been more than nine years old. I found you ten or fifteen meters up a tree, talking to an owl."

Lil rolled her eyes, smiling.

This is a roast. They're roasting me.

I'm quite enjoying it.

"I told the one about you and Claire getting lost in the woods," Nan said. "She thought you were going to leave her there and take off with those wolf pups."

"We were never lost!" Lil protested, hand squeezing Lu's. She felt his body moving beneath her, laughing. She pressed her lips together in some attempt at spite, but she couldn't help joining in with the others.

"I didn't share the one about the kelp," Gunnar said, taking a sip, eyes looking at her over the rim of his mug.

Lil stilled in the cradle of Lu's body.

"We went to Dr. Zhang's lab," Gunnar started. "I got that big bucket of sea water with the string in it... Carried it all the way to that conference room with the piano on our way back because you had a song stuck in your head."

Lil remembered playing, so deep into the song that she hadn't realized what she'd inadvertently initiated.

"I locked the door behind us for privacy," he continued, "Set the bucket by your feet at the bench when you began to play. I sat down on the floor, leaned my head against the wall, and listened." He looked up from another sip of his drink. "Chopin."

Lil nodded.

"I lost track of time," he said. "I heard you gasp as the music stopped. I don't know if I stood or opened my eyes first, but I saw the light fading from around you. I saw the fear on your face, and I saw the kelp that had grown from the bucket, up around your body, around your *neck*, and down your arms."

Lil hadn't noticed the kelp creeping over her, only when it tightened did she became aware, feeling its need for her light, smothering her to get more.

Nan nodded her head, no doubt recalling countless close calls of her own.

Lu's thumb continued to work gently into Lil's palm, emphasizing the connectedness that went beyond their hands.

"I thought the worst was over as I freed you from the weeds, but then the knocking on the door started, people who'd gathered out there to listen."

Gunnar had coached her through her breathing, offered her candy, even made a joke about adding seaweed to his next batch of caramels given their kelp windfall. He made a call and within ten minutes they emerged together to an empty corridor. If he hadn't been there...

"It would have escalated if you hadn't been with me," Lil said. "I can only imagine what could have happened."

"If I hadn't been there, I'm not sure you'd have bothered hauling that bucket in the first place..." He smiled.

The corner of her mouth rose in return. He was right. She would have tucked the bucket away somewhere before going to the piano. Gunnar had been there, though. He always was.

Claire sat up straight; eyebrows drawn together. "Wait, you worked on kelp with doctor Zhang?"

A hush fell over them as everyone looked puzzled, then laughed at Claire's train of thought.

"What?" Claire giggled in protest. "Dr. Zhang's work is *really* exciting!"

"I'm not surprised," Nan said. "Lil always had a way with plants on land... Why not in the ocean?"

"Oh, kelp is plant-like, but it isn't a plant," Claire chirped. "It's a protist. Protista is like the junk-drawer of kingdoms," she continued, to the delight of Gunnar, who seemed fascinated.

Lil took the opportunity to sink into the feeling of Lu's lips along her neck, rolling her eyes back until they closed... when she opened them again, Claire, bless her heart, was still talking about kelp and Gunnar, eyes twinkling, looked at her like she was sustaining him.

Nan didn't appear bored, but her mind had drifted elsewhere. Well," she announced. "I just remembered that I gave up my drink. I'll fix that, and make up a room for you, Gunnar."

His eyes widened as she stood. He probably didn't want to impose, but there was no way he'd turn down the offer. If he was honest with himself, he'd admit he felt compelled to remain there for several reasons. More than one of those reasons was fueling Nan's need to get another drink, possibly all.

"I'd appreciate that, thank you."

*

Lil felt her eyes drift closed again as Lu inhaled deep at her hairline, her body relaxing into his.

I think you need a nap, she barely heard him say. Then with light stroking of fingers on her cheek, he asked, *Are you ready to sleep, or would you like to wait a bit longer?*

Just a little longer.

Lu gently roused her, his hands rubbing up and down her arms. "Let's grab a cup and head to the barn so you can take a nap before we go."

She nodded, leaning into him as they walked to the kitchen.

Claire sipped her drink, watching Lil disappear with Lu into the darkness until one of the little aluminum packages on the table began to vibrate.

"There goes one of the phones," Claire announced. "It's got to be Magnus." Reaching out her hand, she hesitated. "Or Brian."

Gunnar's hand slid under hers, retrieving the parcel and unwrapping the foil. He showed her the screen display: *Magnus Cell.*

"Would you like me to answer?"

"No..." she flushed, "No, thank you. I can get it."

Upon answering, she heard a deep sigh on the other end.

"Nan advised there would be a break in communication, but I couldn't wait any longer."

"What's going on?"

"What's going on is you need to get Lil on a plane *immediately*. I don't care if she's packed. You throw some tea and a sketchbook in a bag and get her to the bloody airport. Lu is with her, thank heavens. Where is she, I need to speak with her."

"Lil or Nan?"

"For heaven's sake, put Lil on."

Pausing as she reentered the living room, Lil leaned against Lu and sipped from her mug. Todd still sat relaxed with his book of puzzles, Gunnar remained focused on Claire, and Claire... she stretched her arm out toward Lil, cellphone in her hand.

"Magnus," Lil said, putting the device to her ear.

"Lily. You're all safe? There have been no other attempts?"

"Yes, safe and together. Gunnar is here too, and Lu."

"I'd like to revisit that bit later. Right now, things are worse than I anticipated. The men from the woods are ghosts, no real records. What identities we found were clearly fabricated." Magnus paused, sighed audibly, and clicked his tongue. He was struggling with something. "Lily, dear, I fear I may have made an error that I had no way of foreseeing the consequences of... And in doing so, I believe I have initiated these events."

Her heart felt for him. "Magnus, you had nothing to do with this," she said gently. She'd been pursued for lifetimes.

"I had a private meeting at my property here, myself and three others. I gave a tour of my home, and one of the gentlemen, Malcom Drake, was intrigued with your most recent painting."

Lu growled against her body, sending low vibrations rippling through her. Malcom Drake. She knew that name.

"I mentioned that the work had been shipped from my Vancouver Island home, that I knew the artist well, and had your work in all my properties. It wasn't until later I recalled that he'd seen one of your paintings at least once before, about a year ago in Norway, you may have seen him at auction when you bought that little ring. He inquired about your gallery presence, and I responded that you were extremely private. I couldn't help myself. Malcom's organization is old, all family at the top, a dynasty. They're on the forefront of technology, as am I, and the other men who joined me here the other day, but his work is, well, the ethics are a little dicey."

They may have known her location for a year. Why wait that long, though?

They've been planning.

And more will come.

"I killed two men today, and there will be more, but I'm sure we have a little time." She looked into Lu's eyes. "Right?"

"Lily, dear, my people found no abandoned vehicle in the surrounding area. Unless the two who confronted you hiked in from a very far distance, there was a driver and at least one more man on the ground here. I think you may truly be in imminent danger."

"Magnus, I-"

"I want you on the next plane out, and not commercial. My jet is here but I'll arrange something for you. I need you in the air. I'm sure Lu will join, Claire too if that is necessary for you. And please, if you can manage to get Nan… the boy can watch the shop. No one would believe he has any information worth pursuing." Magnus let out a sigh, and Lil pictured him rubbing his eyes, running his hand over his beard. "Beautiful, stubborn woman. Will you be alright if I ask Gunnar stay on site with her?"

"Nan is already making up a bed for him. And I, Lu and I, we have a friend. He's like us, and he'll be staying here as well, for security."

Lu winked, placing a hand over hers where she held the phone.

I'll speak to Magnus, he said. *We can pop over and get into details with him after you've rested.* He leaned into her for a deep kiss before releasing her from the wall where she stood, watching her with reverence and hunger as she walked toward the couch.

Her eyes were still on him as she managed, somehow, not to trip over the table.

"Magnus," Lu started. "Indeed, I look forward to catching up in person, old friend. Lil and I should be departing to join you soon if that's alright. No, that won't be necessary, we have transportation. She's exhausted and will take a brief nap before we leave. We won't be traveling by plane. It's best if I explain that bit when we arrive." He paused, listening. "Allowing an hour or so for rest, we should see you in about an hour or so," he chuckled.

Lu, chuckling... It was breathtaking.

"Right, just Lil and I," he said as he walked down to the kitchen. "Can you send coordinates to your location?"

Claire put an arm around Lil as she settled in beside her.

"What's Magnus saying?"

Lil curled her legs under her body, resting her head on the back of the couch.

"Gloom and doom, they're all coming for me, get out now, etc." She said, smiling weakly.

"Lil..."

"Lu and I are going when our friend Uri gets here, after I take a quick nap, apparently. Uri will stay, and Gunnar too."

Claire looked to Gunnar, who nodded.

"We're hoping that with me gone, the threat will be reduced. With Gunnar and Uri here, there will be enough strength to hold things down."

"Rooms are all fixed up," Nan called as she descended the stairs. Taking one of the seats by the fire, she said, "I put an electric lantern on the bedside table in each. Gunnar, I put a toothbrush next to yours. I get a new one every time I go to the dentist, but I use an electric," she shrugged.

"I appreciate the hospitality, Ma'am."

"Lil, sweetie, when do you think you'll head out?"

"We'll wait for Uri then leave the way we came. It's not too late to change your mind, really, Nan. Magnus planned to arrange a private jet. You could all go.

Todd, could stay behind and run a skeleton crew with a couple of friends, work short hours."

"I got your back, Lil. Whatever you need," he said.

Nan shook her head. "No chance. I'm not running from my home. And I'll see Magnus when he gets back."

"Okay," Lil said, eyelids sinking, finishing her thought as they closed. "I'm going to take a nap in the barn before we go, but it doesn't hurt to get a head start."

"He just wants a word before we disconnect," Lu said, holding the phone out as he entered the living room.

Gunnar put out his hand, but Lu curled his lip into a restrained smile, and passed the phone to Nan.

Was that the firelight or did Nan look warmer?

"Hello? Yes," she sighed, deep with relief. "Yes, we are all well." She went on, getting up to walk to the kitchen. "*I'm* well, yes..."

"He wants to touch base with you as well," Lu offered to Gunnar, then turned back to Lil.

Eyes closed and chest slowly rising, her peacefulness radiated, seeping into him. Bending slightly, he slid his arms under her body.

Rolling her toward his chest, Lu lifted, Lil's head falling into place at his neck. With a sigh and a flutter of lashes, she whispered, "No really, I'm up."

"Are you concerned my arms will get tired?"

She smiled and huffed an attempt at laughter, settling into his arms. He was warm, and she lacked both the desire and energy to protest further.

"We'll be back over when Uri arrives," He said.

Lil heard the door close, the rush of cool air around her. As they moved toward the barn, she became very aware of where their skin connected: his arm against her back where the dress draped, her cheek and lips at his neck.

He paused their movement.

She managed to lift her eyelids, seeing they stood in the garden where she'd planted the apple tree as a child.

"This one is yours," he said.

She nodded against him. "Some combination of instinct and curiosity brought my hands and the seed together in the dirt."

"Mmmm," he rumbled, murmuring, "Instinct and curiosity," as his thumb moved up the inside of her thigh, his hand accounting for what was present and missing beneath the dress.

"I thought I was supposed to take a nap," Lil smiled.

"Oh, you'll sleep. Just not quite yet."

His mouth found hers with a growl as his tongue slid between her lips.

A deep Sleep, She heard him say.

Deep indeed. One of her legs squeezed at his arm under her knee, the other slid down.

He leaned his back against the wall of the barn, repositioning her to face him.

The hem of her dress rested above her hips, her movement working the material upwards, her body seeking to replace the cold air where his hand had been. With her knees bent on either side of his waist, her feet pushed down at his pants. When both his hands came to grip her around the middle, she finally felt him against her. With a low growl, he turned them around, thrusting her back against the boards, his body into hers.

The structure shook with the impact.

The frame is strong, he reassured her.

The sensations building in her were powerful, warm, and electric. And around her... She opened her eyes. Their bodies were glowing, pulsing.

I'm going to blow up the barn, she thought, unable to fight the impending blast.

Lu smiled against her mouth. *I'll absorb what I can.*

373

She rose up, squeezing against him, her nails digging, her mouth hovering over his, pushing forward the explosion around her with what conscious effort she could manage.

Lu roared, one arm contracting with her against his chest, the other releasing altogether, the piercing glow of his skin undulating with intensity. Pulling her head back, Lil saw his wings had flared out with a glowing arc between them. She looked down to the hand that had detached from her, where energy shot like lightening from his fingers to the earth.

Lil searching his eyes with concern as the intensity softened and he breathed heavily against her.

"Are you ok?"

"Magnificent," he said, flashing a satisfied smile.

She exhaled, then chuckled along with him as they walked to the shower in the back of the barn, where water fell hot, leaving steam to engulf them where tiny rivers and rain did not.

Upstairs, Lil watched him from the bed where he'd once slept, where, only hours before, she'd heard him tell the story of who she was. Lu donned his pants, placed his shirt on the arm of the chair, and collected the stone cup from the bedside table. He placed it, along with her torn dress, into the bag she'd packed.

"The dress will not recover," he said, "but I'm fond of it."

Lil rolled onto her belly, watching him through heavy eyes as he bent, as he moved, as his muscles served him. She was mesmerized, not because of his size, of his masculinity, his virility, though there was that... But more simply because he *was*, that he existed at all. The miracle of their being was not lost on her, and she was thankful for it, thankful that through the tragedy of their circumstances, he'd been able to make himself tangible, that she was able to sink her fingers into his arms as he sank into her. She was thankful that they were able to breathe deep from one another.

Lu took his place beside her on the bed, hands trailing over her as she closed her eyes again.

"Sleep," he said softly.

Only her relaxed breath answered.

His fingers stroked her neck. They ran over her back and down her legs, returning between her thighs, gliding up to her neck, and down her arm, keeping his movements fluid as not to distract her.

"I do love this form," he whispered.

If Lil had been any less exhausted, his touch may have kept her awake. Instead, she drifted to that in-between place on the cusp of slumber. Content in knowing he would be with her on both sides of consciousness, she allowed herself to be lulled, as if by a song, into her dreams.

32.

Small fires lit the stone room, Lil's body reflecting the warm light. Paintbrushes tickled over her skin, the sensation challenging her ability to stand still. A dream and a memory, from a time when the world sparkled with wonder. Nature dazzled as much as her kind did, a time when she and the others lived among the people, not hiding themselves.

With her skin thoroughly coated in oil, the children dusted shimmering gold over her body, then began painting intricate designs with an opaque liquid gold, the whole of her shimmering. Two slits in her long, flowing skirt allowed the exposure of her legs. Beads hung down from its belt, and from the waist up she wore naught but her necklace and the gold.

She felt him before she saw him leaning against the open doorway. The skirt he wore barely reached his knees, stone cylinder suspended from around his neck resting against bare skin. When she caught his eyes, a deep rumble formed in his chest, moving out into hers, heating her from within.

He shifted his weight to approach.

"Not while it's wet," she pleaded, raising a hand. "Let them finish."

"No."

"They worked so hard," she smiled.

The children giggled as she tried to remain still while thwarting Lu's efforts to make contact. Her left foot slid to the side, toes brushing against a cluster of tiny gold and chalcedony beads. Thousands of them had once been threaded into a dress that had hung over her like a jeweled fishing net. She'd worn it the day before.

Lil floated an image of the dress to Lu's mind, of the garment ripping apart under the strength of his fingers, beads scattering across the stone floor.

"I liked that dress," she whispered.

"It was in the way."

He held his hands hovering less than a centimeter from her body, then rested one behind her head as their mouths met.

Releasing her lips, he moved slowly along her jaw, careful not to come in contact with the painted majority of her body.

"I was on my way to meet with Remi and some farmers to discuss water. You have until I'm done," he purred into her ear. "And then, by my hand or by my mouth, the gold will not remain."

His muscular back taunted her as he walked away, leaving her there to illuminate the little artists with a light far more powerful than the flames scattered about.

"Is it any wonder that this room shimmers?" One little boy smirked to another.

Lil surveyed the space around her, where varying degrees of gold dust, streaks of paint, old and new, reflected back memories of their origin. The children decorated her often.

"Remind me why you never paint him?" She asked, teasing.

"You do that job yourself," one girl smiled. "When we are done."

Your body is the only brush I'll accept against my skin, he said in her mind.

Is your meeting over yet? She asked.

It can be.

Lil eyed a tray of food on a nearby table: little cakes formed from honey, ground tubers, and spices, domed cookies filled with dates, and whatever else Uri had concocted. He was always tinkering. The pastries lay alongside figs, pomegranate and cucumbers.

Give the meeting what time it needs, she said. I'll have a bite to eat when they're through painting It shouldn't be long.

377

With decorated hands, you'll need someone to feed you.

She felt his delighted grin, the provocative rumble.

Remi knows I'm speaking to you,

Of course he does. You're distracted by the promise of gold on your tongue.

He's annoyed. He just rolled his eyes.

They put another layer of paint on my nipples; I can't see the pink anymore.

A crash sounded far down the hall; a low growling echoed through her mind as well as into the room.

You'll terrify the farmers, *she gasped, her heart speeding up as she smiled, shooing the giggling children into an adjoining room with its own exit, that they could escape and rejoin their families for the night.*

Gripping the stone doorway with just enough restraint not to leave it crumbling beneath his hand, Lu paused a moment, drinking in the sight of her.

Lil saw a flash of herself through his eyes, her body lit by both the flickering fires and the glow from within. She stood framed by a backdrop of darkness beyond the wide, open balcony. She didn't need decoration, yet there she was, dusted and painted to shimmer, suspecting it was the game of it that affected him so.

It's you that affects me.

And then he was moving toward her.

She felt each one of his slow footsteps like a pulse in her chest until he stood close enough for the subtle movement of his irises to enthrall; the greens and browns of moss over damp earth. She followed the path they took as he looked down.

The tips of his fingers parted one of the slits in her skirt, revealing intricate metallic details on her thigh. Crisp golden lines and swirls softened, paint moving under his touch.

That sound from his chest rumbled again, felt more than heard, then Lil saw a flash of something. She looked up to catch his eyes reflecting the light from her body, his lips moving in, sliding along her neck and over her jaw, his beard grazing her skin.

"There are still a few children on the balcony," he murmured, in her ear. "I can hear their hearts racing."

"Don't scare them," she said.

He looked down at her chest, thumb tracing the curves that had been promised.

"You may come out," he sighed with elevated volume. "Run along and let your friends know how pleased I am with their work."

A young boy emerged from behind the balcony curtain, Lil's face falling at his expression of fear. It didn't seem proportional to Lu's presence. He was formidable, but never laid a hand on children.

As the boy took another step beyond the fluttering fabric, two men came forward, flanking him. Intruders. One held a knife to the boy, the other with a spear cocked back, aimed toward her.

A deep, penetrating roar erupted from beside her, a roar charged with fury and power. His solid wings sliced out from behind him and through the air, ready to encapsulate her.

Slick with paint, she spun in his arms before he could surround her. Facing the threat, Lil pushed light and energy forward from herself, out through her hands and toward the would-be assassins.

The intruders' bodies were blasted back by the force, catapulted high up and over the balcony's edge. As they were propelled, the frightened boy went with them, a malicious hand holding firm to his arm.

The three had not yet peaked in their trajectory when a great sound came tearing through the night sky. It was a thunderous noise from above, accompanied by a great flame moving so swiftly toward them that not more than an instant went by before Uri's wings came into view on either side of the hovering fire. His bare chest and shaved head reflected the nearly two-meter-long staff of blazing light extending from his right hand.

It looked as though he wielded a flaming sword.

Uri swooped in and grabbed the boy, pulling him safely to his side.

With the child secure, his weapon sliced with clean, unforgiving quickness, the intruders' expressions barely having time to transition from surprise to horror as their heads separated from their bodies.

Uri crashed down onto the balcony with footing solid as stone, releasing the boy with a reassuring squeeze to the shoulder and instructions to go directly to his parents.

"Guards of Eden," Uri grumbled with contempt. The fire had receded from his hand, but his amber eyes blazed with comparable intensity. "They have no idea what happened in the garden." Ticking his head to the edge of the balcony, he said, "There are more down below."

Lil turned within the cocoon of Lu's wings to meet his eyes. His palm cradled her face, thumb working a streak of gold on her cheek.

"Please stay," he said softly. "Az is coming. I know you could level the earth, but if one arrow flies errant..."

She paused the sound from his mouth with a kiss, soft and understanding.

"I'll stay with Az, and remain a distance from the balcony, though I do enjoy watching you."

A hand appeared on Lu's shoulder.

Lil met dark eyes, the border between pigment and shadow almost undetectable.

Az.

His hand slid down, returning to rest by his side as he took a step back. He had deep brown hair like Lu's but short, though not shaved to the skin like Uri. Az was built wide, as were the others, but he stood not quite as tall. There was something about him that seemed impenetrable, though she supposed they all were. He radiated a calm that she only felt with Lu, but without the heat.

The sound of wings moving air announced Remi's arrival.

"There was a set of two on the North side," he said, landing gracefully on the railing.

"Was," Uri repeated.

Remi nodded. "The numbers here are far greater. They knew where she'd be."

Lil wondered if they'd keep any for interrogation.

A Story in Stone

We will listen, and then they will perish, *Lu said.*

Uri pulled the long spear up from the balcony floor to his hand. Looking down over the edge, he asked, "Stop their hearts, or...?"

"No, they'll meet the violent end they wished to deliver, and bathe in the horror of our justice long after death. I'll see to it."

Uri launched the spear downward, audibly meeting its mark.

"The night will still be young when I'm through with this task," Lu whispered with unwavering heat into her ear.

"Go," she sighed. "I'll still shimmer when you return."

Lu released a growl as his body reluctantly slid from hers.

With space between them, she looked over him, eyes wandering from head to toe.

His stone necklace rested against a bare, gold smeared chest. Metallic dust coated his mouth, beard and palms. He wore the paint like battle markings on his skin, and indeed they were. They told of why he brought death to the ground. He wore the story of what was taken, what he would protect, and who he would return to.

A quick breeze snuffed out the flames surrounding them. Moss and earth irises thinned, allowing the black depth of Lu's eyes to expand under a ring of green. Sharp canines lengthened; subtle changes made to provoke fear and facilitate the enhanced discomfort of those he would transition away from their bodies.

Lu effortlessly ascended to the balcony railing alongside Remi and Uri, letting out a roar that called upon thunder to echo in response. He dove into the darkness of a sky undulating with clouds so dense the moon had no chance of breaking through. Only lightning and the raging glow emanating from her beloved were there to illuminate the terror that awaited those who came for her.

Lil closed her eyes and breathed deep, taking in what remained of him until he returned.

33.

With eyes still closed, Lil inhaled Lu's scent, incredibly satisfied by the idea of waking like this indefinitely, with him surrounding her. Spreading her arms, she reached through the blankets, finding no warmth but her own.

Lil opened her eyes.

Darkness rested beside her, the night sky waiting beyond open balcony doors.

Did you dream of me? He asked.

A memory. I was painted with gold, she smirked.

He purred through her thoughts, warring over whether or not to return to the barn.

Where are you, she asked.

At the house. Uri is here, otherwise you'd have woken to my body.

I look forward to napping often.

He chuckled.

How is Uri?

His arrival was quite a surprise for Gunnar. Then, of course, there was the cargo... He's brought a two-kilo brick of his own butter, and has yet to divulge what species of animal he milked it from. All we know thus far is that it was consensual, and must have happened repeatedly to have resulted in the quantity I just witnessed. You'll see for yourself. We'll be over shortly.

A Story in Stone

He's bringing it to the barn?

I believe he will, yes.

No, I'll grab my bag and come to you, then I can say goodbye to everyone before we leave. She paused, inhaling deep from the sheets beside her. *I love breathing you in.*

And I love when you take me inside of you.

Lil blushed and smiled, stretching out from fingers to toes before rising up beneath a falling blanket.

After dressing in a fitted cotton dress, Lil began making the bed. Putting the pillows in place, Lil found herself wishing she had one of Gunnar's candies to leave on top as if it were a hotel bed.

She slipped into a pair of boots and slung her pack over one shoulder, paused for a moment, and then plopped the bag down on the bed. She had to check for candy on the off chance she had some in her bag…

Footsteps.

Lil stilled herself. One set, slow.

You couldn't wait, could you, she smiled, the core of her body warming.

Reaching out to him with her senses, her heart rate picked up, ice replacing heat, spilling out from her chest and down her arms.

It wasn't Lu.

Lil quietly retrieved a knife sheathed in leather at the desk, stag handle with drop point blade. She slipped the knife down into her left boot, a hatchet into the right.

Footfall began on the steps with unsuccessful stealth.

Lil picked up another knife, this one without its sheath. The scaled texture of the grip would stick to her palm in the presence of liquid, warm or otherwise, the modified tanto blade a good fit for what she had in mind.

Left palm planted on the railing, Lil leapt over the barrier and into the stairwell.

She was on him from behind instantly.

Leaning in so he wouldn't throw them both down, she tightened her arm around the stranger's throat, and poised the tip of her blade at the base of his skull. She thought about ending him there on the steps, but she'd changed her clothes too many times for one night, and there'd be the mess after. Better for everyone if he walked himself out instead of having to be carried.

He wasn't terribly tall. Lil figured she could just take him to the balcony, impale him, and throw him over.

The thought of returning while you were in bed did not escape me, but I'm still here at the house. Uri is amused by my suffering, Lu said. His tone started low and suggestive, then, with an edge of concern, he said, *What's happening?*

They're here, above the barn.

A dart hit her in the shoulder.

With quick reflexes, Lil released her arm from the intruder's neck and extracted the projectile from herself. Maintaining pressure at the base of his skull with her knife, she watched as liquid continued to spurt from the needle she'd pulled out. Not all of it had gone into her then.

Lil dropped the dart and grabbed hold of him again, spun them both around, and pulled him down in front of her as she sat on the top step. She sensed his fear and a bit of curiosity bordering on arousal. *Really?* She impaled the base of his skull, released the knife, reached down for her hatchet, and threw it at the second man who'd been reloading his dart gun and rapidly advancing toward her.

Her axe hit him in the face, dead center. He went down quick.

They're here too. Lu said. *Are you safe?*

She grabbed the five unused darts from the vest of the man she straddled before shoving his corpse down the steps. Pausing to steady herself, she stood and, with a firm grip on the railing, stepped over the first body, reaching the man who'd shot her. She pressed her foot into his face, pulling the axe out and then striking down with it into his neck. The initial hit from the axe, though gruesome, was survivable, and she was hardly in the mood to take chances.

Are you safe? He repeated, firm and fierce. *I'm coming. Gunnar and Uri will manage.*

She sent him an image of the aftermath with her mind before speaking.

I'm safe. Secure the house first. I ended two of them. One shot me with a dart but I pulled it out before the full dose was injected. I'm starting to feel a little uncoordinated, but its mild.

You must have worked up a sweat... he said, reassured enough to become playful.
You're terrible... she laughed.
I bet you smell positively intoxicating.
Why don't you come here and find out?
Oh, I'll be coming...

Lil picked up her bag off the bed and headed to the balcony with manageable vertigo. Slinging her legs over the railing, she dropped down. With tresses trailing above her like a dark waterfall, Lil heard the whiz of a shot coming at her as she descended. The muted sound told her the projectile was either silenced or a dart, the impact on her bag indicated the latter.

They were still trying to subdue, not kill.

Lil's feet touched down with the grace of a dancer and the foreboding of something darker than the storm rolling in. With a slight crouch to her stance, she released her bag and surveyed her surroundings. She felt a breeze, sensed unsettled clouds, heard insects singing.

"Nice landing," she heard a familiar male voice say.

Todd stood by the back door of the shop, grin on his face and a box between his two hands. From the clinking of his cargo, Lil knew the box contained a variety of bottled beverages along with the bat sticking out. He really wasn't going anywhere without that thing.

She smiled back, her face rapidly draining of color, mouth transforming into a horrified gape as she watched a gloved hand come out of the shadows, wrapping around Todd's chin and pulling his head back. Before a gasp was able to fill her lungs with air, the box of bottles had dropped, and a blade was at his throat.

She felt too far away, too cold, too hot, everything in her alive and screaming *Stop!*

And so, everything stopped.

Everything.

All sound ceased, insects mute, the air around them paused. The black-clad assailant who'd seized Todd stood frozen, though Todd's blood continued falling to the command of gravity. The steady red stream flowed rather than pumped from the blossoming gash at his neck. *Not Arterial,* she thought as she rushed toward him, that or his heart had stopped.

Over herbs and past the apple tree, she chanted, *"Breathe, breathe, breathe,"* both as advice to herself and as a silent command to Todd.

Halting at his body, she made a quick assessment. Returning muscle control to either Todd or the man holding the knife to his throat could prove dangerous. If either shifted, the blade would continue on its path through Todd's body. As it was, she had them immobile, but holding their positions. Todd had started breathing, but not the stranger, and Lil had no plans of allowing them more oxygen so long as she could work quickly. If she rendered just his attacker's hand flaccid...

With not more than a deep thought, their hand went limp, releasing the knife into her palm.

Lil eased Todd to the ground, putting pressure on the wound while the stranger fell hard, and remained unmoving. She didn't want to obstruct his airway, but the gash was large, the loss continuing.

Todd is down. She started. *Blade to the throat. Alive. I'm with him behind the barn. Nan and Claire?*

Safe inside with Gunnar, Lu replied. *House was clearly the primary target, there are quite a few of them here.*

Todd moved his mouth, attempting speech, but stopped when Lil shook her head.

Life blooms under your hands like no other's, He continued. *You don't require the song, but it might help with focus. Do you need me with you? Uri and Gunnar can-*

No, just stay with me like this.

Closing her eyes, feeling the slippery skin warm under her palms, she stilled herself.

It started as a deep hum, resonating from her mind to her core, through her soul, then moved into a language never written, only existing as sound and intention. Lu sang in her mind, and her body began to sway slightly, as if the song were an ocean and she melting into water, became one, moving with it.

Low and engulfing, lilts where she remembered them, her voice met his.

Threads of hope, promise, and the bittersweet poured out of her, life beneath her fingers having no choice but to mend, to become whole.

As music gave way to breath, she opened her eyes.

Her message of healing must have spilled over to the ground because the patch of clover encircling them had grown considerably, purple blossoms reaching her elbows, leaning over Todd's awestruck face.

Though still operating under the effects of the dart, Lil felt a renewed spark in herself as well.

Moving her hands away, spilled blood remained, but the wound had closed.

"How do you feel?"

He looked to the lifeless body beside them, to the clover. Crickets resumed their rhythm, leaves rustling overhead as Todd's tentative hand rose to inspect the damage she'd reversed, no doubt expecting his fingers to sink into his neck.

"Slowly," she said as he started to stir. "I healed the wound, but you've lost a bit of blood."

The hand on his neck slipped down to cover hers where it rested on his chest, his eyes deep as his heart.

"I thought I was dying," he said, salted tears trickling down his temples and into his hairline. "And that song... I'm not saying I want to die, but just then, how it was... I could have gone and it would have felt right, with the way you were singing. I'm not so sure I'd be all set afterwards, though... I was hoping for more time to balance the scales..."

"Death is a different song, and you'd have nothing to worry about," she smiled, a hint of color reaching her cheeks. "I know a guy."

The slicing sting of a dart spiking into Lil's back sent a fresh jolt of adrenaline coursing through her, along with whatever it delivered into her muscle. She reached for it, but with the placement being so central, she took too long. All of the injection went in.

"Stay down," she commanded.

Not waiting for him to nod, Lil stood up, turning from Todd toward the origin of the projectile.

A shadowed figure crept from behind the barn, reloading their rifle. They may have just come upon them, but more than likely Lil had immobilized them along with everything else, and they'd just regained autonomy.

She focused on her breath, then on theirs.

With the clock running on the hit she'd taken, Lil moved forward, willing the assailant's body motionless before they could take another shot. A man.

Rendering his hands flaccid as she'd done to Todd's attacker, he released the dart rifle to the ground.

The stranger's eyes went wide with terror, while Lil's were becoming difficult to control, their movement uncoordinated.

Raising her left hand, she pressed her index finger against her lips in a silent, *shhhh*.

Holding this new intruder motionless, Lil searched for others from where she stood below the balcony.

She succeeded in finding a figure rounding the front corner of Nan's shop, a second behind them. They moved toward her, ignorant of Todd's position around at the rear of the building.

Clutching the primed darts she'd taken possession of inside the barn, Lil steadied herself, focusing her eyes as best she could, and launched the projectiles with incredible force. One, then a second at the first stranger who'd come around. One, then two more for the shadowed figure following them. Though they sported a fair amount of gear, some flesh had been left exposed, and Lil's aim was impeccable when the ground wasn't undulating beneath her target, even with sluggish eyes.

Lil turned back to her hostage, but detected movement in her periphery. The intruders she'd shot scrambled to pull their darts out. It would take time for the sedative to kick in, enough time for them to aim and fire.

She needed to do something.

Stretching her fingers toward the ground, Lil reached for the earth's energy, calling it to flow into her while maintaining enough focus to retain her hold on the man she held frozen. A current rose toward her, coiling like electric smoke, illuminating her legs pale blue.

Though a surge lifted toward her, Lil felt her body rapidly draining. Through blurring eyes, she saw one figure raise their rifle, then, suddenly a baseball bat made contact with their head. With a great sigh, Lil released her hold on the power she pulled, and watched Todd bludgeon the second stranger by the shop until he stood triumphant over two bodies.

A thunderous crack hit her ears, and as she turned toward the source of the sound, Lil felt her knees nearly buckle at the sight of Lu striding toward her.

Was he wearing a suit?

He flared his nostrils and close his eyes, apparently savoring something as he slid a hand to her lower back, arm snaking around her. Leaning into her neck, he inhaled, slowly releasing the word, "*Magnificent,*" as he released the air he'd taken.

She sighed, eyes rolling back and closing at the sensation of his mouth against her, his tongue. She'd been hanging on by a thread as it was. If she could just relax in his arms for a moment...

I'll take hold of the creature, he whispered. *You've managed beautifully, and you taste exquisite.*

I do enjoy being tasted.

Your needs will be met at length once we've finished here..

Easing into his chest a little further, Lil released her hold on the intruder, allowing Lu to take over.

Nice suit, she said.

His cheeks rose against her skin with a smile, a huff of breath.

I had Uri bring it with him from the mountain, thought I'd clean up a little, for Nan's sake... Then this nonsense started. Uri has already removed his shirt. I'd like to do the same.

One of Lil's hands rested on an exposed patch of Lu's chest, in agreement with his sentiment on shirts.

"Nan ok?" She asked.

"Yes. The house is secure. Gunnar is standing by with six down. Uri is out looking for strays, and it seems Todd has been busy."

Todd leaned against the exterior wall of the shop, bat in hand, presumably watching the bodies for movement and catching his breath.

A burst of air moved over her from above, calling her eyes upward to the shaved head, bare chest, and wings spread wide against the night sky. Catching her eye, he winked, the sight of him warming her heart like a kitchen rich with the fragrance of fresh baked cookies. Uri, carrying one haggard man in each hand.

Though he could have landed light on his toes, the earth shook as Uri's came down beside the one Lu kept motionless.

"Hey, Lil," he smiled, throwing the two men he carried to the ground. Too timid to stand, they righted themselves but stayed low on their knees.

"Hi Uri," she smiled back.

How hard it must have been for him to walk away from her that night in the bakery. She wanted to wrap her arms as best she could around his wide frame, but it seemed they had work to do.

"They were down the road a ways, by their truck," Uri said. "There must have been a second vehicle, given the bodies we've amassed, but I just found the one. Would you like it brought in?"

"Yes," Lu said, quickly adding, "It should remain drivable…"

Uri flashed a grin, then pushed off into the sky,

"You came to have a word with my wife," Lu said, directly addressing the man he held still.

The man's eyes moved; his brows high as they could go.

"Speak." Lu commanded.

Tentatively, the man flexed his fingers and dared to answer.

"We came to retrieve her. Were instructed not to damage-"

"Who is your team leader on the ground here?"

"Goose, Sir."

"Goose? Like from *Top Gun*? Is your team leader aware that Goose dies in that film?"

"He's... He's in the barn."

"Ah. Already dead, then."

Lu sent frost creeping up the man's fingers and legs. "Should we call you Ice Man, perhaps?"

"Lawson."

Lu stared at him intently, waiting.

"Ed Lawson, sir."

"Edwin? Edward?"

Lu was clearly playing with his food. He didn't need to know the man's name any more than his shoe size. Lil couldn't blame him after what they'd been through, but she was tired. Even with her metabolism, she still felt off from whatever the darts carried. Eyeing the balcony, she thought about her nap from earlier… couldn't wait to be sleeping again.

I'll have Uri interrogate him so we can get going. I'd probably kill him prematurely anyway.

"Emmett. Emmett Drake Lawson."

"Working for the family business. Tell me, Emmett *Drake* Lawson, what was to be done with my wife after you'd poached her?"

He shook his head, teeth chattering from cold and fear.

"I'm on retrieval team two. A guy on team one knew the details, and our team two leader was back-up for him, as far as after... I... It was need to know for me."

"You'd be surprised at how useful small details can be."

The boom of a Suburban being dropped into the parking area interrupted Ice Man's shivering, forcing him into a startled crouch.

Uri grinned, flashing a thumbs-up as he swooped down beside Lil.

She beamed drowsily as he pulled her into a hug, spinning her around.

392

"Good to have you back," he sighed.

Lil closed her eyes, her head drooping as Uri continued to spin.

"She's still dizzy from the darts," Lu growled.

Uri's smile faded as he released her.

Deep and slow, Lu said, pulling her against his body. *Eyes closed.*

"Well, Ice," Lu said, remotely crushing the hearts of the two men kneeling beside him, their lifeless bodies slumping to the ground. "Looks like your ride is here."

I'm going to let him watch us leave, Lu said. *Uri will interrogate him, then send him back to wherever he came from with a message that you've gone.*

Will buy us some time at least, she thought.

Enough time for you to take another nap.

I'll be expecting more than one, she smirked drowsily.

I will provide as many naps as you need.

Uri chuckled.

Can he hear us?

I don't think he needs to...

A light glow pulsed around them.

The bodies... she thought. *Throw them in the truck for Ice to take with him. Nan shouldn't have to deal with that.*

Uri shot up in the air, the half-frozen man following his trajectory with frightened eyes.

Gunnar and Uri to load them. Todd will want to help.

Of course he will... she smiled. *He's having the time of his life, though he gave me a bit of a scare earlier. Will Uri follow this man back?*

Most likely.

Lu continued massaging her neck, the base of her head as two bodies dropped from the sky by the Suburban. Uri made a couple more trips, relocating the six from Nan's house to a pile by the vehicle before swooping down and heading into the barn.

Gunnar can help Todd with the two by the shop. Claire and Nan are on their way over with him now. He tried to dissuade them, but they're both strong-willed.

They were indeed.

Uri came out of the barn dragging the two men she'd bloodied, one on either side of him.

"Axe?" He asked, head tilting toward the corpse with the oozing vertical gash in the center of what was once a face.

Lil nodded.

Uri smiled wide, nodding back to her in a wordless response of acknowledgement and pride.

Gunnar and Nan arrived with Claire between them, her eyes wide, hand firmly planted high on her chest as she caught sight of the intruders' remains, the work being done.

Gunnar leaned in to whisper something to her and, only after she nodded, he moved to meet Todd. Clapping him on the shoulder, they stood assessing the bodies, then started in on moving them over to the truck.

"It's probably for the best I'm seeing it now," Nan said. "Know what we're up against."

Lu nodded, Lil's head still leaning against him, watching together as the intruders were stripped of their gear, and the vehicle loaded.

"You'll drive back with your dead, to wherever it is you came from," Lu said, addressing the terrified man before him. "Todd," he continued. "Would you relieve this man of his vest and anything else you feel appropriate?"

"On it," Todd replied with palpable enthusiasm.

Lu turned his attention to Nan. "They were here only to retrieve her," he said, pointing to a pile of discarded weapons. "You'll notice, though, that they were equipped with more than the tranquilizer guns. Their mission was to bring her back viable, collateral damage of no consequence."

"You could still come with us to Iceland," Lil offered. "Or at least stay at Magnus's here."

But Nan shook her head. "No, you go where you are needed, and we'll be here, keeping the hearth warm for your return." She gave Lil's shoulder a squeeze, then lovingly cupped her cheek. "I'll have a full house now, and we'll face what comes together. Uri is with us, Gunnar as well." Her voice lowered to a whisper. "Though he appears keen on Claire, and I suspect he'd not go far anyway. I'll have to make up a room for Todd; there'll be no keeping the boy away after what he's seen tonight. He can't surf in the field, so I suppose I'll have a few moments of peace now and then when he hits the waves or whatever the kids are calling it."

Claire, distracted and distant, let out a series of sighs, each progressively shakier, eyes glistening with tears not yet fallen. Disregarding Lu, to his amusement, she wrapped her arms around Lil.

"There was no one with you," Claire said. "In the woods when they came for you, and just now when you woke. And it was after such a beautiful time, all of us together." Her eyes widened again as she gasped, "And when you were little, they came for you when you were so little..." She squeezed Lil even tighter somehow.

Lil sighed. "You with your big heart."

"And I can't believe you didn't tell me about the kelp!" Claire stomped, sniffled, and laughed. There was snorting involved as well, eliciting relief and laughter from the others.

"The vehicle is loaded," Uri announced, approaching with Gunnar and Todd.

Lu nodded.

Shall we?

Yes, I just want to say goodbye.

We're coming back at some point…

It's what people do.

Can you stand on your own?

Lil took a step away, tested her balance, and nodded.

I'll lean on Claire if I need to.

"This is all so big," Claire said. "Bigger than I imagined it could be, even after growing up with you for a cousin." She twisted to where Uri stood, then back to Lil, face serious as her eyes widened. Her arms went out, hands flapping twice at her side. "Like, really big."

Right. She'd seen Uri flying.

Lil shrugged and nodded.

"You should have seen Lu, he moved so fast. One minute he was talking with Uri, and then he'd be staring off smiling to himself. Uri thought it was hilarious, but then he became scary serious, and he was gone. The next thing I knew, Uri was *in the sky,* and Lu, he was somehow both graceful and terrifying. And Gunnar… it was like a dance they'd all rehearsed ahead of time. I *knew* we were safe, but Todd had gone to the shop, and you were off in the barn. So many came for you, and you defeated them alone."

"To be fair, I was connected to Lu the whole time."

Claire scrunched her nose.

"We can talk to each other, in our minds. Distance isn't a factor. And I only ended the lives of two on my own, well, three. And Todd was incredible. He took two down with his bat, and that was after being knifed. I patched him up; he's good. I was darted, though, twice. I am exhausted, have a touch of vertigo, and I honestly don't know how I'm still able to stand at this point."

"Because you're you, I suspect," Claire smiled.

"And now I'm off to remember how to be whatever that is."

"Wait..." Claire's face morphed into an expression of serious curiosity. She put out her arms again, flapping her hands much slower than before, eyebrows lifting with silent question.

"Yes, wings, and no, you can't see them... yet. I need practice, but it shouldn't take more than a couple days. I promise to scoot back and give a demonstration. We'll have a *lot* to talk about."

Lil gave Claire a squeeze. "I'll see you soon. You can text and call anytime. I'll try to do the same, but I'll be overwhelmed a bit at first. You might find yourself experiencing distraction as well... It's going to be a full house here," she winked.

The darkness of the hour couldn't hide Claire's blush. It brought warmth to Lil, knowing she'd be leaving behind something bright along with the chaos.

Nan raised the corners of her mouth as she listened in. There'd be no shortage of amusement for her over the coming days.

"I expect to hear from you every day, and if you *scoot back* to see Claire, I'll not be left out of it." Nan said, eyeing Uri. "I've given him a hard time since he arrived, but I'm rather excited to see what he can do."

"He has a lot to offer, but don't forget that you do too," Lil started. "Uri has been around a long time, long enough to recognize when he is the student, and wise enough to value the experience. You're not the only one who's excited, trust me."

Nan pulled her into a tight hug. "Love you,"

"Always."

Todd had meandered over, and Lil wasted no time in throwing her arms around him next.

"You are very much a part of this," she said. "A part of this family. You belong here, Todd, and I'm proud of you."

When she stepped back, he put his fist over his heart. "See you when you get back."

"Keep that board waxed," She winked.

"I'll have Nan do it," he said with a wicked smile.

Lil chuckled as Nan burst out, scolding.

"This white hair is your doing, Todd. It may have been grey to start, but the white is you're doing, and I must be crazy because I wouldn't change you one bit." She shook her head and turned to Claire, whispering, "I've never needed a drink more in my life. When we go in, I'm pouring a glass of port and taking it straight to bed."

Lil sighed, turning from Todd to the small white paper bag outstretched toward her.

"You'll have to ration them," Gunnar said. "We went through a lot today."

She took the bag and wrapped her arms around his waist.

"I'm thankful to have you here." She looked up at his face, curling her lip into a smile. "You're not going anywhere, are you?"

His eyes flicked to someone behind her.

"Not a chance, kid."

"Oh, he's not going anywhere," Uri grinned, putting one arm around Gunnar's shoulders, using the other hand to muss his hair.

"Our roots run strong through this one. Haven't smelled anything like it since the old days, and it's not just my line running through him. You must have felt it."

Lil paused, reaching beyond Uri to the calm emanating from Gunnar, the grounding stillness.

"Az," she whispered with excitement. "But did he...?"

Uri nodded. "Just the once. Remi must have known immediately upon recruiting him."

Lu hadn't said anything about the lineage of her *guardian*, but other things had understandably come up before discussing Gunnar's origin.

"Who is Remi, and what is an Az?" Gunnar asked.

Lil figured she could start him off and leave Uri to fill in the rest.

"The man who recruited you," Lil began. "The one who was in the bar with Lu..."

"Master *Remmond*?"

She nodded, "Remi. And do you remember the names of his two predecessors?"

"Masters Artturi and Azemi..."

"Uri and Az."

Gunnar's eyes went wide. Attention on Uri, he whispered, "Artturi?"

"I was for a time, baked with Magnus when he was a boy. The name *Uri* has been with me the longest. And Az is just Az. Tell me, do you see things before they happen, know where to find things?"

Gunnar looked to Lil, then back. "Just with her. I can sense where she'll be, where she's gone in her mind, what she needs."

"A skillset we're thankful for," he said, clapping Gunnar on the back.

"He's not too bad in the kitchen, either," Lil chimed in, holding out the bag of confections. Uri raised an eyebrow, plunged his large hand in, and pulled out a piece of candied ginger. He popped it into his mouth, eyes looking off to the side, then closed.

"Greatness indeed."

"He has grapefruit in there too," Lil grinned. "His caramels, though... that's where the magic is."

"I might make candy," Gunnar protested, gesturing to Uri, "but have you *seen* this guy? *Wings!*"

"She hasn't showed you hers?" Uri laughed.

Gunnar's wide eyes silently asked, *seriously?*

"I just found out tonight. I didn't even know how to put them away once they emerged," she said, shaking her head, cheeks heating up.

"It comes back quick," Uri said. "Control has always been the biggest challenge for you since, but you've done well, considering. Of course, I was no help to you at the bakery. Your proximity was a distraction…"

"You closed your eyes," she said. "I still ended up exploding lights, but that moment helped me to calm a little."

"You were on the verge of blowing out the windows, and it still took strength for me to break eye contact. It's not easy; seeing you, knowing you and not being able to spin you around. Lu knew better than to go crashing in… It's harder on him than the rest of us, obviously, and more so when you're close with another male and he can't access you. I probably should've stayed outside, but when Lu gave me the green light, I couldn't resist." He shook his head, smiling a little. "It'll all come back as you acclimate to who you are, wield what you've got instead of tamping it down."

Lil looked over to see Nan cupping Lu's' cheeks, the tender smile between them warming her heart.

"The orchard here," Uri said, his voice low. "He planted it before you were born in this life."

Lil nodded toward the solitary apple tree in the garden. "And I grew that one. I took a seed from an apple I'd picked in the orchard… I wasn't conscious of whether it was possible, just felt the need to take it in my hand, and put it into the earth."

"The story sings to my heart. I'll bake something when you get back, with fruit from both trees."

I'd like that," she smiled.

He paused, surveying the night. "It's a beautiful garden you've brought me to. A worthy garden." Uri smiled softly, placing a large hand on her shoulder for a moment before turning away. "C'mon Ice," he called out. "We need to have a chat in the barn before you head back."

A hand slid down Lil's back, heat spreading through her. Lips brushed along the rim of her ear where Lu stopped briefly to whisper, "Let's go take a hot bath."

How hot?

Geothermal.

She leaned into him as they strolled away from the group, walking in the direction of the orchard where the familiar roaring of a great ocean storm filled her ears again, giving way to stillness.

A Story in Stone

Acknowledgements

Massive thank you to Kerry and Melissa. You are my original champions. You read my chapters when they were chunks of thoughts. You imagined the taste of Gunnar's caramels and laughed at Todd's shirts before anyone else. You sent me The Rock. You sent me a Story in Stone gift basket (Shout out to Our Green House.) Kerry, you made me one of Lil's mugs! You both encouraged me to keep writing, and took this journey seriously when I was unsure. You've been gracious with your time, gave me tough love when I needed it, and I am beyond grateful to have you both in my life. So much more than a book club. Colleen and Caroline too, you came in after these stories were born, but have been there for my triumphs and my tantrums, cover design and (insert vomit emoji) formatting.

Thank you to my parents for reading my first draft… steamy bits and all. As a daughter, feeling your enthusiasm and pride was everything.

Thank you to my spouse. You helped me make an office in our closet, you provided a sleeping bag for when I write outside and it's cold. You pull my leg, you cut my grapefruits, and you do all the little things. Extra special bonus thank you for your last-minute editing services!

Thank you to my daughters for enriching my life and keeping things beautiful, interesting, and sometimes a little bit gross. I love you.

About the Author

Kristen Cornwall is a writer, an artist, and a great many other things. She likes maple in her tea when she wants it sweet, enjoys the seasons in New England, croissants, and listening to birds (though it's a little love/hate when days are longest and they are awake before she really wants to get started.) She likes being in the woods and by the ocean, and reads often. She occasionally makes crepes.

www.ingramcontent.com/pod-product-compliance
Lightning Source LLC
Chambersburg PA
CBHW020011120726
47903CB00004B/1239